Sing for Me

Brittany Ann

Cover Design: Brittany Ann

Editing & Proofreading: The Fiction Fix

Formatting: Sam Penrod

Contents

Trigger Warnings

This book contains graphic and violent scenes.
Sex. Sexual assault. Murder.
Characters in this book were victims of **mental, physical, and emotional abuse**.
Mental Health issues such as: **PTSD, anxiety, suicidal thoughts, and depression** are present in this story.
Child loss and death are mentioned in this story.
If you have an issue with any of these topics, please proceed with caution.

Playlist

Sleeping on the Blacktop by Colter Wall (*Hallow Ranch Theme*)
God Made Airplanes by Jason Aldean
Man in the Box by Alice in Chains
Outlaws and Outsiders by Cory Marks (*Mason's Song*)
Never Comin' Home by Bailey Zimmerman
Brother by Kodaline
Drunk Driving by Koe Wetzel
On the Edge by Zachery (*Harmony's song*)
Still a Few Cowboys Left by Ben Gallaher
Bad Bitch by Dylan Wheeler

To the broken ones who feel unworthy of love.
To the damaged ones.
You are worthy of love, regardless of your scars.
Happiness will find you in the healing.
Cherish it.

Prologue

Eleven Years Ago

"Where's your fiancée tonight, Langston?"

I looked up from the saddle, the beast beneath me thrashing against the pin. I grunted and adjusted, tightening my thighs on either side of him. He was the biggest fucker in the rodeo tonight, and he had been challenging me with his dark eyes all afternoon.

I looked up at my competition, smirking at his attempt to rock my focus by bringing up Cathy. I adjusted my hat and clicked my tongue. "She's at home, waiting for me in bed...naked," I said. The truth was, I didn't know where she was. The plan for tonight was for her to drive out here with me and then we would stay the night before going on a mini vacation. The bull bucked, trying to throw me off before the gate opened.

"Whoa, there," I drawled, tightening my grip on the rope.

The announcer came over the shitty loudspeaker and everything around me drifted away. The only things on the planet were me and the animal trying to kill me. The roars of the crowd faded away along with the judgmental eyes of the other riders and my shitty manager. The bright lights above me dimmed, and I focused on my hand, the strength in my muscles, and the beast's breathing. He was pissed, and I didn't blame him.

"Mason Langston is the youngest rider here tonight, riding the biggest and baddest..."

I closed my eyes for a moment.

Every single time, just before the gate opened, I would close my eyes, and every single time, I would see him. My father. The hate in his eyes, gray like mine, when he looked down at me. The fury in his eyes the night he avenged Momma. I would hear the words he used to throw at me just because he felt like it.

Like every other time, the buzzer would sound, and he would disappear for eight seconds.

For eight seconds, I would be at peace.

For eight seconds, I was just Mason.

For eight seconds, I was free.

The gate flew open at the same time as my eyes. My arm shot up, and the fight began. The beast bucked and kicked, throwing my body around like a rag doll. I grunted and clenched my teeth.

"...FIVE, SIX, SEVEN, EIGHT! MASON LANGSTON HAS DONE IT AGAIN, FOLKS!"

Immediately, I released my hold and was thrown from the bull. The dirt greeted me, and I rolled expertly. Then, I was on my feet, backing away from the bull as it charged at me before the wrangler came forward on his horse and turned the beast away from me. As I watched him move back into the holding area, the world came flooding back. The sounds came back, the colors returned, and then the pain came with them. I was a prisoner again, and I already craved my next taste of freedom.

The crowd was chanting my name, so I did a slow turn, taking my hat off for them. A smile spread across my face, the same as always, practiced and perfected. Fake.

A show.

A trick.

When the night was done, and they announced me as the winner, I looked to the cheap, worn-out bleachers, hoping Cathy would be there. She wasn't. As I was heading back to my truck, my phone rang.

"Langston."

"Bro, you need to get back to Hayden." It was the bartender from the local bar.

"What's wrong?" I demanded, jogging to my truck now.

"Your fiancée is fucking plastered. Cut her off an hour ago and she won't leave."

"Fuck," I clipped. "I'll be there in thirty."

"Appreciate you."

I flew back into town, the high of tonight's win gone. My hand gripped the steering wheel as I clenched my jaw to the point of pain, staring at the dark road ahead. "Dammit, darlin'," I muttered.

Cathy and I had been engaged for a few months now and the wedding was set for the middle of autumn. I cared for her, truly. I met Cathy over a year ago at a rodeo. She was a buckle bunny, but that didn't bother me. She was kind and listened to me. She seemed to care, and fuck, if that didn't feel good. There were some things that seemed to be missing in our relationship, but we were still young, and I had faith that they would come as we got older.

I was excited to marry her.

I just wished I felt like Momma did when she told me about falling in love with Pop. He wasn't always a monster. Before she died, Pop was a good man, the kind of man that every little boy wanted to be someday. That all changed after the fire, after the ashes settled.

I finally made it into town and pulled up to the bar. When I was near the front door, a man stepped out. He worked down at the car shop, so we were familiar. He turned to me, his eyes going wide.

"Mason! Hey! Congratulations!"

I raised a brow. No one in this town ever congratulated me after a ride. They didn't care enough. "On?" I prompted.

The guy looked at me like I was crazy before laughing it off. "Man, I forget how much you like to joke around. Congratulations on Denver coming back home safe."

My stomach plummeted, crashing down to the warm concrete below my boots. The man put his hand on my shoulder, giving it a squeeze before walking off. It took everything in me not to punch him. Without a second glance, I went back to my truck, my heart pounding in my chest.

Cathy was at the back of my mind, and Denver was at the front of it.

The one thing I didn't expect was to come home and see my brother for the first time in five years with my fiancée in his bed.

Chapter One

Harmony

March

"Hey, Harm? Could you take this to the supply room for me?"

I looked up from my charting to the head nurse, Claire.

There were lots of things one could say about Claire, number one being that I didn't like her and probably never would. She was one of those girls who pretended to be your friend but talked shit behind your back. I didn't have the energy for that, and I knew she was a snake the second she smiled at me on my first day. Of course, that was just the nonwork-related stuff. There wasn't enough time in the world to go over everything she did wrong on the floor.

My eyes held hers for a few moments before I looked back down at my screen, my fingers still adding patient information to the chart. She cleared her throat, reminding me of nails on a chalkboard.

"Harm? Please? I'm really swamped," she pleaded, attitude lacing her voice at the end. When I looked back up at her, I decided to take in her appearance instead of answering. She wore her brown hair in a high ponytail, curled and teased to make it look bigger. Her brown eyes were bright, dark makeup surrounding them, her fake eyelashes adding extra flare. She had straight white teeth, perky breasts, a slim body, and a cute ass, the kind of person who stepped into the sun for five minutes and came back with a golden glow. Even her voice was sweet.

That was the thing about Claire, she was perfect.

I was perfect once, too.

Now, I couldn't stand the thought of being perfect ever again. In fact, I hated the word.

The medical supplies were in her arms, and she was standing three feet from the supply closet. *No joke.* Three feet. She probably wanted me to do it for her so she could go press her body against Dr. Mitch. Rumor has it, she has been trying to get in his pants since the day he started two years ago. I, on the other hand, had only been working for the clinic for a year. I wasn't trying to get into anyone's pants. I wasn't trying to draw attention to myself. I was here to help people, go home, sleep, repeat.

The old me would've told Claire to fuck off and stop being lazy. Unfortunately for me, that wasn't me anymore.

That girl died a long time ago.

Besides, I needed a refill on my water.

I plastered on the biggest, fakest, brightest smile I could muster and stood, closing my electronic charts and logging off the computer. My water bottle was right there, and my hands itched to grab it. Claire was impatiently waiting, and when I held my arms out, she dumped her contents in, and spun on her heel without even so much as a thank you.

"Thanks so much, Harm. You're a big help," I grumbled, rolling my eyes. I looked at my water bottle, double checking it was where it was a second ago before making my way to the storage closet.

Once inside, I put everything where it belonged. It took a few minutes, for two reasons that greatly annoyed me. Number one, it was a lot of stuff. Number two, my OCD wouldn't allow me to leave until everything was in its place. After putting everything away, I went to the door and pushed.

It didn't open.

I wrapped my hand tighter around the handle and pushed again. It didn't budge. The light above flickered, and the monster with a slick smile that liked to torment me in my dreams lingered over my shoulder, its cold breath against my neck.

Panic.

Before I could stop it, I felt the walls closing in. Even though I knew, somewhere in the back of my mind, that everything was fine, that someone would come open the door in just a moment, the monster's sickening, stomach churning chuckle was louder than my logic. I tried to breathe as I squeezed my eyes shut, pushing on the door. It wouldn't open. I was trapped. My phone was in my locker, and my water bottle—

My pulse quickened as my throat dried.

Before I knew it, I was pounding on the door with my fist. "Please! Please!" I cried.

I didn't know how much time had passed, but when the door swung open to reveal the janitor, tears were running down my face and fear had me in a chokehold. My hands were shaking, and I had tunnel vision. The janitor, Mr. Steele, took me in with wide eyes. He opened his mouth to say something, but I pushed past him, rushing to the nurse's station. My eyes landed on the teal metal water bottle, and I scrambled to have it in my hands once more. My fingers wrapped around the smooth metal, the coolness reminding me of the precious liquid inside.

An unsteady breath escaped me as I clutched it to my chest.

One, two, three. One, two, three.

Red, blue, green. Red, blue, green.

One, two, three. One, two, three.

I repeated the patterns under my breath until the monster growled low in irritation before sliding back down to the depths where it belonged. When I calmed, I lifted my eyes to find Mr. Steele staring at me. He was an older man, probably about my father's age. His caramel-colored skin was warm, and every time he passed me in the hall, he reminded me of sunshine and summer. His dark hair was speckled with gray, and his dark eyes had smile lines etched around them.

"*Querida*, are you okay?" he asked softly, stepping up to the counter.

I nodded and gave him a weak smile. "Yes, sorry. I don't do well in small spaces."

The old man looked back to the closet and then to me. When his eyes dropped to my water bottle, I tensed.

Don't ask. Don't ask. Don't ask.

When his eyes moved back to mine, his features softened. "Hold on. I have something for you," he said before turning back to his cart. I watched as he pulled something from the top and turned back to me, his hand outstretched.

A door stopper.

"Oh no, that's okay," I said, laughing slightly to try and play it off. He probably thought I was crazy.

Because you are.

I was only in the fucking closet for a minute, and I lashed out like a lunatic. Sucking my bottom lip between my teeth, my eyes dropped to the floor.

"*Querida.*"

Something in his tone brought my eyes up. He was closer now. "Take it. Then you won't get trapped anymore."

I'll always be trapped, Mr. Steele.

I didn't argue as I took it from him. "Thank you, Mr. Steele."

"You're welcome, Harmony. You have a good night now." With that, he drifted down the hall. Once he was out of sight, I turned around, flipping the straw up on my water bottle. I gulped the cold, refreshing fluid down my throat until it was gone.

I needed more.

No, you don't. You'll make yourself sick, Harm.

My best friend's voice rang in my ears. I took another breath and headed to get a refill. Shift change was in a few minutes, my patients were taken care of, and my charts were updated. I was ready to go home.

To hide.

"You have to come out with us, Harm!"

I finished tying off my braid and threw it over my shoulder. "Just because I'm back home doesn't mean that—"

"Harmony Green, you are twenty-eight years old," my best friend, Billie, snapped through the phone. This was what she did, my Billie: she pushed. She was instructed to push me, gently but firmly, back out into the world after years of hiding from it. She was instructed to help me find my voice again, be my own person. I'd agreed to this because I knew I needed it.

Just not tonight.

No amount of snapping would get me to leave.

No amount of begging would convince me that getting dressed up to go to PBR was a good idea.

Cowboys and I have a long history, not a particularly pleasant one. It wasn't sunshine and rainbows—more like tears and shattered dreams.

Anyways, I planned on spending the weekend unpacking my music room and kitchen. Having take-out every night was getting old, and I was ready to get settled. I was ready to get my life back.

It had been years since I'd stepped foot in this city. Years of torment. Years of nightmares. Years of running. Years of healing. I was tired of running, tired of being a coward.

I missed my home.

So, a year ago, I gathered up all my courage and moved back home to Houston. Up until two weeks ago, I lived with Billie and her boyfriend, Cabe. I was comfortable there, I felt safe there, but I knew Cabe wanted to propose to Billie. He wanted to start a family, and having a trauma-ridden nurse in the house was a huge roadblock. They didn't kick me out, they told me I was welcome for as long as I needed. Still, there was a huge part of me that would need them for the rest of my life, and they had their own life to build together. I was standing in the way of that.

The truth was, I was tired of holding other people back, of holding *myself* back. I was tired of being a burden. Two weeks ago, I moved into a two-bedroom apartment by Spotts Park. Two weeks ago, I was handed a set of keys to a space I could make mine, a space where I would be safe, comfortable, that I could make my own.

Something I wouldn't be ashamed of.

A place where I could be myself.

"Are you even listening to me?" Billie deadpanned.

I blinked, shaking thoughts of my past away as I lifted a box. "I don't know why you're trying to get me out. I told you I wasn't going anywhere for a bit."

"But it's PBR!"

Professional bull riding. The place would be crawling with cowboys, cowgirls, drunk rednecks, and buckle bunnies.

I shook my head as I walked into the second bedroom, my music room. I'd spent the last six years trying to discover who I was and who I needed to be. My therapist said I needed a creative outlet, something to take my mind off everything when it became too much.

Some people got lost in books.

Some people got lost in writing, creating their own worlds to run away to.

Some people lost themselves in painting or drawing. Hell, even pottery.

I got lost in music, and I discovered myself through songwriting, before everything went to shit. With this new beginning, I've tried to pick it back up again. Bille and Cabe say I have a talent for singing, that my raspy voice gives me an edge, but I didn't have the confidence to sing anymore, not with this voice.

My voice wasn't always raspy.

Once upon a time, my voice was actually smooth and light.

The voice of an angel.

"Harmony..."

I sighed. "Billie, I'm not budging."

A knock sounded at my front door.

"Then let me in so I can help you get your place together, babe," she sighed. I smiled to myself and pulled out my AirPods. I went to the door, grateful for her, grateful for the roof over my head, and grateful for the breath in my lungs.

Two hours later, my music room was unpacked, and the sun was setting.

"Now I get it," Billie murmured from beside me, staring out the window. I looked at her from my place on the floor and smiled.

Apartment hunting had been a chore, to say the least. It had taken me three months to find the right spot. I needed light, natural light. If I didn't have it, I would've gone insane. I needed to see the sun rise and a set from my new place. I needed to know when the day was starting and when it ended.

When I came across this listing, I couldn't believe it.

It seemed almost too good to be true, like the heavens above had finally started to look out for me, to make up for lost time.

My place was a corner unit, only minutes away from the clinic, in a secure building, with underground parking, a gym, a pool, a coffee shop, and a courtyard. From my living room and bedroom, I could see the sunrise, and from the music room, I could see the sun set. It was wonderful. Sunset was the time my creativity blossomed the most, and I knew I was going to be spending hours in this room after my shifts.

My antique, dark wood, piano sat against the far wall. I didn't know how to play, but I planned on learning. I saw the instrument two years ago at an estate sale in Michigan. I brought it on sight, and for the last two years, it had been sitting in a storage unit. Now, it was in its rightful spot—my home. Next to the piano was my Gibson guitar, worn down from hours of practicing. It had been my first purchase when I rediscovered my interest in music, and I realized quickly how much it soothed me. My therapist, Giana, told me it was an excellent idea, so I'd been playing guitar for the last five years, and I was fairly good at it.

Not great, but good.

We'd hung the sheer cream curtains together, which took a bit of time without a power drill. Then we assembled the chair in the opposite corner. It was a dark green, wide enough for me to sit crisscross applesauce if I wanted to. I'd angled it to face the window slightly. There was a bookshelf to the left of it, against the wall closest to me, filled with my favorite books and the ones I wanted to read.

"It looks really good in here," Billie whispered to me, taking my hand and giving it a squeeze.

"I think so too," I replied, my eyes going back to the room, taking everything in.

Billie turned me to face her, and I groaned at the puppy dog look she was sporting. *Here we go.*

"Please? Please can we go?" she fake cried, tugging on my arm.

"How does Cabe put up with you?" I snapped, pulling my hand free. I turned, heading to the kitchen, she followed me down the hall, chanting my name. Thoughts of being in a crowd swarmed by my mind, my anxiety picking up, ready to take control. My eyes immediately went to my water bottle sitting on the counter, and I swiped it up. After taking a drink, I lifted my chin to her.

"What are you doing?" I asked, getting to the point.

Billie looked at me with a smile, her blue eyes sparkling. "I'm hyping you up."

"I don't need to be hyped up to tell you no, but thanks for offering."

She glared at me, and I glared back. There was no way I was backing down from this. The movies, maybe. A concert? Probably not. PBR rodeo with people who hated people like me? Not a chance in hell.

"Come on, this used to be our thing, remember?" she started.

I held my hand up. "I have no desire to get dressed up and make fun of the buckle bunnies," I said, shutting her down.

That had been our thing back in high school. We would go to the local rodeos and watch the bull riders. We couldn't decide what was funnier, the rodeo clown or the buckle bunnies chasing after cowboys. There was a part of me that envied them, their simple life.

My life had never been simple.

"We are past the buckle bunny stage, babe. Remember, queens lift up queens. So, if the buckle bunnies want to chase cowboy dick, that's their prerogative," she replied, clearly not ready to give up this fight.

"Good," I replied softly. "I always hated girls laughing at me as a kid, and I don't know why we did it as teenagers."

Billie squared me with a look. "Because we were young and dumb."

"Exactly, so there is no need to go tonight," I finished, fully prepared to sit down on the couch and read my new vampire romance.

Chapter Two

Mason

"Wanna tell me where the fuck you are?"

Keeping my eyes on the flat road ahead, I sighed, "Abilene."

"*Abilene?*"

My lips tugged up into a smirk at Eddie's outburst. I switched my hands on the wheel and leaned back in the seat, getting comfortable as I drove through the ass crack of Texas. I'd been all over the world, seen the good, bad, and the ugly. This part of Texas wasn't ugly. No, it was hell: flat, dry, and boring.

"Mase, you were supposed to be in Houston *last night*," he clipped, reminding me of my schedule.

"Don't give a shit, Ed," I mumbled.

"You never do." He hung up.

Silence filled the cab.

He was right. I didn't give a shit about anything anymore, hadn't given a shit about anything but bull riding for the last decade.

Now, I was starting to not give a shit about bull riding.

If I was being honest with myself, there was no logical reason for me to still be bull riding. Money wasn't an issue. I was getting older, and my body was feeling the pain of being thrown around like a fucking rag doll. My name was known in households all over the world. I was an inspiration to thousands, loved by millions, and hated by the other millions in the world.

That was the thing: you either loved me or you hated me. There was no in between, but the shitty thing was, no one loved the real Mason.

Hell, no one really *knew* the real Mason. I buried him years ago in an empty field with two bottles of Jack.

Mason Langston, the best bull rider in the world.

Mason Langston, the loneliest bastard in the world.

"What a joke," I grumbled, taking a sip of my now cold coffee. I'd stopped in Dallas three hours ago for gas and coffee. I'd been on the road since five this morning.

I should have been hauling ass to get to Houston...but I wasn't.

I would get there when I got there.

They would let me ride, like they always did. It wasn't because of my manager, nor because of the fans. No, they would let me ride because of my title, my fucking name. They would let me ride because I was a study subject to them. The PBR leaders and my fellow riders wanted to know how the fuck I managed to stay on the beast for eight seconds. No matter the size of the bull or the location of the show, I would hold on.

In the last eleven years, I'd only been thrown off three times: once right after leaving Hayden, Colorado for good, once right after receiving a phone call about Pop's death, and once five years ago, when my brother begged me to come home.

I never responded. I never went home.

Not after that day.

I swore off the ranch the day my older brother, Denver, took the one good thing I had going for me, the one thing Pop was actually proud of me for. He ripped it from me without a second glance, then again, that was Denver: headstrong, and set in his ways, just like Pop, who got whatever he wanted, not giving a fuck if he left his little brother in the dust or not.

The phone rang again through the Bluetooth of the truck cab. My eyes dropped to the dash. *Great, now fucking Richard was calling.*

Richard Tompson was my manager, the newest addition to the Langston team of bullshit. He'd only been on for about six months, and I was probably going to fire him after this season. He was annoying and liked to talk like he was better than me. I was the one bringing in his money, yet he still belittled me. That shit didn't fly with me, not with him or the last fifteen managers I had.

Pamela was my PR manager, or, as I liked to call her, "the crabby bitch from hell." I couldn't even take a piss without her griping at my ass. Sometimes she could be cool, but other times, I wanted to rip her fucking head off.

"Langston," I answered.

"Where are you?" Richard demanded with clear anger in his voice.

"Just passed the great town of Abilene, Texas, Richard," I drawled. "It's lovely here this time of year. The brown dirt is a little richer in color."

Silence and then, "Are you fucking kidding me? You're riding in four hours and you're telling me you're five hours away?"

See? The yelling?

Who the fuck did he think he was?

"That's exactly what I'm telling you," I replied coolly. "Keep yelling at me, Rich. I *dare* you."

He mumbled something under his breath, and I found myself smirking. *The little bitch.*

"Get here as fast as you can," he ordered.

"Sir, yes, sir," I taunted.

"Mason, I swear to—"

"Goodbye, *Dick*," I sneered. Shaking my head, I turned up the radio station to try to drown out my anger.

Two hours later, I stopped for gas.

I was in a small town in the middle of Ass Crack, Texas. There were only two pumps at this station, and an old man snoozing in a rocking chair by the front door. A feeling of home tugged at my chest; Hayden's local gas station had an old man, too. His name was Paul, and he always wore jean overalls and a straw hat. The man before me was dressed in dirty jeans, a dirty white t-shirt, and a worn flannel.

I hopped out of my truck and started the pump. There was a pulsing, dull, pain at the back of my skull and I knew a headache was forming. Ignoring it, I reached into the cab and tugged on my cowboy hat before heading inside. Once I was by the door, the old man lifted his head.

"Afternoon to ya," he said, his voice withered and shaking.

I tipped my hat to him. "Sir."

The convenient store was small, crammed with shelves of junk food and off-brand shit your body didn't need. That didn't stop me from swiping up some cheese crackers before heading to the old fridge in the back, though. I also grabbed two waters and headed to the counter. Two young boys were behind it, and the oldest set his phone down and approached the register.

"That all for you, sir?" he asked, scanning my items.

I smiled. "Need forty on pump one as well, bud."

The younger one was staring at me, his little brow furrowed. "I know you."

"Probably do, kid," I said, holding out some twenties to the older boy. There was a small TV above them and the local news channel was on. In that moment, my name was said, a picture of me plastered on the screen.

God's timing pissed me off sometimes.

"Mason Langston, the number one bull rider in the world is riding tonight in Houston, Texas. I don't know about y'all, but I am excited to see him ride the newest monster..."

The other anchors began discussing my ranks and the bull I would be riding tonight—one of them anyways. The two boys in looked at the TV and then back to me.

"Holy shit," the younger one breathed.

That snapped the eldest out of his trance, his little mouth thinning into a hard line. He turned and scowled. "Don't say 'shit.' I'll tell Momma."

"You just said it!" his brother snapped back, embarrassment coloring his cheeks.

"I'm older than you," the older one declared. "I'm in charge while Momma is gone."

Pain slammed into the organ in my chest as I stared at them, reminding me it would always be there. The memories would never be lost. The flashbacks would always come, and the nightmares always returned. My eyes looked back and forth between the two boys, noting the determination in the older one and the rebellion in the younger one.

Two brothers.

Two brothers with an unbreakable bond...

That was kicker, though, because that bond could be broken. It would take a lot to break it, but it could break. In fact, that bond could be destroyed in an instant.

I prayed it didn't happen to them, that their bond would survive the trials of becoming a man. I hoped they would stick by each other, protect each other. The ache in my chest was becoming more annoying and I couldn't take it anymore.

"Keep the change, boys," I said as I turned for the door.

"Wait! If you're supposed to be riding tonight, what're doing here?" the young boy called out to my back.

It was time to put on a show, to do what I did best. I turned my head, looking at them over my shoulder, and gave them my signature smile.

"Cowboys do what they want." Then I was gone.

"Shaking your head at me ain't gonna change a damn thing, Eddie. It's just going to piss me off," I called as I stepped out of the truck.

He was standing a few feet from me at the back entrance to the arena. The show had already begun, the lights illuminating the dark sky above the open dome. The arena was packed tonight, the crowd more massive than what most riders were used to.

Not me, though.

The glitz, the spotlight, the glamour—all things this sport shouldn't have—were things that I'd grown used to.

I'd been in this stadium time and time again. I rode in this stadium. I drank in this stadium. I'd fucked in this stadium.

It'd been years since I fucked a buckle bunny against the wall in the back hallway, pressing her caked up face into the cement as I used her body for my pleasure, not giving a fuck about hers. She wanted pleasure? Then she needed to find a man to fuck who gave a damn. That wasn't me.

"Did I say anything?" Eddie asked, holding up his hands, pulling me from the past. He was dressed in athletic shorts and T-shirt. The clown make-up had worn off a bit since the show started about an hour ago.

"You look like shit, Ed," I noted, slinging my bag over my shoulder, and flashing him a teasing smirk.

He glared and pointed his finger at the door. "Please, for the love of steak, get inside, put on your gear, and remember to smile pretty for the crowd when you reach your eight seconds."

I chuckled and went through the door as I heard him call, "Please, for the love of a baked potato on the side of that steak, no fucking fighting tonight!"

Throwing my hand up in the air, I gave him the bird. "Okay, Ed!"

Eddie was the rodeo clown. He was in his sixties and had been my only friend for the last ten years. He was the only one who seemed to tolerate my bullshit, and for that, I was grateful. Without him, I was certain I would have died from liver failure or in a fight years ago.

That was another bad habit of mine: fighting.

I had a short temper, and a lot of fuckers liked to piss me off.

I headed to the locker rooms and changed. A decade ago, when I was still fairly new to bull riding, I would take this time to pray. I would pray I got to come home, that the beast I'd be riding that night wouldn't throw me off and kill me. I would pray I would make my family proud. I would pray my girl would give me a kiss when I saw her. I prayed Pop would see me give my girl a kiss and smile at the sight.

Now, I didn't pray.

Now, I didn't give a fuck whether I died.

The problem was I was damn good at holding on.

The problem was the *eight seconds of peace* I felt when I was on a bull.

The problem was that despite the money and fame, I couldn't quit.

I could quit because I was addicted to those eight seconds. Why? Because when I was on a bull, my head was silent.

I stepped out of the room and headed to the main area, ready for my seconds of peace.

My eyes looked up from my boots and my jaw tightened.

Fuck me.

Richard and Pamela were walking by the bullpen, daggers in both sets of eyes. Pamela was a little thing, five-two with short, chopped black hair. She was in her forties now, married with two kids. Her children loved me, they idolized me. Her husband on the other hand, he couldn't stand me. Probably has something to do with the fact that I broke his nose three years ago, but I couldn't be too sure. He didn't exactly have a bubbly personality.

My latest manager was a head shorter than my six-seven frame. He was older, fat, and balding. Why the PBR gods above thought to send me an off-brand sausage king in the hopes of controlling me was beyond me.

I couldn't be controlled.

Not anymore.

"You're over an hour late," Dick barked, folding his arms right above his protruding stomach. He took a step towards me, and I adjusted my hat, wrapping my rope around my fist.

"You sure you want to take that next step, Dick? I'm not in the mood," I warned. I wanted my eight seconds of peace, then a bottle of whiskey. I didn't need this bullshit today.

He froze before smoothing his hand over his bald, sweaty head. "You aren't worth this much trouble and stress," he snapped.

I barked out a harsh laugh, stepping by him. "Tell that to your six-figure salary, dipshit." I didn't bother speaking to Pamela. There were no words I could say to make her happy. She either tolerated me or she didn't.

When I got into the bull pen, my *colleagues* were leaning against the railings. All eyes landed on me just in time to miss the youngest of the bull riders get tossed off his beast. My eyes shot up to the clock: six seconds. Not bad for a newbie.

"Well, look who finally decided to show up," the cowboy at the far end of the line drawled. Matthew Colby.

I didn't bother responding to him. I never talked to any of them. If I did, it would end up with me hurting feelings or breaking bones.

These cowboys would come and go like everyone else in this industry. There was no point in making friends, and I wasn't looking for any. Eddie, though, he didn't count. Eddie would be with PBR until the day he died, which I hoped wasn't anytime soon. The man stuck to me like glue the first time I got knocked off after leaving home a decade ago.

"Hey, I'm talking to you, Langston!" Colby called.

I was about to pass by him when a hand landed on my shoulder.

I didn't like people touching me, especially this arrogant, big *yee-yee* truck driving, small-dicked motherfucker.

A sigh left me, and I set down my bull rope on a bench beside my head before slowly turning. His hand fell away from me, and he raised his brow, challenging me, trying to show the guys around us that he was boss. Colby was about my height, but not quite. He was leaner than me, that was for damn sure. He was a scrawny, thin man who seriously lacked muscles. That's why he kept getting thrown off. His arrogance was just a burden for everyone else to bear.

"Don't touch me again, boy," I growled, leaning down.

The rest of the riders knew better. This fucker, on the other hand, he was dumber than a sack of rocks. He's seen the damage I can do, and yet...

"You ain't shit, Langston," he clipped. My eyes drifted to the scoreboard to the right of us. My name was still on top, despite me being an hour late. Colby had already ridden twice, and he'd got thrown off before five seconds...*twice.*

A low, dark chuckle left me. "Why don't you take a seat, Colby? Pay close attention, and maybe you'll learn a thing or two."

I turned away from him, heading to the front. My sponsor rep from Evergreen Feed was standing close by, a smirk playing on his lips.

"Mason," he greeted. Evergreen didn't give a shit when I showed up, just as long as I did and held on for eight seconds. I tipped my chin to him and handed the guys my bull rope. For my first ride, I was given the youngest, biggest, meanest bull. I mounted him in silence as the crowd cheered, ready to see me do what I did best.

The bull fought me, bucking while we were still in the cage, slamming me against the railing. The cheers stopped and gasps filled the arena. I ducked my head, giving the cameras my hat and focused on the monster underneath me. He huffed through his nose, letting me know he wasn't having this shit. I clenched my jaw, closing my eyes as my fist tightened around the rope.

Peace.

Eight seconds of peace.

I raised my hand in the air, the gate opened, and the battle began.

Chapter Three

Harmony

This.

This was the reason I didn't want to come here tonight. I did only because my best friend, the most annoying person in the world, somehow convinced me to.

After cleaning up the kitchen, Billie sat me down and pulled *the card*, the one you shouldn't pull on your best friend when they don't want to go someplace.

The therapist card.

Part of my therapy was to find the courage to go places other than work, home, and the store. Once a month, I was supposed to go a place out of my comfort zone with someone I trusted.

That was my homework, assigned by Dr. G. Billie knew about it because she was usually the person I dragged along. When I was in Michigan, I rarely went anywhere, mainly staying in the shelter when I wasn't working. That had to change when I moved back to Houston, according to Giana. She told me life wasn't worth living if I had to hide from it.

I didn't have an excuse anymore because Billie was here, and tonight, she pulled that fucking card.

"You know…this would count as your homework. The month is almost over, and you haven't done anything in March." She shrugged, an evil smirk forming on her lips.

She was right, of course.

"I really hate you," I hissed.

Two hours later, there we were or rather, there *I* was.

Billie was using the bathroom.

I, however, got stopped by security.

The man who stopped me was a tall, Black man with kind eyes and a beard, but he looked more annoyed than anything. I was against a wall in a smaller hallway, away from the crowd, and he was in front of me, his hands on his belt.

"You can't have that in here," he stated, nodding to my bottle.

"I'm sorry," I said softly. My hold shifted on my bottle, needing to feel it with the tips of my fingers. "I have to have this, sir. I have a health condition."

It wasn't exactly a lie. It wasn't the whole truth either.

His eyes softened for a fraction of a second. Then, in the next blink, it was gone. "Ma'am, it's the rules. No outside food or drink."

The crowd was dwindling now as everyone headed back to their seats. There had been a break in the show, and everyone jumped up to get refills and food. I hadn't got to see a single bull rider yet because we were late getting here—due to my resistance. Then Billie wanted to get snacks, plus we had a hard time finding our seats. Then of course, small bladder Billie, had to fucking pee.

In the middle of the crowd, filled with buckle bunnies and wannabe cowboys, I felt the monster trying to swim to the surface, no doubt ready to drag me back down.

I didn't do well with crowds but the old me—*the dead me*—thrived in them. The old Harmony thrived on going out every Friday and Saturday night to dance and sip on colorful drinks in crowded bars and clubs. The mere idea of that terrified me now. If I thought about it too long, panic would set in, and I wouldn't be able to function for an hour.

After Billie convinced me to go and assured me we would only be in the crowd before and after the show, I felt good about it. For the first time in years, I felt good about being normal again.

Then, she and I got separated.

She sent me a text informing me she was in the bathroom. I needed to get away from the crowd. I just wanted a moment of quiet. So, I ducked into this little hall and decided to people watch for a moment, thinking that maybe if watched the sea of people, it wouldn't be so damn terrifying when I had to join it again.

The security guard just happened to be walking by and got the wrong idea, seeing my bottle in my hands.

"It's just water," I tried to reason with him.

My eyes silently pleaded with him to let me go, to let me be. I wasn't bothering anyone. I was just carrying my bottle. It wasn't like I was hitting people with it. It wasn't a gun or a knife, yet he was treating me like it was.

He shook his head. "We have water for sale here."

There was nothing I could say to that. Of course, they had water here. Concession stands were littered all along the sides of the arena; hell, you could smell the junk food from the back of the parking lot.

Not able to hold his eyes, I looked down, taking in my dark jeans and Fleetwood Mac shirt. I didn't wear boots tonight. I didn't own boots anymore. Everything the old Harmony had was most likely in a landfill or littered through the Goodwills of Texas. Instead, I was wearing a new pair of dark green Converse. I thought they went well with the colors on my shirt and contrasted against my hair. I felt cute before leaving the apartment—confident, even. Cabe came by to pick us up, and he beamed at me, probably happy to see me in something other than scrubs or leggings. He'd whispered in my ear how beautiful I was, giving me an extra boost of confidence.

Focus on the now, Harm.

Look the guard in the eye.

Be fucking brave for once.

When I looked back up, the guard was closer, holding out his hand. Alarm bells went off in my head, my spine stiffening, my throat drying.

"Give me the bottle please, ma'am."

Never again. Never again. Never again.

I shook my head in desperation. "I can't lose it," I argued, holding it closer to my chest. My raspy voice was shaking at the thought of the bottle being taken away from me. The man stared at me, his hand still in the air between us. I looked at the crowd and back to him.

Where in the hell was Billie?

"I'll lock it in the office, and you can come find me after," he said, sighing. He was growing impatient, and so was I. I was being a nuisance—*a burden.*

I didn't understand why I couldn't *just* be normal again.

Why I couldn't be like everyone else on this stupid planet? It was just a water bottle, Harmony. Why was I so fucked in the head? Why couldn't I just pick myself up and dust off my shoulders like everyone else?

My lip trembled and I looked away from him, my fingers flexing around the metal cylinder. A weight settled on my chest as his words washed over me. He wanted to *lock it in his office.* He was the only one with the keys.

He.

Wanted.

To.

Lock it away.

He wanted to keep it from me. Control me.

I stepped back, trying to create some distance. He couldn't take it. It was mine. If he took it, then—then—

He stepped closer, the movement derailing my train of thought.

"Ma'am, give me the bottle," he snapped. I flinched at his tone. A normal person wouldn't flinch. A normal person would just give him the bottle—

A normal person wouldn't even have the bottle in the first place.

I squeezed my eyes shut, shaking my head again. My back was against the wall, and he was crowding me. I felt small. I felt weak. I felt like a prisoner.

I felt trapped.

Billie, where are you? "Either give me the bottle or leave," he growled.

I nodded quickly, relief washing over me.

I didn't have a problem with leaving. I could go home to the quiet and lock my door.

"I need to wait for my friend," I whispered, opening my eyes and gesturing behind him. "She went to the bathroom, and then we'll go."

The man shook his head, looking to the crowd and back to me. "Do you think I'm stupid?" The kindness in his eyes melted away. I shook my head immediately. Not stupid; he just lacked compassion.

He continued, "Give me the bottle. Now!"

"I can't."

He closed the distance between us, and his arm snapped out. His hand was on the bottle now, the tips of his fingers brushing against my chest. "Give it to me!"

"No! Get off me!" I said, twisting my body. He grabbed my arm with his other arm and slammed me back against the wall. Flashes filled my vision, the monster breaking the surface with an evil laugh, its talons reaching for me.

I needed to breathe. I needed to count.

One, two, three. One, two, three.

Red, blue, green. Red, blue, green.

One, two—

The guard yanked on the bottle and pinned me to the wall with his body. His other hand was now gripping one of my wrists, trying to wretch my hand from the bottle. I opened my mouth to scream, fear taking over my trembling limbs. Memories from the past came rushing forward as the monster gripped my skin, ready to pull me down and drag me under into the darkness.

Ready to drown me once and for all.

Fight, Harmony. Fight.

The man growled when I tried to kick him. He backed away for a moment, his eyes wide with shock. I swallowed, ignoring the dryness in my throat as I tried to run but he grabbed me *again,* pinning me against the wall *again.*

"Give me the fucking bottle, lady!" he hissed. I tried to bend over, needing to get away, but his forearm came to my chest, slamming my top half back against the wall. A short scream left me.

"Get off me!" I cried, grunting as I tightened my hold on the bottle. I wouldn't let him have it.

Never again. Never again. Never again.

"What the *fuck?*"

Before I could register who spoke, the guard was pulled from me and thrown—*yes, thrown*—against the opposite wall. His body slammed into it, and he slid down to his ass with a grunt. I adjusted my hold on the bottle, my chest rising and falling faster and faster. The monster was back above the water, coming around behind me. For the second time this week, he sported that same greasy smile as he looked at me over my shoulder. I shook my head and kicked my feet, suddenly in the deep pool of tar that the beast escaped from.

"No, no," I whimpered, my chest heaving.

"Whoa, darlin', whoa," a deep, rough, voice said gently. Heat enveloped me and I stood up straight. My eyes flicked to the source, and my breath caught. The monster glared at the man towering over me, a low growl ripping from its lips.

The man in front of me was a bull rider.

Not just any bull rider.

A tall, gorgeous one.

He was still in his gear, his vest hanging open to reveal a black and grey flannel. The black hat on his head did a horrible job of making him appear unattractive, only adding to the intensity of his gray eyes. His jaw line was dusted with stubble, adding to his roughness. He had high cheekbones, a straight nose, and thick brows.

Those brows were furrowed as he looked down at me.

The cowboy tilted his head slowly, taking a step closer to me. My body flinched.

"Gonna need you to say something to me," he demanded gently.

How could this tall, huge man be gentle?

It didn't seem possible. His boots clicked on the concrete as he stepped up to me. My eyes met his, and I felt my lips part. He was angry.

Holy goodness, he was angry.

The storm that raged in the gray of his eyes was proof enough.

"Did he...did that man over there touch you?" he asked, still gentle.

The anger in his eyes told me he was anything but *gentle*. The anger in his eyes told me he was the kind of man to destroy everything in his path and walk away, leaving nothing but debris behind.

He was the kind of man the woman I once would dream about, the kind I wanted to end up with.

Gentle but fierce.

A protector and a fighter.

Once upon a time, if a man like this flirted with me, I would have flirted back.

Not now. Now, I just wanted to run away.

"Darlin', answer me," he ordered, his deep voice shaking slightly. He was having trouble containing that anger.

That scared me. Everything about this experience scared me.

I nodded.

Lightning flashed in the cowboy's stormy eyes, and he turned to face the guard, who was now on his feet, staring at the cowboy with wide eyes.

"She said no, man. I heard her," the cowboy started, his voice low.

"M—Mr. Langston, it's not what it looks like. She can't have *that* in the building." The security guard gestured to me.

The cowboy—*Mr. Langston*—looked back at me over his shoulder. His eyes dropped to the bottle against my chest. Instinctively, I tightened my hold on it. "Darlin', you got liquor in that bottle?" the cowboy asked. When his eyes met mine again, my heart skipped a beat.

I shook my head.

"Soda?"

Another shake.

"Drugs?"

I shifted my feet. *God, I was so lame.*

"Water," I whispered, my raspy voice shaking a little.

The cowboy stared at me for the beat, his eyes trying to assess me in a way I didn't want to be. Then, he turned his attention back to the security guard.

"Let me get this straight, man. You saw this *woman* carrying a *water bottle* and decided that's what you needed to focus on?" There was a growl in his voice when he said the word 'woman' and sent shivers down my spine. "There are fist fights going on outside, and the red-head is who you decided to focus on?" the cowboy deadpanned.

"It ain't like that, Mr. Langston," the man stammered on, not looking at me anymore.

The cowboy chuckled darkly and took a step towards the man. "Let me make one thing perfectly clear: *ever* touch another woman who doesn't want to be touched in my presence again, you'll wake up in the hospital sucking shitty food from a straw," the cowboy threatened. His voice was menacing, causing my pulse to quicken again.

The guard nodded.

"Get the fuck out of my sight," the bull rider clipped, his hands balling into fists at his sides. The guard nodded, then ducked out of the hall.

I watched as Mr. Langston pulled off his hat and ran a hand through his short, dirty blonde hair. His presence was devasting.

In the middle of my gawking, he turned to me, slowly putting his hat back on, but couldn't focus on that. No, I was focused on the tension in his neck, the golden tan of his skin, and the way his throat bobbed.

Why did he have to have a gorgeous neck too?

I didn't understand it.

"Darlin'," he called softly, snapping my attention back to him. My spine straightened, my body on alert again now that we were alone.

He held up his hands, the storm in his eyes calming a bit. "You alright?"

I nodded.

His handsome features softened, causing my belly to flip, and my heart to skipped another beat. How could a man like this be soft?

"Need to hear you say the words. If you don't, I'm going to go after him."

"W—why?" I asked. The damage was done. It was over.

"Men don't hurt women," he stated, his jaw tightening. "Men who do pay."

Emotion swelled in my throat at his words, at his promise of justice. This was the kind of man this planet needed to be filled with. Unfortunately, a man like this was a rare breed. He was a protector, that was clear, but there was a softness within him.

Someone in the world got to see that softness.

That someone wasn't me.

It would never be me.

I wasn't worthy of softness, period.

Unable to handle his eyes, I looked down at the ground again, focusing on my feet. I inhaled a shaky breath as tears threatened to form in my eyes.

No. Please, not here. Not in front of him.

Then, I felt a rough, warm finger slide under my chin, the touch sending a rush of electricity through my body. He lifted my head up and he was right *there*, in my space, leaning down close. My eyes dropped to his large hand, noting the scars and dried blood on his knuckles.

How had I missed that?

My nose filled with his scent, and that frustrated me, too.

Cowboys were supposed to stink. He didn't stink.

He smelled like a rainy day in the spring, after the sun had come out and the flowers had started to bloom again. He smelled like happiness. He smelled like my life before it turned dark, before I became this fucked up version Harmony.

The damaged one.

The basket case.

This cowboy smelled like that, but his stormy eyes told me that he wasn't happy. In fact, I was sure there was no sunshine in his life at all.

I found myself nodding again, unsure if he asked me a question. He focused on my lips for a moment, causing my heart to stop completely. Then those eyes lifted as he scanned my face slowly, like he was trying to engrave it into his memory. I didn't need to study his face.

One look and I knew I wouldn't be forgetting this cowboy.

His eyes held mine as he said softly, "Say it for me, baby."

Baby.

My core hummed for the first time in what seemed like forever, shocking me like I was sucker punched to the gut. A whimper threatened to escape, but I swallowed it down. He didn't need to know that. He didn't know that his words, his voice, the look of him, his scent, it all just flipped a switch inside of me, a switch I'd thought was ripped from the wall.

"I'm okay," I finally rasped.

Suddenly, his finger was gone, and my skin burned. I missed it.

His touch felt like the sun, and I wanted more.

Why did I want more?

Mr. Langston flashed me a smile that seemed too beautiful and too practiced to be real. "Good," he muttered. Then he, with his burning touch, stormy eyes, and intoxicating scent, was gone. I stood plastered against the wall wondering what just happened.

Why the hell did my body respond to him like that?

A second later, I heard a low, country drawl come across the loudspeaker. "As usual, folks, your winner tonight is Mason Langston! Let's give it up for the man who can't be thrown, ladies and gentlemen!"

"Harm, you don't have to watch this," Cabe said, moving around my coffee table. I held up my hand and shook my head.

"Wait—Cabe. I want to know what happened," I returned, my eyes not leaving my TV screen. Bille and he were over for SFB—Sunday Friend's Brunch, the day after the I was saved by Mason Langston.

The man was now plastered all over my TV as news anchors discussed the events that unfolded shortly after his win was announced. A video recording, taken by an onlooker, was playing by the news anchor's head.

"Well, another surprise from the top bull rider in the world took place last night. Our favorite cowboy had just closed on yet another win when a fight broke out at the arena security office," the first anchor stated.

My stomach dropped, but my heart skipped a beat.

"The crowds were leaving the arena when the fight started. Security guard Greg Wyatts was in the middle of a conversation with his manager when Langston approached them," the female anchor continued.

My eyes drifted to the recording. Mason was stalking over to the two men, ignoring the fan following him with his phone. The guard who approached me—*Greg*—looked at Mason, his brown skin visibly paling at the sight. The cowboy didn't give him a chance to get a word out before he picked Greg up off the ground and shoved him against the nearest wall, his fists gripping the guard's collar.

"Words seem to have been exchanged," the anchor commented as the video dragged on. Mason pointed a finger in the man's face, and though I couldn't see Mason's full face under his hat, his jaw was clenched with fury, his muscles flexing under the fabric of his flannel.

A surge of desire rushed through my body, and I gasped softly, bringing my fingers to my lips.

What the hell was wrong with me?

"The video gets pretty violent after that, folks, so we're going to stop it there. It is yet to be determined whether charges will be pressed, although Mason Langston was arrested last night. We'll have more to come as this story develops."

The TV was flickered off, and I looked up to Cabe standing in front of the coffee table, hands on his hips. I liked Cabe. He was good for Billie, two peas in a pod. Cabe was the dark to Billie's light. He had brown curly hair, cut short on the sides and long on top, and Billie had straight blonde hair. I envied her straight hair.

Meanwhile, I looked like the fucking princess from the Disney movie *Brave*. My head was a mop of unruly coils and curls of bright orange, making it easy for childhood bullies. I stood out in the crowd when all I desperately wanted was to blend in.

I didn't blend in last night. I caught the attention of a cowboy—the last kind of attention I wanted. Still, I couldn't figure out why I reacted to him the way I did. This morning, when I woke up, did my meditation, and journaled for a bit, I just brushed it off as an adrenaline rush.

If it was just that, then why are you staring at the TV like you want it on again?

"Mason Langston is the bad boy of the PBR world," Billie said, whistling low as she emerged from the kitchen, carrying a small tray with three glasses of orange juice. Cabe took it from her and placed it on the table.

"That guy is fucking nuts," he grumbled, shaking his head.

I looked between them wondering if I should say anything or not. Last night, after the bull rider left me in the hallway, Billie found me. She apparently got caught in the crowd and ran into her boss. She was in a frenzy, apologizing and breathing heavily. I waved it off and put on a fake smile; she didn't need to have that heavy guilt on her shoulders. It wasn't her fault her best friend was damaged.

As I was getting ready for SFB, I was wondering why I hadn't told my best friend about the angry cowboy last night. Normally, I told her everything, but for some reason, I'd held back.

Because he's a sliver of sunshine that you wanted for yourself.

"He won last night," I noted stupidly, taking a sip of my juice and shaking off my previous thoughts, thoughts that had no business being in my head. Thoughts my head didn't deserve in the first place.

Billie plopped down beside me, tucking her legs in with a huff. "He wins every single time," she deadpanned, sounding unimpressed.

I blinked.

I hadn't really followed bull riding the last six years. In fact, anything to do with that lifestyle, I avoided. Then again, I hadn't really followed or kept up with anything in the last six years.

"Really?" I asked in disbelief. It didn't seem possible that he'd win every single time. A lucky streak, sure, but no man was that lucky. Right?

Cabe took a seat on the floor in front of the coffee table, stretching out his long legs. "Yes, really. They're studying him like he is some damn science project. He has only been thrown off three times, I think." I looked to my best friend, who nodded in agreement.

Holy shit.

"That doesn't seem possible," I murmured, looking at the black TV again.

Cabe snorted. "Yeah, I know. That's why they're studying him. Seriously, they look at old videos. The younger guys either worship him or hate him. The older ones know not to mess with him."

"What do you mean?" I asked with a blink, looking at them.

Billie sighed. "A few years back, PBR was in Houston, and we went. It was like his second ride of the night, and the guy before him lasted eight seconds. The crowd was cheering, and Mason even clapped for the guy," she explained. I could see him doing that, supporting his fellow riders. He seemed like that kind of man: a protector with a soft side. Billie's voice pulled me from my thoughts. "Harmony, the guy got cocky. I think it was the first time he lasted eight seconds. Anyways, he approached Mason and mouthed off to him. Next thing you know, Langston hopped the gate and *beat* the guy *into the dirt*."

My mouth dropped open. "Really?" It came out as a whisper.

She nodded, tucking a piece of her blonde hair behind her ear. "He has a reputation for fighting. Anyone who gives him lip gets an ass whopping. That's the thing about Mason Langston: he doesn't take any shit—from anyone. He just hired a new manager a few months back, like the tenth one, right, Cabe?"

Her boyfriend grunted, taking a sip of his juice.

"That doesn't make any sense," I said under my breath.

"What doesn't?"

Oh, shit.

My eyes snapped up to meet hers, and I gestured to the TV. "He—uh—he looks like a nice guy."

Billie tilted her head and Cabe twisted his neck, both of them looking at me with confusion now. I cleared my throat. "You know, for someone who looks like that."

Cabe shook his head. "Mason Langston is unhinged. Nothing about that man is nice, except for his stats."

Three hours later, the conversation about Mason Langston had faded away, brunch was over, the kitchen was cleaned, and my friends were leaving. Billie told me to have a good week, followed by a tight embrace. Cabe pressed a kiss to my cheek and promised he would drop by after work on Wednesday to help hang the painting in the living room. I wouldn't be seeing Billie for the rest of the week, the first week since I returned to Houston that I wouldn't see her. Cabe was only stopping by on Wednesday because Billie was making him. After Wednesday, I would only see my friends on the weekends, as instructed by my therapist.

I needed to stop using them as a crutch.

They left and I locked the door behind me, enjoying the silence that filled my apartment for a moment. It called to me immediately: the need to create. The need to make something beautiful. My feet carried me to my music room, where I picked up my guitar. I sat in the chair, staring out the window, grateful to be where I was today. The sun was high, white clouds scattered across the blue sky; a beautiful Sunday. My fingers strummed the strings mindlessly for a few moments as I gathered my thoughts.

Thoughts of my growth.

Thoughts of friends.

Thoughts of mundane things I'd lost, such as laundry. I had to do the laundry tonight, and I was grateful for it.

Then my mundane thoughts drifted into dangerous territory as my fingers strummed a melody. Mason's face flashed through my mind, and in the quiet of my apartment, I allowed my body to feel what she needed. The notes filled my ears as my eyes closed.

Music was a way to process my pain, but that afternoon, I found myself writing lyrics about a cowboy's pain and the storm in his eyes.

Chapter Four

Mason

Say it for me, baby.

Baby.

Say it for me, baby.

What the actual *fuck* is wrong with me?

I tilted my head slightly, raising my brows. *Wasn't that the question of the fucking decade.* Fuck. I scrubbed a hand down my face before shaking my head. I called her *baby.*

I called that woman in the hall *baby.*

I never call anyone *baby.*

Ever.

Not fucking once in my entire life have I used that term of endearment.

Last night, I did. Last night, I saw that woman with bright red hair, the color of fire—untamed and begging to be touched—cowering against the wall, and I called her *baby*. It just slipped out, before my mind could register what my mouth had done.

I *touched* her.

Fuck, I touched her. She was trembling in fear from another man, and I touched her without her consent. My jaw tightened at my stupidity. Me, the asshole who hates being touched, touched her without consent.

I didn't mean to touch her, but she was terrified, hiding her eyes from me.

The last thing I wanted was her hiding those eyes from me.

She had the brightest blue eyes I'd ever seen, like a cloudless sky in the middle of summer. They reminded me of simpler times, times when I was innocent and free of torment. I'd never seen eyes like hers, not anywhere else in the world. I could stare at them for forever, if she let me.

I wanted those eyes on me and me only, not the fucker who scared her. Fear had been dominant in her endless blue pools, and it was the last thing I'd wanted to see. I never wanted fear to be in her eyes, not around me. I wanted to see how bright her blue became when she was happy, to see how her pupils dilated when her body was overcome with desire, and then earth-shattering pleasure.

I wanted to see those eyes again.

No—I needed to see *her* again.

"You really can't help yourself, can you?"

I smiled, Eddie's voice filling my ears, bouncing off the private holding cell that I sat in. Slowly, I turned my head to him. I was lying on the metal cot, hands behind my head, boots crossed.

"Took you long enough," I drawled, not moving from my spot. I'd been in jail all night, and the fucker strolls in here the next morning.

Some best friend.

Eddie's face was clear of last night's clown makeup, and he was wearing jeans and a PBR shirt, along with a Cubs hat on his head.

I pointed to it, "They've sucked ever since Dean Connors was murdered."

"Yeah, yeah, I know, asshole," he barked, and then grumbled something under his breath. My chest shook as a chuckle came from me.

God, I loved giving this guy shit.

"You done talking about baseball, or did you want to stay in here another day?"

I looked back to the ceiling. I hadn't slept a fucking wink, and my body was sore from last night's ride, but I would never show it. No one would ever know how tired I was or see the bruises on my body.

"The company wasn't ideal," I drawled out.

Guys from the cell next to mine started in on their shit.

"Fuck you, cowboy!"

"Pretty boy's only talkin' shit cause he ain't in here with us," a voice boomed back. I smiled at the ceiling again, knowing damn well I could kill every single one of them with my bare hands.

"Can we go?" Eddie clipped.

"I've been waiting for you all night and you're rushing me?" I deadpanned.

He glared at me. "I should just leave your ass in here."

"Then you wouldn't have any fun," I returned.

Eddie shook his head. "Mase, they pulled the security video from last night."

My hair on the back of my neck stood on end. The red head. I sat up, swinging my legs over the cot, my boots hitting the floor. "And?" I pressed.

"You were right, as usual. They're dropping the charges, letting you go, and they fired Greg Wyatts."

I didn't give a shit about that or Greg. Good riddance. He put his hands on a woman over a water bottle.

In truth, I only cared about the woman in the video. the one with flaming red hair and blue eyes. My mind drifted to last night, how I took my time drinking in her hair, her eyes, her pale, freckled skin, and her curves, wishing that we'd met under different circumstances. That woman had curves, mainly on the lower half, but—

"You listening to me?"

The image of her body, full pink lips, and face disappeared at the sound of Eddie's voice.

"Yes, Your Highness," I drawled, getting up from the cot.

My gear was off, no doubt with my team and not in the evidence room. They made me take it off before shoving me into the back of a squad car.

I was still in my boots, jeans, and flannel. The police took my hat, which pissed me off, but I was too angry to argue with them last night. I had just beaten the shit out of that guard, and I just wanted quiet. When I'd found him talking to his manager, he was telling him about how I threw him against a wall.

"I'm here to do it again, bud," I hissed as I gripped his collar, shoving him up into the air and against the wall. His feet were dangling as he pleaded for mercy, but I was seeing red.

Red like the color of her hair.

He touched her.

He fucking scared her.

I pointed my finger at his face. "It's time to teach you some manners, Greg."

Eddie and I approached the front desk, where the officer from last night stood. My hat was on the counter next to the paperwork I needed to sign. I lifted my chin to him. "Appreciate you taking care of this," I said, grabbing the hat.

He smirked. "Could've sold that shit on E-bay and paid for my daughter's college tuition."

I gave him my fake smile. "Well, fuck me. Here." I held the hat out to him, and he laughed, shaking his head.

"Nah, man. That's yours."

"Mr. Langston."

I looked over my shoulder to find Pam and Dick standing up from their chairs. I shot a glare at Eddie, and he held his hands up in innocence. "Don't look at me, fuck nut. They followed me." Clearing my throat, I went back to the paperwork. Then, I spent the next few minutes shooting the shit with a few cops and signing autographs, dragging it out just to see Dick sweat a bit more.

This was Texas; I was a fucking god here. I hated it. I hated being in this state more than being in Colorado. The attention I received was overwhelming; I couldn't even walk to the store without getting swarmed by fans. Still, I never skipped the shows in Texas, just Colorado. I made the most money here, and the whiskey was strong.

"You mind if I come back by in a little bit without the leeches?" I asked the officer who arrested me. Last night, his face was set in stone. Now he was grinning, happy to be talking to me.

He held out his hand. "Sure thing, man. Anytime." He gave me his name—which was Steve—and I turned to the people who hated me most.

"Alright, let's get this shit over with," I called out to my team, putting my hat back on.

Pamela had her arms folded over her chest, tapping her high-heeled shoe on the dirty, white tile floor. She shook her head and pursed her lips. Walking up to her, I dipped down to her level and gave her a wink. "Good morning, Pam."

She snapped her fingers and pointed to the door. "Go."

"You got any gum?" I asked, ignoring her.

"Mason," she snapped.

I sighed and stood back up to full height, looking back at the police officers. "Thank you for what you do."

Everyone started clapping and I ducked out in the sunshine.

"Fuck! Why can't you just be—"

I stood from the couch, pointing to the door as I fumed at my manager.

"Get. The. Fuck. Out," I growled, tired of his bullshit. I was tired of being lectured over something I needed done. I was a cowboy. If there was a lesson that needed to be given, my fists were going to be involved. It's as simple as that, especially if it came to defending a woman, even more so a woman like her.

A heavy, uncomfortable silence settled over my hotel suite. Pamela was on the other couch, typing on her laptop—most likely a statement for the press. Eddie was leaning against the mini bar in the corner, though he was only here as a friend. He was the last person to judge me, and I him. He had his demons, and I had mine. Mainly, we ignored those demons together, but there were times like this when I needed him more than he needed me. I just couldn't let him know that.

Richard gaped at me, his eyes flashing with anger. His face was red, dripping sweat from yelling at me. His suit was baggy and worn. He never bought new suits, despite all the money I made him. The fucker wore the same two, old, loose suits over and over again. He was lecturing me for no reason.

I'd done what was right.

"Show me the footage," I demanded.

"That's not important, Mason! You beat up a security guard last night!"

"That woman was in danger, *Dick.* I know you don't respect women, but some of us in this room do," I challenged, taking a step closer to him. He stiffened for just a moment, his tomato-red skin paling a bit.

Yeah, I know about the fucking strip clubs. I also know about your whore in Georgia and your wife in Tampa.

"That's not what this is about, Mason! This is about you not being professional!" he shouted back at me, the bulbous vein in his face neck pulsing.

I looked at the ceiling and pointed to the phone in his hand. "Check your bank account, and you tell me if it looks professional or not."

He flinched. I smirked.

I was the one in control here, not him, management title or not.

"He's right, you know," Pamela said from her place on the couch, her eyes never leaving her computer screen.

"What?" *Dick* barked.

What?

"She was in danger, the girl from last night," she returned calmly. I didn't take my eyes off Richard, but I could feel Pam's on me.

My manager glared at her, ready to lay into her. "Pam, please, for the love of God, tell me you aren't buying into this bullshit!"

"There is nothing to buy into, *Dick*. The video is proof enough," she reminded him. He huffed, and my upper lip curled. Fuck, this guy got on my nerves.

"Show me the video," I repeated with a growl.

The man turned to me again, pointing a chubby, sausage finger at me. "You are so *full of shit*, Mason Langston! Everyone in this room knows you were only using that opportunity to get your cock wet!" he sneered.

I stilled, my spine snapping straight as hot anger, slid down my back like molten lava. My jaw clenched and I balled my hands into fists.

Control it.

Control it, Mase.

Pamela's head snapped. "Richard…"

Eddie pushed off the bar, coming to me slowly. "Mase…"

My voice was cold and low when I spoke to the fat, low life fuck in front of me. "You're fired."

The man exploded. *"What?"*

"Eddie, get him out of here before I—"

"On it," my friend assured me, jumping in front of my now former manager and pushing him towards the door.

"Good luck finding another manager, you cocky piece of shit!" he bellowed. I shook my head and went to the mini bar. It wasn't even noon yet, but fuck, I needed a drink.

Or the whole fucking bottle.

The door slammed behind me.

My hand shook as I swiped up the brand-new bottle of whiskey from the granite countertop; black labeled, a gift from the owner of the PBR. He sent me one in every city. I was making him millions and he thought a bottle of whiskey was sufficient repayment. Greedy ass.

Fishing out a glass, I poured two fingers before lifting it to my lips. My eyes focused on the city before me, the city I hated.

"Bastard," I muttered before throwing back the burning liquid, relishing in the pain as it trickled down my throat.

"Mason."

My head swiveled to Pamela, who was standing up to face me. Her laptop was discarded on the couch, and I knew what was coming. She had been with me for years, and even though I gave her shit, and she gave it right back, she stayed. A few years back, her firm offered her a contract to represent another rider. She stuck by me. Most of the time, we couldn't stand each other, but then there were days like today.

Days when I wasn't such a disappointment.

"Thank you," she said softly as I poured myself a second drink.

"For firing that fucking sleaze? Or something else?" I quipped, still hot with rage. I didn't want to fire her, but if she gave me bullshit, I would.

"For standing up for women."

The glass was halfway to my mouth when I stopped.

Lowering it, I turned to face her fully. "Hurting women isn't something I'm a fan of, Pam. You know that," I reminded her. "Despite everything, you should know that. I'm a decent fucking human."

Something flashed in her eyes as she flinched at my words. She looked away from me, focusing on Houston instead. "When I was given the tape this morning, I didn't know what to expect, Mason. You're a hothead," she said softly.

My jaw tightened.

She sighed, looking to her feet and then up at me. "I'm sorry. He shouldn't have said that to you. Saving that woman was not a conquest. I know you better than that."

No, she didn't. No one did.

"You got the statement ready for the press?" I asked, not wanting to talk about this. I threw back the last of the whiskey and took the glass to the sink. Pam's eyes following me as I moved across the hotel suite.

"The video is the statement, Mason."

A chill ran down my spine. "No," I said, looking at her. "Do *not* put that video on the news."

She scoffed, crossing her arms over her chest. "I know you think it's going to damage your bad boy reputation, but you need to think about—"

Like I said, she didn't know a thing about me.

"Pamela do not put that on the news. I am not a bad boy with a fucked-up hero complex. That woman was attacked," I practically growled at her. "That woman has been *through enough*."

Her eyes widened as her arms fell away slowly. She was stunned to say the least. *How typical.* Her head tilted, her brows coming together as she stepped up to the counter. "How do you know what she's been through, Mason?"

Because I saw it in her memorizing blue eyes.

Because I read her body language like a fucking book.

Because she was holding onto that teal bottle like it was a fucking lifeline.

I didn't tell Pam any of these things, though. She didn't need to know about the red-headed woman's pain. That was for me to know, not her.

So instead, I shrugged. "If you were attacked like that, would you want to see it plastered over every news outlet in the country?" I asked, raising a brow.

Pamela's lips thinned.

I nodded. "Exactly, Pam. Just write something. I'll play nice for the cameras and dazzle everyone with my smile," I assured her, smiling wide.

She opened her mouth to say something, but then her phone rang.

Thank fuck.

My eyes lifted to Eddie, who was leaning against the wall by the door. He and I were waiting for my PR queen to wrap this shit up. I needed a fucking shower and then a nap.

"This is Pam—yes. Okay, I'm on my way down. No, he needs to rest," she said into the phone, looking at me. I nodded. She began gathering her stuff while listening to whoever the fuck was on the other side end. When she turned to me, she pulled the device away to say, "Evergreen Feed wants to do a photoshoot."

Evergreen Feed was my *biggest* sponsor, and because of them, I was able to make it big after leaving Colorado. I owed them everything.

"Set it up," I replied, shooing her away.

When she was out the door, I looked at Eddie.

"The woman from last night."

He looked at me expectantly.

I looked out the window again, focusing on the overcast skies of March. "I'm going to find her, and I need your help to do it." When I looked back at him, he was closer, shaking his head.

"Mase, what are you doin'?" he sighed. "What is she to you?"

Someone I needed to know.

"Don't ask me that, man. I don't have an answer for you."

Houston Police Station.

The chief of police, Donald, lingered in the hall corner, watching his men laugh at something the bull rider said. Yesterday, that cowboy had been locked up, and now, he was shooting the shit with the officers who put him in cuffs. Shaking his head, Donald raised his coffee to his lips, settling in to observe until the cowboy made his departure.

When the time finally came, Mason Langston shook hands with each officer. His hat tipped up, scanning the bull pen for a moment before his eyes landed on Donald. The cowboy took in Donald's uniform and ranking before lifting his chin. The chief lifted his hand, giving the man a wave.

Ten minutes later, one of his deputies approached his office door.

"Chief, you wanted to see me?" Steve asked.

Ten minutes after that, Steve having returned to his duties, Donald was on edge, nervous about the phone call he was about to make. He prayed that he would be able to leave a message.

"I assume your call is important, Chief," the man answered.

Donald swallowed, sitting up in his chair. "Yes, sir."

Silence and then, "I don't have all day," the man growled.

"She's back."

"Back," he repeated, slower than Donald liked. Sweat trickled down the back of Donald's neck as his eyes darted to the picture of his wife and their two children on his desk.

Clearing his throat, the chief confirmed, "Yes, sir."

"I'll deal with this later." The line went dead as the man hung up.

Donald sat back in his chair wondering if he just made the biggest mistake of his twenty-year career.

Chapter Five

Harmony

May

"I think you're making excellent progress, Harmony."

A rare, real smile formed on my lips as I stared at Giana on my laptop screen. "I feel really good, Dr. G," I whispered, pride coursing through my veins at her statement.

My therapist was a middle-aged, Hispanic woman from Detroit. Since moving back to Texas, I'd been doing my sessions over Zoom calls. Giana Rodiquez was my saving grace; without her, I don't know where I would be.

Probably still broken, lost, and rotting in the dirt.

When I first moved to Michigan, I'd been hiding in a shitty hotel room. I had been there for about three weeks when my first panic attack hit me, shattering the already broken pieces of me into even tinier ones. It was so intense, I passed out on the sidewalk on the way to a laundry mat.

I woke up in a hospital a day later.

As much as I hated my attacks, I was grateful for that first one, because it led me to Giana. She didn't like being addressed as Dr. Rodiquez. She told me during our first session that it was too formal for the conversations that we'd be having. From that moment on, I called her Dr. G.

"How's work at the clinic going?" she asked, crossing her legs and adjusting her tablet to rest against her thigh.

My mind drifted to my watcher. The cowboy.

"He still comes by," I admitted, ignoring the way my heart skipped a beat. Every time I thought of him, my heart malfunctioned. Every time I saw him, I felt like I couldn't breathe or think.

"Do you feel threatened by him?" she asked, raising a dark brow.

I shook my head.

Threatened? No. He would never hurt me; I knew that in my soul.

I felt drawn to him, like a moth to a flame.

A flame I had no business looking at.

My hands sunk into my hair, and I lifted it off of my neck, twisting the mass into a bun on the top of my head. "The truth is, I know he doesn't come to the clinic for me. Hell, I don't even know if he remembers me..."

But he looks at you.

He looks at everyone. *Especially Claire.*

"Why do you think that, Harmony? Why do you think you're forgettable?" she pressed, doing a damn good job. She knew how to dig deeper with me.

I stared at her, swallowing the lump in my throat before whispering, "Because for so long, I wanted to be."

I wanted to be hidden, forgotten. I used to dream of it, and the peace that would come with it.

She hummed and jotted down a few notes. "I think you should talk to him," she finally declared, looking up at me again.

"What?" I screeched, my eyes going wide.

A smile tugged on her lips. "You said he was good looking, right?"

He wasn't just good looking.

He was the first ray of sunlight that peaked through the clouds after a storm.

He was a beautiful chord in a song that sent goosebumps across my skin.

He was every note in the music I'd been writing for the last two months.

I shook my head and looked down at my lap.

I was sitting at my kitchen counter on a Saturday morning. Normally, Giana doesn't do weekend sessions, but I had to work late last night. Avoiding her eyes, I looked up around my kitchen, noting the ways I'd settled in, the progress I'd made. Being in this apartment for the last few months was an adjustment, but finally, it was starting to feel like home. At the end of the day, I couldn't wait to get home and be in my space.

I hadn't felt that way in a long time.

I never really had my own space, and now, I do. There was something powerful and beautiful in that, something I treasured.

The girl who never stopped running never thought she would have this.

That same girl never thought her body would react to a man again. Yet here I was, six years later, confused about my watcher—I liked to think he came into my life to look out for me, to protect me like he had that night two months ago.

The week after the PBR incident, Mason Langston showed up at the private practice clinic I worked at. It was a fairly large clinic, and the owners had plans of expanding in the next two years. The day that cowboy walked in, I thought I was seeing things again. I immediately grabbed my bottle and ducked into the breakroom to call Dr. G.

I wasn't hallucinating.

He was there. In the flesh.

An unfamiliar feeling of excitement rushed through me, but it quickly died when he didn't even look at me.

He never looked at me.

I had been forgotten by the person I never wanted to forget me.

Now, it'd been almost two months, and he stopped by once a week to talk to the doctors and owners. Apparently, according to Claire the Great, he was looking to invest. He never stayed for more than ten minutes and he never, *never* looked at me. At least, not when I was looking at him, which I tried not to do, but like I said, moth to a flame. A *stupid* moth to a flame.

"This is crazy...I'm—"

"Harmony, look at me," Dr. G urged gently.

I lifted my eyes and found her sitting forward, her tablet gone. Her kind brown eyes were studying me. "You are stronger than your trauma. You are braver than your fears. You have blossomed over these last six years, and the progress you've made should be proof enough that you're an incredible, strong, resilient woman."

I stared at her, and I felt the tears coming. She was used to seeing my tears, used to hearing me cry out in agony as I relived the most heinous, nightmare-fueled memories. Of course, that was when I lived in Michigan.

"I don't want to push you, but I have one more question, okay?" she said softly.

I nodded, knowing what was coming. It was the same question every session. Six years ago, the answer was always no—it still was.

"Harmony, do you feel like you are deserving of love?"

"Maybe," I whispered before I could think about it, shocking myself. My bottom lip trembled as emotion clogged my throat.

A wide, gorgeous smile spread across her face. "I like that word coming from you. Maybe is good."

"It is?" I blurted.

She winked at me. "It's a hell of a lot better than no."

Our session ended a few moments later, and I blindly reached for my water bottle, needing a drink. As the cool, crisp liquid ran down my throat, my body grateful for it, my phone rang.

"Hello?"

"Harm, I need your help," Cabe groaned.

A short chuckle escaped me as I wiped a stray tear from my cheek. "What did you do?"

I already knew what he did, because Billie texted me late last night. I wasn't going to let him know that though; he needed to admit it himself. He sighed and I stood from the stool, taking my breakfast dishes to the sink. "I forgot about her work anniversary," he whispered.

"Oh, crap," I giggled.

"This isn't funny. She's pissed at me; you know how much she cares about her work. She came home last night and just looked at me. I didn't know why she was staring. Anyways, she left this morning to go have a celebratory lunch with her dad." Billie worked for her father's company, and her five-year anniversary was yesterday.

"Even *I* didn't forget it," I boasted, walking to my bedroom.

"Thanks for reminding a fella," he snapped.

I rolled my eyes. "Just do something nice for her tonight."

Another sigh. "That's why I need your help. I'm gonna cook for her. but I need more spices."

Excitement bloomed inside my chest. "Cabe, are you asking me to go to the farmer's market with you?"

"Get dressed. I'll be there in ten."

"These are so pretty," I mused softly, picking up a bouquet of pink tulips.

The stand owner smiled at me, and I gave her an easy smile back. Years ago, I wouldn't have been able to look her in the eye. I felt another set of eyes on me and I looked up to find Cabe staring down at me. He was a few inches taller than me and way taller than Billie, as the shortest in our little group. Today, Cabe wore a plain blue shirt, jeans, and a baseball cap on backwards, of course, making him look like a teenager.

He looked from me to the flowers to the owner.

"What?" I asked.

He shrugged, a smile playing on his lips as he wrapped an arm around my shoulders. "Love seeing your growth and strength, Harm," he said softly.

Tears formed in my eyes for the second time today, but I blinked them away quickly.

No more tears today, Harmony Green.

Shoving him away playfully, I addressed the owner. "Can I have these and those yellow ones over there?" I asked sweetly. Another thing about me getting comfortable in my space: I loved *flowers*. I wanted some in every room. These would go on the coffee table and in the music room.

Flowers added some brightness to a room, and it was time I'd had some.

"Sure thing, sweetheart. Let me get you a baggie so those don't drip all over that pretty dress," the old woman said, giving me a kind, warm smile. When she came back to me, she looked up to Cabe and then back to me. "Y'all are a cute couple," she noted like older women do, wanting to know more.

Cabe and I looked at each other for a moment before we burst out laughing.

It was a real laugh, carrying through the beautiful day like a chorus.

Those were rare too, but man, they felt good.

"I'm sorry," she said, "I didn't mean—"

I waved her off, shaking my head. "He's in love with my best friend and is in the doghouse right now. We're here to get her something special."

She nodded in understanding. "Then the flowers are a good choice."

"Oh, these are for me," I informed, handing her some cash.

She looked at Cabe, her lips turning into a frown. "Boy, rule number one: always get your woman flowers. Any time, any day. Just because. Flowers are a must in a house," she said, turning to hand me the pink and yellow tulips.

Flowers are a must in a house.

Yeah, I agreed with that.

I lifted the beauties to my nose and closed my eyes, reflecting on the morning, grateful for it.

Today was a good day.

The sun was shining, promising us that the warmth of summer would scorch us in a few weeks. Spring was the only bearable time in Texas, in my opinion. A breeze came by, brushing up the skirt of my maxi dress and my curls over my shoulders. The dress I wore was cream, with tiny black flowers on it. I found it at Goodwill a few weeks ago. It had spaghetti straps, but it wasn't hot enough for that, so I paired it with a blue jean jacket and my black combat boots.

I felt girly but tough.

I felt like I was finally discovering who I was. I discovered that Harmony Green was a pretty cool person. I was glad to finally meet her after years of slamming the door in her face.

"Here you go. Thanks," Cabe said, causing me to open my eyes again.

The Farmer's Market was bustling with people of all ages. Children were running and giggling, parents were watching with cautious eyes, small smiles on their lips. Young couples were looking at those parents and their children with thoughts of the future buzzing in the back of their minds. The older generations were smiling, reflecting on their own lives. Sellers were being discovered. Friends were meeting. Dates were being planned. Life was good at the Farmer's Market. It was simple, humble, and downright beautiful.

To think I'd missed years of this because of that monster.

Shaking my head, I pulled my cloth bag off my shoulder and tucked the flowers inside next to the fresh strawberries and cucumbers, double checking that my water bottle was, in fact, still there.

I looked at Cabe. "Where to next?"

He looked around, scanning the tents. "I need to find that spice lady."

I looked at the flower lady, tipping my chin slightly. "Do you know where the spice lady is?"

Everyone knew who the spice lady was. She was from New Orleans and grew her own herbs and she created her own spice blends as well. Instead of calling her the spice lady, we should call her the Food Fairy, because cooking with her spices adds a little magic to your dish. The flower lady gave us directions: it was on the other side of the lot. We thanked her and she called, "Make sure you don't go back into that doghouse, son!"

I giggled. Cabe's jaw tightened.

As Cabe and I made our way to the spice tent, both of us chatted about work and our love for Billie. We were halfway across the lot when I felt the hair on the back of my neck stand up at attention, my body warning me of something nearby. Alarm bells started to sound in my head, and a rumble emerged from the dark depths inside me, threatening to ruin my perfect day.

Cabe was going on about a movie he wanted to take Billie to as I twisted my neck to look behind me.

I sucked in a breath at the sight, my body reacting immediately, shocking me yet again.

My body hummed with glee. My nipples hardened.

My body reacted to only *one person*, one person in my entire dark, messed up life.

He was here.

My eyes scanned the small crowd, looking for him. Of course, in a crowd, he would stand out like a shooting star in a dark sky. He wouldn't be standing here out in the open. No, not him. My eyes drifted to the tents and sellers.

My breath caught once more as my heart skipped a beat, ignoring her bruises and scars.

There, standing in between the tents, in the shadows of the alley, was a tall, dark figure. He stepped forward, and I saw the outline of his cowboy hat.

I felt his stormy eyes land on me, beckoning me to get lost in the storm with him, rain, wind, thunder, and lightning be damned.

My watchful dark cowboy.

He did remember me.

"You didn't have to walk me up here, Cabe," I said, shaking my head as I unlocked my door.

"Billie would kill me if I didn't. Besides, I like knowing that you are safe," he replied from behind me. I turned and smiled at him as he stared down at me, his Adam's apple bobbing. "I know...I know we don't talk about this a lot, but I am so fucking proud of you."

My throat thickened as I stared at him. Normally, I would brush this off, but Dr. G told me that if someone was complimenting or praising me, I needed to listen and accept it.

I needed to believe it.

My soul needed to believe it.

"Thank you," I whispered, tears springing to my eyes.

Suddenly, he pulled me into his arms, crushing me to his chest. "I love you, Harm. Billie and I both love you. You are amazing. You are worthy. You are strong—"

"Cabe—"

"Hush," he snapped, his hand going to the back of my head, pressing my curls in.

I hushed.

I hushed because I wasn't the only one healing.

I hushed because Cabe and I didn't have a lot of quiet moments.

I hushed because his hug felt good.

I hushed because I was finally getting comfortable being touched again.

A few moments later, I pulled back and smiled. "I'm okay," I assured.

"I know, Harm," he whispered.

Later that night, as I was getting ready for bed, washing my face in the bathroom, I heard a noise by the window. I stilled, my blood rushing to my ears.

Breathe, Harmony. It's okay, it was probably just the wind.

Taking a slow breath, I quietly wiped my wet face and stepped into my bedroom. My mind drifted to when Cabe bought me a gun last year. It was in my nightstand, loaded and ready to go. Even though I wasn't comfortable with it, he told me it was the best protection from...

A tap on the window caused me to yelp, and panic surged through my blood, spreading through my body in a matter of seconds. Immediately, I started chanting in my head, trying to chase it away. If an attack happened now, I would be helpless.

One, two, three.

One, two, three.

Red, blue, green.

Red, blue, green.

I slapped a hand over my mouth to keep from whimpering and rushed to the nightstand, grabbing the weapon. It was heavy; a different kind of heavy—a powerful, dark kind of heavy. I hated it. This was a weapon of destruction and terror, and I wanted nothing to do with that. Not anymore.

Okay, focus, Harm.

All the lights were on in the apartment, and my room was quiet, except for the low hum of my humidifier on the dresser. I gripped the gun with both hands, just how Cabe taught me, and began checking the apartment. The front door was locked, the doorstopper in its place.

Nothing was moved.

Everything was fine.

Everything was fine.

I shook my head, my curls brushing over my bare arms.

"Jesus, Harm. It was probably just a bird," I mumbled to myself, walking back to my bedroom. I stashed the weapon and began my "closing shift." I shut everything down, turned off the lights, and double checked the front door again. Okay, maybe I checked it three times, but still.

When I came back into my bedroom, I walked to the window to inspect the glass. My eyes scanned over the corners, then the middle, checking for chips or cracks.

Nothing.

Everything was fine.

I was fine. I was safe. Everything was okay.

I was about to turn away when something caught my eye across the street.

My heart raced and my stomach dropped.

I waited, for the second time today, for the monster from the depths to rise and take over my senses, but it didn't. Any opportunity it had to cause me pain would not be missed.

Still, the monster stayed in the depths, where it belonged— it didn't like what I was staring at. It didn't like the feelings my body developed as I stared at the cowboy, leaning against the light pole across the street, arms crossed over his chest, the brim of his dark hat hiding his face. Even then, the monster didn't come.

I knew Mason Langston was staring at me. I knew those gray eyes were on me and nothing else.

He found me.

He found where I lived, and he was *watching me.*

I should be scared. I should be running to the phone and calling the police, not staring back at the cowboy. Not wondering why I liked the way my body felt when he was near. Not wondering why he called me 'baby' that night in the arena. I should be scared. The monster *should* be taking over, and I *should* succumb to the panic and fear.

It never came, not even a single rumble.

My eyes on the cowboy, I remained still as a feeling of warmth washed over me, destroying whatever fear I'd felt a few minutes ago.

I was...*happy* to see him standing there, *staring at me.*

"You're crazy," I whispered to myself, my eyes not leaving his shadowed ones. My body tingled, my core hummed, and my nipples hardened as I stood in front of the window in just my satin tank top and panties.

My breaths came out shorter as my chest rose and fell, my nipples brushing against the cool glass. He didn't move.

Did he like what he saw?

Did he like the wild curls I could never seem to tame?

Did he like my wide hips, my pear shape?

Did he like me staring back at him?

"Jesus, Harm! Listen to yourself," I scolded, shaking my head and backing away from the glass. With all the strength I muster, shut the curtains and turned away from the window.

That night, I got the best sleep of my life.

Because I knew that he was out there, watching over me.

My dark cowboy.

Chapter Six

Mason

I was addicted to her, and I didn't know why. I didn't know what I was even addicted to. There was something about this woman that I was drawn to. I'd never felt anything like it before. It'd been two fucking months since that night in the arena.

For two months, I watched her.

For two months, I tried to convince myself she needed me.

For two months, I shown up at her clinic once a week, bullshitting with the owner, Chadwick Dalys. He was a fan, and my smile gave me things that I wanted. I wanted her.

Fuck, but I wanted her.

There was a strange need that flared inside of me the second I saw her pressed against that wall, trembling in fear. After getting out of jail and dealing with Pamela, I had Eddie bring me the security footage. Every time I watched it over the last couple of months, I was fueled with more burning anger, like an endless river of lava. Seeing her backed into that wall, shaking her head, pleading with him...I wanted to kill him.

She tried to reason with him. Over a water bottle.

Why?

I wanted to know why she was clutching that bottle to her chest like it was her first-born child. I wanted to know why she had tears in her eyes when he told her he would lock it in his office. Then, she tried to leave and said that she needed to wait for her friend. He didn't believe her. Then again, with the job he had, bullshitters were a dime a dozen.

She wasn't like that. No, she wasn't a bullshitter. She was just a girl with a bottle.

The day after I was released, I ended up going back to the police station, working my smile, charm, and status to get Officer Steve to run facial recognition on her. I told him I wanted to give her flowers and tickets to the next event because of the trouble she'd dealt with. He bought my story, of course, just like I knew he would.

Anything for you, Mr. Langston. Congratulations on another great ride.

Over the last two months, because I couldn't just sit and watch her like I wanted, I travelled across the country riding the high of those eight seconds of peace. Next month, we were supposed to go to Spain, and I couldn't leave the country, not without knowing her.

Seeing her.

Smelling her.

Touching her.

Claiming her.

I felt like a madman just thinking about her.

I'd never felt like this about anyone, not even my ex-fiancée.

Twelve years ago

"Why are you even dating that girl? She isn't your type," Brody, one of the bull riders sneered. I looked to the blonde girl in the stands, the girl who was still a stranger. She was the key to everything. She was going to help me and I her. Brody was right; she wasn't my type.

She was a buckle bunny, a fame chaser, but I was desperate, and she was willing.

A deadly combination.

I smirked and looked at the guy. He was a year younger than me and couldn't hold on to the bull for more than five seconds, but I respected him. Why? Because he kept getting back on the fucking bull.

"She gives great fucking head, man," I lied. I didn't know if she gave great head or not.

Probably not but I could teach her, right? Sort of like a "I scratch your back, you scratch mine" kind of a deal.

"Really?" he blurted, his brows rising. He looked across the way to the girl in the stands, the blonde girl with brown eyes. She was pretty, with good bone structure, but she covered it with cheap makeup. I didn't have the heart to tell her that I didn't like a lot of makeup, especially since she was mainly doing it for herself. It was a way for her to feel something, other than her piece of shit father dragging her down with his harsh words and violent hands.

"Yeah," I grumbled.

I wasn't interested in her. She wasn't my type but maybe, in a few years, we will be attracted to one another, and maybe that would blossom into something more.

Maybe…but when I looked at her now, I felt nothing.

When I obtained Harmony's address, I held off, even though it took everything in me not to knock on her door.

My desire for her was all consuming, like an ocean in the middle of a hurricane, waves crashing into me over and over until I drowned in the fear of never truly knowing her. I wanted to know the significance of that bottle. I wanted to know why she was still fearful after I threw that man off her. I wanted to know why she couldn't hold my eyes. I wanted to know how to make her smile. I wanted her to tell me who hurt her.

I needed the fucking names of those who wronged her, hurt her, damaged her…

I would bide my time, for now.

When I wasn't chasing my eight seconds of peace, I was chasing the high of her.

When I got back to Houston, I would go into her clinic and bullshit with the owner just to catch a glimpse of her. That's all I wanted. Just to make sure she was okay.

That's the bullshit I fed myself.

She had a spot at the nurse's station, her teal bottle by her computer. Sometimes, if she was busy, I would watch her work, moving from room to room, stopping by her desk every few minutes to have a drink. She seemed fine. I wanted to know her name. I told Steve that I didn't want it when he offered.

I wanted her to tell it to me herself.

When I wasn't riding or travelling, I was at her clinic or at her house, standing in her street like a fucking lunatic. Any chance I could get, I was there, which was only a few nights a week.

The first week, I memorized her schedule. I found out she liked to meditate in the window facing the rising sun in the morning. I found out she spent her evenings in the other window of her corner unit, facing the sunset. I couldn't see what she was doing with her hands, but I saw that she was sitting in a chair.

The second week, I found out it was a guitar. She liked to play guitar during the evenings. I found out the janitor at her clinic, Mr. Steele, liked to watch over her too. He was an old man, and the kindness in his eyes gave me comfort.

By the beginning of May, I knew she was a simple woman. She was a hermit with a good job, helping patients and spreading her light where she could. She had a good home. She didn't go out often. Work and home. She lived a peaceful, boring life.

So why the fuck couldn't I give it up? Why did I feel the uncontrollable need to watch her every fucking second I wasn't on the back of a bull?

This past Saturday, I needed food, fresh food. I was tired of take out.

I'd rented out a skyrise condo in Houston...*why?* I couldn't seem to leave this fucking city for long because she was in it.

I was obsessed with her, and it pissed me off.

I was obsessed with her, but I couldn't stop. I ached to see her.

I couldn't get her out of my head.

At night, after getting back from her apartment, my head would hit the pillow and I would see her auburn curls and blue eyes. Dreams of her haunted me. Dreams of her playing guitar in her sunset window calmed me. Dreams of the way she looked at me after I called her baby aroused me in a way I couldn't explain. It also pissed me the fuck off.

Like every morning, I woke up starving last Saturday. There was only take-away in the fridge, and I didn't want that shit. I had to keep my body in shape for the monsters that like to throw it around.

There happened to be a Farmer's Market downtown that day.

I never expected to run into her and see another fucking man's arm around her shoulders. In that moment, jealously boiled up inside me, its toxicity melting my insides as I watched her throw her head back and laugh.

I wanted to hear that laugh.

I wanted to be the cause of that laugh, not the motherfucker next to her.

Then, I did the unthinkable. *I fucking stalked her in broad daylight.* Before, I would just stop by in the mornings and the evenings, trying to convince myself there was nothing wrong with that.

There was.

I was a fucking psychopath when it came to my red-headed woman.

So, I followed them to her apartment building, and when the guy came out on the phone with some girl named Billie, telling her he loved her and he would see her at home—I felt a rush of relief.

I should have left then, gone back to my condo, minded my own fucking business.

But I didn't.

I watched the windows of her corner unit for six hours, waiting to catch a glimpse of my addiction. Then, she saw me. I don't know what possessed her to come to the window, but when she did, my cock twitched at the sight.

She was the most gorgeous, illuminating creature I'd ever seen. Her curls were everywhere, unruly and wild. She had on a flimsy little tank top I could easily rip off with my teeth. I felt like a sick fuck, watching her, but I just *couldn't stop.*

I still felt like a sick fuck today as I walked into her clinic, but my desire to see her overrode that feeling.

"Hello, Mr. Langston," a brunette nurse purred at me as I walked through the waiting area to the back. I tipped my hat and carried on. That woman had been trying to hop on my dick from the moment I set foot in this building.

Her desperation smelled like a rotting corpse.

My girl was sitting at her desk, typing on the computer, her water bottle beside her. I took my usual seat in the hall, my eyes still on her. Someone would let Mr. Dalys know I was here, and he would come running, like always he did.

She knew I was here, though; she could sense my presence. She knew I was looking at her. I could see the pink in her cheeks deepen beneath her freckles.

There was a pull between us.

Maybe that was the addiction, the way I felt when I was near her.

I wanted this red-head with bright blue eyes...

She was the first person I'd ever truly wanted.

The sad fact was, I never wanted Cathy. She was just a means to an end for me at first. Then, through the loneliness, we clung to each other. My ex had come from a shitty home. We both hated our fathers and bonded over that. I cared deeply for Cathy, but I never loved her.

No one knew that.

No one would ever know the truth.

This girl might, if she asked.

Fuck.

The countless women who came after Cathy were just a quick release, nothing more. Sure, the women I fucked could touch me, worship me, but they couldn't ever kiss me on the mouth.

The last person who kissed me was Cathy.

I hated it even then, because it felt forced. It didn't feel real.

My eyes drifted to my girl as she stood from her chair, a chart in her hands. Those blue eyes that haunted my dreams and thoughts were on the papers before her as she moved around the counter. My body tightened at the sight of her, like it always did. She stood tall, around five nine, curvy, her amber hair piled on top of her head in a messy bun.

My girl pulled that shit off.

Fuck, it was cute.

I shifted in my seat, fighting my growing erection. Those purple scrubs were going to be the death of me. My girl had the most luscious, wide hips I'd ever seen. My hands itched to grab onto them, my fingers digging into her skin as I brought her back onto my aching, thick co—

"Mr. Langston!"

Time for the show.

I put on my fake smile and tore my eyes away from the person I was really here to see. I looked up to see Mr. Dalys coming to me with his hand held out, and a megawatt smile painted on his face. We shook hands, and he walked me back to his office. I was investing half a million dollars in the clinic's expansion. Pamela thought it was great for my image. Eddie thought I was fucking crazy.

I agreed with Eddie.

Mr. Dalys showed me the new building my money bought him, it was on the other side of the city, in a different tax bracket. He was excited about the project, that the people of the lower background would have good, decent healthcare without costing an arm and a leg. He also had plans to open a pediatrics wing in that building. I nodded along, asked questions when needed, but my mind was at the nurses' station.

An hour later, I was saying goodbye and making my way down the hall. It was my longest visit, but there was a lot to go over. Next week, the interior designer would be taking over.

Halfway down the hall, my body tightened, causing my eyes to snap up. My heart pounded in my chest as I scanned over her again, greedy, taking in every inch of her. My girl was looking down at her phone, her bottle tucked close to her chest, her car keys in her hands.

Mostly likely leaving for the day.

Not before I had a taste.

My eyes darted around quickly and spotted an open closet. I stepped in front of her, and she ran into me, the collision causing my heart to jump, heat spreading through my body.

"Oh my goodness, I am so sorry," she said, her raspy voice going straight to my dick. She was adjusting her hold on her belongings and hadn't looked up yet. I needed those blue eyes on me, and I needed them now.

Fuck it.

"Baby," I drawled, my voice lower than it had been with her fucking boss.

Her head snapped up instantly.

There's my girl.

Smiling, I pulled her into a nearby closet quickly and shut the door. I flipped on the light to discover she was pressed against the shelves of supplies, trying to get away from me. I leaned back against the door and crossed my ankles.

She didn't scream.

She wasn't afraid of me.

She just stared, her chest rising and falling rapidly.

I didn't want her scared of me. That was the last thing I wanted.

A thick silence stretched between us before she broke it.

"You've been watching me," she stated.

God, that fucking rasp.

I wanted to hear more of it, every day, every minute, every second.

I would never grow tired of it.

"Yes," I answered, smirking at her.

"Why?"

Something sinister and dark stirred inside me, something almost *primal.*

Because I want you.

"You fuckin' that guy from the Farmer's Market?" I clipped, folding my arms over my chest. Despite the phone call I'd heard, I needed to hear the truth from her own lips. Hell, he could be having an affair. That didn't sit well with me.

No one would use my girl like that.

"Excuse me?" she breathed, her blue eyes going wide.

I licked my lips. "Gotta say, darlin', a man should be at your side if he's fuckin' you. If you are in *his* bed, he shouldn't let you get attacked by a fucking security guard."

She lifted her chin, the light from above showcasing her freckles, presenting themselves to me like a priceless work of art. They were scattered all over her face like angel dust. I wanted to kiss every single one. *Every. Single. One.* My eyes trailed down the length of her body, wondering if all of her was covered in those cute angel marks.

"You can't talk to me like that," she spat.

I tilted my head. "Sure, I can," I replied calmly, shrugging a single shoulder.

She stared at me for a moment. "What do you want?"

"You." *Just you, darlin'.*

She wasn't expecting that answer. "What?"

"You heard me, baby. Don't like repeatin' myself," I warned her, testing the waters.

Let's see if she can handle me.

"Stop calling me 'baby'," she hissed. Fuck, she was feisty.

I smirked again, pushing off the door to close the space between us, enjoying the way she sucked in a breath.

"I'm gonna touch you again," I murmured as I moved my knuckle down the side of her face. My finger felt electric from the touch, and I wanted more. I wanted to feel that same rush all over my body. Her breath hitched, and her arms loosened, the bottle shifting a bit. "You're going to tell me about that bottle, but not today. Today, we are going to dinner."

"D-dinner?" she stammered, breathless.

I hummed, bending my head a bit.

"I can't see your eyes," she whispered.

"Give me your name and I'll give you my eyes," I promised. I was an inch from her face now, and her sweet scent engulfed me.

Plagued me.

Ruined me.

My girl smelled like melons.

Fuck, it was sweet.

She was sweet.

My jaw tightened. I wanted to touch her again, but I didn't want to scare her.

"My name is Harmony," she said softly.

Of course, it was. She was the song running through my head for months, over and over, like a broken record. I couldn't get enough.

"It suits you," I whispered, my voice gentle, my eyes dropping to her lips. Pink.

I never wanted to kiss a woman before, but I needed to know what she tasted like. I needed to know if she would cling to me like she clung to that bottle. I needed to feel her against me. I needed to know if she was just as soft as she looked. I needed to know if her pussy tasted just as sweet as her mouth.

"Mr. Langston—"

"Mason, baby. Call me Mason," I reminded her softly, meeting her eyes again.

"You need to step away from me now, please." Her raspy voice was trembling a bit. "I can't see your eyes."

I stepped away and pulled off my hat. Her breath hitched again as she drank me in.

Feeling is mutual, Harmony.

Harmony.

"Well?" I prompted.

She shifted on her feet. "I don't want to go to dinner."

I opened my mouth to speak, but she cut me off. "It's Friday night."

"Yeah, it is," I drawled, my lips twitching.

"I make pasta on Friday nights," she stated.

I smirked and took a step closer to her again. *She cooked?* Fuck, even better. I liked to cook but there was something about a woman who knew how...

"I like pasta," I murmured.

"You going to follow me home if I tell you no?" she asked, attitude lacing her voice now. I almost smiled at that. It was cute as fuck.

"Yep."

She looked down to her feet. My jaw tightened, and I slid my finger under her chin. It was time to cut the bullshit. For two months, I kept my distance. I was done with that. She was here, inches from me, and damn it all to hell, I wasn't letting her go now.

"I'm drawn to you, Harmony. That doesn't happen to a man like me."

There was no point in flirting around the obvious. I wanted her, and she wanted me, whether she was willing to admit it or not.

"You're very direct, Mr. Lang—"

"Little Song, I will spank that ass if you call me Mr. Langston again," I growled.

Chapter Seven

Harmony

"Little Song, I will spank that ass if you call me 'Mr. Langston' again."

My brain misfired.

Everything about me misfired.

My logic was ready to jump out the window, with no parashoot strapped to its back.

My heart was beating so fast, I was certain I would have to call Dr. Williams in here to revive me.

My eyes were stuck on Mr. Langston—*Mason*—memorizing every single inch of him, like I had every chance I got for the last few weeks. The chords of his voice reminded me of Bohemian Rhapsody, ringing in my ears, the haunting melody seeping into my soul. His words settled over me, his rough voice louder than his music, and my skin felt hot. I felt heat rush into my cheeks, and I knew that, under my mass of freckles, I was redder than a setting sun.

Little Song.

Baby.

Darlin'.

"You hear me?" he asked, drawing me away from the chaos inside my chest and head.

"Sir—"

He stepped forward again, backing me into the shelves behind me. His nostrils flared as his scuffed jaw tightened, and lightning flashed in his eyes. He planted his hands on the shelf above my head and leaned in close, his scent sweeping my logic out the window.

"Say my first name," he demanded.

We held each other's eyes and Dr. G's advice echoed from somewhere outside that window, telling me to take the chance.

You only get one life, Harmony Green. You can sit here and remain broken, or you can get up and heal.

I was ready.

Years of my life had been stolen from me, precious time that I would never get back; days, weeks, months, and years, of torture and painful healing. That was the thing about healing and fighting your demons: it hurt like a motherfucker.

They don't call them growing pains for nothing.

I was ready to stop hurting. I was ready to replace the hurt with *something else.*

Something that gave me butterflies.

Something that made me blush.

Something that excited me.

Something that made me feel beautiful again.

Desired.

Wanted.

"Mason," I whispered.

Another bolt of lightning flashed. Then, his eyes darkened as he inched down closer to my face. His lips were an inch away from mine, and I could practically taste him. I wanted to taste him. I wanted—

I blinked, and logic was climbing back in the window, just to remind me I wasn't scared of him.

Two months ago, you got locked in a supply closet, and you panicked. You are here with him, and fear is nowhere near you, Harm.

"You said you liked pasta?" I asked.

He nodded, his face still stern, darkness brewing in his stormy eyes. My eyes dropped to his full, lush lips. I wondered, if he kissed me, would the roughness of his beard make it better?

"Stop looking at my lips like that," he hissed, baring his teeth.

Immediately, I cleared my throat and adverted my eyes. He pushed off the shelf. "You got everything we need at your place, or do we need to stop at the store?"

I found myself blinking again, this time slower.

It wasn't the question; it was the sense of normalcy within it. I liked it.

My healing soul smiled to herself. *Normal.* Oh, how wonderful it would be to be normal again. There was something lingering within the everlasting storm in his eyes, telling me I could trust him.

"I have everything," I answered.

Twenty minutes later, I parked my car in its spot, and Mason's black Chevy Silverado pulled into the spot next to it. I gathered my things and exited the vehicle to find waiting in front of my car.

"Need me to carry anything?" he asked, his gray eyes on my full arms, mainly on my water bottle.

I shook my head. "I'm good," I said as he fell into step beside me.

If we were a normal couple, and I was a normal person, he would have taken the items from me like the gentleman he is, but he respected my boundaries, and for that, I was grateful.

"Okay, baby," he muttered.

Baby. My stomach flipped again, excitement buzzing throughout my body.

When he got to the front door, I felt his big, warm hand at the small of my back, and I nearly moaned at the contact. Yes, that's how touch deprived I was. When Cabe or Billie touched me, it was different. When a patient touched me, it was different. When this hotshot, bull riding cowboy touched me, I felt my world tilt on its axis.

"Harmony."

I shook my head and looked up to him as he towered over me. "Yes?" I breathed.

His lips twitched, and amusement filled his eyes under his cowboy hat. "I open doors for you, got me?"

I nodded, still not moving. I was being sucked into his storm, ready to get lost in it forever. He bent down to get into my space. "That means you gotta let go of the handle for me."

My hand dropped from the handle, and as he pulled it open, I swear I heard a low, toe-curling, chuckle from him. The ride in the elevator was silent. I kept my eyes straight ahead on the metal doors, but I knew he was staring down at me. His dark reflection was twisted towards mine. Once I put the key in my door, his long, tanned forearm shot out, pulling my hand gently away from the knob.

"Let me check first, okay?" he demanded.

"But—"

Rough fingers gripped my chin, and suddenly, I wasn't looking up at the door anymore. No, I was looking at him. In that moment, I discovered I wanted to look at him and only him for a long time, perhaps the rest of my life.

"This is the first of many dinners for us. There are things we need to discuss, baby. A lot of those things center around the way you reacted that night at PBR and the bottle in your arms," he said lowly, tipping his hat. "I'm not going to push you, Little Song, but you need to know you're safe with me."

You are safe with me.

You are safe with me.

You are safe with me.

One, two, three.

One, two, three.

Red, blue, green.

Red, blue, green.

The monster growled within the dark depths, pissed that this cowboy was telling me I was safe with him. Against my monster's judgement, I believed him. Thus, I nodded, absentmindedly chewing on the inside of my cheek. Mason smiled and entered the apartment before me, holding out his hand in silent command. I lingered in the foyer, as I watched him walk away.

How could a man make a basic pair of jeans, a faded Chevy T-shirt, and boots look good?

Because his ass looks good.

Because his tanned, muscular, veiny arms, looked better.

Because his chest was broad and strong in that shirt.

Because you want him to kiss you.

A minute later, he returned, and I grumbled, "So much for me giving you a tour." I tried to pass him, but his arm shot out, stopping me.

"You wanna give me a tour? Give me a tour, darlin'," he returned softly.

This cowboy.

I stood up on my toes, getting up in his space. "Thank you," I whispered. I thanked him for a number of things, and he knew it, too.

Mason blinked and his jaw flexed. His arm wasn't touching me, and I really wanted it to. I wanted his touch.

Holy shit, I wanted his touch!

I couldn't wait to tell Dr. G.

"You're welcome," he said after a moment.

After that, he stepped away and I gave him a tour. It didn't last very long, but when I opened the door to the music room, something passed over his face, something that looked an awful lot like pride. His gray eyes landed on the antique piano.

"You writin' and singin'? Or just writin'?" he asked, stepping closer to my most prized possession.

"I'm learning to play. I know how to play the guitar, but I just got this piano out of storage when I moved in," I explained. He'd bent down, looking at the books on my shelves, the classics mixed in with romance books. All my favorites.

Without looking back at me, he said, "Need to know if you sing, baby.".

He wanted to know if I sang.

For some reason, a chill slithered down my spine, comfortable in its path, like it had done so countless times before, years ago, when the old Harmony was dying. Clearing my throat, I made my way to the window where my guitar sat. My fingers grazed over the top of it as I focused on the sunset.

"See that question made you uncomfortable," he muttered. I heard his movements, and my body sensed him moving closer to me.

"It's an honest, good question, Mason," I replied. When I looked back at him, he wasn't far, but he wasn't close, either. He seemed to have no problem crowding me in public spaces, but in my space? He was keeping his distance.

I couldn't figure out if I liked that or not.

"If I ask you a question that makes you uncomfortable—"

"Yes, I sing," I informed him softly. His mouth snapped shut, and I saw his jaw flex under his stubble. "Though, I don't think I've very good at it." *Not with this new voice. Not with the rasp.*

He took a step towards me. "When you sing for me, I'll let you know if you sound like shit or not."

A laugh bubbled up in my chest and escaped my mouth before I could stop it. It felt *so good*. So wholesome. So free. My head fell back, and it continued.

After a few moments, it was done, like everything good in life, it came and went before I could savor it. I looked back to the cowboy to see his eyes were slightly dilated now, his nostrils flared, his hands shoved into the pockets of his jeans.

"What?"

He closed his eyes for a moment, muttering something under his breath. When he reopened them, they were back to normal, and he smirked. "You ready to feed me?"

Yes. In bed.

Jesus, where did that come from?

I lifted my chin. "Maybe I'll poison you."

He looked at the ceiling and then back to me. "Darlin' you've done something to me because I can't seem to get you out of my head."

My heart froze. My soul froze.

Hell, I froze.

There was nothing I could do but sit there and watch as his eyes trailed up and down my purple scrubs slowly. He was so direct. Had I been right all along?

Was he watching over me?

"Why did you come to the clinic?" I found myself asking.

"You."

"Why did you invest half a million dollars in the clinic?" I breathed.

He chuckled and took off his cowboy hat, sliding a hand over his short, dirty blonde hair before looking at me. "Had to find some excuse to be near you, Little Song."

Mason calling me that while we discussed something so raw in my place of solace, my place of peace, was stirring foreign emotions inside me, emotions I was afraid to explore. If I did, I would give into this cowboy, much sooner than I anticipated.

"But it's half a million dollars," I blurted, trying to understand why he would waste that money, although, technically, he wasn't wasting it. It was going to a good cause, one that would help people. The ones who needed it.

He shot me a look that I felt in my core. "For a woman like you, that ain't nothin'. Now come on, you have to feed me."

"None of the boxed shit, huh?" Mason drawled from behind me, chuckling slightly. It wasn't a demeaning chuckle; more of an impressed one. I smiled to myself as I shut the fridge with my hip and turned to the island. The smile stayed as I remembered the first time I attempted to make homemade pasta.

It had been an assignment from Dr. G.

"Ms. Green, I know you're still a fairly new patient, but I'd like to assign you some homework. That is, if you don't mind."

"Homework?" I parroted, picking at the string on my jeans. I couldn't meet her eyes. I haven't been able to look anyone in the eye for months. I missed the connection, the recognition, the respect that came with looking someone in the eye, but I couldn't. Fear had its tight, unrelenting hold on me and it wasn't going to let me go, not for a very long time.

"What's something you have always wanted to make?" she asked, encouragement lacing her gentle voice.

My answer had been pasta.

The process had always fascinated me since I was in nursing school, but I never had the time. Now, every Friday, I woke up an hour or two earlier than normal to make pasta dough. It gave me something to look forward to, a treat for making it to the end of another week. The first couple of times I tried, years ago, I'd failed. Badly.

Now, I considered myself an expert. Well, Billie and Cabe certainly thought so, and maybe, I'll convince the cowboy sitting in my kitchen.

After showing him the music room, we moved back into the living area. I told him to make himself comfortable while I went to change. Once in my room, with the door shut between us, I allowed my heart to skip all those beats it'd been wanting to. I allowed myself to feel like a normal woman, one who grew up in a normal household and had normal female experiences. For moment, I was just a young woman, pressing herself against a door, blushing like crazy because of the beautiful man in the living room.

I wasn't fucked up. I wasn't damaged. I wasn't broken.

I was just...normal.

I allowed myself this moment before pulling off my scrubs and heading into the closet.

I changed into an old Nickelback T-Shirt, and yoga pants. I didn't do yoga, but damn, yoga companies made comfy pants. My hair was in a wild pile on top of my head and that's where it would stay until I was done cooking. When I came back into the living area, Mason's jaw tightened. I turned on some jazz for background music and offered him a drink.

Now he had a beer in front of him and I was preparing the meal.

"Pasta is something I love," I told him, sprinkling flour on the countertop.

"How long have you been making it?" he asked, interested. *Very interested*. I looked up to meet his eyes only to find they were studying me.

I shrugged a shoulder. "A few years." I didn't want to tell him the truth behind it. If I did, I would have to tell him everything and I wasn't ready for that yet.

"What else can you cook?"

"Looking for a personal chef, Mr. Langston?" I asked coolly, dropping the dough onto the surface.

"If it's you, yes. Anyone else, fuck no," he deadpanned before taking a swig of the beer—I always liked to keep some on hand for Cabe.

I laughed as I worked the dough. A comfortable silence stretched between us as I worked, getting lost in the usual routine of it all, but I felt his eyes on me. I *liked* his eyes on me.

Today, when I felt him watching me, I felt good. There had been a weight on my shoulders, bearing down on me for a long time, but knowing that he was watching me, that weight seemed to get a little lighter each time.

"Harmony," he called.

I looked up to find him sitting on one of the barstools, leaning back, a large, tanned hand wrapped around the base of the beer bottle, his hat hanging on the coat rack by the hall. He was a wonderful sight. I liked him in my space.

He stood out like a sore thumb, but he looked good doing it.

"Yes?"

"Thank you for letting me come over," he whispered gently, surprising me once again, showing me the softness he desperately tried to hide from the world.

Chapter Eight

Mason

Fuck.

Fuck.

Here I was trying to be a gentleman, and she changed into yoga pants. Yoga. Fucking. Pants. The thin, black tight material clung to her wide hips and ass like a second skin. My cock was begging for mercy against the zipper of my jeans.

Christ, it was like I was fifteen again.

Thank God there was an island separating us.

Harmony started setting pots and pans on the stovetop, clearly a comfortable routine for her. I watched her in part fascination and part confusion. When she said she was going to go change, I never expected yoga pants. I expected a dress, jeans, or hell, even a full on "going out" outfit. That's what I expected, not what I wanted.

What I wanted was someone who was comfortable in front of me, like Eddie was.

I was Mason Langston, a rebel, an asshole, and a player.

As the years of my career went on, when people were around me, they weren't themselves. It was something I gathered pretty quickly. First, it was the admirers who were secretly begging to the big man above that the next bull I rode would throw me off. Second were the people who saw me as a paycheck and nothing more. They didn't give a shit about my bad days or my good ones; they just wanted me to stay on the bull. Third were the ones afraid of me, who felt like they had to walk on eggshells around me. Finally, there were the women.

Women who also saw me as I paycheck. Women who would flaunt themselves at me, shoving their tits in my face and swaying their hips so I could marvel at the ass they thought they had. They would dress themselves up like Cinderella every time they were around me. Early on in my career, after the sting and betrayal of my brother dulled, I thought about dating someone again.

That was the end goal, after all, to find someone. Someone who didn't see me as a paycheck. Someone who didn't think I'd fall off. Someone who didn't see me as a monster. Someone who didn't need to impress me with their looks every second of the day. Someone who wasn't afraid of a decent conversation. Someone who wasn't afraid to let me see the good, the bad, and the ugly.

In turn, I wanted to do the same for them.

Eddie was like that, in a way.

However, Eddie also had a dick, and I wasn't gay, so, Eddie was a friend and nothing more.

My eyes grazed over Harmony's body, from her fuzzy purple socks to her pile of wild red curls on top of her head. She was comfortable here—*with me.*

She didn't care that she had a bull riding legend siting in her kitchen. She wanted to be comfortable and cook a meal she loved. Fuck, she was willing to share that meal with me. *After stalking her for two months.* My throat tightened, and I desperately tried to swallow the lump forming in it. When that didn't work, I took a swig of the beer she gave me.

"Do you drink beer?" I found myself asking, my voice gruff.

Harmony twisted her neck to look over her shoulder at me. "I do, but it's not my favorite. I have to be in the mood for it," she answered, her raspy voice causing something in my chest to ache.

Fuck, that voice was intoxicating.

"That's Cabe's beer," she informed me.

"Who is he to you?" I asked, bringing up the conversation from the storage closet. She turned away and stirred the sauce she'd just started making. A moment later, she turned back to the island, her hands immediately going to the dough.

"He is my best friend's man. Billie and Cabe have been together for years," she replied, her eyes trained on the dough. There was a hint of pride in her voice that told me they were good people. I liked that. I liked knowing that she had good people in her life, that she wasn't alone.

"So, you three are from Texas? Born and raised, I'm assuming." I took another pull of my beer, my eyes never leaving her.

She nodded. "Yeah, Billie and I met in elementary school. Cabe came in later during college. He's from a town called Abilene."

A chuckle came from me. *Fucking Abilene.*

"You've heard of it?" she asked, looking up at me. Those blue eyes were going to be the death of me.

A smirk formed on my lips as I said, "Abilene is a dirt town with nothing but trouble."

She smiled; it was a small one, but still, it took my breath away. "Pretty sure trouble is sitting on my stool."

I leaned forward to grasp her chin in my fingers, causing her hands to freeze. My eyes held hers, getting lost in her seas of blue, reminding me of all the beautiful places I'd been. None of those places could compare to this apartment. Her pink lips parted, and her chest heaved under my scrutiny.

"You a woman who likes trouble, Little Song?"

"Only your kind of trouble, Mason," she whispered back immediately. Her eyes widened a fraction, letting me know she hadn't meant to say that. Fuck, but I liked hearing it.

I was going to kiss her. I was going to slam my lips against her pretty pink ones and claim her with my mouth. I was going to devour her.

Not yet, asshole. You just got here.

My jaw ticked, and I pulled my arm away. "Lucky me," I murmured, truly meaning it.

I was a lucky son of a bitch.

She got back to cooking, cutting the dough into strips and wrapping it into a bundle. When she turned to face the stove, I rose from my seat and went to the fridge to her left. I leaned my shoulder against the wall beside it, folding my arms over my chest. The blush stayed on her skin as I watched her, as I took in the way she moved, the way her fingers tapped against the spoon as she stirred the sauce, the way her lips pressed together as she hummed to the low playing jazz in the background.

Comfortable.

She wasn't comfortable around me at the clinic or at the arena. At the farmer's market, she was laid back but still on edge. I was beginning to realize that probably wasn't because of me.

"You're different here, Harmony," I noted softly. She looked up at me while stirring the sauce and smiled.

"I'm home."

Two words.

Two little words, and envy pooled in my gut.

I didn't have a home, not anymore. There wasn't anything I could say to that and the feeling inside wasn't a good one. I was happy for her, sure, but my own selfishness morphed into something green. I hated this feeling.

Instead of replying, I nodded in understanding.

She went back to cooking, and I watched her for a few more minutes, in a trance. The ache in my chest only intensified the longer I watched her.

Tearing my eyes away, I looked around her apartment once more. It was charming—small—but cozy. The smell of dinner filled my nose, soft music played in my ears, and I was overwhelmed with a feeling of contentment. I was content here with this woman—*Harmony*.

"Tell me something else," I requested.

"What do you want to know?"

"Everything," I replied, pushing off the wall and coming to stand behind her. She stiffened, her back straightening, as if she was bracing for something. My brows furrowed and my jaw hardened.

I wasn't even touching her, and her body was on high alert. *Why?*

"You're safe with me, baby," I assured her.

I came around to her side to find her eyes were squeezed shut. I wanted to touch her cheek, but there was something about her body language stopping me. "Harm?" I called softly, concern coating my voice.

Her eyes snapped open, and, after blinking a few times, she shook her head a bit. "I'm so sorry. "I—uh...," She stopped and set the spoon down before she taking step back from the stove—*from me.*

"Harm—"

"Excuse me for just a moment. I'll be right back," she said, her voice shaking a bit at the end. Even though I was on alert and the urge to comfort her was strong, I nodded. There was something about her reaction that scared me.

It scared me because once upon a time, I used to tense up like that.

With my father.

Twenty-three years ago. Hallow Ranch.
"Dammit, Mason!"

I flinched at my father's harsh tone, backing away from the kitchen counter and spinning to face him. He was coming in from the front door, his spurs clicking with every pounding step. Each step he took, the more afraid I became. He had his brown cowboy hat and jacket on.

Pop probably just got done for the day.

Denver finished about an hour ago, came back to change, and then left for football practice. School was starting in a few weeks, and he was the second-string quarterback. Rumors spread throughout the school about my brother, saying he was going to start this year. I didn't know if that was true or not, but either way, I knew the upperclassmen wouldn't like that.

I, on the other hand, had no interest in football. That was Denver's thing, not mine. Last weekend, Jigs took us to the rodeo in the next town over, and I really liked watching the bull riders. Denver said he didn't understand why men would willingly put themselves on beasts like that. He didn't get it, but I did. I saw it in the cowboy's eyes when they jumped from the beast after the buzzer sounded.

Thrill.

I was interested in that, but when I mentioned it to Jigs, he told me I was far too skinny. The bull would throw me into the sun if I got on one now. He told me I needed to put some weight on, bulk up, gain strength.

"I'm talking to you, boy," Pop growled. I looked up to him.

"Yes, sir? Did you need me to do something?" I asked, raising my chin a bit higher.

My father and Denver looked a lot alike, Denver cut from Pop's cloth. I wasn't. The only thing my father gave me was my height, even though I wasn't as tall as him yet, and his eyes. The rest of me belonged to Momma and that sucked for me—she wasn't here anymore.

It sucked for me because I was her boy.

It sucked for me because it had been years and I still cry every day.

It sucked for me because no one else seemed to cry about it. Pop caught me once and told me cowboys don't cry. I thought that was a load of crap.

"You're good for nothing, you know that," Pop growled, crowding me back into the sink.

The day Momma was murdered, Pop changed. Jigs told me once that every man had a monster inside him, and that what makes a man is how they contain it. The day Momma was taken from us, consumed by fire and lifted into the heavens, Pop's monster broke free from its cage.

I got to see it firsthand when he dragged us to hunt down the men who killed her. Bison hunters. They set fire to the forest around her because they were hunting on our land, hunting animals they shouldn't. Because of their greed, two boys lost their mother, and a man turned into a demon. That day, Pop told Denver to cover my ears and for us to close our eyes. I knew Denver did, he listened to Pop, he respected Pop.

But me?

I just wanted to see the men who hurt Momma suffer.

I didn't close my eyes. Even though I didn't hear their screams, their blood lingered in my nightmares, coating it.

"You didn't feed the fuckin' horses before you came up here to sit on your ass," he barked down at me, bringing me back to the present.

"Yes, I did," I argued. I fed the horses every damn day.

I shouldn't have done that.

I really shouldn't have done that.

Good thing Denver decided to spend the night at his buddy that night. He didn't have to see Pop shove me to the ground and kick me in the stomach. Pop left me on the kitchen floor, curled into a ball, grinding my teeth to stop the tears.

That was the day I learned not to talk back, not until my growth spurt hit. Then, the old man stopped fucking with me and left me alone. We avoided each other, and Denver was unknowingly the barrier between two men who wanted to kill each other.

Denver had a great childhood.

I didn't.

Harmony excused herself over ten minutes ago. I sighed and headed down the hallway in search of my little song. I found her in the second bedroom, standing in the center with her arms around herself, her back to me, her head bent. I leaned against the doorframe and shoved my hands in my jeans.

This room was a safe place for her.

I understood that.

I'd had a safe place to run to once too.

There were a lot of things I missed about Hallow Ranch, things I occasionally allowed myself to think about, things that weren't tainted by Pop's monster and his hatred for me.

Momma's photo room was one of those things.

My brother didn't know this; in fact, I was certain Pop didn't know either. I used to sneak in there after her death, every morning in summer. Early, of course, so no one would catch me. Usually by then, Pop and Den were either sleeping or already gone for the day.

I would push the door open and slide in. Then, I would go to the center of the room, much like Harmony, and curl into a ball on the floor. The first few months after her murder, I would only sneak in there to cry. After the funeral, Pop told me and Denver that cowboys don't cry. He didn't have an issue repeating that statement as the years went on, but I was young. I was just a boy who lost his momma with father who couldn't look at him without getting angry.

Momma's photo room was my sanctuary.

I never touched anything while I was there.

That was her space, and I was just a guest, much like now—this was Harmony's space. So, as I made my way to her, I reminded myself not to touch anything or her without her consent.

"Wasn't going to rush you, baby, but I need to know," I said gently.

She knew what I was asking. I didn't have to spell it out for her.

"I'm healing," she hiccupped.

My eyes closed for a moment as I clenched my jaw, I did that a lot around her. Nevertheless, I was pissed.

A woman like her shouldn't be healing. A woman like her should have a life filled with nothing but happiness and love. A woman like her deserved to have a reason to smile every day, her only tears being happy ones. A woman like her needed the world placed at her feet.

I would be the one to give it to her.

"Gonna touch you, Harmony," I murmured before putting my hands on her shoulders. She didn't flinch, thank fuck, and I turned her around to face me. Tears were pooling in her gorgeous eyes, some running down her cheeks. Her skin was red from her pain and trauma, and fury flared inside me at the sight.

My little song should never have tears in her blue eyes.

My hands remained on her shoulders for a few more seconds before I slid them up to cup the sides of her neck. "Tell me this, Harmony," I whispered. "Are you afraid of me?"

I braced for her answer, preparing for the worst, like I had most of my life.

I didn't know what I would do if the woman I felt drawn to protect feared *me.*

I knew I would have to leave her, honor her wishes, but I wouldn't stop watching her. I would plant myself against that light post on the sidewalk every fucking night to ensure she was safe and happy, even if I wasn't the one to make her that way.

Her blue found my gray, and suddenly we were lost in an unforgiving ocean of pain, fear, and trauma, our pasts demanding control. Then, like a lighthouse, shining like a beacon, she called out to me, the boat beneath us steadying at her words.

"My soul trusts you."

Not her.

Her soul.

Jesus.

Pain sliced through me like a hot poker, like my father's words used to.

Unworthy little shit.

Don't know why we even had you, you useless fuck.

You don't care about Hallow Ranch, boy. If you did, you wouldn't be hopping on those bulls every chance you got.

I only have one son, and he ain't you.

"What are you doing to me?" I asked, my voice thick with emotion and confusion.

Her breath hitched as I brought my forehead down to hers. She held my eyes as she whispered, "I was going to ask you the same thing."

She felt it, too. It wasn't just my imagination. The last two months had been my own personal brand of torture to fuel an addiction I shouldn't have. I wasn't worthy of a woman like her, and yet, she wanted this. She felt this, this pull between us, and damn it all to hell, whether I deserved her or not, I wanted her. *Right now.*

I dropped my hands and took a step back. Confusion washed over her beauty, but not before a short wave of hurt. My gut twisted.

"Did I say something wrong?"

"No, baby. You said everything right," I admitted roughly, my control slipping.

"Then why—"

"Gotta create some distance, or I'm going to take you right here." The words came out as a growl that didn't intend. Then again, I didn't intend to become obsessed with her, invest half a million just to have an excuse to see her, then stalk her. There was a need swirling inside me, it was strong. Primal.

She wasn't ready for that, and I didn't want to push her, not after everything she was giving me today.

"Take me?" she parroted, her brows rising.

"Yeah, Little Song. *Take* you." Another growl. I took another step back. *What the fuck was wrong with me?* "Claim you, Harmony."

"Mason," she rasped, the sound shooting straight to my dick.

God fucking—

I needed to leave. "I'm going to go. I'll be back on Sunday," I informed her, turning on my heel.

"But what about dinner?" she asked, her voice so weak, it was hard to miss the disappointment.

I looked at her as I went back into the hallway. "Sunday," I promised.

"Mason—"

I turned to walk to the living room, where I grabbed my hat and keys. As I put my hat on my head, she came out into the hallway, only a foot away.

"I don't want you to go," she stated, her voice stronger than it had been a few minutes ago.

I didn't either, but I was trying to be a gentleman. I was trying to be a decent man, like she deserved.

"Dinner is almost done. I'm sorry I freaked out and probably freaked you out, but I..." She trailed off, looking at her purple socks.

"This has nothing to do with you, Harmony," I assured her gently, my fist tightening around my keys.

She was still looking down at her socks, and I knew she wanted to say something.

I waited.

Fuck, but I waited.

"I like having you here, Mason," she whispered. She looked back up at me, her beauty hitting me in the gut. "I liked you watching me."

The darkness in me smiled—something that I'd been trying to keep at bay for years. Around her, it was difficult to control. It was vile and twisted, always had been, born from the trauma I'd endured as a child. It wasn't good. It wasn't worth her time. Then again, she brought it out of me. I wanted to know why? I wanted to know why this woman. Why was she so intoxicating to me?

My mind drifted back to when she pressed herself against her bedroom window, giving me a better look at her body as I watched her from down below.

Take her.

Claim her now.

She wants it.

"Harmony," I warned, my upper lip curling.

She took a step towards me, looking down for a moment again, perhaps to gather the courage. Finally, her eyes met mine again, desperation and pain painting them. "You can go, but just tell me this one thing."

Anything you want, Little Song. Anything.

"What?"

Inhaling a shaky breath, she began to whisper, "Tell me I didn't freak you out. Tell me my brokenness didn't scare you away. Tell me—"

Fuck it.

My lips crashed down to hers, my hands cupping her face to hold her where I wanted her. A whimper came from her as she staggered back, hitting the wall behind her. My tongue pressed against her lips, begging to be let in as my fingers dove into her mass of curls. Soft, like I knew they would be. Soft like her. Her hands fisted my shirt at the sides as she opened for me.

Fuck, but she opened for me.

I didn't waste time. A growl left me as the taste of her hit my tongue.

Melons. Sweet, ripe, and fucking delicious.

She was timid, her tongue softly dancing against mine as my lips moved with hers. The world around us was still spinning. Cars outside were still moving, the people inside of them heading to their destinations. The sun was still shining, setting soon as it always does. The moon would rise tonight as darkness blanketed the sky, and the stars would shine. None of that mattered to me. I didn't care about tomorrow. I didn't care that I had a ride I needed to get to. I didn't care that my family was a shitshow. I didn't care that I needed to find a new manager.

I didn't care about any of it.

All I cared about was this, *right here*, this kiss that seemed to stop time. Harmony, my little song, kissed me back, giving herself to me. It was the greatest gift I'd ever received, and it was just a kiss.

This is more than just a kiss, Mason.

I pulled back, needing to end it, but a broken, pleading whimper left her lips. "Mase, more."

Mase.

She called me Mase.

"Fuck, baby," I groaned before capturing her lips again. We devoured each other, both of us starved for affection, broken and trying to heal. The kiss shifted into dangerous territory as her hands snaked up my chest to wrap around my neck. She was anchoring herself to me, and I found my hands dropping down, slowly, to her shoulders, to her waist, to her hips, before sliding behind to grab her fantastic ass that haunted my dreams.

I broke away and pressed my forehead against hers. "Harmony," I whispered gruffly.

"Yes?"

"You kiss like a fucking angel," I said, opening my eyes, only to be surrounded by blue.

"You aren't so bad yourself," she breathed.

A chuckle escaped me, and for the first time in a long time, it was real one—not some fake shit I'd gotten down with years of practice.

This woman.

Things were starting to look up, but I was still waiting for the other shoe to drop.

Chapter Nine

Harmony

"Harmony. Fuck, baby. You feel so good," Mason rasped against my ear, his hand going to the back of my neck to hold me against the window. I arched my back more, giving him more access as he pounded into me.

"Mason," I moaned, my eyes closing in ecstasy.

"Really, darling? A cowboy?"

My eyes shot open, and he was there, sitting on the bed, watching me. As always, he was dressed in the finest suit money could buy, his hair slicked back, and his dead eyes on me. Then, they dropped down to where Mason and I were connected. Mason wasn't stopping. With a groan, he dropped his forehead to my shoulder. "Ignore him, Little Song," he urged.

The source of my pain and nightmares smiled at my cowboy's words. It was cruel. It was vicious. It was a downright evil. It was the same smile he used to give me right before he lost his temper.

"She can't ignore me, boy," he laughed. "I'm the one who marked her soul. Do you not understand that?"

Mason's hand gripped my jaw, burying himself in me to the hilt, as he forced me to look at him. The storm within his eyes was calling out to me, begging me to stay. "Focus on me, Harmony. I got you. I will always have you," he promised softly.

I wanted to believe him. I wanted to know everything was going to be okay.

"She barely knows you!" the man on the bed roared.

Mason's eyes flicked to him, his jaw tightening. "She knows my soul, and I know hers. We are the same. Broken always finds broken."

"She isn't broken, boy. She is my perfect girl."

A gunshot rang in my ears, and Mason's body jerked. His hand fell away from me as did his body. Blood dripped from his mouth, a mouth I'd grown to love kissing and feeling all over my body.

"Mason!" I screamed.

"Baby, why?" he groaned in pain, clutching his stomach. My eyes dropped to the bullet wound as his hands clutched it to try and stop the bleeding. He coughed, blood splattering all over my legs.

I felt a presence behind me, and I knew.

I knew it was time.

He found me again.

I was a fool to think that he wouldn't.

My hair was brushed from my shoulder and cold, chapped lips pressed against the skin there as I watched my cowboy bleed out.

"See what happens when you run?"

I shot up in my bed, screaming. "No! No! No!"

You are safe with me.

You are safe with me.

You are safe with me.

One, two, three.

One, two, three.

Red, blue, green.

Red, blue, green.

You are safe with me.

My cowboy's words whispered through my head, promising me something that couldn't possibly be true. Blinking a few times, my mind registered that I wasn't naked and covered in an innocent man's blood. I was in my apartment. My space.

My safe space, unknown to *him.*

Away from him.

"You're okay, Harm," I whispered to the darkness, my voice unsteady. The rasp in my voice was worse at night, and it made me hate it even more. My voice wasn't always like this, raspy and quiet.

Before, I had a wonderful voice. Everyone told me so, including my music teacher in high school. She told me my voice would set records, but that was a dream that was too far out of reach for me. So I went into nursing, thinking my life would be small but filled with love. There was nothing wrong with living a small life. I would put my mark on the world by healing people, helping the sick. I set my "what if" dreams aside for something more stable. Then, I went to hell, straight down, and I was still trying to claw my way out of it.

This was the first nightmare I'd had in a long time.

I needed to call Dr. G.

My eyes shot to the old-fashioned alarm clock on my nightstand. Yes, it's clunky. Yes, it's old. It's also the only thing that will wake me up when I am in a deep sleep. It was five in the morning. I fell back against the pillows, and my fingers touched my lips, thinking of the man who just died in my dream.

It had been a week since that kiss. A week of daydreaming about it. A week of missing him. He came over Sunday as promised, but he didn't touch me. He was keeping his distance, and I respected that. On the other hand, I hated it.

I hated it because Mason Langston, the rebel bull rider and cowboy, was the best kiss I'd ever had.

Just like the storm in his eyes, he loomed over me and rained down promises of pleasure, pleasure I'd never felt.

That man knew how to kiss.

That man knew where to put his hands.

That man made me feel things I hadn't felt in ages, things I didn't know I would ever feel again.

Mason Langston was bringing me back to life, despite the insanity of it all.

On Sunday afternoon, we were sitting on the couch, watching a movie. Cabe and Billie wanted to come over, but I made an excuse, lying about how I was sick. If they came over, they would meet Mason, and I wasn't ready to share him yet. I wasn't ready for reality to crash into this dream.

Instead, Mason had brunch with me, continuing the tradition, and then, after the kitchen was cleaned, we settled in for a movie. During that time, Mason swiped my phone off the coffee table and put his number in. Then, he looked at me with his intense gray eyes and demanded I talk to him every day. I made him promise he would return the favor.

"Already planned on it, baby," he murmured, putting his hand on my thigh.

We talked every single day, unless I was busy with work, or he was off doing...whatever Mason Langston did when he wasn't riding a monster. Cabe told me Mason was a wild card, and it was rumored that he didn't show up to the PBR shows until it was his time to ride. When I asked how he could get away with that, Cabe simply told me that Mason was Mason, and he did what he wanted.

Throughout the day, it was mainly texting.

On Monday morning, he wanted to know what time I went to lunch, which was twelve. He called me at twelve and stayed on the phone with me for the whole hour. At night, we would FaceTime. He would watch me cook dinner, grumbling about not having decent food. I then reminded him he could've had decent food had he stayed Friday night.

After that amazing kiss, he pressed his lips to my forehead, thanked me, and left.

Today was Friday again. I was off today, and of course; I woke up from a nightmare. The plan was to sleep in, clean, order groceries, and stay in the music room all day. There was a song I was currently working on, but I was still struggling with the melody. After I worked it out, I wanted to get lost in a book and take a scorching hot bubble bath. Then, Billie was supposed to join me for pasta night.

I laid in bed for a few more minutes, hoping sleep would bless me again, but she didn't. With an exhausted sigh, I rolled over and grabbed my phone finding two messages from Mason.

I miss you, gorgeous girl.

Eddie wants to know your hair care routine.

A laugh left me, and I shook my head. Eddie was a nut. Over the last week, he had interrupted our FaceTime sessions, telling Mason that he needed the screen to get his clown makeup just right. The man was funny and damn good at his job. Mason told me Eddie was his good buddy, and that even though they were eighteen years apart in age, Mason was the mature one.

I quickly typed out a message back before getting out of bed. Like every morning, I set about my routine: bathroom, kitchen, bedroom, back to the living area. I set about my skincare routine and then put in some hair oil and conditioner before I twisted it back, put a claw clip in, and headed to the closet. Dr. G told me life was about finding peace and beauty in small moments.

Romanticize everything you can, Harmony.

So, instead of reaching for a pair of sweats and a baggy t-shirt like old me would have done, I reached for a light blue maxi skirt and a cream, cropped t-shirt. Once the outfit was on, I turned to look in the mirror. The blue fabric clung to my hips, letting the world know just how wide they were, and the skin of my stomach was showing. I didn't have a flat, toned stomach. I liked cookies and pasta too much.

I used to hate my body.

He drove me to hate my body. *He* never missed a chance to tell me what *he* would change, because I wasn't good enough just as I was.

The only thing *he* really enjoyed were my eyes and hair.

My eyes dropped to my little tummy, to the faint pink stretch marks poking out of the maxi skirt. With a sigh, I pulled it up higher to fully conceal them. Maybe one day, I would be able to look in the mirror and love the person staring back.

One day, one thing at a time.

About an hour later, I was in the kitchen, rolling up the second ball of pasta dough when my laptop dinged. It was Dr. G calling, so I set the ball down, rinsed my hands, and rushed to it.

"Good morning, Dr. G," I exhaled.

Her dark brows shot up and her red lip turned up on one side. "Good morning. I just got your text and thought I could squeeze you in before my first appointment. Is this a bad time?"

I shook my head and brought the computer to my lap. "No, I was just making pasta dough."

She smiled and made a note. Before, during our first few sessions, I used to despise her when she jotted something down. Now, I'd grown used to it. "What kind are you making tonight?"

"Fettuccine alfredo," I answered. "Billie is a basic pasta girl."

I watched as she continued to jot stuffed down. I knew it was coming. There was no prolonging it, so I sat there, waiting.

When she looked up, she reached for her mug. "Tell me about the dream."

"It started out as a sex dream with Mason," I blurted.

Her eyes widened just a fraction. It was barely noticeable, but I saw it.

This was big. *Huge.*

Years ago, I feared I would never be attracted to another person again. She knew that over the last two months, Mason had been on my mind, but this was the first intimate dream I'd had about him. She also knew about the kiss and about how I didn't want him to leave.

She saw that as progress, but a part of me feared exactly that.

"Tell me about it," she requested, setting her mug down and giving me her full attention.

I swallowed and began, leaving out the explicit details. When I got to the part about *him* being on my bed, her dark eyes flashed with anger as her jaw tensed. The anger wasn't directed toward me, and it took me a long time to realize that. It was towards *him*. When I finished, there were tears forming in my eyes as visions of Mason bleeding out in front of me filled my brain.

"I just—I don't know how it got so dark so quickly. It was such a good dream," I whispered, my bottom lip shaking.

"Take a breath, Harmony," she ordered softly, studying me. I did as she said and calmed myself. As I wiped away my tears, I waited for her response. She was leaning forward now, jotting down notes.

"This is a generic question, but how did that make you feel?" she asked.

"Scared." I feared for Mason's life, because I knew *he* wouldn't hesitate to rip it from me.

"No, not the last half of the dream. I want to focus on the sex, Harmony," she stated.

I blinked.

She waved her hand, sitting back and crossing her legs. "Here's the thing about *him*, Harm. *He* is gone. *He* is in the past. *He* can only hurt you if you continue to relive the past, and you aren't doing that anymore, correct?"

I nodded. "Correct."

"Right. So, you are here in the present. Mason is also *with you* in the present. You told me last week that the kiss you two shared made you 'feel alive again.' What did the dream make you feel? The beginning. Block out the last half and focus on the good," she instructed.

My eyes dropped to my lap, remembering our kiss, how his big, rough, warm, hands felt holding me in place and then sliding down the back of my body. How electricity shot through me when he squeezed my bottom and pushed his hips into mine. How I felt his growing erection against my body and how that made me wet—for the first time in years.

Then, I thought of the dream, combining those feelings with it, my cheeks heating.

"It was amazing, Dr. G.," I began softly, "For the first time, I felt like a woman again. I felt powerful. Yes, he was the one...you know...to me, but he couldn't get enough. I've never felt that before."

When I looked back up at her, she was smiling.

"This is progress, Harmony. I know the second half of that dream might've been scary, but you have to understand, your mind plays tricks on you."

I nodded, my throat suddenly feeling scratchy. All this talk about *him* made my body want to retreat into the past, back into survival mode. I reached for my water bottle and took a long sip, grateful for the coolness and nourishment.

Dr. G watched this, her eyes on the bottle. "Are you still carrying it everywhere?"

Years ago, when I got out and escaped to Michigan, I wouldn't let this bottle out of my arms. I would shower with it, sleep with it, and I couldn't even put it in a bag to carry it. It had to be in my arms. I even dressed with it *in my hand*. That was a difficult task, but I did it, because I couldn't let the bottle go.

It was mine, and I wouldn't lose it again. That went on for nearly seven months before I could finally put it in a bag or on a table. Now, I was to the point where I didn't have to carry it from room to room, unless I knew I was going to be in there for some time.

"I didn't carry it into the bathroom this morning," I beamed. This was new for me, and I have only been able to do that since I moved into the apartment. This was my space, and I was the only person here.

No one could take it from me.

Never again.

Dr. G hummed in approval and jotted down some notes. "That's wonderful. How much are you drinking a day?"

I looked down to the bottle and said, "Only a gallon or so." That was another thing we had to monitor. The doctor at the shelter said I was drinking so much, I was about to drown myself, washing away all the nutrients that food and vitamins provided. So, I limited myself to a gallon day.

Another hum. "That's good, Harmony." She sighed and set her pad aside. "The dream is significant, that much is certain, but you need to understand that it's not *him* anymore. It's your trauma that *he* caused you. Your body and mind are healing. Clearly, they're ready to let go based on what you have told me when it comes to Mason."

"Yes, I feel it. Never—Dr. G—not since before..." I looked out the window. "My body hasn't been aroused in such a long time," I sighed, tired of the journey as I looked back at her.

She smiled at me, giving me all her perfect teeth. "You are doing wonderful. This is progress. This is good. This is healing. Here's your homework for the next week. I want you to start a new dream journal. Write down everything you remember about the dream and then write how you feel about it. Reflect on it. Then we'll go over it together during out next session, yeah?"

I nodded and smiled. "Sounds good."

"Tell me more," Billie hissed, sounding pissed off.

"B—"

"I was over at your place for *four hours last night*, Harm, and you didn't say a word," she snapped. This was true. I had been meaning to tell Billie about Mason last night, but every chance I had, I found myself stopping—holding back.

Reality wanted to crash into my little bubble that was Mason Langston, and that terrified me.

"I mean, seriously, babe! You kept this from me for *over two months*! The best bull rider in the world beat up that guard because of you, and you didn't think to tell me about it? Let alone everything else you've been keeping from me!" she huffed.

I could hear it—the pain in her voice. I'd kept something major from her, the person I'd leaned on the most in my life, and she was hurt because of it. She had to know it had nothing to do with her.

"Because I'm not ready for it to end," I whispered, leaning back against the headboard.

"Harmony, what are you talking about?"

"I don't—I just..." An unsteady sigh left me. "Billie, what if I tell you and then it goes *away*? What if I put it out in the universe that I actually....*that me*, that my body finally feels something again, and then it gets ripped from me?" I wasn't ready to lose that. The moments I'd shared with Mason, though they were few, were precious to me.

She was silent for a moment. "The universe isn't that cruel, honey," she promised.

God, I hoped so. I don't know what I would do if it was.

"Tell me everything, from start to finish. Don't leave anything out," my best friend commanded.

I looked out the window, soaking in the sunshine and the green leaves on the tree outside my building. Then, I reached for my water bottle on my nightstand and tucked it in my lap before telling my best friend all the thoughts and events that had been plaguing my mind for the last two months. This lasted awhile.

Sometimes, I was timid.

Other times, I was excited and giggling.

When I told her about the kiss, I felt like a sixteen-year-old girl who'd just had her very first kiss.

When I told her about the dream, I cried.

Once I was finished, she was silent, and nerves were eating away at me.

"Is it stupid?" I asked, taking a sip of my water to ground myself. I was here. I was safe. I was healthy. Billie was my best friend, and she was a safe haven. I was okay.

"Considering the man forked over half a million just to watch you, no. I think you should go to a show," Billie noted.

I blinked and looked at my bedroom door. "Isn't it too soon for that? I mean, technically, we haven't even had a date yet."

She scoffed. "No, he just pulled a grown man off you, threw him a few feet and then watched over you for the last two months. Not to mention, he practically inserted himself into your life in the most Alpha-male way possible and kissed you so good, your body rose from the dead."

My heart skipped a beat.

"This is crazy," I muttered, shaking my head as I looked to my lap.

"I think it's sweet."

My eyes widened. "Really?"

She hummed. "Don't you want to see him live?"

"I do. I don't want to only see him on a TV, and Dr. G thinks—"

"Harm," she sighed. "This is your life. You don't have to use your therapist's advice—or mine—as justification for something *you want.* I can hear it in your voice, honey. You want Mason Langston."

I said nothing, but that was okay because she wasn't done.

"I owe Dr. G everything for saving you from your past when I couldn't—"

"Billie," I whispered, my lip trembling.

"But you are your own person, Harmony Green."

I sucked in a breath as she continued.

"If you want to go see the hot, bull riding cowboy who makes you blush and kisses you dizzy, then do it. If you don't, then don't. It's that simple. You don't need anyone's approval to live your life the way you want to live it," she finished softly.

"I don't deserve you," I admitted.

"Yes, you do. I'm sorry you felt like you couldn't tell me all this. I knew that something was up the last few months, but I wanted to give you space while you navigated the adventure of living on your own again."

"You're right, you know, about everything," I told her.

"Cabe is going to want to meet him. I already do," she stated.

Suddenly, the monster inside me stirred my anxiety just the right way. I huffed a laugh. "What if this is a fluke, Billie? What if he was just bored and—"

"Babe, the top bull rider *in the world* stood in your apartment and told you he wanted to fuck you after you said something sweet to him. That's not a fluke. Mason Langston is hot for you."

With a sigh, I flipped my covers back and headed into the kitchen to turn on the coffeemaker. I heard a door shut on the other end of the line.

"Fucking finally," Billie groaned.

I heard rustling and then she said, "Cabe finally left to go help my dad, and now I can dig up dirt."

As I headed into the bathroom to do my morning routine, she dug up everything she could find on my cowboy. She told me she would call me back. It was early, only six in the morning, and Billie had called me an hour prior, demanding answers. She was right; I *had* been drawn away last night. I kept looking at my phone to see if Mason's name had popped up.

I was in my music room, my second cup of coffee sitting on the bookshelf as I strummed some chords on my guitar, when she called back.

"Hello."

"Okay, I have everything I could find on your bull rider," Billie boasted.

Chapter Ten

Mason

Eleven years ago. Hallow Ranch.

"Mason! Mason, please!"

I looked over my shoulder at the man I called my brother, then to the woman who, no less than ten minutes ago, had my ring on her finger. She was standing on the porch—my porch—her hair now a fucking mess from my brother's hand being in it.

My gut twisted at the sight.

We had a deal, her and I. I was gonna make life easy for her, and she was going to get me something I should've already had.

"Mase," Denver clipped.

My eyes swung back to him, anger seeping into my bones, anger for him being the perfect golden boy. The first-born son. The only son Pop wanted. He had everything, and yet he took the one chance I had—

"I hate you," I sneered, hating the way the words tasted on my tongue. "You are no brother of mine!"

You are no son of mine, Mason!

Pop's words echoed in my head over and over as I stared at my brother, his gray eyes flaring with something I didn't have the patience to decipher.

"Brother, think about this for a fucking second," he barked, stalking towards me.

We were nose to nose now, our anger swirling around us like a fucking tornado, destroying everything in its path, including our foundation of brotherhood.

"Don't call me that," I growled.

"You haven't talked to me in five fucking years, Mase! Hell, how the fuck was I supposed to know you were engaged? I didn't even know you had a fucking girlfriend!"

It wasn't about that. He could have Cathy; I didn't give a fuck about her. She broke the deal, and whatever feelings I was forcing my heart to conjure up for her vanished the second I saw her in my brother's bed.

"Back off," I warned, seeing red. He didn't get it; then again, how could he?

"Boys? What's going on?" Pop's old, tired, confused voice called from the porch. Before I could look at him, Denver's hands came to my chest, and he shoved me. "What the fuck are you going to do about it, huh? You pissed I'm calling you out on your bullshit? You can have anything you fucking want, Mase! Anything!"

Oh, how wrong he was.

I lost everything I needed the day Momma died. Now, I just lost everything I hoped would heal the brokenness inside me.

Denver's jaw tightened as he took another step towards me. "You don't got anything to say to that?"

My hands balled into a fist at my side.

Don't hit him.

Don't hit him.

Walk away.

Control it, Mase.

Walk away before you do something stupid, like kill your brother.

"Mason, baby, I'm sorry," Cathy rasped, coming up to both of us. Denver looked down at her in disgust. Her brown eyes met mine, pleading for mercy. We had a deal. She knew that. We had a fucking deal and she just shattered it by opening her fucking legs for my brother.

My.

Fucking.

Brother.

"We're done, C. Deal's off," I told her, my voice dead. She flinched as panic clouded her features.

"Mason—Mason, please! Listen to me, baby. I didn't—I just wanted—"

"I was busy building a future for us, and you were looking for attention from another man—my brother!" I roared. She flinched again, but I didn't care. I pointed a finger in her face. "Don't you ever speak to me again."

"Get off Hallow Ranch," Denver barked at her. "I don't ever want—"

"Fuck you," I spat to him. He looked at me. "Fuck you, fuck Pop, and fuck this ranch!" My eyes lifted to the old man on the porch, his hand on the railing, and his gray eyes confused. I looked at Denver, then down to his boots.

Fuck this place.

I spit on my brother's boots before I turned to my truck, and without looking back, I left Hallow Ranch for good.

"Mason Langston has done it again, folks!"

The crowd roared, cheered, and chanted, calling out my name like it was a fucking prayer.

I shot up off the ground to my feet just in time. The bull turned and bent its head, charging toward me. This bull was a beast, young, fresh, and rightfully pissed off. Eight seconds. That's all I needed to win. I held on for eleven because the high was *so fucking good*. I smirked at the beast before jumping back up on the railing. I lifted my legs at the last second before the bull rammed into the fencing, sending me flying back.

The crowd gasped.

I held on and sat back up with a groan, clenching my teeth.

Jesus, I need an ice bath.

Once the bull was contained, I hopped down, and the crowd began chanting my name again as I headed back into the pen. Eddie came up to me, butt first, and started twerking on me for the crowd. The men laughed, and the women hollered. My friend righted himself and turned to face me. His clown makeup smudged off and cracking as he smiled wide at me.

"Good ride, buddy," he praised, clapping me on the shoulder.

"Always is," I replied, giving me a smirk. I lifted my hat and flashed my signature smile before disappearing from the crowd's view.

The next rider was on the bull, gearing up for the longest seconds of his life as Eddie and I headed to the back hall. I was done for the night, and I was ready to leave. For the last two months, I didn't bother staying until the end to hear my name called. I wasn't focused on that prize. Eddie knew the drill and always walked me to the parking lot.

"You heading back to Texas?" he asked, stopping at the exit.

Honesty slammed into me like a wrecking ball, and emotion gathered in my throat at the thought of Harmony. Being away from a woman I barely knew but who consumed my every thought was getting to me. That kiss had been playing in my head over and over for the last week.

Hell, I even jacked off to the memory of her sounds, her taste, how her soft body felt against mine. Multiple times.

Eddie didn't need to know that.

He didn't need to know Harmony Green consumed my every waking thought. Even on the bull, I was thinking about her—something I'd never imagined. When I was on the monsters, my head was clear.

Swallowing the sudden lump in my throat, I said, "That's the only place I want to be."

Eddie looked at me for a moment, studying me. "Thought that was on the back of a bull."

I looked back to the arena then back to him. "You're right, but the ride is done, and I want to see my woman." Something passed over my only friend's face, and I chose to ignore it.

Hours later, the plane finally touched down in Houston.

It was three in the morning.

Fuck.

It was three in the morning and all I wanted was to see her, to get lost in her blue eyes and auburn curls. She was an itch I couldn't scratch. I could feel her in my blood, wreaking havoc and twisting up everything I thought I knew, everything I thought I wanted.

I couldn't show up at her apartment at this hour.

Why not? She's yours.

I shrugged off that possessive thought and headed to my condo.

Someday soon, she would already be in my bed when I came home.

Until then, I would wait.

A couple hours later, I was heading to Harmony's apartment, showered and charged with energy. My hand tightened on the steering wheel of my truck at the thought of her smile, how it took my breath away, and how that scared me. We had been talking every day this past week. Before I left on Sunday, I gave her my number and instructed her to do so, but I still anxiously awaited her calls and texts. Hearing from her was a new drug for me.

Harmony Green *was a drug to me*, foreign and stronger than the drug of bull riding.

Why would I need to ride bulls when I have been riding the high of that kiss for the last eight days?

About a block away, was a flower stand. It was still early, but I managed to busy myself with mundane shit for the last few hours so I wouldn't knock on her door at five in the fucking morning. It was now eight—a reasonable time to knock on a woman's door.

My phone rang, breaking me from my thoughts. Pam.

Fucking hell.

"Yo," I answered.

"Mason," she hissed through the speakers of my truck.

"Good morning to you too," I muttered, stopping at a red light.

"Don't. Don't you go and try to be cute. That shit doesn't work on me," Pam warned. My lips tipped up on the side.

"What do you need, Pam?" I asked sweetly.

She huffed. "What I need is for my bull rider to *remain* at the PBR event until the end, that's what I need."

The light turned green, and I switched my foot over to the gas. "Pam, I'm a busy guy. I don't have time to sit and watch everyone else ride their bulls."

"It's about being supportive, Mason," she quipped.

Supportive, my ass.

"Pam, half those assholes want to learn from me, and the other half hopes a bull will crush me," I deadpanned. She sucked in a breath, and I knew I'd caught her.

"Mason, that's—"

"I'm not welcome there. Never have been." A decade ago, I was the new guy beating all the experienced ones. Now, I was the experienced bull rider who couldn't be matched.

She sighed, and what came out of her mouth next really pissed me off. "You are set to ride in Nashville and Charleston next week, then in St. Louis the week after that. In St. Louis, the Cards are playing. PBR has purchased a box for you and some of the cowboys. They want you all to attend the game together and get some photos for social media."

"I'd rather have my cock dipped in acid."

"Mason!" she snapped.

"Pam," I returned calmly.

She sighed. "Look, you can fire your managers, but you can't fire me. I am your image, Mason. When you do stupid shit, I clean up your mess. I do that a lot, mind you. Do this for me."

"Pam—"

"Please," she begged. "Just go hang out with the guys in St. Louis."

Fuck me.

"Fine," I snarked and hung up the phone.

I slid my truck into an empty spot, swung out, and walked to the flower stand, remembering the tulips in every room of Harmony's house.

My woman loved her tulips.

"Good morning," the old man behind the stand greeted as I approached.

"Mornin'," I replied, eyeing a bundle of yellow tulips. "I'll take those please."

The man smiled. "Good choice, son."

I gave him a tight smile, ignoring the word that made my skin crawl. He handed me the flowers, and I pulled out some cash for him. Then a question slipped from me before I could stop it. "Why are you open so early?"

The man chuckled. "My wife operates our secondary flower stand at the farmer's market down the way. I learned a long time ago, that flowers are good anytime, anyplace, and for anyone," he explained.

My mind drifted back to a place it shouldn't have, a memory that escaped from behind the lock: Momma in a cream dress and her jean jacket—she loved that outfit. So did Pop. She was cutting the stems off some pink roses Pop had picked up for her that morning. She looked at me and smiled, her eyes bright with love.

Shove it back, Mase.

"Thank you," I mumbled. "Keep the change."

As I turned on my heel, the man called out, "Good ride last night, son."

Years ago, I would've begged until the air in my lungs ran out to hear those exact words from Pop.

Chapter Eleven

Harmony

I waited for Billie to tell me what she found on Mason as I swayed my upped body back and forth in my green chair.

I didn't feel good about this. There was a little twist in my gut telling me this was wrong. I shouldn't be digging up dirt on a man I was interested in, right? Was this the normal thing to do in the dating world?

He's a famous man.

A very famous man, Harm.

"Well?" I prompted, ignoring my thoughts.

Billed sighed through the phone, sounding off. "He was engaged, Harm..."

My back straightened, and my hand fell away from the guitar strings. "What?" I breathed. *Was?*

Mason was engaged.

"Yeah, to a woman named…Cathy. This was when he was just starting out in the bull riding world. It says here in an article that he was the love of her life—"

My stomach full on twisted at this point, a cold, slick whoosh of anxiety running down my spine. "Wait, what article?" I pressed, needing more information.

"One published about nine years ago, and the magazine interviewed Cathy herself," she explained as my throat dried. My eyes immediately started searching for my water bottle.

Billie continued, "According to her, they were high school sweethearts, and he promised her the world. She said there was something personal holding her back in Hayden, Colorado—where they're both from—and that she couldn't go with him on his first PBR tour. So, he left her, and later, she states that 'I showed up at one of his shows, ready to convince him I was ready and that we could be together, ya know? Find our spark again. Sparks like that don't truly ever go out, but it was too late.'"

"Too late?" I whispered.

Why would Mason leave the girl he loved to bull ride?

Maybe because it's his dream and nothing should hold him back from that, Harm.

My eyes drifted to the guitar in my lap, then slowly over to the piano I had yet to play.

Why wouldn't she go with him? Why didn't she support her dreams?

Did that monster of a man support yours? No. He wouldn't even let you chase them.

"There's more," Billie whispered, pulling me from the surface of the depths where the monster lurked.

"More?"

"Yeah, I went deep, babe. According to the Hayden public library, your cowboy owned a ranch, a big one."

Past tense again.

A ranch.

He was a rancher.

The monster chuckled inside me, reminding me that it would never leave. No matter how many exorcisms, therapy sessions I attended, or years that passed, it wasn't going anywhere, all because of *him*.

"Owned?" I parroted, setting the guitar down, swiping up my empty coffee mug and water bottle. I needed more coffee for this. I headed into the kitchen and started my Keurig as Billie told me about Mason's ranch.

"Hallow Ranch, owned by the Langston family for over a hundred years, is one of the largest cattle ranches in the state of Colorado. It turns over a good profit, so I don't know why Mason signed over his share over a decade ago..." My best friend trailed off.

I swallowed and focused my eyes on the bottom of the mug.

This changed things.

Mason wasn't just a bull riding cowboy. No, he was an *actual cowboy* who grew up and owned a ranch—*Hallow Ranch*.

I was poison to ranchers, raised to be that way by my father and the generations before mine in my family line. My eyes squeezed shut, my thoughts running wild with fear, anxiety, and regret.

It was times like these that made me hate the life that I was given. "Billie, he was a rancher," I whispered, my voice shaking.

"I know, Harm, but—"

"I can't...that's—this, it's too—"

"Harmony," she scolded. "Stop it."

"Billie, I can't." Shaking my head, I opened my eyes. "Why did he focus on me?" I asked, watching the coffee drip down into my mug, its strong, addicting scent filling my nostrils.

"Harmony, you are gorgeous," she said softly.

It wasn't that. I knew I was attractive—even if I wasn't in *his* eyes. Despite the verbal lashes *he* threw out about my appearance, I knew my mother passed her looks down to me, making me stand out among my siblings, who took after our father. I was the black sheep of the family, standing out with my freckles and red hair. "No, that's not—"

"Honey," she snapped, "Mason is not *him*."

Silence stretched between us. My coffee was done, and it was time to pour the creamer in, but I couldn't move. The monster wouldn't let me, lurking near the surface now. My hands shook as I braced them against the counter.

"Fuck, Harm, I'm sorry. I just wanted you to know some things about him, just so you weren't blindsided. I had a feeling he was probably a real cowboy, and I knew how that might affect you."

"Billie—"

"That being said, I think you should pursue this. It would be good for you. It's been six years, babe. I think Mason is genuine—*good*. I also think that even though he's travelling all over, he only has eyes for *my girl*," she said softly, love dripping from her voice.

Before I could respond, a knock at the door had my head snapping to the hallway.

"Someone's at the door," I whispered.

"Stay on the phone with me while you answer it," she demanded. This was something we had been practicing since I moved in with her and Cabe. When I was at the shelter in Michigan, I didn't have the responsibility of answering the door, which was a small sample of bliss.

Now, I was on my healing journey, living on my own, and someone was knocking on my door. No one was going to answer it for me. The rule set in place for me was that if someone knocked on the door, I called Cabe or Billie before answering it.

I left my coffee and headed down the hall. There was another knock, and goosebumps spread across my skin. I looked through the peep hole, and my breath caught.

"What? Who is it?" Billie pressed.

"Mason," I breathed.

She laughed. "Perfect timing. Enjoy your cowboy, babe. Remember, we want to meet him," she said simply, like we hadn't been discussing his past, before disconnecting

I sucked in a breath and opened the door.

Mason was leaning against the door frame, dressed in jeans, a white T-shirt, his boots, and his black cowboy hat, also holding yellow tulips and a brown bag. His gray eyes met mine, his storm calm, and a small smile ghosted his tempting lips.

"Harmony," he greeted, his deep, rough voice causing my goosebumps to spread all over my body again.

"Mason," I whispered.

"You gonna let me in or leave me standing out here?" he asked softly. The monster growled, sinking back into the depths. My heart jumped with glee again, ignoring the scars and bruises.

Instantly, I opened the door wider for him to step through. He flashed me a smile, before heading straight down the hall as I closed the door and locked it.

When I found him, he was in the kitchen, standing at my island, pouring creamer into my coffee. He slid the mug across the surface to me.

"There you go, darlin'," he murmured as he turned to the brown bag. I stared at the coffee; it was the right color. He knew how much creamer I took.

He came into my apartment and finished making my coffee...*for me.*

My heart pounded in my chest as I watched him pull out containers of food. My eyes went to the fresh tulips resting on the counter, then to the tulips that needed to be replaced in my living room, then back to the cowboy who bought me said tulips.

No one has ever bought me tulips before.

He used to buy me red roses all the time, as an apology to erase the pain *he* caused, thinking it would be enough. It never was and *he* always did it again. *He* knew tulips were my favorite, but *he* didn't care. *He* said I was a woman, and that women wanted roses.

Period. Dot. End of story.

But the cowboy in front of me brought me tulips...

"What are you doing here?" I blurted, my emotions swirling inside me like a hurricane that was about to make landfall with no way of stopping it.

His gray eyes flicked up to mine. "Breakfast, baby," he answered.

"Why are you—you could have any person in the world," I blurted again. He stared at me.

"You could buy breakfast for anyone in the world. Why are you—" I cut myself off, and looked out at the sun, which had just risen, sucking in a breath.

What was wrong with me?

You aren't normal.

You are a broken, damaged charity case.

"Harmony," Mason murmured, his voice soft, calling out to me like the sweetest song. It was gentle at first, and then it would build into a crescendo that caused another round of goosebumps to cascade over me. The way my body reacted to him was a miracle, one that I was struggling to understand.

I didn't deserve to hear that song. Some other person, maybe, but not me.

"Look at me. *Now*," he demanded.

When I looked back at the cowboy, the thunder in his eyes shook the floor beneath me, and the look on his beautiful face caused my heart to stop for a moment. *Yeah, I definitely wasn't worthy of that.*

He was a rancher, down to the bones. It was in his soul. He loved that Cathy woman, the love of his life, and left her. That was their business, but I knew about guys like Mason. I also knew evil men who wanted everything they laid their greedy eyes on. Mason wasn't that, but he also couldn't be for me.

I was damaged goods.

He deserved someone good—*whole*.

So, not wanting to, I tried to push him away. "I don't want to be another notch on your headboard. I don't want to be something you need for your image, and I appreciate everything you've done for the clinic, but..." I let out a shaky breath and looked at the floor. The last part I gave him caused my heart to beg me to stop, before it was too late.

"I don't want all your words to be lies. I don't want—"

Suddenly, a large, rough hand gripped my jaw and forced me to look up. My vision was filled with a powerful storm, unrelenting and angry, overpowering my emotional hurricane. Mason's nostrils flared as his scruffy jaw jumped under his tan skin.

"I'm going to kill him," he promised, his voice filled with a dark promise.

"What?" I blinked.

He bent his head lower and brought his other hand up so they could cup the sides of my face. His eyes held mine, pulling me into his storm, and then my back was against the wall.

Mason surrounded me, raging and intoxicating. "I'm going to kill him, Harmony. That piece of shit, whoever the fuck he is, I'm going to kill him for what he did to you," he growled.

My stomach twisted into a dark, unforgivable, painful knot as panic coursed through my body, pulsing faster than my blood. He had no idea, *right?* He couldn't even begin to imagine what that monster did to me. How could he possibly know?

"How do you—you—"

"You told me you're healing, Harmony."

I was silent.

A lightning strike flashed in his gray eyes as he said, "Doesn't take a genius to see it was man who hurt you, baby. It was plain as day in the fucking hallway, just as it is now."

"You don't know me," I whispered, my voice shaking.

His eyes softened, but not much. "*I want to know you*. I want to know the passions and secrets behind those mesmerizing blue eyes. I want to know everything that makes you smile. I brought you tulips because I saw how happy they made you at the Farmer's Market. I stood in the shadows and watched your beautiful face somehow become even more stunning as you smiled. My eyes want to see that smile every fucking chance I can get. I want to know what makes you laugh; I want to drown in the sound of it. Hell, baby, I want to be the reason," he admitted, his voice rough. His thumbs stroked my cheeks. "I want to know the name of the mother fucker who hurt my little song, who made her afraid to sing."

"Mason," I gasped.

He pressed his body into mine, and instantly, wetness pooled between my legs, ignoring the emotions swirling in my mind and chest. My body was drawn to him. My heart wanted to reach out to him but didn't know how. My mind? My mind didn't know how to process him and that scared the shit out of me. My soul? She was still struggling to pick up the pieces of herself.

"Harmony, you weren't part of my plan. Meeting you the way I did...baby, I was on my way back to my hotel room so I could get hammered and pass out when I heard your cry," he explained.

I stared at him, and after a few quiet moments, his intense gray eyes dropped to my lips.

"The second I saw you pressed against the wall, scared beyond comprehension, I wanted to shield you from him. Not just him, Harmony, but everything else in this shitty world. I wanted to protect you, make you feel safe."

He wanted to protect me. He wanted to make me smile.

Don't try to push him away again.

"Why?" I croaked.

"Fuck if I know. All I know is that I gotta," he growled as his lips slammed down on mine.

Six years.

Six fucking years of not being kissed without being forced.

Six years of not being touched.

Six years of nightmares, loneliness, and healing to get here, where a man looks at me like Mason does.

Six years of having to protect myself, and now I have a man wanting to do it for me.

His lips moved with mine, demanded control, and I submitted to him. Oh, but how I gave into him.

Mason's hands slid into my hair and yanked my head to the side, causing me to whimper. He pulled away and gruffly ordered, "Look at me."

My eyes fluttered open to find him glaring down at me with an undeniable heat in his eyes, causing my core to flutter.

As I tried to focus on what he did to me, the damaged parts of me wanted to focus on something else. "I'm sorry," I whispered. The words slipped out before I could stop them.

His brows came together. "For what?"

Everything.

For being a freak who can't seem to get her emotions under control.

For letting my best friend dig up your past so I wouldn't be blindsided by it because I went through something so terrible, it would give you nightmares.

For freaking out because you grew up in a place called Hallow Ranch and I was born from the poison that destroys them.

For being broken when you deserve someone whole.

I was lost in all the ways I wanted to apologize to him, and apparently, I was taking too long to come up with the words, because he sighed and pulled off his hat. He tossed it on the couch, and when he turned back to me, he pressed his hips against me, allowing me to feel *every single inch* of him.

"You feel that?" he clipped, his jaw tight.

My lips parted. He flexed his hips again, sending a wave of desire throughout my body. "Answer me."

I nodded immediately.

He dipped his head lower, setting a hand on the wall above my head. "You like that?" he asked, softer this time.

Oh, yes. So much.

I nodded again, still unable to find the words.

"I need your words, Harmony. I need your verbal confirmation you like my cock pressed against you, that you like knowing what you do to me."

"Y-yes," I breathed.

"Good," he murmured as he pressed his lips against mine again.

All too soon, he pulled away and stepped back, leaving me against the wall. I gave a small whine of protest, wanting more but he wasn't going to give it to me.

The cowboy folded his arms over his chest. "Right, gonna cut through the bullshit now, so we're on the same page. Truth is, Harm, I don't know what the fuck I'm doing with you, but all I know is that whatever *this* is, I don't want it to stop. For the past week, I've looked forward to your texts and calls. For the past few hours, I've been holding myself back from barging in here just to be near you. I've been back in Houston since three this morning and the first place I wanted to go was here, with *you*."

My stomach swarmed with butterflies, something else that was new to me. "Mason—"

"The last time I was here, you told me you were healing. That tells me some fuckwad hurt you, and I've been thinking about that for the last week too. I told you I was going to give you time, but I need to know something, Little Song."

I waited, enjoying the way he called me *Little Song*, the way it made me feel.

He lifted his chin. "Do you want this?"

My eyes dropped to his chest, the fabric of his shirt stretching over it in the most delicious way, then to his abdomen, down his long, jean-covered legs, down to his black boots. He was everything I'd ever wanted, once upon a time.

He was the kind of man I'd pictured myself marrying, before the poison got to me.

"I want those blues on me," he rumbled. I looked back up to his face and again, I was struck by the pure beauty of him.

Mason Langston was the kind of man you could fall in love with quickly.

Mason Langston was also the kind of man my mind was telling me to stay away from.

The mind plays tricks on you, Harmony.

"Define this," I requested, my voice raspier than usual.

His eyes nostrils flared again, as he unfolded his arms, and came back to me slowly, closing the distance between us. "*This* being the strong pull we both have to each other and don't try to bullshit me like you did at the clinic. You feel *this*, Harm. You do, and so do I. *This* would consist of me going off to ride bulls and coming back here to you. *This* would be, instead of knocking on your door and taking the shit into the kitchen, I would press you against the nearest wall and kiss you until you were dripping for me as a hello. *This* would be, eventually, baby, you in my bed, taking my cock, coming on my cock, and loving every fucking second of it. *This* would be me taking you out and showing you off to every unlucky motherfucker who wishes they were me. *This* would be me meeting your friends and family. Now, I only have one friend—Eddie—and he is a fucking nut. I don't talk to my family and never will again. So whatever holiday shit we gotta work out, we will go to yours, because mine isn't a fucking option."

What the hell happened at Hallow Ranch?

Mason continued, not giving me a chance to speak, which was fine—he'd rendered me speechless with his next words.

"*This* is also, eventually, me getting down on one knee and putting my ring on your finger. *This* would be us starting a family, because I do want children, always have. If you don't, I'll learn how to deal, because that's how much I fucking want *you*. That's how much I want *this*, Harmony. You weren't a part of my plan, but I have been thanking the heavens above every single day for hearing your cry for help."

I was silent, in shock possibly. Tears stung my eyes as my chest heaved with my short breaths.

"That's what *this* is, baby. You get me?" he asked, dipping his head to mine. "If you don't want *this*, then say the word, and I'm gone."

"What if I want to come with you?" I blurted out suddenly, surprising not only him, but myself as well.

His brows came together. "Come with me?"

"What if I don't want you to come back here to me because I want to be with you?" I asked, knowing damn well that I shouldn't have. I was putting myself in that woman's shoes. If his fiancée would've gone with him, would he be standing in my living room right now?

Don't think about that, Harm.

He's here with you in the present. Be present.

His throat worked, drawing my eyes to his tanned, thick neck.

Goodness, why is his neck attractive?

"Look at me, baby. Won't tell you again. We're having a serious conversation, and I want those eyes on me," he ordered. My eyes snapped up to his instantly, my cheeks heating at the tone of his voice. His rough hand came out to push a stray curl away from my face, holding my eyes as he replied, "You want to come with me, then come with me."

"It's that simple?"

He nodded once. "Yeah, it is."

I needed to trust that. I needed to trust him. Most of all, I needed to trust myself.

"Thank you for the tulips. They're beautiful," I whispered.

"Don't gotta thank me for anything, darlin'. Just give me a smile and a kiss," he whispered back. "That's all I need."

In that moment, I knew two things: one, I needed to talk to Dr. G about my emotions again. I could just chalk all of this up to the dream I had two nights ago, but I knew that wasn't the issue. *I* was the issue. I needed to learn how to process my emotions, especially if I was going to move forward with the cowboy in my apartment.

That was the second thing I knew.

I wanted Mason Langston. I wanted him just much as I wanted to sing again, and I had a feeling he would be the reason for me finding my voice after losing it to that monster who tried to destroy me.

Chapter Twelve

Harmony

"That was beautiful."

I looked up from my guitar to the cowboy standing in the doorframe.

I'd just finished strumming through the song I was working on. It still needed work, but it was improving. I just wished I had the courage to sing the fucking lyrics.

"Thank you. Everything okay?" I asked, closing the notebook on my knee and sitting back in the chair. I didn't want to talk about my music, not yet.

Mason smirked, and I knew this was a practiced routine. In fact, during the time I'd known him, I was certain that every smile or smirk he gave was fake. "Pam is being Pam. She's pissed I left the event early to get back here."

"Pam?"

He nodded and scratched his jaw.

This, I found, was another thing I shouldn't find attractive, but I did.

It was after breakfast, mid-afternoon now, and we had been talking on the couch for the last two hours. I found out Hallow Ranch was indeed a real place, not a fantasy land Billie made up in her head.

I also found out Mason hated Hallow Ranch with every fiber of his being.

He told me two sentences about the place where he grew up and shut it down. I let him, God, how I let him. There were things I wasn't ready to tell him yet, things he would need to know, but not now. Not while whatever was between us was still new. Not until I knew he wouldn't run when I told him the truth, that he wouldn't turn me away, disgusted at the sight of me. Instead of jumping into his past, he changed the subject off Hallow Ranch. He told me about some of the places he'd been, some of the adventures he'd had along the way. His stories were beautiful, filled with excitement, also with an underlining loneliness that had my broken soul's attention.

Then, the conversation turned to me. I told him I grew up here, then went away after college, leaving it at that. A simple, normal life story. There was a look in his gray eyes that told me he knew there was more, and when I couldn't handle it any longer, I broke his stare.

He didn't push me, and I didn't push him.

After that, the conversation was easy, even comfortable. He made me laugh a few times, and when I was done, I would find him staring at me with a that made my body hum with need.

I told him about my music room, and he told me about how his mother used to be a photographer, how she had a darkroom in their house when he was a kid. I didn't miss the hint of sadness in his voice when he told me that, but again, I didn't push.

Then, he got a phone call, and I left him in the living room to give him privacy. As always, I drifted into the music room, where I sat, strumming the guitar, until he found me again.

"Pam is my PR guru. When I do something stupid, she cleans it up," he explained, stepping further into the room.

"Well, what you're doing for the clinic is wonderful. I'm sure that—"

"Harmony, I did that for purely selfish reasons," he told me, his voice low. He was staring down at me with humor in his eyes.

"Yeah, but you're helping people who need it. That means everything, Mase," I replied softly, needing him to know just how much his contribution would help.

Something flashed within his gray eyes, and he got down on his haunches in front of me. "Like that about you, baby," he murmured, his hand on my knee.

"What?"

He looked out the window for a moment, his jaw ticking. When he looked back at me, the *something* in his eyes had grown more intense. "You care about people you have no business caring about. The world needs more people like you."

My hand fell on top of his, and I gave it a squeeze. "You care too, Mason."

"Know that, Harm. I'm just not as nice as you," he said with a wink.

Something in my gut told me there was a side of Mason that wasn't very nice, and that was the side of him that would kill for me.

I'm going to kill him, Harmony. That piece of shit, whoever the fuck he is, I'm going to kill him for what he did to you.

Three days later

I stared at the number on my phone as fear crawled up my throat, rendering me speechless. I squeezed my eyes shut, hoping it would go away—that this was just a dream.

A horrible dream.

My father just called me.

My fucking *father*.

After six years.

Immediately, I texted Dr. G and reached for my water bottle. I stood, clutching both items to my chest as I mumbled to Stacy, another nurse, that I was taking a break.

"Okay, girl!" she called to my back, but I couldn't respond. My eyes scanned the hall in front of me, glancing over patients waiting for the lab, and the doctors and nurses walking past me. I needed a place to breathe.

I needed quiet.

My body knew where to go, because seconds later, I was standing in front of the storage closet Mason pulled me into over two weeks ago. Barreling inside, I twisted and locked the door before I put my back to it and slid down to the floor.

One, two, three.

One, two, three.

Red, blue, green.

Red, blue, green.

"You're okay, Harm," I whispered, flipping the straw of the bottle so I could take a drink. The cool water ran down my throat, grounding me, reminding me I was safe. I was okay.

You're safe with me.

Mason's words echoed in my head, his deep voice comforting me in a way I didn't think was possible. My phone rang. Dr. G.

"I'm sorry for bothering you—I know you—"

"Harmony, take a breath," she ordered gently.

I did as she asked, holding it in for three seconds like she taught me.

"Where are you?"

"Work, in the supply closet," I answered.

"Did you answer it?" she asked softly, timidly.

The thing about my father was he only believed in three things: money was power, men were the superior sex, and daughters were chess pieces. That's all I was, a clay chess piece for him to mold and shape into whatever he needed before putting me on the gameboard. I wasn't a daughter to him, never had been, even when I was in my mother's womb.

I was burden to him simply because I possessed a vagina.

My father reminded me a lot of ancient kings, daughters were of no use. He wanted sons only, sons he could train to take over his empire.

My throat tightened, and before I could stop it, my mind went back in time.

Seventeen. I turned seventeen years old today. I should be out celebrating with my friends like a normal teenager, not standing in the middle of my father's office waiting to be inspected. The housekeeper told me the pink dress she'd chosen for me would be a nice touch.

It was a sweet thought, but nothing about me impressed my father.

His cold, dead eyes assessed me slowly, from top to bottom, like a snake slithering over my skin, looking for the perfect place to strike.

"Your hair is always going to be a problem, isn't it?" he drawled, sounding bored.

I tried to ignore the twinge of pain his words offered. Tried and failed. I just wanted to be good enough for him. That would be a great birthday present; finally being good enough.

"Perhaps there's a hair treatment of some kind, one that would straighten out all those hideous curls," his current mistress purred. She had her flat ass perched on his desk as she filed her nails.

I wanted to gag.

My father came around to grip my jaw firmly in his hands. He and I were around the same height, so those cold eyes were directly in front me now. "I don't care what you have to do. I don't care if he wants to fuck every single hole on your body. You let him. You make sure that boy marries you."

I didn't answer, I couldn't.

I felt sick to my stomach, and I wanted to die.

I'd been wrong though, to think I'd wanted to die on my seventeenth birthday. I wouldn't truly want to die until years later, on my twenty-second birthday, when I was on the brink of death and the monster wouldn't let me go.

"Harmony!"

I snapped out of the past, out of my thoughts, into the present. The storage closet came back into focus around me, and I realized Dr. G calling out for me.

"I'm here," I rasped. "I'm here, Dr. G."

"Are you alright?" she asked firmly.

"Yes, I just—" I swallowed, my throat dry again. "I just had a—a flashback."

"Of *him* or your father?" she pressed.

"My father," I answered before taking another drink.

"A flashback of what?"

"The time right before he introduced me to *him*," I said, my voice barely a whisper as the past threatened to surface again.

I heard her sigh softly before asking, "Harmony, is Mason still in town?"

Her question surprised me. Why would she need to know that? "Yes, he leaves tonight."

"Call him," she ordered.

"W-what?"

"I want you to call him. You are getting to the point where you are learning to trust people other than Billie, Cabe, and me. Mason is one of those people. Your updates and journal entries are promising. This is one of those times where you need to lean on those around you, Harmony."

I shook my head, biting my lip to stop it from trembling. My hands squeezed the bottle, the cool metal unmoving, unwilling to bend for me. It was solid, strong, reminding me of what I needed to be. Dr. G's words sank into my skin, and my heart skipped at the mention of Mason.

Yesterday, we spent the entire day together in my apartment. He kept his distance from me physically, except for a kiss here and there. He was trying to be a gentleman, and I found it sweet. Since meeting him, I've heard nothing but horrible things from him through the media: he's a player, an asshole, he's selfish...

In the time I'd known him, he wasn't any of those things.

My soul trusts you.

"I—he doesn't know *anything*, Dr. G. Not about *him* or the—"

"You don't have to tell him everything right now, Harmony," she began. "You just had a bad thing happen, and you need to know it's okay to lean on him for comfort. You don't have to tell Mason anything; just call him. Let him take your mind away from your past."

I found myself nodding. "Okay, okay, I'll do that right now."

"Good," she murmured. "I'm going to make some notes, and I'll see you for our session on Wednesday, okay?"

"Okay," I whispered.

"Call Mason," she ordered before hanging up.

I took a breath, pulling my phone away from me to pull up his contact. I hit dial, prepared to listen to it ring.

It only rang once.

"Little Song," he greeted, his voice rougher than normal. The sound of it instantly calmed me in a way I wasn't prepared for.

"Mase," I breathed, my voice shaking as my emotions swarmed through me.

I was such a basket-case. A freak.

A waste.

"What's wrong?" My cowboy sounded more alert, concern lacing his voice.

"I—" My mind drifted back to Dr. G's words. *You don't have to tell him everything right now. Just lean on him.* "I just wanted to hear your voice."

There was rustling in the background, and I heard a door slam. "You at work?"

"Uh, yes," I answered pushing up to my feet.

"Stay there."

"Mason—"

"Stay. The. Fuck. There," he growled. The phone disconnected and I stood there dumbfounded.

What the heck was that?

I decided to ignore it and distract myself with work. When I got back to my desk, I pulled up the missed call from my father and blocked the contact. Just as I set my bottle back by my computer, Claire the Great approached.

"Okay, I need to know something," she declared.

I pulled my hair into a bun, leaving some of the curls to fall around my face. "What's that, Claire?" I asked, sounding bored. I didn't have time for this. I needed to see my patients.

She tilted her head and plastered on her signature *Mean Girl* smile. "I just want to know how you got Mason Langston to talk to you."

My spine stiffened.

"I mean, honestly, Harm, the man is a legend and yet he can't keep his eyes of you when he's here. So, what's the deal?"

Anger sparked inside me, a short, bright spark. Girls like her frustrated me to no end. I couldn't understand it. "What was the point of you walking over here?" I asked.

She blinked.

"I have a job to do, and unlike you, I don't need to stick my head up anyone else's ass to do it," I snapped and walked away from her.

"Mason Langston is the biggest player in the industry! He is just gonna use you and throw you away," she hissed to my back. I ignored her and knocked on my first patient's door.

"Hi, Ms. Carter," I greeted, giving her a smile. "I apologize for the wait."

The middle-aged woman looked up from her book. "Don't worry about it. I just had more time to read." We shared a gentle laugh, and then I dove into her exam.

A few minutes later, Dr. Williams approached me. "Hey, Harm, can you show Ms. Carter where the lab is?"

"Sure," I said, standing from my desk. I was about halfway there when I heard.

"Mason! What a pleasure!"

My neck twisted, and excitement surged through my body—Mason wasn't paying attention to my boss. No, he was heading straight for me, his gray eyes flashing with an intensity that should've given me chills.

Instead, it made my core spasm.

"Mason..."

He ignored me, his big hand wrapping around my wrist as he pulled me to my desk. "Get your shit," he clipped.

My mouth opened but nothing came out. All I could do was stare at him. Get my shit? Why?

In the middle of my attempt to process what the fuck was going on, my boss approached us, a big "thank you so much for your money" smile plastered on his face. In truth, I knew this was his genuine smile, because he, like the other who ran this clinic, weren't money hungry. They were passionate, caring people. The most important thing to them was patient care, and they wanted to ensure everyone, no matter race or class, got the medical care they deserved.

It just so happened that my selfish, dark, bull riding cowboy was the key to that.

"Ms. Green is taking the rest of the day off," Mason informed my boss, his voice stern, leaving no room for bullshit.

If my eyes could pop out of their sockets, they would've in that moment. I looked at my boss, ready to apologize on Mason's behalf when his eyes snapped to mine, his brow furrowing in concern.

"Are you alright, Harmony?" he asked.

Again, I opened my mouth to speak but I couldn't. This time, Mason answered for me. "My team has been in touch with you about the build, yes?"

Mr. Dalys looked back to Mason. "Yes, Pamela has been the point of contact."

Mason looked down at me, jerking his chin. "Get your stuff."

"But I have to—"

He cut my protest off by leaning down as his jaw tightened and his gaze darkened with a different kind of intensity, the brim of his hat concealing us from the world. "Get. Your. Stuff."

"Is something going on here?" Mr. Dalys cut in.

Slowly, Mason's head turned in his direction. "No offense, sir, but my relationship with Harmony is none of your business."

Now, Mr. Dalys' eyes got wide. "Relationship—"

"I am heading out of town tomorrow morning. Got bulls to ride. Harmony is taking the rest of the day off," Mason stated, rising back up to his full height.

Now I was getting angry. Angry because the last man who ordered me around like this, broke my spirit and beat me into submission.

Never again.

This cowboy just came into my place of employment and made a scene. Now, he was telling my boss who I was to him and where I was going to go. I looked up at him again, and that dark intensity was still there. It was so dark, it had the power to scare me.

Mason wasn't supposed to scare me.

Mason never scared me, not once in the last few months. Not when he pulled that man off me, not when he stood outside my apartment, not when he told me what this was between us, and definitely not when he told me that he wanted me. In those moments, I was scared of my feelings. I was scared of myself, of not being good enough, worthy enough.

In this moment, I was scared of him. I was scared of him because he was trying to control me and the life I was trying to build for myself. A life I'd worked so damn hard for.

Mason saw me for who I was. *He saw right through me.*

He knew I was healing. Hell, I was the one who told him so. I let him in. I let myself believe he was a decent man, a good man. Instead, he was man who liked control and was trying to take advantage of a broken woman. I called him to lean on him, not for him to uproot my life and embarrass me in front of my boss and colleagues.

Grinding my teeth, I reached over to the counter to grab my bag and water bottle. I looked at Mr. Dalys, my cheeks heating with embarrassment. "Excuse us for just a moment, Mr. Dalys," I said, yanking my wrist out of Mason's grip. I brushed past concerned-looking boss, and that only added to my embarrassment as I headed down that hall. I heard Mason's boots following me. Turning the corner, I headed out backdoor to the employee parking lot. Without a second glance, I pushed the door open, and the heat of the sun hit me.

I was a few feet from my car, his truck parked beside it, Mason grabbed my arm. I whirled on him, throwing my finger in his face, rising on my toes. "You don't control me!" I snapped, ready to fight for it, even if it meant letting go of the first man I cared for. "I am not some fucking bitch you get to put a leash on! No man will ever get that power over me again, and I swear to—"

I was cut off by Mason yanking me towards his hard body and spinning us. In the next second, my back was against the side of his truck, his front pressed into mine, his hand was at my jaw. He forced my head back, and the air left my lungs.

The sun was directly above him, his hat blocking it, but that didn't stop its rays from pouring out all around him. The storm in his eyes was a full-on hurricane now, raging with a power not even God could stop, destroying everything in its path. That included every thought my brain conjured up in the last three minutes.

"How dare you," he seethed.

I *flinched.*

Lightning flashed in his eyes, and he growled, "You scared of me?"

I didn't respond.

He huffed a harsh, unkind laugh as he looked away from me, giving me his profile, half—hidden by his hat. I watched as his nostrils flared and his jaw worked as he inhaled deeply through his nose. Slowly, his hand fell from my jaw, and instantly, I missed his touch. My stomach dropped as he braced his hands on either side of my head, caging me in against his truck. When he looked back at me, he not only looked angry, but he looked hurt.

"I would never lay a hand on you with the intent to cause you harm," he whispered, his voice rough.

My throat tightened, and my eyes stung.

"That fucker put a leash on you, didn't he?"

Not a leash—chains. Ones I was still trying to break free from.

"You're scared *of me*? You have no idea how much you scared me when I answered your call," he continued, making my chest ache. His eyes scanned my face for a moment, and then dropped down to my bottle hanging from my hand at my side. "You told me that you wanted this," he stated, his voice getting angrier.

"I—"

He bent his head, his lips brushing against my ear, his breath sending tingles down my spine. "You needed me, and I came, baby. I'll always come. Don't give a fuck who I gotta go through. You call, I come."

Oh, God.

"Mason, I—"

"You said you wanted *this*, Harmony," he growled. "Gonna have to clue you in, seeing that fucker still has his claws in you so deep, you don't know what's standing right in front of you. *Me.* Let me erase that doubt you've got swirling in your head, doubt that fucker put there. You. Are. *Mine.* You've been mine from the moment I saw you in that damn hallway. Gave you time, Little Song, even gave you a choice. You said *yes*. You want me—you get *all of me*." He pulled away from my ear and came to my face, the brim of his hat pushing against my high bun. My heart was pounding too hard for me to give a damn.

"Mason, I—"

He shook his head, bringing his hand to my face so his thumb could brush over my lip. "Pains me, darlin', you thinking I would ever hurt you. Thinkin' I was anything like that monster who stopped you from singing," he murmured.

My chest cracked open at his words, and the tears came. He tilted his head as his thumb moved from my lip to cheek so he could wipe the tears away.

"I don't want to be controlled," I whispered.

"You're free with me. You just gotta trust me," Mason promised. "My sweet girl called me, something in her voice told me something was wrong, and I came. Didn't think anything of it. Just needed to get to you."

God, I was such an idiot.

"I'm sorry," I breathed, bringing my hand up to his chest.

"You gonna let me take care of you?" he shot back, his jaw tightening again.

I looked down to our feet, feeling like a fool. "I don't know if I'm even worth the trouble," I admitted, my tears falling to the concrete.

"Harmony Green, you are worth every ounce of trouble you throw my way." His words crashed into my soul, oozing over the shattered pieces. Slowly, oh so slowly, those pieces started to come together again.

Fingers gripped my chin, and then I was looking up at him again, the storm in his eyes quieting.

"I'm a cowboy, and we protect our own. You are mine. Therefore, I protect you. Simple as that. Don't give a fuck who I'm protecting you from; if they hurt you, they deal with me. When I said you get all of me, you get *all* of me, including the cowboy. It's who I am, Harm. Down to the *bone*," he said, his voice fierce.

My father's face raced into my mind, along with *his*. Two powerful, evil men, fueled by greed and hate. I came from that. I was born from that, raised in it, and nearly died because of it.

"I'm poison to cowboys, Mason."

He shook his head again, his throat bobbing. "How can you be poison when you're my cure?" he asked.

I didn't get to answer.

I couldn't, because his hands came to my face, cradling it like I was the most precious thing in the world as his lips came down on mine. With each stroke of his tongue, he chased everything away.

The doubt.

The poison.

The fears the monster from the depths sent to the surface in hopes to push Mason away.

Newsflash: this cowboy wasn't going away. Even if he was fighting for his life, he wasn't going away.

Chapter Thirteen

Mason

"I'm sorry if you felt controlled," I whispered to her once I broke the kiss. "That wasn't my intention. I just knew something was wrong, and I ran in there seeing red."

Harmony's blue eyes shined with tears as she looked up at me. "How did you know something was wrong?"

"Your voice, baby," I answered.

A door slammed in the distance causing both our heads to snap in the direction of the clinic. The bitchy brunette was standing there, her skinny hip popped out, her arms folded over her tits. Her eyes were on Harmony, jealousy evident within them.

"You want to go back to work or come with me?" I asked the woman in my arms. Her head snapped to me, gratefulness in her eyes.

"What?"

Before we got to that, we needed to clear some things up.

"Few things to note, darlin'. I'm a man."

"I know," she breathed, the sound going straight to my cock.

Fuck me.

Here I was, trying to be a gentleman…

"There's gonna be times when I'm a dick, and I want you call me out on it. You did it here, but you also assumed I was the type of spineless man who laid their hands on women."

She opened her mouth, but I talked over her. "Forgiven, baby. Don't think about it anymore. It's over. Done. You don't wanna be controlled, and I don't want to control you." *Except for in my fucking bed.* I left that part out. "I'm sorry for going in there and pulling you from your job. You enjoy it, you're good at it, and I disrupted that because I was seeing red."

Her features softened. "I forgive you."

"Get used to saying those words. This isn't the last time I'll piss you off. That's the cowboy in me. Cowboys piss off women."

"Is that y'all's moto or something?" she asked, teasing me.

My lips twitched, wanting to give her my real smile, but I settled for sarcasm. "Haven't been to a monthly meeting in a few years, so I'm unaware if they adopted a slogan or not."

As soon as the words were out, I watched my little song's face break out into a brilliant, blinding smile as she tossed her head back as a soft, raspy, throaty laugh came from her. I watched in awe, pondering what type of bastard would hurt a woman like this with a laugh like that. Add in her smile, her beauty, her curves, and her sass…I was still coming up blank.

I did know one thing, though.

I was going to kill him.

"I don't want to go back in there and face Claire," she said finally, her laugher subsided.

"The hard-looking woman at the door?" I asked.

She nodded. "Yeah. She's not the best person, but I can handle her. She's a typical Regina George."

"Who's that?"

Harmony blinked. "Regina…George."

I chuckled. "Dragging her name out isn't cluing me on anything."

"She's—how the hell do you not know who Regina George is? *Mean Girls?*"

I put some distance between us, my shoulders shaking at the shock on her face. Jerking my thumb to Claire, I asked, "Regina is one of her friends?"

"Mase, Regina is from the movie *Mean Girls*," she deadpanned. I ignored the way my chest ached at the sound of my nickname on her lips.

"That a chick flick?"

"You're impossible," she giggled.

"Cowboy, baby. I don't do chick flicks."

"Oh, you're watching it," she declared. "It's your duty as a human being to watch that movie."

I shook my head, scratching my jaw. "Rather eat dirt."

"Mason!"

I closed the distance between us, cupping the side of her face. "As much as I love standing here in the sunlight, your beauty taking my breath away as you tell me about some stupid chick flick, you need to tell me what you want to do."

Her eyes dropped to my lips. "I want to go with you."

Heat surged through me as that primal need formed in my chest. "Then let's go."

Harmony looked up into my eyes and said, "We can watch *Mean Girls* and laze on the couch."

"The fuck we are," I clipped, opening her car door for her.

Hours later, when I left her apartment, she asked me if I enjoyed the movie. We didn't watch the damn chick flick, but it was playing in the background as I kissed her until she was gasping my name, her hips grinding against my thigh. As much as I wanted to take her, to claim her, to fill her with me, I didn't.

I didn't because of the fear she had in her voice when she called me earlier and that's all I could think about. That and what she said in the parking lot.

I'm poison to cowboys, Mason.

Nashville, TN.

"You need to hire another manager, Mason," Pam noted from her spot at the table. I was staring out the window of my suite, watching the storm clouds roll in the distance. I had just finished today's ride and had the rest of the day free.

There were things I wanted to do, all of them having to do with my little song and absolutely none of them having to do with hiring a new, money sucking manager. Keeping my eyes on the dark clouds, I answered, "Pam, you and I both know hiring another manager would be a waste of fucking time. Besides, I'm not the only one who doesn't like those guys. You hated Dick, remember?"

I heard a soft sigh, and a smirk formed on my lips. *Got her there.*

"Be that as it may, Mason, you need a manager."

I turned my head to face her. "Then you be my manager, Pam."

Her dark-stained lips parted, and her eyes went wide. "What?"

"You heard me. Hell, you practically *are* my manager," I explained, walking away from the window. I took a seat on the arm of the couch and pulled off my hat. "Pam, you are the one who keeps me in line most of the time—"

"No one and nothing can keep you in line Mason," she deadpanned.

I flashed her my signature smile. "You clean up my messes so well, Pamela."

"But—"

Time to cut the shit.

"Look, hire an assistant. Take the manager position and I'll double your salary," I offered before I jerked my head to the door. "That last thing I need is another Richard barging in here pretending like he gives a damn about me or you. Those guys just want the ego boost and the challenge."

She blinked and slowly closed her laptop. "And what challenge is that, Mason?"

"Breaking me," I spat.

"Mason," she said softly.

I held up my hand. "I don't need some fat ass in a suit telling me how to ride the bulls I've been riding for over a fucking decade, Pam. I'm the best there is, and that's because of me—*no one else.*"

She nodded but continued to stare. Irritation crawled up my spine.

"What?" I barked.

"You're in a mood," she noted. "I've never seen you like this."

That's because the woman I'm obsessed with has something dark in her past, thinks she's poison to a man like me, and I know nothing about the fucker who tried to break her.

I didn't want her to know about my past, but not because it wasn't worth her knowing. That part of my life was over and done with, but I needed to know about hers. That fucker tried to break her and failed. If she was broken, she wouldn't have snapped at me the way she did, with a fire in her blue eyes that made me so fucking proud.

"Look," I sighed, pinching the bridge of my nose. "I'm sorry."

Pam slowly stood, clearly, in awe. "Did you just apologize?"

My head snapped up so I could shoot her a dirty look. "You act like I'm an asshole to you or something. Just because I make messes you have to clean up doesn't mean I've treated you badly, right?" I raised my brows, awaiting her answer.

"No, you don't treat me badly. You just stress me out more than my sixteen-year-old son."

Part of me wanted to smile at that, but I held it in. My jaw tightened as she put her small hand on my forearm. "You're different because you aren't walking around here like a ghost today—let alone the last few weeks."

The tension in my shoulders dissipated. "What?"

She gave my arm a squeeze. "In all the years I've worked for you, I have never seen any real emotion from you. That handsome smile you flash to the crowd is fake, the 'asshole' act doesn't match the kindness in your eyes, and when you aren't smiling or pretending to be an ass, you look lost."

Dammit.

"Pam," I warned, pulling away from her. "Keep talking, and I'm gonna fire you."

She scoffed, pushing her dark hair back. "Oh, please. We both know you need me."

I glared at her, and she held her hands up in surrender as she walked back to the table. Watching her gather her things, I let her words sink into my skin. Of course, I put up a front for the millions of people who watched me. The public eye didn't' deserve to know the real me, but the fact that Pam saw right through me made me feel exposed.

I hated it.

When she headed to the door, she turned to look over her shoulder. "It's just nice to see there may actually be a human underneath that hard cowboy exterior."

"Get out," I drawled, pointing to the door. "Before I fire you for the night."

She laughed. "Have a good day. Don't do anything stupid between now and tomorrow's ride, and please for the love of all that is holy, do not bail after your eight seconds!"

I made no promises. The only thing I wanted to do was call my girl and ignore the ache that Pam just put in my chest. I walked over to my phone, pulling up the text from Harmony I'd gotten before my ride earlier.

I can't wait to see you ride! Billie, Cabe, and I are having a watch party at their place!

The ache in my chest intensified.

She watched me.

My girl watched me.

Houston, TX. Police station.

Donald wanted to get home soon. His daughter was at a sleepover tonight, and he had a special dinner planned for his wife. He stood from his desk, shutting his computer down and locking his case files in the drawers. When he turned to get his lunch bag, there was a knock on his office door.

"Yes?" he called, turning around to find one of his younger officers, fresh out of the academy, poking her head in.

"Someone here to see you, Chief."

"Anyone important?"

"No, sir. Just said he needed to talk with you about something. Didn't seem urgent," she explained.

There were multiple cases open, and lots of people came to see him, anywhere from witnesses to nosy neighbors, to players looking for immunity, or even news reporters. However, it was six in the evening, and he was ready to go home to his family. He'd given enough to this city today.

So, he gave her a smile and whispered, "I'm not here."

She shook her head, a smirk forming on her lips. "Okay! Have a good night!"

Once he was in the parking deck, a few feet from his truck, he beeped the locks. That's when he heard it—when he felt it. He was being watched. Slowly, he reached for the gun at his side but kept moving, eyes on alert. Two decades of this, and he knew when trouble lingered.

"Tell me about the girl," a deep voice called from the shadows just past his vehicle.

Fear crawled up Donald's spine, knowing this was about the phone call he made two months ago—the one after the bull rider got done flashing his white smile to his officers.

"Don't know much," Donald said, opening the door of his truck. It was true—Mason Langston never returned to the police station, and the news about him having a woman in his life was non-existent.

He felt something cold and metal press against the back of his neck. A gun.

"Take your hand away from your gun, Chief. Boss wants to talk."

He did as the stranger asked and held his hands up. Then, a phone was pressed to his ear, and a familiar voice filled his ears.

"I don't have time to collect. Busy with things here. So, you are going to do it for me," the man ordered.

The Chief's blood ran cold. "Sir, without probable cause, I—"

"You will do what I say, Donald. You don't, and your little girl won't wake up at her little friend's house tomorrow morning," he clipped. The police chief didn't get a chance to respond, because the man gave him an order. Fear swept over Donald that he hadn't felt since the late ninnies, when his wife was taken by the Bratva. He'd made a deal with a different kind of devil to get her back.

"Bring the woman to me, or your family dies. You have three days," the man ordered through the phone.

The phone disconnected, and the gun was pulled away from his neck. The stranger behind him chuckled, and then he was gone.

Chapter Fourteen

Harmony

"The King of the Underworld isn't supposed to be hot," I whispered, heat rushing to my cheeks as I turned to the next page of *A Touch of Darkness* by Scarlett St. Clair. Hades was playing cards with Persephone in his club, and I was falling in love with the devil.

Mason had left for Nashville last night, after a deep parking lot conversation, banter, and a heavy make-out session on the couch. Needless to say, cowboys didn't watch chick flicks. This morning before work, I called Dr. G with a mini update.

"This is actually very good, Harmony," she declared shortly after I finished. I didn't tell her everything Mason said, just about how he laid it out and apologized to me.

"I think the dream and my father calling messed with me, and I'm afraid he—that Mason will see that I'm—"

"We don't say that word," Dr. G said sternly. *"You are a beautiful, intelligent, young woman. A person having darkness and pain in their*

past doesn't make them unworthy of happiness. I've told you this before, Harmony, you are not unworthy of anything. You deserve love and happiness just like anyone else."

"But Mason—"

"—handled the situation well. You're new to this, and no doubt he is too. You mentioned he was engaged some time ago, correct?"

I bit my lip, not wanting to think about Cathy or why they ended. "Yes, over a decade ago."

She sighed. "I'm not a bull riding kind of woman, but I do know who Mason Langston is."

My eyebrows shot up. "You do?"

Dr. G chuckled softly. "My father is a sports man, as is my partner. It's hard not to know who the greats are. Dean Connors, Travis Remington, and Mason Langston are in that category."

Travis Remington was the quarterback of the Los Angeles Rams; experts say he might be the next Tom Brady. As for Dean Connors, he was the biggest baseball star in the nation. Just last week, he reappeared after five years, playing for the Yankees. He came back and the world accepted him.

I came back, and I was still struggling to accept the world.

"Though, I will admit, I blindly assumed Mason was a hockey player," she admitted shamefully.

I laughed, trying to imagine my wild cowboy in hockey gear—and in skates.

"My point is, I know he hasn't been in a relationship for a while. If he has, he kept it off the media. This relationship is new to both of you, and it's going to be bumpy. No one said the journey to love was a smooth one."

"I hear you, Dr. G. I do have another question for you..."

Now it was after work, after I apologized to Mr. Dalys for yesterday, after the watch party, and I was in the bath reading a Greek Mythology retelling.

"I'm going to hell for enjoying this," I muttered, sinking my body deeper into the bubble bath, the hot water reddening my pale skin.

I was also going to worship Billie for the rest of my days for introducing me to this book. I got lost in the world St. Clair created, and I never wanted to leave. If Hades asked Persephone if *she was well* one more time, there was a high possibility I would be fainting in my bathroom.

Minutes or hours later, my cellphone rang. I reached for it and set the book down on the ledge of the tub.

"Hello," I breathed, still thinking about the bath scene between Hades and his future queen.

The line was silent for a moment.

"Fucking hell," Mason muttered.

"What?"

"What the fuck are you doing to make your voice sound like that?"

"I'm in the bath reading a book," I answered, my cheeks getting hot. *What did my voice sound like? Shit, could he tell?*

"Eddie!" he yelled, "I'm not riding tomorrow!"

I sat up, the water sloshing around and spilling over the tub. "Why aren't you riding?" I asked, my brows going up.

He scoffed. "Because I have a gorgeous woman on the phone telling me she's in the bath reading a book."

I stared at the bubbles around my knees, noting the freckles on my skin. "What's wrong with that?"

His voice lowered. "That's something I want to see in person, Little Song."

My stomach flipped as the rest of me grew hot. I looked to my chest to see a blush creeping up my skin—not from the heat of the water. My mind drifted back to yesterday, when he had me pinned down on the couch as his trailed hot, burning kisses down my neck. I'd wanted him to go further, but he never did.

He respected me, making my damaged heart like him even more.

"You can't leave Nashville," I gasped, panic setting in. He was there for two more days, and after a discussion with Mr. Dalys, we concluded that—

"I do what I want, Harmony," he grunted lowly.

"Boy, you're riding! I am not your manager! I am a fucking rodeo clown. So, tell me why I gotta spend half my fucking time worrying about your fucking messes!" Eddie yelled on the other side of the phone.

"Just a minute, beautiful," Mason muttered to me. "Listen here, you old man..."

"Listen here, pretty boy. I was raised on the streets. I'll fuck your shit up!" Eddie shouted.

"What streets you talkin' about? Eddie, for the love of fuck, stay off social media..."

I laughed and sat back in the bath, listening to the men bicker and argue. It warmed my heart that Mason had someone like that when he was on the road. From what Cabe and Billie told me, Mason was a "lone wolf" in the bull riding world.

"Get the hell out of here and let me talk to my woman," Mason commanded.

My breath caught, and my stomach swarmed with butterflies.

My woman?

My blush resumed taking over my skin, spreading its as my heart pounded in my chest. My body felt like it was coming to life after floating in an abyss for ages.

"Harmony?" he called. I heard a door close in the background.

"Yes?" I whispered.

"You take bubble baths all the time?" he questioned, his voice rough.

"Your woman?" I breathed, my hand drifting to the center of my chest. I didn't even know what he just asked me. All I could focus on were those two little words.

"Been over this, darlin'. Yes, *mine,*" he damn near growled.

My exposed nipples peaked at the sound, and I stared down at them in awe. That'd never happened to me before, unless it was self-induced—which didn't happen...hardly ever.

Sucking in an unsteady breath, trying not to get my hopes up, my fingers drifted across my wet skin, skimming over one of the dark, pink peaks. A zap of pleasure went through my body, shooting straight down to my core at the contact, and a small whimper came from me.

Oh, *God*.

That felt...

"Jesus," he murmured. "What in the hell are you doing to me?"

"Mason, I...You need to know something," I stated, my breaths becoming shorter as I went to the opposite nipple, testing to see if my body would have the same reaction, needing to know this wasn't a dream, that my body *could* feel this way. The same zap of pleasure shot deeper into my core, causing me to clench around nothing. I whimpered again.

"Fucking hell," the cowboy growled through the phone. "You touchin' yourself?"

I cupped my breast fully. *Oh*. That felt good. Too good. I let out a breathy, quiet moan.

"That's it, baby," he whispered, his voice rougher and deeper than before. My core spasmed, and I felt a different kind of wetness between my thighs.

It was Mason. All him. I had nothing to do with this.

I put the phone on speaker before setting it on top of the long-forgotten book.

Persephone could have Hades; I wanted my bull rider.

"Mason, I...I haven't in a long time," I admitted, ashamed.

God, what he must think...

He was gorgeous, no doubt he had women in every city, waiting for him to show. A man like Mason Langston knew how to pleasure women. A man like him probably got off on it. A man like him was someone who caused alarm bells to go off in my head, but I ignored them—had been for weeks. The monster that took years of my life away wasn't going to get this.

Never again.

I wanted to feel pleasure. I wanted to make a gorgeous man to feel pleasure.

I wanted to feel like a woman again.

I thought back to Dr. G's words this morning.

"That's alright," he said softly, his voice void of judgement. My soul whimpered at his words, his acceptance.

"Y-you turn me on, Mase," I whispered, bringing my free hand to my other nipple, dusting my fingers over it and closing my eyes.

He cleared his throat. "Tell me what you're doing, baby," he demanded gently.

My fingers pinched a peak at his words. "I'm touching my nipples," I rasped, opening my eyes again.

He growled and cursed under his breath, the sound sending bolts of electricity down my body.

"Close your eyes and do exactly as I tell you."

"But—"

"Are you going to be my good girl or not?" he clipped.

My good girl.

More wetness gathered between my thighs, and my clit throbbed with need. Need to be touched, stroked, and licked. My body was humming with need. Hades made me blush, but Mason Langston, he sent sparks through my body.

"Yes," I whispered closing my eyes.

"I want you to hook your knee over the edge of the tub," Mason ordered gruffly. "Spread yourself for me."

Before doubt could take over, I did as he commanded, my breaths coming quicker now. I was sure my entire face and chest matched the color of my hair. My hands were still at my breasts, cupping and squeezing.

The sad truth was, I haven't done anything to my body in years. I couldn't bring myself there, no matter how many times I tried. Reading smut would make me feel things in my head, but my body would never become aroused. Not like this.

I hadn't touched my *body in years.*

I hadn't found *pleasure in years.*

At first, it was because I didn't want it, the trauma I'd suffered was too catastrophic. Then, I didn't believe I could be sexually pleased again, because I was too broken, too much trouble for what I was worth.

Eventually, I stopped trying, accepting my body was just a shell for my soul.

That all changed the second Mason Langston pulled that man off me.

"You spread for your cowboy, Harmony?" he asked, his voice sending goosebumps across my body.

"Yes," I rasped.

"You still playing with your little nipples?"

"Yes," I replied, pinching the right one. My back arched slightly, my body resurrecting itself. He hummed, pleased with my answer.

I liked that. I liked that he was pleased—because of me.

"Don't ignore that little pussy of yours, darlin'. She needs attention too."

Now, a whisper of doubt, sent by the monster, shot straight up to the surface, ready to whisper in my ear and ruin this.

Pinching my nipples again, I moaned, focusing on what I knew felt good.

I wanted this.

I needed this.

"Take a hand and slide it down your belly, Harmony," he growled. "I want to listen to you play with that wet cunt."

That doubt sunk back to the bottom, Mason's heavy anchor on top of it.

His words were filthy. *Rotton.* All new to me. I'd never had a man dirty talk me before.

Be his good girl, Harmony.

I wanted to do anything Mason Langston told me to.

"Okay," I whispered. I took my right hand, sliding it down until it dipped into the warm water, then down to the apex of my thighs. My fingertips brushed against my curls and, unlike the countless times before in the last couple of years, excitement filled my veins.

Then, I realized I needed his words. "I—um, Mason, I—"

"Touch your clit for me, baby," he murmured. His voice. Those words. Exactly what I needed.

Holding my breath, I spread my lips open, skimming my middle finger over my bud. *Oh, goodness. Sweet goodness.*

My body arched in pleasure as I let out a long, raspy moan. *Years.* I'd lost years of this because of that monster. Fuck him.

"That's it," Mason growled. "Again."

"Mason," I whimpered.

"Rub your finger in a circle over it, baby. Make yourself feel good. My good little song deserves to come," he instructed. His voice was thick with need, like it had been after he kissed me. I did as he asked, whimpering and moaning in the bathroom as he listened.

"Beautiful," he groaned. "You like that?"

"Yes, but..."

"But what?"

"I wish it was your fingers, Mase," I whispered. I didn't know if I could get to the finish line.

His voice lowered, becoming rougher, darker. "They're mine, baby. I'm standing over you, stroking *my* little pussy, watching your body react to me."

The image filled my mind, and pleasure zapped through me, building and building.

"Oh, God!" I cried. My hand squeezed my breast, and I moved my fingers faster and harder. It wasn't going to take me long.

Finally.

"My little song, singing for me," he growled. "She is going to come for me, right on my fingers. Move your hips, Harm. Fuck my hand like good girl."

My body did as he commanded.

I loved it.

My mind imagined him standing over me in his undone jeans and black T-shirt, his cowboy hat on his head. He had one hand between my legs and the other braced on the ledge by my head. His scent wrapped around me; I could see his gray eyes and held them as his hand moved faster. Mason's head tilted to the side as I writhed for him in the water, my thighs starting to shake.

"Gorgeous," he called softly.

"Yes?" I whimpered, nearing the peak. I was so close—so damn close.

"Be my filthy girl and come for me," he whispered.

Alive.

I was alive again.

Pleasure warped my mind, body, and soul as white dots sprinkled across my vision. My back arched as cried out his name, over and over, chanting it so the whole world would know that Mason Langston was the cause of my first orgasm in six years. "Mase, Mase, oh God, Mase! Yes!"

"*Fuck*," he growled.

As I came down from the heavens, I opened my eyes and Mason was no longer here. His voice sounded gruff as it came from the phone.

"That was the most beautiful thing I've ever experienced, and I didn't even see it," he admitted.

My breathing was labored as I whispered, "Thank you. Thank you so much, Mason."

Pulling my leg back into the water, I sat up and wrapped my arms around my knees, astounded my body could feel that again.

All at once, emotion filled me as if a dam had burst, freeing things I'd thought I'd lost. Pleasure, warmth, excitement, need—*feeling wanted*. I rested my head against my knees, my eyes closing.

"Harmony."

My bottom lip trembled as my eyes filled with tears. He didn't need to know I was about to cry after I orgasmed for him.

How lame is that?

God, I was such a freak.

"Harmony," he called, his voice stern now.

I snapped my head up and stared at the phone. "Yes?" I whispered, a single tear sliding down the side of my head.

"You don't thank me for what *you just gave me*, do you understand?" he growled.

What I gave him?

I—

"Mas—"

"That was a *gift*," he told me, his voice thick. "I should be the one thanking you."

My heart constricted. I opened my mouth to say something, but the words were ripped from me.

"Now, I gotta go deal with Eddie before he gets arrested. You have a good night, okay? I'll call you later, darlin'."

I nodded.

A chuckle came from him. "You gonna give me luck for my ride tomorrow?"

"You and I both know you don't need it," I croaked.

He chuckled again. "Bye, baby." The phone disconnected as I unfolded my body, and I slipped my head under the water.

Chapter Fifteen

Mason

"Jesus, what are they feeding these things?" Eddie muttered, referring to the bull that just chased him around the arena so the rider could get to safety, as he leaned against the gate. I rested my forearms on the top bar beside his head, and whispered, "The blood of virgins."

"They get yours yet?" he shot back.

My shoulders shook as a chuckle came from me. "Not yet."

The announcer sounded on the loudspeaker, congratulating the cowboy who just rode. He lasted eight seconds. My eyes shot up from Eddie, and I tipped my hat to the rider as he entered the bull pen. He was a new guy, young as shit, stupid as shit—*fearless*. I remembered those days. The boy tipped his hat back to me, a sign of respect. The other guys shook their heads as one called out, "He ain't your friend, boy!"

Eddie turned to me, pulling his mic back down to his mouth. "I didn't know this was the set of *Mean Girls*." His words echoed throughout the stadium.

The crowd started laughing and I shook my head. "You've seen that shit?"

Eddie gave me a wide smile, holding out his arms as he backed out into the spotlight. "Regina got hit by a bus. Of course, I've seen it. Who hates Regina George?" The crowd roared with laughter, and then music came on over the loudspeakers as Eddie started dancing. "Y'all see that bull almost kill me? Tom, I want a raise!" More laughter.

My lips tipped up in a smirk.

Fucking Eddie.

It was our last night in Nashville, and then we would be heading to St. Louis.

Pam still wanted me to take the boys to the Cardinals game, and I told her I would do my best. I wasn't taking them to a fucking baseball game.

My eyes drifted to where she was sitting in the crowd. Her husband had driven their kids up for the show, and she was laughing at something her youngest was saying. I studied them for a moment, noting how her husband's arm stayed around her shoulders as she conversed with her children, a smile on his lips as he watched her. Eddie was putting on a good show, but the man only wanted to look at his wife. Their eldest, the sixteen-year-old who acted like me, was sitting back in his seat, arms over his chest, his eyes on a girl three rows down from me. Then, his brother climbed into his lap, and the girl was history.

From my point of view, you could see they weren't faking it, not like my father did with me. No one knew about the way my father turned after Momma died; that was a secret he took to the grave. I looked back to Pam, who was now looking at her husband, her eyes filled with love.

My chest ached, and I thought of my little song, the time we'd spent together, and the gift she gave me yesterday. Riding a bull with an aching cock is not recommended, but I couldn't get that phone call out of my head. In fact, it's the only thing that didn't leave my head when I got on the back to the beast.

My eight seconds of peace was filled with Harmony.

I wanted more.

Just when I thought I was getting control of my addiction to her, too.

"Alright, I'm tired of dancing for y'all," Eddie said to the crowd, signaling that it was my time to mount the bull. I pushed off the gate as the crowd booed Eddie. Adjusting my hat, I looked to the ceiling, knowing what was coming.

"Hey! Unless you got some dolla-dolla bills, I ain't shaking it anymore!" he snapped, moving his hips slowly. *Fucking Christ.*

The crowd laughed as he looked at me. "Besides, y'all don't wanna see me. Y'all want Mason Langston!"

The crowd stood and jumped, shouting my name as the lights dimmed, flashing red as "Man in the Box" played throughout the arena. The bull was waiting for me, bucking against his restraints in the cage. The cowboy beside me gave me the green light, and I hauled up, climbed over, and positioned myself on the bull, tuning out everything and everyone around me.

My bull rope was placed in my fist, and I put my hand on my hat, tipping my chin down, concealing myself from the crowd as I closed my eyes. Pop's voice filled my ears, his hatred trying to distract me like it always did.

You are no son of mine.

Why can't you be like your brother?

Your mother is gone; stop crying about it!

Boy, I'm talking to you!

My jaw tightened, and I knew the gate was about to open. I lifted my hand in the air, my other tightening on the rope. The deafening crowd was chanting my name but that didn't matter to me. I opened my eyes, the gate shot open, and the battle began.

The bull was instantly bucking, jumping, spinning, trying to throw me off. My grunts and his harsh sounds filled my ears, but I held on, keeping my eyes on my fist. Just like last night, my mind didn't quiet, and my peace didn't come.

Her raspy, intoxicating voice did.

Mase, Mase, Mase.

Thank you, Mason.

Mason, I...I lo-

The buzzer sounded, and just like that, eight seconds were up. I shook my head, and the bull bucked again. I growled and tightened my thighs around his body. I wasn't done. I wasn't done with Harmony.

She was about to say something to me.

She was about to tell me—

"Mason Langston, the legend is still holding on! Twelve seconds on the clock, folks!"

I closed my eyes, trying to find her voice again, but it was gone. With a frustrated grunt, I released my hand and jumped from the beast. I landed on my back and rolled, getting to my feet and running. The bull was behind me, no doubt ready to kick my fucking ass.

Eddie and the wranglers jumped in so I could get up to the fence.

A minute later, the bull was guided back into the pen, and the crowd roared once more, their noise drowning out the music. "Let's give it up for Mason Langston everyone!"

Sighing, I jumped down, boots hitting the dirt as I pulled off my hat so the crowd could see my face while the announcer spoke about my sponsor. I went to the center of the dirt, hat in my raised hand, slowly spinning as I painted on my fake smile. As I came full circle, something to the right of me caught my eye at the same time as the overhead lights dimmed, and Eddie started in on his skit.

I shook my head, certain I was seeing things—*she couldn't possibly*—

Pulling my hat on, I looked down in search of my bull rope, made my way to it, and swiped it up before raising my head again. My eyes went directly to hers, her fire red curls standing out like a sore thumb in a sea of blonde and brunette.

The organ in my chest pounded as my ears began to ring, the arena around me fading away in a blur, and all I could see was my little song. She was smiling at me, wide and bright, knocking the fucking wind out of me.

You waste your time riding those bulls. Why the fuck would I waste mine watching you do it?

Pops never bothered. He hated that I was different, that I didn't want to remain at Hallow Ranch for the rest of my life like Denver.

Denver, though, he supported me—cautiously—before he enlisted in the Marines without telling me.

Fuck. That hurt. I rolled and jumped to my feet.

"Dammit!" I growled, running from the small bull who was still bucking, pissed at me for getting on his back.

I couldn't blame him. I jumped on the top of the fence right as the bull rammed into it, rocking me. Without looking back at the animal, I swung my leg around and jumped down, landing on the outside, safe from the pissed off animal.

"That's not a bad time," Jigs called out from opposite the small corral. We were currently in pasture four, on the furthest side of the ranch. We had this set up for me a few months back, and Jigs brought in a bull from a ranch on the other side of the county.

This place had become my sanctuary in hell.

We'd been out here for the last half hour so I could get some practice in. My chores were done, the herd was settled, and the barn was clean. The sun was about to set, and then the cold would settle over the valley, warning of the brutal winter to come. The grass was brown, the trees orange, red, and yellow, covering the mountain in warmth as the wind cooled more with each passing day.

Ranches from all over the state had been talking about it for weeks. We were preparing to lose some cattle, and even though we didn't want to, we couldn't fight mother nature.

My eyes swung to Jigs.

The old man had one boot on the lowest bar of the fence, his arms resting atop it. He was chewing on some tobacco, a nasty habit he should've quit a long time ago. His son, who was a year older than me, had been begging him to stop for years.

"Gotta remember, kid, you still gotta put on some weight. When you do, that'll help," he reminded me as I walked around to him.

I shook my head, pulling my hat off and adjusting it. "Six seconds ain't going to get me anywhere, Jigs."

"No, son, but it's a fucking start. You're still a kid."

I opened my mouth to say something when the sound of a running horse filled my ears. As I put my hat on, we turned to see Denver charging up to us on his steed. My brother, already eighteen, with plenty of muscle and weight on his frame, wouldn't have a problem lasting eight seconds on a bull—but he had no interest.

"Jigs, Pop needs you up at the house," he called.

The old man sighed, looking at me. "The work of a cowboy is never done."

I grunted in response, and Denver swung off his horse as Jigs got on his. Neither of us spoke until Jigs was out of ear shot.

I spoke first. "Where'd you sneak off to yesterday?"

"Madison's," he answered quickly—too quickly. He was lying.

"Thought you dumped her over the summer," I noted.

"Changed my mind," he returned.

Whatever secrets he was keeping, I let it go. "Alright."

My brother tipped his chin to me, "You get it?"

My upper lip curled, pissed at myself. Six fucking seconds.

"No." I turned and rested my arms on the top rail, watching the bull pace back and forth in the enclosure. Denver stepped up beside me, resting his arms as well.

A deep sigh left him. "You know, if Pop don't kill you for being so stupid, the bull will. You are playing with God, Mase."

"That's the idea," I muttered.

I knew what he was saying, where he came from. He was trying to be a good brother, and he was—for the most part. I couldn't be mad at him for being Pop's favorite. Our childhood was never a competition. Denver loved the ranch; it was his life. I loved the ranch too, but I loved riding more. I wanted that to be my life.

Denver supported me because that's who he was. I tried not to be mad at him for not noticing. I tried to remember he had his own life. I tried to remember all that, but we were under the same roof, and he had no idea.

He probably wouldn't believe me anyways. He worshipped Pop.

I couldn't worry about that right now. I was trying to be the best. To prove myself, but the only thing I could focus on was my failure.

Still wasn't good enough.

"What the fuck is that supposed to mean?" he clipped, turning to face me.

I looked at him, his eyes the same as mine, and saw it.

After years, he still had no idea. He had no idea his little brother wasn't part of the family—just the punching bag for an old man with a broken heart.

"Nothing," I sighed. "Just in my head."

"Don't talk like that again," he ordered, anger and fear in his voice.

I looked at the bull. "I won't."

He didn't go see that girl, but I wouldn't find out until later. Three weeks after that, Denver shipped out to basic training in California, leaving me to deal with Hallow Ranch and the wrath of my father, alone.

I made my way to the pen, my eyes never leaving Harmony.

What the fuck was she doing here? Did something happen in Houston? Did she need me? Did Eddie know?

She's here to support you, sweet boy.

Pain struck my gut like I'd just been punched at the sound of Momma's voice, which I hadn't heard in months. I used to hear her voice after my rides or right before I would pass out, my body filled with too much whiskey and pain. Now, I was hearing her again, and she was referring to Harmony.

Why?

I refocused on Harmony, pushing my mom to the back of my mind.

She was wearing a dress. Fuck.

She dressed up for me.

She came all the way to Nashville—*to watch me ride*.

My jaw tightened, and I looked up to her, pointing to the door. Her smile only brightened, and my heart pounded faster. She gave me a thumbs up and started moving from her seat, her teal bottle in her hands. I went to the back of the pen, ignoring the dirty looks and backhanded congratulations from other riders. Instead, I went straight to our security guy, Marco.

He lifted his chin to me, unfolding his arms from his chest. "What's up, Mason?"

Cutting through the bullshit, I stated, "Red-head, curly haired woman. She's coming down here. Let her in."

He nodded once. "Okay, I'll let the boys know."

Before I turned away, I got close to him, baring my teeth. "She has a teal bottle with her, don't you fucking touch it. It's hers. She needs it. We clear?" I clipped, not understanding why I was so angry. His eyes widened a fraction before muttering he understood.

"Appreciate it."

Then, I turned on the heel of my boot, leaving him confused, in search of the woman I never saw coming.

Chapter Sixteen

Harmony

"Mason," I cried as he crashed his shoulder into my mid-section, lifting me up over his shoulder. My curls dropped around my face as his arm banded around the bottom of my dress, securing the fabric so it didn't fly up.

My bull rider grunted in response, the sound giving me butterflies.

I was in Nashville.

The plan had gone without a hitch.

With the help of Billie and Cabe, approval from Mr. Dalys, and the reassurance I needed from Dr. G, I'd planned a trip to see Mason Langston ride bulls in person. I'd gotten to the arena an hour earlier than needed, my water bottle with me and my nerves swimming in my gut, anxiously waiting to catch a glimpse of Mason.

Halfway through the event, Mason showed up, propping himself against the railing, his eyes on Eddie. Then, it was his time to ride. That's when the fear set in, a fear I'd never experienced before.

Fear someone I cared about would get hurt.

In my soul, I knew that he wouldn't, but the fear wouldn't go away.

I'd watched as he mounted the nastiest, meanest looking bull with ease. I watched as he adjusted his hat and bent his head. Seconds later, his hand was in the air, the gate swung open, and they were off.

The bull trashed, bucked, swung, yanked Mason anyway he could in a fleeting attempt to get him off. The crowd around me had been cheering and shouting praises at Mason.

All I could do was stand there in part horror, part awe at the man I was slowly falling for.

Yes, falling for.

When the eight seconds were up, I felt like I could breathe again, but I stopped short. This was because Mason continued to hold on, for four more seconds. It had been the longest twelve seconds of my life, and I couldn't even cheer him on because I was frozen, praying to God above that nothing would hurt him.

After it was over and the bull was returned to the pen, I didn't think he would see me.

But my Mason did.

He locked eyes with me, giving me his storm, and it was then that I knew.

Mason wasn't riding bulls for the fun of it or the money.

Mason Langston rode bulls to fight his demons.

While he flashed the crowd his jaw-dropping, dazzling smile, I saw the war within his eyes. My cowboy was in *pain*, and I knew it had everything to do with Hallow Ranch. He saw me, and even though the storm in his eyes scared me, I gave him a big smile, feeling grateful he was okay—physically, anyway.

Now, here I was, on his shoulder as he carried me through the back halls of the arena. He was still in his riding gear, and that made me even more nervous. The man was sexy in basic clothing, for fuck's sake.

Mason turned right, and I cried out again.

"Mason!"

"Hush," he clipped.

A rush of cold shot down my spine as I noted the anger in his voice. Was he angry at me for coming?

Did he not want me to watch him?

You aren't worth his time. You aren't worth anyone's time.

I flinched at the monster's harsh tone.

How in the world had it come up from the depths? Fucking bastard.

Mason turned us down another hallway and shortly after, he grunted, lifting a leg and kicking something that sounded like a door.

"Mase! Mason, where are you—oh," a male voice said in front of me. My head snapped up as I brought my arm up to hold my hair back. The man before me was in his late forties or early fifties and stood a few feet away. He was dressed in red basketball shorts, a Nashville t-shirt, and a straw cowboy hat. Clown makeup painted his face, but it was wearing off.

Eddie.

Awkward as ever, I let my hair fall so I could prop myself up to give him a wave.

A warm, kind smile spread across his face. I only got to enjoy it for half a second, though, because Mason turned around. The breeze from outside hit my face and I heard, "Harm's here."

A soft chuckle came from Eddie. "I can see that."

"Pam asks, tell her that," my cowboy ordered, his deep voice firm.

"Will do, bud," Eddie replied, his voice softer than before.

The tone of his voice, no matter how soft, couldn't hide the pride laced within it. Silence stretched between the three of us for a moment, and I let it. This was a moment between them, and I had a gut feeling Eddie had seen the storm in Mason's eyes before.

"Get her out of here before the boys find her," Eddie finally said. "She's too pretty for you, and damn too pretty for those assholes."

I smiled at Mason's ass.

Mason spun around again, ready to head out the door. I looked up to find Eddie smiling down at me.

"Nice to meet you in person," I whispered as Mason carried me through the door. I was unsure if the rodeo clown heard me, but his laughter was a good indication he had. When the metal door slammed behind us, I waited a few beats before trying again. I could feel anger radiating off of my cowboy in powerful waves, his muscles tense beneath me.

"Mason?" I called.

His hand slid up the back of my thigh, not stopping until his palm was resting over one of the globes of my ass. "Don't push me, baby," he growled.

"But—"

His fingers tightened, digging into the cotton of my dress, providing a delicious pressure. "Shut that pretty mouth before I *fuck* it," he warned. A whimper escaped me as my core throbbed, instantly wet. My heartrate climbed higher with each pounding step his boots took against the pavement. I rose again, tilting my head back to get a good look at the arena. The PBR was indoors, but I knew when he went to St. Louis, the location wouldn't be covered.

I scanned the area behind me, my hand tightening on the handle of my bottle on instinct. My brow furrowed and I pulled it up, wondering when I would have the strength to leave it behind. I had to have special clearance to bring it on the plane with me. Don't ask me how Dr. G pulled that one off, because I don't know.

That woman was a miracle worker.

Then again, look at all the progress she'd made with me.

It was dark, the sun having set about an hour ago. We were in the back of the arena, a private lot for the trailers and bull riders to park. There weren't many cars, mainly pickup trucks with trailers attached to them. The was a sound in the distance, like a car door slamming, and I yelped.

"You're safe with me," Mason grunted.

You're safe with me.

You're safe with me.

You're safe with me.

I remained silent, not wanting to piss him off even more, my eyes going back to scanning. The lights of the arena shot up into the night sky in reds, blues, and yellows. Even though it was enclosed, you could still hear the announcer and the roar of the crowd. This parking lot looked like a ghost town, if I was being honest.

Meanwhile Mason was dragging me out here like...like he was ashamed of me.

Wasn't he?

I was just some girl with a water bottle.

He was a superstar, his name known in households across the world.

Exactly. You are an embarrassment to him.

A burden.

A waste.

You're nothing without me, darling.

Tears filled my eyes at the sound of *his* voice in my head.

Aside from the dream the other night, this had been the first time I've heard it in *four years*. My grip tightened on my water bottle as Mason made another turn, stopping shortly after. I looked up to find a tree towering above us. I sat up and twisted my neck to see Mason's black Chevy parked by the base of it. We were in the far back corner of the lot.

He parked as far away as possible from the other trucks and trailers. The locks beeped, and I heard a click. Before I could see what it was, Mason shifted me, and then I was sitting upright on the back of his truck. He stared down at me, moonlight shining around his cowboy hat, making him look like a nightmare.

I pulled my water bottle to myself and suddenly, things became clear.

He didn't want me here. That's why he looked mad. That's why he was talking to me the way he was.

I wasn't wanted here.

Suddenly, a different kind of emotion took over. I was angry. Angry at him for treating me this way. Angry at myself for being so foolish. My eyes dropped to my lap, my stomach twisting painfully.

"Look at me," the cowboy ordered.

My eyes snapped up, taking in his tall, muscular frame, his gear, his hat, his painfully handsome face, the storm in his gray eyes. His hands were on his hips, his nostrils flared and his jaw tight. There wasn't much light over here, but those features were hard to miss in the moonlight.

"You don't have to be such an asshole, ya know?" I snapped, hopping off the tailgate. "I just wanted to surprise you—I wanted to watch you do your thing. I wanted to experience *the great Mason Langston* in person, because I didn't get the chance months ago. Even if I did, it wouldn't have been the same, because you were nothing but a stranger to me. Tonight, you weren't a stranger! You were mine!"

You were mine, and I was yours.

That's what we decided on, right?

You and me?

This.

I glared at him. "You don't get to be an asshole when I was just trying to support you. You don't get to scoop me up and haul me out of there like you're a fucking caveman! Hell, I didn't even get to properly introduce myself to Eddie, which was something I was looking forward to! Actually, I was looking forward to this whole night!"

His face didn't soften, but the storm in his eyes calmed a bit. It was so subtle, anyone would've missed it, but not me, the woman who'd been dreaming about his stormy eyes for months. "Harm—"

Shaking my head, I talked over him, on a roll. I was finally standing up for myself, and it felt damn good. I lifted my finger and pressed it into his chest. "You know, Dr. G told me to take a leap of faith with you! That what I was experiencing with you was *normal*? I've never *had* normal, Mason. My life has *never been* normal! Tonight, I put on a pretty dress, and came to see you, the cowboy who bought me flowers—" My voice cracked as my throat thickened. "You don't get to call me your little song and do what you just did. You don't get to push me to sing when you are so fucking ashamed of me that you had to get me out of your world the second I stepped into it."

My hand fell away from him as tears filled my eyes. "You don't get to be mean to me, Mason Langston! I've been around mean—"

I was cut off when his hand shot out to the back of my head, fisting my curls, yanking my head back. I cried out, but he wasn't done. Releasing a growl, his free hand gripped one of mine, and he brought it to the front of his jeans, pressing my palm against the bulge there.

My breath hitched.

My heart stopped, and suddenly, everything I was just saying went out the window.

Oh, goodness.

His eyes snapped up to my face as he leaned down, only an inch away, anger flashing in his gray eyes. The bull rider bared his teeth as he clipped, "I ride bulls *alone*. Been doing it *alone* for over a fucking decade. You hear me? Over ten God damn *years*. Never—*never* has anyone been in the stands *for me*."

"Mason—"

"Shut the fuck up," he snapped, his fist tightening in my hair. He pressed my hand further into his crotch, against his erection. "This is what you do to me, Harmony Green. *Fucking beautiful*. Too damn beautiful, and the kicker is that you don't even know it. You don't *know* how beautiful you are. What a treasure you are, with your red curls, blue eyes, a smile that could blind a sorry motherfucker, curves that make a man like me believe in God, and the voice of an angel. You being in those stands tonight—*for me and only me*—not as a fucking fan, buckle bunny, or a person who wants me to fail, damn near killed me. You sitting there in *this dress*, supporting me, because *you care about me*...this is what *that* does to me. I can't fucking think about *anything but you*," he growled.

No one had ever been there for him. No one had ever supported his dreams. He wasn't mad at me; he was mad at everyone else in his life—the ones who didn't care. My anger melted away and the monster was shoved back down as my heart began to swell for this cowboy, this lonely, deserted cowboy.

Softly, I whispered, "Mase—"

"Another thing, baby; when I set you on my truck—you stay on my fucking truck," he growled, releasing me and lifting me in one second. All I could do was stare as he plopped my ass back down on the tailgate, the cool metal against my thighs sending a shiver through my body.

"Mason—"

His hands shot out again, one in my hair and one pulling my hand back to his erection.

"I got you out of there because the second I saw you; I knew this wasn't a fucking game. Not anymore—never has been to me, Harmony. You're healing, and, darlin', I respect that, I really do. You need space. You need a man who's patient with you. You need a gentle man, one who will take you slow and sweet. I'm not slow and sweet. I'm hard and fast. I don't make love—never have. I fuck. Hard."

The twisting in my stomach stopped and turned into something else entirely. Something heavy, lustful, and dark. Something that shouldn't be inside me but was anyway. Something I shouldn't have wanted, but damnit, I did.

Mason continued, "Rode a monster tonight to get my eight seconds of peace—of *silence*. Didn't get that, baby. I got your voice; it was the only thing I could hear as that fucker tried to throw me off. When it was all over, I looked up and saw you there—*here*—watching me."

"Yes," I whispered.

He pressed his hand harder against mine, thrusting his hips into my palm. "Had to get you out of there because if didn't, I was gonna fuck you in front of those cowboys. Those underserving sons of bitches shouldn't see beauty like yours."

"Sweetie," I whimpered. His eyes flared again, and he dropped his forehead to mine, his fingers tightening in my hair. I knew my scalp would be sore tomorrow, but I didn't care.

"Do you trust me?" he demanded, his lips an inch from mine.

There was a storm forming around us now, trapping us within its eye, and as everything around us was in chaos, we held on to each other, our souls, finding each other after braving the storm alone for so long. We met in the center of it, broken, hopeless, and desperate.

Desperate for a connection.

Desperate for acceptance.

Desperate for love.

"My soul does, Mase."

"Fuck," he groaned as his lips slammed down on mine.

He released his hold on my wrist at his crotch, wrapping that arm around me instead. I spread my legs, and he stepped into them as my hand traveled up to hook around his neck. His lips moved against mine in a frenzy, and when his tongue shot out, teasing my bottom lip, I let out a moan. He wasted no time diving into my mouth and claiming it. Our tongues danced as I blindly made sure my bottle was standing upright on the tailgate before letting it go.

My free hand came up to his face, my thumb stroking his cheekbone as the palm of my hand pressed against his scruffy jaw. He grunted and dropped both of his hands to my ass, pulling me to the edge of the tailgate, where I collided into him, his erection pressed against my mid-section. I whimpered at the contact, at his size, at what his hands were doing. The hand on his face slipped back, and my fingers ran through his short hair under his hat, loving how soft it was.

This was it.

I was going to give myself to him, right here under this tree, with the moon shining down on us.

Mason's hand was in my hair again, breaking our kiss by yanking my head to the side so his lips could explore me. During our make out session on my couch last week, we discovered together that my neck was sensitive. I liked it; he *loved* it. His teeth grazed against the soft skin as he trailed kisses up and down the column of my neck. My hands dove under his hat, knocking it forward as I arched for him. He reached up and pulled the hat off, setting it beside my bottle. The sight of it caused my heart to skip, and my broken soul picked up another piece, slowly repairing itself—*healing*.

My bull rider's teeth grazed against the shell of my ear. "Little Song," he rasped.

"Mase," I breathed, electricity shooting through my body, right down to my clit, as he held me against him.

Something inside him snapped because he brought his head up and released me, stepping back.

Both of our chests heaved as we held each other's eyes before his gray ones moved, descending, pausing at my cleavage, then down until they reached where my legs were spread, the fabric of my dress still covering me.

In that moment, my cowboy looked like a man starved. His eyes were dilated as he stared at my center with a hunger that should've scared me, but it didn't. I'd never had a man look at me like that before, like I was the forbidden fruit.

Like I was the only thing he wanted in the world.

"You wear that dress for me, darlin'?" he asked, his voice gruff and thick with desire.

"Yes," I whispered, my nipples hardening under his gaze.

"You wear those Docs for you?" he asked, tipping his head down to my shoes.

I looked down at my Docs, remembering why I chose them—because they made me feel badass. The dress made me feel beautiful, but the Docs gave me an extra layer of emotional protection. My eyes drifted back up to him. "Yes."

"Turns me on so much that you don't try to change yourself for me, Harmony," he whispered. His eyes snapped to my chest, and I knew without a shadow of doubt he could see my nipples.

"Sweetie," I murmured.

His jaw tightened, and he shook his head once. "Fucking killin' me, baby, you know that?"

"Mason—"

"You gonna let me fuck you on the back of my truck wearing that dress?" he clipped.

My heart stopped, my lips parting at his words. "Fuck me?"

Had to get you out of there because if didn't, I was gonna fuck you in front of those cowboys.

He closed the distance between us, his lips going straight to my ear as his fingers skimmed over my bare knee. "You gonna let me fill you, Harmony? Or do I have to fuck my hand again tonight?"

Oh, God.

The desire in my body intensified, my core slick as my clit throbbed, begging for his touch.

My body was ready to be his.

My heart was already his.

My soul was reaching out to his, broken or not.

"I...I..."

His hand snaked under my dress, pushing the skirt up until his fingers grazed over the lace of my panties. I stopped breathing. My knees widened for him, and a dark chuckle rumbled from him, "You wanna know why your body reacts this way to me?"

I nodded, leaning back on my hands so I could look into his eyes.

Suddenly, he fisted the edge of my panties and tugged, not once, but twice. The sound of fabric ripping caused me to gasp. My eyes widened as I breathed, "Did you just—*oh*!"

His fingers were *on me.*

Yes, on me—*there*, moving up and down through my sensitive, drenched folds.

Heaven. This was heaven on Earth. It had to be.

He looked down and back up to my face, lightning flashing in his eyes. He braced his other hand next to my hip so he could lean down further.

"Because you belong to me," he hissed, dropping his finger down and pushing inside me.

My back arched, my hands shooting up to grab his shoulders as I let out a cry. His free hand shot over my mouth, silencing me. Then, my back was against the bed of his truck, my legs pushed up at his sides, the leather of his chaps digging into my skin. He leaned over me, settling his weight on me, shielding me from the outside world.

It was just us.

A broken artist and a broken cowboy, lost in a storm we never wanted to end.

"Quiet, Little Song," he taunted as he began moving his finger in and out of me.

So good. He felt so good. My body was on cloud nine as pleasure washed over me, ready to release, bolts of lightning shooting through me with every pump of his finger. I moaned against his warm, rough palm, my eyes holding his. He stared down at me, clearly enjoying the view.

"Such a wet girl, aren't you?"

Mase pulled his finger out, and when he entered me again, there were two. I cried out once more, my nails digging into his shirt. I wanted skin. I wanted to feel him against me—I wanted him inside me. My hips began to move against him, the need for pleasure taking over my body.

"That's it," he murmured, grinning at me. "Such a good girl."

My eyes fluttered closed at his words, his beauty too much for me, and then I felt his lips brush against my ear, his breath caressing my skin. "This cunt is mine, do you understand me?"

I whimpered at the filth in his words as he began to finger-fuck me faster—*harder*.

Yes. Oh, yes.

My hips lifted slightly, giving him more. I needed this. I needed him.

He pulled his other hand away from my mouth and dropped it down to my throat. I opened my eyes, and he was in my space, centimeters away from me. "Wanna hold you down while I fuck my little pussy, baby. You gonna let me do that?" His fingers pull out and then they were on my clit.

"Mase," I pleaded, my voice raspier than usual—damn near trembling—as he began to rub in circles.

"Yes or no?" he pressed as his fingers stilled against me.

Images of us flashed in my mind, his big body over mine, one of his hands on my throat and the other holding my legs open as he fucked me. I wanted that. I wanted to be fucked like that but only by him.

I trusted him.

With everything I had, I trusted this cowboy.

But would I be enough for him?

Swallowing, I admitted, "I'm not—um...I've never—not like—"

He pulled away, pushed off me. Instantly, my body missed the heat of his. Before I could utter a word, I was pulled further down until my lower half was hanging off the tailgate, the skirt of my dress flipped up to my stomach. My eyes dropped from his face to his waist, where with a single hand, he was working his belt.

"Mason, what—"

"Look at me," he barked.

My eyes snapped up to his face. Now that he was standing over me, my pussy bared to him, it clicked.

Mason Langston could do anything he wanted to me, and I'd let him. I'd let him.

My heart pounded in my ears, but I didn't miss his words, and they didn't miss me. They struck true—a direct hit into my soul.

"Let's get one thing clear, right the fuck now; I am *the only one for you.* Do you understand? That fucker—the one who hurt my little song—he doesn't get *this.* He isn't between you and me, Harmony," he growled. "You don't talk about any other men when you are with me, not like this. Not when you are spread open for me like a damn goddess, willing to give me something precious." He reached for me and yanked the front of my dress down roughly, my breasts spilling out, my nipples hardening even more in the night air. His hand cupped my right breast, squeezing hard. He grunted and moved to the other, messaging it.

"Oh, goodness," I gasped, my eyes closing.

"You belong to me now, darlin'," he hissed, releasing me.

I felt the tip of his cock press against my entrance.

"Say it," he spat, leaning over me, his hand going to my throat. I couldn't focus on his words, only on the heat of his hard cock against my core, ready to claim me.

Six years.

Six fucking years.

Six years of my life lost—I wasn't losing another second.

"Not fucking you until you say it, Harm." His voice was different now, not soft by any means, but I knew he was trying to be gentle. His control was about to break, and he was still thinking of me—making sure that I consented.

When my eyes met his, I knew what to say—down to the depths of my broken soul.

"I'm yours, Mase." It was barely a whisper, but it was out there, hanging in the air between us.

My wild bull rider's gaze darkened, and he snapped his hips, thrusting into me fully with a force that rocked my entire body, shoving me further up into the bed of the truck.

Bliss.

Utter bliss.

My neck arched the same as my back, my arms reaching for him, my legs trembling as my pussy quivered around his rigid length, trying to adjust to his size. My eyes met the stars above as I let out a long, low, raspy moan. "Oh, God!"

A dark chuckle came from him as his rough hands snaked under my ass, his fingers digging into my cheeks as he lifted my hips. "God ain't here, baby. If you wanted God, you should've stayed away from cowboys," he ground out as he snapped his hips again, pulling out of me and thrusting back in. "Ironic, seeing as how your wet little pussy is the closest thing to heaven I've ever fucking felt."

"More," I begged, trying to move my hips against him. He groaned, the sound giving me another zap of pleasure.

One of his hands fell away, and a second later, pain radiated through my ass cheek, straight up to my clit. *He just spanked me.* I raised my head to see his eyes on his cock buried inside me before they flicked up to my face, his upper lip curling in the most savage way.

"*Mine.*"

"Yes," I groaned, trying to move.

His hand slapped my cheek from underneath again, harder this time. "Brace yourself, Little Song."

He didn't give me a chance to brace.

He didn't give me a chance to even breathe before he began *fucking* me.

My head fell back as I let out a cry. His hand went to my throat, cutting off my voice, holding me down like he said he would. His cock rammed into my pussy over and over at an unforgivable pace, hitting the right spot with every single thrust. My legs wrapped around him over his jeans and chaps, my hands going to his arm, nails digging in.

He growled and squeezed my neck harder, a short lock of his dirty blonde hair falling onto his forehead. "Look at you. Fuck, *look at you*," he groaned, teeth bared as he looked between us, my breasts bouncing with every thrust. It was too much: him, his eyes, me being spread for him, the overwhelming need that stretched between us.

We just started, and I felt it coming—

"Mase, I—I'm going to—"

Instantly, I was yanked up, his arm around my back and the other braced on the tailgate behind me. He didn't slow his pace as he pressed his forehead against mine, our eyes never breaking contact. "My good little whore gonna come for me already? Huh? She gonna soak my cock?" he asked roughly.

Whore.

His whore.

Only his.

"Mase!" I gasped.

He kissed me, his tongue stroking mine. When he pulled away, his lips still against mine, he whispered, "You feel so fucking good, baby. This tight pussy is gripping me so hard, not wanting me to leave."

Pleasure shot through me, hot and fast like lightning, and I needed *more.* I hooked one arm around his neck as my other hand dropped down between us, my fingers pressing against my clit, rubbing in circles just like he told me to over the phone as his eyes dropped to watch.

He pulled out and slammed back into me, his cock hitting deeper than before as he pressed a kiss to my lips before going to my ear. "Filthy girl. Can't get enough, can you, Harm?"

I whimpered, my fingers moving faster, his cock fucking harder—so hard that his truck was rocking back and forth. I should've been worried someone would see us, but all I cared about was him—*Mase.* I moaned his name again, my arm tightening around the back of his neck.

"You had to call and play with your needy little cunt for me, didn't you? Wanted to tease me, show me what I left behind, how badly you wanted my cock," he growled, his hand at my back snapping to my hip, gripping me as his pace began to pick up. "That's how badly you wanted me, isn't that right?"

My eyes were about to close, my peak nearly reached. I could feel it coming and I knew it was going to be the most beautiful thing I've ever been given in this life. "Yes," I gasped, holding on.

He pulled away to look down at me. "You gonna give me what I want?" he demanded, his voice rough, deeper than ever before.

"Always," I whispered.

His gray eyes flashed, and his jaw hardened. "Milk my dick, Harmony. Give me it to me," he growled. He pulled out, slammed into me once more, and I was *gone*.

Blinding white filled my vision as my back arched as far as it could, my face to the sky above, my neck exposed to him as I cried out my release, a release I'd been holding in for six years—stronger than anything I'd ever felt. In that moment, I was fully resurrected, given a new life, my soul a new light, my heart nearly healed. White hot tingles spread through my body as I tightened around Mason, not wanting him to leave me.

I wanted him to be connected to me always. "Mason," I whispered, my eyes closing as I drowned in him.

My cowboy's body jerked against mine as his thrusts slowed, and I heard, "Harmony! *Jesus, Harmony.*" I felt him swell inside of me as his fingers flexed against my hip.

Bliss.

I fell forward, my head hitting his chest as my heart still soared in heavens above, my body still trying to recover from the pleasure. My eyes remained closed, and my ears were filled with a wonderful beat, a steady rhythm.

Mason's heartbeat.

The most beautiful song ever written.

Chapter Seventeen

Mason

"I can—"

"Darlin', no offense, but you just took my cock, milked it like it was your fucking purpose in life, and told me I was *yours*. You're staying with me tonight," I said, taking her suitcase and tossing it on the couch.

Her blue eyes met mine as she pushed some of her curls back.

Fuck, she was so beautiful—how was she even real?

I was starting to think she wasn't.

Despite the nonsense that just came out of her mouth, I took a moment to soak her in, burning this image of her into my memory. Her blue dress was wrinkled now, her curls wilder than before and hanging down to her breasts, her freckled cheeks tinted a deep pink, her lips swollen from me.

"That wasn't very nice," she noted.

No, it wasn't, but she was pissing me off.

"You want nice, then you get your ass in my fucking bed. You don't, and I'm going to be an asshole. Laid it out for you, baby," I deadpanned, pointing back to the king-sized bed. We were back at my hotel, and she'd just told me she didn't want to overstep.

This fucking woman.

She just gave me the greatest gift, and she was worried about *overstepping.*

"But—"

"Do you honestly think I would take you and leave you?" I spat. "I'm not that kind of man."

Not with you, my precious Harmony.

"I haven't slept with a man in six years," she blurted, her eyes going wide. She didn't mean to tell me that. A slip up.

My features softened, my red-hot anger dimming a bit. "Know it's been a while, darlin'. You told me that."

Harmony shook her head, backing up until she was standing in the hallway, pulling her bottle to her chest. "No, you misunderstand me. I've been sleeping alone for the last six years. I don't—I don't know if I will—" She cut herself off, and looked to the windows, the color in her cheeks deepening.

I closed the distance, pulled her fully inside the room, shut the door, and locked it. *Not a chance in hell.*

Then I turned her to face me, my hands cupping her face, thumbs stroking her cheeks. "We don't have to do anything you don't want to, Harmony. You are the one in control here, not me. You don't want to sleep together, then I'll take the couch. Regardless, I want you with me tonight—in this room."

Her bottom lip trembled as she dipped her chin, mumbling something about not being normal. My mind drifted back to her words from earlier, when she was letting me have it.

You know, Dr. G told me to take a leap of faith with you! That what I was experiencing with you was normal? I've never had normal, Mason. My life has never been normal!

"Who's Dr. G?"

My little song's head snapped back up. I could see the panic. I could see the desire to run—fuck, it was plain as day. I'd seen that look every time I looked in the mirror before I left Hallow Ranch.

"No, no, Harmony. None of that," I whispered.

My thumbs stopped stroking, my fingers snaking into her hair so I could hold her in place. Her blue eyes watered, tears filling them. I knew she was working through a lot of emotions, I knew she was healing, and I also knew I just claimed her in a very exposed way not even an hour ago.

I told her she deserved a patient man, a gentle man, and I wasn't that kind of man.

That changed the second I was inside her.

She was mine, and I was hers.

She'd been mine for months. I was in too deep to turn back now, and this journey to her heart was going to be a long one.

So, I would have to be patient. "You don't have to tell me tonight, but at some point, I need to know about your past."

She inhaled deeply before answering. "She's my therapist. She specializes in trauma victims, mainly victims of domestic violence."

Victims.

Trauma victims.

Domestic violence.

Her words struck me, and not even a second later, I was compelled by it. A nasty chuckle came from the darkness inside me, the darkness born from watching Pop avenge Momma. I was suddenly overwhelmed by it.

Rage.

Blinding, blood red rage filled me as the darkness tried to take over.

No, keep it together.

For her. Don't scare her.

Normal. She said she wanted normal.

She didn't want normal—she wanted *safe.*

Trying to get a handle on my bloodlust, I pushed out, "Okay, baby."

Her brows came together, confusion washing over her face. "That's it?"

"For now. Tonight is ours, like I said, and that fucker isn't going to come between us. When you decide to tell me, we'll sit down and talk about it. I do need to know something, though, okay?"

"What?"

No bullshit. My gut tightened as I asked softly, "Do you have any triggers when it comes to sex?"

Harmony held my eyes for some time, her bottle between us. I would give anything to know about that bottle.

The only thing she would accept is time.

She would have it.

Minutes passed, but I remained patient with her, knowing that if I'd done something tonight that hurt her—or took her to a dark place—I'd never forgive myself.

When she answered, her words were a punch in the gut. "Don't hold my face down," she whispered.

Rage felt like a brand on my skin, and the scar on my back ached. "Earlier, when I said—"

"I loved every second of it," she cut me off, her raspy voice gentle.

Fuck me.

"You're perfect."

She flinched at my declaration, and I stilled, cold washing over the hot rage. I immediately released her.

My girl just *flinched*.

She stepped away from me, and I let her. A single tear fell from her eye as she begged, "Don't call me that." Her voice was shaking, filled with pain.

"That word is no longer in my vocabulary," I assured her. "Never again, got me?"

She didn't move.

"Gonna touch you now, Harm, okay?" My voice was soft, low, gentle as I closed the distance between us. My fingers gripped her chin, tipping her head up as I bent down to kiss her.

My lips moved with hers, promising her something she didn't ask for. *I was going to kill him.*

My hands would be tainted with his blood as I gave her the life she deserved.

"Mason?"

I twisted my neck to find Harmony standing just outside the bathroom. I swallowed the lump in my throat as my dick twitched in my jeans at the sight of her in my shirt. My eyes dropped down to where it bunched above her wide hips, following the curves of her toned legs, down to her painted toes. Freckles were dotted all over her pale skin, every inch of her kissed by angels. Her curls were in a bun on the top of her head and her makeup was gone—not that she wore much to begin with.

She was a work of art, made just for me.

"Fuck me, baby," I muttered, rubbing the back of my neck.

"I—um—if you want—I can change," she stammered, twisting her hands together, her eyes darting to her bottle on the nightstand. I moved, coming around the bed, not stopping until she was against me, her back against the wall. She avoided my eyes as I caged her in.

"Look at me, Harmony," I ordered softly.

When she did, I let it out: everything that'd been running through my mind since she decided to stay with me and wanted a shower. "You can say anything to me. You're mad, you let me have it. You've done that a few times already, so don't stop. You've got a problem, you voice it. You've got a question, you ask it. Nothing is off the table with me. You are safe with me. Under no circumstances, do you have to walk around eggshells with me."

She remained silent, so I dipped my head lower. "I'm a hot-headed, bull riding cowboy, beautiful. I'm gonna say stupid shit. I'm gonna do stupid shit. Someone crosses me, I got no issues handing them their ass. Someone crosses you, I got no issues with going to prison."

"Mason—"

"Been fighting majority of my life, Harmony," I whispered. "Fighting for my life. Fighting for my right to be here. Fighting to prove myself to someone who's not even on this fucking Earth anymore. Fighting my past. Fighting my demons—yeah, I got 'em. Fighting the cowboys who want me hurt, gone, or just plain dead. Now, I have you, and darlin', I'm fighting for you. I'll never stop, you have my word on that." I paused and dropped my eyes to my shirt on her body. "You're wearing my shirt."

"Yes," she whispered.

"No other woman has gotten to wear my shirts, Harm. Gave it to you for a reason. So don't you dare think you have walk on eggshells around me. You speak your mind with me, ya hear?"

Her lip trembled, and her eyes drifted to my shoulder. "This was supposed to be a happy trip—a fun one."

She didn't get it. That was fine; in time, she would.

"Having the time of my life being with you, baby." Her eyes shot to mine, and my lips twitched. "Get in bed. Gotta shower and I'll be there, okay?"

She nodded, and my lips found hers. I kissed her for a long time, addicted to her mouth. When I finally pulled away, she was breathless and flushed. Ten minutes later, I came back into the bedroom in boxers to find her asleep, her bottle tucked into her chest. I stepped up to the bed, my eyes never leaving her. She was on her side, curled into a ball, her pink lips parted, her face relaxed.

I trailed my finger down the side of her face. "Nothing's ever gonna hurt you again. You're safe with me, Harmony," I whispered.

Leaving her in the room, I headed into the living area and grabbed my phone. Without thinking twice, I made the call. It was midnight, but he answered on the first ring. He always did, even though it'd been years since I called him.

"Mason?"

His voice caused my chest to ache, but I pushed through it.

"Don't have much time," I began.

"Mason, we need—listen—Denver—"

"Don't," I warned, my voice low. "Didn't call for that."

A beat of silence and then. "Alright, Mason. What do you need?"

I braced a hand on the nearest wall and bent my head. "Tell me again."

"Mason..."

"Say it, Jigs," I begged, my voice shaking.

"Cowboys don't cry."

I hung up.

Chapter Eighteen

Harmony

"Mason," I gasped, my back arching as my eyes fluttered opened. I dipped my chin, and time stilled.

The cowboy beside me released my nipple from his mouth with a pop, a wicked smile playing on his lips. My—his—shirt was pushed up on my body, bunching just below my throat.

"What are—"

"Put your bottle on the nightstand," he ordered. My eyes dropped to where it lay beside me and back to his face. His hand was an inch away from it. He could've easily grabbed it himself, but he didn't.

Jesus, this cowboy.

I did as he asked and when I twisted back to face him, his gray eyes were on my exposed breasts, and my clit swelled with need. My nipples weren't a pinky pink like most women had in the movies. They were a darker pink, almost brown, and now that those gray eyes were studying them so closely, I suddenly felt self-conscious.

Then, he obliterated those thoughts with a single sentence.

"I'm gonna fuck these pretty tits, Harmony," he whispered darkly, bringing his hands up to cup the sides of them. "Gonna leave my mark on them." His hands were massive, engulfing them completely as he pressed gentle kisses on my stomach. With each touch of his lips, I felt more and more electrified. My hand reached out to him, my fingers running through his hair.

"Good morning," I whispered.

His head snapped up, his jaw tightening as the morning sun seeped through the windows beside us, making him glow. He was shirtless, his sun-kissed skin gleaming as the muscles of his shoulders worked underneath it. My hand dropped down to cup his jaw, my thumb stroking against his rough scruff.

"So fucking sweet," he murmured as his gray eyes scanned my face.

"Say it back."

His features softened. "Good morning, Little Song."

My eyes drifted to the window; the sun was just rising. My plane would be leaving in a few hours, and I wasn't ready to say goodbye. My throat tightened. This trip was more than just a surprise for Mason; it was the final hoorah before he left for Spain.

"Hey, where did you go?" he asked, his fingers gripping my chin.

I blinked, shaking my head. "I was just thinking about how much I'm going to miss you."

A shadow fell over his handsome features, and he pushed himself up on his hands, hovering over me. "I don't have to go," Mase whispered.

I didn't want to respond to that. I didn't want to think about him leaving for a month. I didn't want to think about anything but him being here with me—in this moment.

"Kiss me," I whispered.

Time stilled.

The world stopped spinning, our lives frozen in time, movements halted, thoughts evaporated, dreams drifted closer. The universe stilled to give me this moment, allowing me time to study every single centimeter, burning the image into my retinas so that from now on, when my eyes closed, I wouldn't be surrounded in darkness. I would only see him as sleep came, instead of the nightmares.

The universe was apologizing for the torture that was thrusted upon me, the darkness I was drowned in, filling my lungs and leaving them tainted. The universe was apologizing for the years lost, the sleepless nights, the screams of terror.

The universe was apologizing for breaking me and taking away my light.

It came in the form of a smile—a real, genuine smile.

It was a smile that stretched so beautifully across a man's face that my soul sighed in awe, the bruises on my heart healing, the doubt in my mind vanishing

Mason Langston was smiling at me.

The storm that lingered in his gray eyes parted, giving me a hint of sun and a dash of blue. It was faint, but there—around his pupils was a thin line of blue I'd never noticed before. The skin around his eyes crinkled, telling me that if he smiled more, they would become more permanent as the years went on. A dimple on his right cheek appeared, saying hello and giving me a glimpse of a younger, happier cowboy—a boy free from pain. His white teeth gleamed in the early morning sun, so bright that I knew this was a gift from heaven above.

"Mase," I breathed, bringing my hands up to either side of his face.

The smile began to fade, causing my stomach to dip. "Harm."

"I..." I trailed off, my cheeks heating as he shifted, settling in between my parted legs, giving me some of his weight. "Kiss me," I repeated.

"Don't gotta tell me twice, darlin'. Just getting settled," he chuckled, the sound so gloriously rich, I knew that it was another gift from the universe.

That was when I lost it.

My logic.

I yanked him down as I pushed up, our lips crashing together somewhere in the middle. Desperation washed over me like summer rain in the middle of Mason's storm, and my lips moved against his, tasting and seeking. Needing more, I shot my tongue out, tracing his bottom lip tentatively. A low grunt came from his chest, vibrating against mine as he opened for me. Wasting no time, his tongue met mine, leading the dance. My hands slid up, locking my arms around his neck as his hand snaked under me, holding me against him as we devoured each other. His head tilted, another growl coming from him as he pushed further into my mouth. My clit hummed with need as my pussy clenched around nothing—missing him.

I angled my head, my fingers drifting up into his short hair as he bent, his mouth immediately going to my neck, kissing all the way up to my sensitive spot. His teeth nipped at the skin there, sending goosebumps across my body as my nipples ached against his hot skin.

Mase's lips found my ear. "Hungry, baby."

Disappointment pooled in my gut and my hold on him loosened. "Oh, right," I whispered as my back hit the mattress again. He pulled back, but instead of getting up, his mouth latched against my nipple, sucking deeply. A moan left me, and my hands snapped back to the back of his head, holding him to me.

So good.

"I thought you were hungry," I noted breathlessly as he moved across my chest to my other breast, his hand engulfing the one he just left, squeezing it. Gray eyes flicked up to meet mine as he sucked and nibbled. He released me only to pinch the nipple with his thumb and forefinger before rolling it. A gasp left me as a dark chuckle came from him, his eyes drifting down my body.

"Been starving since the moment I saw you," he stated gruffly as he drifted downward, his rough hands leaving my breasts and trailing down my stomach.

I sat up, my eyes going wide. "Mason—"

His eyes came to mine instantly as he declared, "I'm hungry." Suddenly, my panties were shredded with a vicious tug.

"That's the second pair you've ripped," I noted, wetness coating my inner thighs. The bull rider tossed the fabric over his shoulder, his eyes on my core, his nostrils flaring. Memories of last night on his truck flashed across my mind and I whimpered.

Mase's eyes came back to me. "Be as loud as you want, baby," he murmured as he dropped down. I watched—stunned—as he lifted my knees over his shoulders slowly and gently, one by one. When that was done, his large, muscular arms curled underneath me and with a vicious, quick tug, he yanked me down the mattress. His face was right there, a breath away from my clit.

He inhaled deeply, causing my mouth to fall open. "Smells like addiction, Harmony."

"Mason, I've never done this—I mean—I don't—"

He lifted his head, smirking at me. "Lie back and let me eat my breakfast, darlin'. That's all you have to do."

I nodded.

He dropped his face, inching closer and closer to my pussy. "That's my good little whore," he growled and then he was *on me.*

My body arched, and I let out a sound, guttural and pleading, as Mase dragged his tongue through my folds, flicking it at my clit. "Oh, God!"

His hold tightened on my thighs, his fingers digging in as he sucked, nibbled, licked, and devoured me. He dropped down lower, his tongue impaling me as the scruff on his jaw rubbed against the soft skin of my inner thighs. My hands drifted over my skin, stopping at my nipples, electric shocks shooting through me and down to my clit.

"Mase," I begged, pinching my nipples and arching further into him.

"Fuck," he hissed against me before rising slightly to latch onto my clit. My head dipped and I saw his eyes on me, scanning over my face before dropping down to my hands. He pulled away, his chin glistening with my juices. "Taste like fucking heaven, did you know that?" he said his jaw tight, his muscles flexing under his warm skin.

"Please, please," I whimpered, lifting my hips.

He looked own at my pussy and then to my moving hips. "Needy little thing, aren't you, Harmony?"

I nodded, one of my hands leaving my breast and snaking down my stomach. Mason's hand clamped over my wrist and my eyes snapped to his. He shook his head. "Did I say you could touch my pussy?" he asked, his voice low and dangerous.

"I need more," I begged, my voice ragged.

Suddenly, he released my hand, brought his down, and shoved a single finger into me. My body was still sore from last night, my walls fluttering around his digit. "Yes!" I cried, my hand returning to my breast as my eyes closed. He began moving his finger in and out at a steady pace, but it wasn't enough. "More, please!"

"If you are going to beg, I want those blue eyes on me," he purred.

When I looked at him, his head was tilted, studying me.

"Mase, please," I whimpered, moving my hips in time with his hand.

"Such a dirty, needy girl." He didn't give me more.

"Please! Please! Please!" I chanted, breathlessly.

"Tell me what you want," he demanded.

"Your mouth."

"Where?"

"On me," I whimpered, his finger still moving as my clit ached to be touched.

He leaned down, his breath skating across my clit. "Right here, darlin'? That where you want my mouth?"

"Mason..."

"Say the words," he growled.

"Please put your mouth on my pussy," I rasped.

"That's a good girl," he whispered before adding another finger and dragging his tongue against my clit.

"Yes!" I screamed, my back arching, my hand squeezing my breasts hard.

My hips moved against his face as he finger-fucked me faster and faster, my body so close. I moaned and chanted his name, nearly there. He pulled away, his lips grazing my clit as he growled, "Give me that sweetness."

When he latched on, I was *there.* "Mase! Oh, fuck! Oh, Mase!"

He growled as he began to eat me like a man starved, addicted. His scruff burning my skin as his jaw worked, adding to the pleasure. As I climaxed, screaming and thrashing, white spots filled my vision while warmth pulsed through my body.

When it became too much, I tried to break away, but he wasn't done with me. His arm shot out and banded around my middle, holding me down as he pulled out his fingers and dipped. He tongue-fucked me, not giving me any mercy as I flooded his mouth, my hips moving erratically.

"Sweetie," I breathed.

That did it.

With a growl, he released me, and in the next second he was over me completely, his hand at my right thigh, holding my leg open. My eyes opened and I was in the middle of his storm again. With a flash of lightning, thunder clapped in my ears, and he thrusted into me, filling me completely with his cock. My back arched again as pleasure overwhelmed me, cascading down my body like never-ending rain. My arms moved under his, my hands pressed against the base of his shoulder blades.

"Oh, Mason," I moaned.

"You keep those eyes on me, Harmony," he ordered, his voice ragged and thick with need. "Don't you dare shut yourself off from me. Let me see you."

His forehead settled against mine as he pulled out and slammed back in, the slapping of our skin echoing across the room.

"You—you feel so good," I stammered, my hips lifting and grinding against him as my pussy stretched for him.

Mason moved faster, fucking me with abandon, showing me no mercy. "You gonna miss me, huh?" he taunted, gripping my jaw, dipping his lips down to mine. "You've plagued my thoughts—my entire sense of being from the moment I saw you, Harmony Green. You have no idea how much you consume me." Our bodies were moving together, colliding over and over again, seeking the ultimate connection.

My nails dug into his skin as he pounded into me. I opened my mouth to respond, but the emotion building in my throat prevented me from speaking.

That was okay, because Mason wasn't done.

Not with my body, not with my soul, and definitely not with my heart.

"Let me tell you how this is going to work, baby," he began, thrusting into me and remaining fully inside me, the tip of his cock pressed against my cervix. I gasped his name before he pressed a kiss to my lips and dropped his hand down to my throat.

"We are going to talk every single fucking day."

He pulled out.

"You are going to tell me about your dreams in the morning when I call you. You are going to tell me about your day when I call you in the evening."

Thrust.

"Every night, you are going to Facetime me so I can see you—every fucking inch of you," he growled, dipping his mouth to my ear.

Thrust.

"You're going to touch my little pussy for me every single night like the good little whore you are. You're going to come for me *every single fucking night.* Don't give a fuck how tired you are—I'm gonna see my girl scream for me," he purred.

Thrust.

Pleasure coursed through me as I let out a pleading cry.

"If you think I'm going to go a *single day* without giving your body the pleasure it deserves, you're out of your fucking mind," he growled.

My pussy spasmed and I felt myself tip over the edge again.. "Mase, I'm—"

Thrust.

He chuckled again. "Trust me, baby, I know. This cunt is squeezing my cock so tight, I can barely think."

"Mase," I breathed.

He was done fucking around. His hands dropped to my hips, gripping me tightly, holding them in place as he *fucked* me, harder and faster than last night. The headboard above me was slamming into the wall, the sound of our skin echoing at the same pace, my cries and pleading carrying through the rooms of his hotel suite, his grunts filling my ears like they were for me and me alone.

"Calling me that like it's nothing," he hissed. "Like it doesn't mean something to me."

"I—"

He dropped his face in my neck, his tongue licking my skin. "My little heaven, blessing me as I pound her into the bed like a whore."

My second climax hit me like a bolt of lightning striking my body, its heat shooting through my veins, down to my core, causing it to spasm. "Mason!" I screamed, my thighs tightening around his waist, his heat against me as my nails dug into his skin, drawing blood.

"Fuck yeah, Harmony. Give me that—all of it, baby," he groaned. "That's it. Milk me, darlin'."

My eyes closed as my neck arched, my body swept up in pulsing waves of pleasure. Mason's thrusts become slower but more powerful as I heard him groan my name into my neck, his arms snaking under me and holding us together.

We stayed like that for some time, connected and breathing—in sync.

We were one.

We were more than just Mason and Harmony.

We were *everything*.

It wasn't until a bit later, when he detached himself from me, pressed a sweet kiss to my lips, and exited the bed that I saw it. I saw the evidence and I knew why Mason, my grumpy bull rider, never wanted to talk about his home—let alone return to it. My eyes were glued to it as he walked into the bathroom naked, and my stomach twisted painfully.

There, seared into his right shoulder, the skin a deep, ugly red and scarred over was the brand of Hallow Ranch.

Then, as tears filled my eyes and rage burned in my blood, I knew I was in love with Mason Langston.

Chapter Nineteen

Mason

St. Louis, MO. Oasis.

"Dontell," I drawled, tipping my hat to the man walking towards me.

Dontell Vance Michealson was one of the three owners of Oasis, a street racing hub in the baseball city of St. Louis.

The African-American man smiled at me, his white teeth gleaming against his dark skin. His partner, Leon Torrance, was flanking him, along with a white man one the other side. That man had dark hair, a dark beard, and dark eyes. That wasn't what stood out the most, though. No, that would be the snakes tattooed on his arms, one black and one red.

Leon was an Asian and African-American man, with light mocha skin, similar to Jeremy Jones, the leader of Oasis. The only difference between the two was that Leon was covered from head to toe in tattoos, complete with a teardrop in the corner of his eye. Leon Torrance wasn't a man you messed with. Everyone knew that and steered clear of him.

Dontell looked harmless, but he had the power to kill a man in seconds with his bare hands.

"You finally get your ass knocked off tonight?" Dontell asked, bullshitting with me. This wasn't my first visit to St. Louis. Over the years, after riding, I would venture out into Ballpark Village, and one night, I got pulled into a group of guys and we made our way into Soulard.

That's where Sullie's bar was located.

That's where I met a bartender named Jeremy and his pretty sister, Kay.

They were good people and I liked good people. From then on, anytime I was in St. Louis, I made a point to stop by and say hi to my buddy. Come to find out after my third visit that my buddy Jer was more than just a bartender. He was also the prince of a street crew, one his uncle ran.

Eventually, he roped me in with his boys, Leon and Dontell, and the rest was history. Pam wanted me to be friendly tonight with the other bull riders. She told me to take them to a bar or the Cards game, and I made her a promise that I would hang with them. I knew this shit was just a PR stunt, prepping for the shows we had lined up in Spain. After saying goodbye to Harmony, riding the bulls, and playing nice, Pam still expected me to take the cowboys out to a game tonight.

Clearly, that shit didn't happen.

I smirked at Dontell. We both knew I never got knocked off. He shook his head. "Crazy ass white boy," he muttered.

"We both know you're crazier than me, Donnie boy," I shot back with a laugh. I held out my hand to him, and we shook, clapping each other on the shoulders.

Engines fired up in the distance, the roars echoing through the large lot, which was filled with countless cars and people.

This place was a haven for street racers, and even though that shit was illegal, that didn't stop Jeremy and his boys. They owned this city, their names etched into the streets. Once, he'd told me racing to him was what bull riding is to me. He told me that when he got behind the wheel of his Challenger, the rest of the world faded away. It was an escape. A release.

I respected that.

This was my first time at Oasis since it opened a few years back. Apparently, some shit went down with the Italian Mafia, and everyone was on edge. Even the racers from out of town were tense. I knew Jer's uncle, Sullie, was going head-to-head with the Mafia boss, but that was all I knew.

"How are things?" I asked Leon and Dontell, my eyes darting back and forth between them.

Leon, quiet as always, dressed in his signature black hoodie and pants just shrugged, not giving anything away. Then again, he never did. Dontell and Jer grew up in the St. Louis, while Leon was from the Houston area.

Small world.

The man standing beside him was studying me, and I let him. If this were any other place, I'd have shut that shit down by now. However, this wasn't my turf. I was a guest here, and he may be a new recruit.

Dontell answered for them both. "We got some shit going on."

A chill ran down my spine, and I was instantly on alert, my brows coming together. "You boys need anything from me?" I asked, my mind drifting back to the Mafia shit Jer told me about years ago.

"We'll handle it," Leon promised darkly.

My eyes snapped to his, and I could see the pain within them. I didn't know much about Leon Torrance, only that he was from Texas, and ran in the street racing rings there. There was another thing that I knew about Leon.

He was the fastest street racer in the world.

He never lost.

People from all over the world came to race him, and he never lost.

Just like I never got thrown off a beast trying to kill me.

"Listen, Mason, we need to talk. Think you could leave your boys for a minute?" Dontell asked, breaking into my thoughts. I looked back to where the bull riders were standing—the fuckers. I'd barely spoken a fucking word to them on the way here. Even if I did, they only wanted to know my secret or accuse me of cheating.

Don't know how a cowboy could cheat in bull riding, but a jealous mind can make a person blind.

"Those aren't my boys. My PR woman wants me to play nice with the other kids," I informed, crossed my arms over my chest.

"Come with us," Dontell muttered.

Leon chuckled darkly and turned on his heel, heading back inside the large abandoned factory Jer had bought years ago.

It now served as the meeting spot for their underground street racing organization. The building had a bar area on one side and a garage on the other, cars parked in what looked like a showroom set up in the middle. One of those cars happened to be a 1969 Eleanor, a car I couldn't keep my eyes off of, a car I would kill to drive. However, Jer told me four years ago when I saw it for the first time, that it wasn't for sale.

He was storing it for a friend who had gone away on business.

The four of us walked through the space, and once we were on the garage side, away from the crowd, Dontell turned and rested his ass against an electric blue Porsche GT3. He leaned forward, resting his hands between his knees, his jaw tight. His dark eyes snapped up to the Snake Man, "Mason, this is Joseph Grayson."

A warning bell went off in my head, but I ignored it—for now.

I looked at Grayson, who was already staring at me again as I lifted my chin. "Good to meet you," I declared, holding out my hand. Not sparing a second, he took it and gave me a firm shake as the corner of his mouth tipped up.

"Don't know how good you'll think it is in a second," he rumbled.

My spine stiffened as our hands dropped. Leon cleared his throat and leaned against the brick wall, crossing his arms over his massive chest. I looked at each of the men, the hairs on the back of my neck standing at attention.

"Is Jeremy okay?" I asked, worried for my boy.

"This isn't about him," Leon said, shaking his head, dismissing my concern. "This is about you."

"Answer my question, brother, because he isn't here right now," I ordered, my voice low.

"Jer's in New York, working with the FBI," Dontell answered. Leon shot him a glare, which earned him a scowl in return. "You know damn well that this cowboy cares about our people. Don't give me that shit, Torrance."

"It's the Mafia, isn't it?" I asked and all eyes shot me. "That shit isn't over with, is it?" Jer told me something went down years ago, but that things were settling down. He told me he was helping a friend raise a little boy, a blessing born in dark times.

"It's being handled," Leon said darkly, confirming my theory.

My eyes met his, and he gave me a short nod.

"While I can appreciate this reunion, I have a job to do, gentleman," Grayson said, drawing my attention back to him.

"And what is that?" I asked.

"You."

My blood ran cold, the alarm bells in my head ringing louder than before as the man continued. "I was hired by your brother, Denver, to deliver a message to you."

The air around us stilled as my spine stiffened.

Rage swallowed me whole at the mention of my brother. My mind thought of Jigs, of the call I made to him the other night. It was a moment of weakness, but I needed to get my head on straight—get my emotions in check before getting back into bed with Harmony.

Now, my brother was reaching out, exhausting every angle he could. I left that part of my life behind for a fucking reason, and he had the audacity to— "You're a bounty hunter," I growled.

"Yes."

"What's the message?" I spat, wanting to get this over with. Thankfully, Grayson spared no time, cutting through the bullshit.

"Hallow Ranch is being threatened by a pipeline—Moonie Pipelines Incorporated, to be specific. Your brother has been trying to contact you for a while now, and you've been silent—"

"There's a fucking reason for that," I spat, anger lacing my voice. A damn good one too.

Grayson continued, "Don't give a fuck what that reason is, Langston. Your brother hired me to find you, and I did. You need to—"

"I don't need to do shit."

The man stopped mid-sentence, staring at me. He took a moment to assess me, taking in my body language and the look in my eyes. A wiser man would've walked away. Clearly, Joseph Grayson liked playing my favorite game.

Fuck around and find out.

"You do realize your brother wouldn't have gone through such trouble if it wasn't important, right?" he noted, raising a brow.

I shook my head, folded my arms over my chest and got right to it. "Right. Were you there? At Hallow Ranch?" I clipped.

"Yes."

"Anyone dead?" I pressed.

Dontell looked at his shoes and cleared his throat. Leon shifted, crossing his ankles, his eyes bouncing back and forth between us. Grayson's eyes never left me. "No," he answered.

"You see any fucking cows?"

"Yes."

Good. Denver's herd was fine. The ranch was fine. *Why the fuck was he reaching out to me about a pipeline?*

"Denver has dealt with pipelines before," I informed the bounty hunter. This wasn't the first time Hallow Ranch had been sought after by greedy men. It had been for generations, and every single time, Hallow Ranch came out on top. "He's a big boy. He'll handle this one."

I looked at Leon and lifted my chin, then to Dontell, giving him the same. "Good to see you boys. I'll be in Spain for the next month or so. You need anything, you call me."

"If they do, are you going to answer?" Grayson snapped, clearly annoyed with me.

I looked at him and then to the ceiling, adjusting my hat. "Stop while you're ahead," I warned, looking back at the man.

His jaw jumped underneath his short, dark beard. "You offer them help, but not to your own brother," he judged.

A dark smile spread across my face before I could stop it, the darkness within me taking control. "Now ya done it," I drawled. In a flash, the distance between us was closed, and my fist connected with his jaw. Pain shot through my hand, but I ignored it.

Grayson flew back but righted himself quickly. He didn't touch his jaw, not giving me any clue as to whether I hurt him. His eyes slowly came back up to me, his upper lip curling. "Not here to fight you, Langston. Just here to deliver a message."

I was in his face again, nose to nose. "Great. You've done your job. Now get the fuck out," I hissed, baring my teeth.

"Seems I have," he muttered, taking a step back from me, his features calm. It wasn't a sign of weakness, I knew. In fact, I knew he was holding himself back. His face may paint the picture of calm, but his eyes told a different story, fury swirling within his dark pools.

Joseph Grayson was a dangerous man—more so because he possessed such control.

Without breaking eye contact with me, he said, "Mr. Michealson. Mr. Torrance. Thank you for your patience and your time."

Leon remained silent.

"Not a problem, man," Dontell muttered, his voice genuine. That was the thing about the St. Louis crew: they accepted everyone from all walks of life. Despite what just occurred between the bounty hunter and me, he showed respect and that went a long way here.

"I'm not your enemy," Grayson stated. "Your brother isn't either."

My jaw tightened. "Do me a favor, bounty hunter: stay the fuck out of my business," I clipped.

I watched as the man turned and made his way across the showroom, disappearing into the crowd beyond.

"You good, brother?" Leon asked. My head snapped to him, my brows coming together. In all the years I'd known him, he'd never called me that. Only Dontell and Jeremy did. I nodded.

"You know anything about that pipeline he's talking about?" Dontell asked, rising to his full height, his eyes on the crowd where the bounty hunter disappeared. My eyes followed his.

"I know he's nasty," I declared.

Leon pushed off the wall and came to stand beside us. "Moonie Pipelines originated in Houston. Don't know much about his father, but Tim Moonie used to show up at the races back in the day," he explained, shoving his hands into the pocket of his hoodie.

My head turned to him. "Houston?"

He nodded. "Yeah. The guy who runs it, Tim, he was a spoiled rich boy—probably still is. He used to bring his daddy's cars to the races. Heard from my sister a few years ago that he took over the company from his father. It was all over the papers."

"Your sister in Houston?" I asked.

Leon's jaw tightened as he looked to the crowd. "Yeah. She is."

There was something else there, but I wasn't going to push it. Not my business.

"Alright, cowboy. What are you going to do?" Dontell asked.

Nothing.

"Hallow Ranch isn't a part of my life anymore," I said, my voice void of emotion.

Days later. Denver, CO.

"It's done," the gruff, voice confirmed through the phone.

Tim Moonie was standing in his hotel room, his cock currently down a prostitute's throat, on the phone with his man, the one who was ordered to kill Valerie Cross. Without missing a beat, he reached for the remote and turned on the local news, the headline dragging across the top of the screen.

Wildfire on Hallow Ranch.

The fire started this morning, ingulfing half of Denver Langston's mountain, scorching everything and the cowboy's lover with it. She'd been an excellent employee, but, as always, they were replaceable. Tim's eyes watched as the camera tilted to show how high the smoke rose in the sky.

"Where are you? I need you back here," Tim said, biting back his groan as the woman choked on his cock.

"An hour away, sir. What do you need?"

The woman pulled back, gasping for air. Moonie looked down at her. "You done?" he asked softly. Her eyes were filled with tears, her cheap makeup running down her cheeks.

"Yes, sir," she whispered.

He tipped his chin to the couch. "Go. Now," he growled. His eyes followed her, watching as she bent over the arm of the couch, fully expecting his cock. However, Tim didn't want his cock wet with used pussy. He wanted his perfect girl again.

He was going to play with the blonde another way tonight.

The man on the phone waited patiently through all of this, familiar with the routine. Tim turned around and faced the windows, his eyes on the mountains, barely visible in the moonlight. "Someone has been digging."

"Digging, sir?"

"Yes. Don't know who he is. He is good, the fucking best if we're being transparent, old friend."

The man grunted.

"Need you to take care of that, too. He hacked into the system and accessed our payroll files," Tim sighed, bored. There was always some nosey fuck after him and the kingdom his father built. It was just another day for Tim Moonie. What he didn't like was how quickly this hacker got through his firewalls.

"Yes, sir."

Tim didn't bother responding, hanging up instead. He stroked his cock, already limp. Frustration burned in his chest, and he turned to the woman on the couch.

Fucking didn't do it for him anymore. Never had.

He wanted pain and blood.

Dropping his limp dick, he smiled at her. "Such a beauty," he whispered sweetly as he came to her.

An hour later, Tim's hitman showed up just as he was coming out of the shower. He emerged from the hotel bathroom, wrapping a towel around his waist.

"Hello, old friend," he greeted.

The man didn't respond. His eyes were on the woman in Moonie's bed, or more specifically, the pool of blood she was laying in. Tim chuckled, satisfied. "Take care of her for me, would you, old friend?"

Tim left his man to it, walking into the living area of the suite, his eyes on the news coverage of Hallow Ranch. There was still an ongoing search for Valerie Cross, Denver and his men scaling the mountain as the flames spread like a vicious and ruthless disease.

Tim smiled. "You'll never find her, Mr. Langston," he boasted as he reached for his phone. Without sparing a second glance at the TV, Tim called his favorite police chief.

Chapter Twenty

Harmony

Two Weeks Later

"Have a good night, Ms. Green!"

I turned and waved at Mr. Dalys standing by his car. Since Mason's outburst in the clinic weeks ago, my relationship with my boss had grown. In fact, he was actually including me in the discussions of the new clinic build, asking for my input. We'd had a lunch meeting with the contractors, and they were set to break grown next week.

Once I was in my car, like clockwork, my phone rang. Shaking my head, I turned on the car and answered the phone, putting the call on speaker. "Hi," I greeted.

"Little Song," Mase drawled, his voice deep and rough from exhaustion.

"You should be sleeping," I noted, putting on my seatbelt.

"Not until I hear your voice, darlin.'"

"I miss you, Mase." So damn much, it physically hurt. I was worried I'd gotten too attached to Mason too quickly, and when I expressed these concerns to Dr. G, she simply smiled and told me something I already knew.

I was falling in love with Mason.

"Tell me about your day, baby. Don't leave anything out," he ordered.

"Did your ride go well?" I asked, pulling out of the parking lot.

"Harmony," he deadpanned.

I laughed. Every single one of his rides went well. On the ride home, I told him about my day and the meeting with the contractors, explaining to him that Dr. Dalys was very adamant about my opinion. "I think he is just trying to suck up to you," I informed Mase with a sigh.

"He'd be a fucking idiot not to take your advice. You see the clinic from a different perspective than he does, Harm. You're a fresh set of eyes."

"I hope so. I think it would be good to make the waiting room colorful. Ours is so dull; it reminds me of morgue."

He chuckled. "Oh yeah? Because that's your usual hangout spot?"

"Well, yeah, where else am I going to meet a tall, dark, and handsome vampire?" I shot back as I pulled into my building parking lot, swinging into my spot.

He was silent for a moment. "One thousand, five hundred and two," he stated.

My stomach fluttered, heat rising in my cheeks as my chest ached. "Mason," I breathed, the distance between us hitting harder than before. Today was Friday. One more week down, and only two more to go.

"That's how many times I have to kiss you when I get home."

My chest caved in. *Home.*

I opened my mouth to say something, but I was cut off by a loud crash on the other end.

"It's my turn to talk to Harmony, pretty boy!" Eddie shouted.

"Jesus, fuck," Mason sighed.

I burst out laughing.

"Give me the phone, ya selfish cowboy!"

"Eddie, for fuck's sake! It's nearly midnight!" Mason clipped.

There was shuffling on the line and then I heard my cowboy mutter, "Call you back in a second." The line went dead.

I shook my head, gathered my things, and got out of the car. After locking it and swinging my bag over my shoulders, a chill went down my spine. Instinctively, I tightened my hold on my bottle. Quickly, I turned and made my way to the front door of the building, and just as I was about to round the corner, I slammed into something. A wall.

A chest.

I jumped back immediately, losing my footing. Two large hands clamped down on my shoulders as a voice said, "Woah there, gorgeous. Steady." Ice filled my veins at the man's touch, and his voice made my skin crawl. Without looking up at him, I jerked out of his hold and darted around him. Once I'd made it to the door, my hands were shaking and I couldn't keep my keys steady.

"Are you alright?" the creepy voice asked.

I nodded. "Yes. Thank you. Sorry."

Keep it short. Don't engage beyond that.

"You live here, gorgeous?"

One, two, three.

One, two, three.

One, two, three.

Red, blue, green.

Red, blue, green.

Red, blue, green.

You're safe with me.

You're safe with me.

You're safe with me.

I chanted the words in my head, trying to seek comfort in Mason's words.

"Hey, I'm talking to you," the man clipped, anger filling his voice.

I knew that voice.

I didn't want to know that voice.

I never did.

Steady, Harmony. Just open the door and shut it behind you. You'll be safe.

I felt the man's presence at my back, standing just as close as Mason had the first time he came over.

This wasn't Mason.

One of the man's hands clamped down hard on my shoulder. "I know you hear me, bitch—"

"Yo!"

Relief filled my body at the sound of Cabe's voice. My head snapped up to find Cabe standing less than three feet away, anger masking his features. "Step back, man," he ordered darkly.

"This your woman?"

"Yes," Cabe spat. "Get the fuck away from her." My friend stepped forward, closing the distance quickly as he yanked the man's hand from my body.

I was frozen, the monster swimming up from the depths, sporting a demonic smile on its face.

Gotcha, darling.

The air in my lungs left in a whoosh as the monster surfaced, gripping me by the throat, its claws digging into my skin, drawing blood. He leaned down and whispered the words.

The words that cost me my sanity and my light.

My perfect girl.

The door to my building faded away, replaced by a cold, damp, stone wall. The warmth of the afternoon Texas sun was replaced by darkness, the chill of it seeping into my skin. The smell of dirt and rot filled my nostrils, and bile rose in my throat. Pounding footsteps from above filled my ears, each one getting louder and closer to the stairwell. Dread claimed my soul months ago, and the need to survive faded away much like the red blood stains turned to brown on the concrete floor.

I'd given up days ago.

I had nothing left to give him.

Nevertheless, the familiar sound of the basement door opening with a low and eerie creak still caused a small flare of panic inside me. Despite my soul being ripped to shreds and my heart being beaten to a pulp, my body could still feel pain. The nerves hadn't died like my soul had. No, that was the universe's special treat for me. My body was sore, of course, but the looming anticipation of new pain always caused that little flare inside of me.

The door fell closed, and those heavy footsteps descended the stairs. I didn't bother looking up; I couldn't see anyways. Both of my eyes were nearly swollen shut. A smooth, male chuckle filled the space around me. "Good morning, darling."

"Harm! Harmony, look at me. Honey, I need you to look at me..."

I shook my head. Stupid voices in my head, always trying to give me hope.

"Harm!"

Billie.

My head snapped up, and my eyes were open, no longer swollen shut. Billie wasn't in front of me, and my skin felt hot. My eyes scanned the scene before me: long stretches of concrete, the heat of the sun rolling off it in waves, rising to the cloudless blue sky above.

"Harmony, look at me." A sweet voice. One I hadn't heard in years.

My mom's voice.

I twisted my neck to see her. She was crouched down in front of me, dark sunglasses on her face to cover the bruises Daddy gave her. There was a silk scarf wrapped around her auburn hair, and she was wearing a navy-blue dress. My eyes dropped to the bruises on her arms.

Daddy liked to hit Mommy when she did bad things. I overheard the maid talking about it once. I looked down to find I was wearing a fluffy yellow dress and shiny black shoes.

I was a little girl.

This was memory—*right?*

"You need to listen to me," she whispered, pulling me in close. "You stick to yourself, do you understand? You keep your head down and be good. If Daddy tells you something, you do it, okay?"

My bottom lip trembled. I didn't like Daddy. I was scared of him, him and my brother. "Mommy—"

She looked over her shoulder at the small white plane that sat on the runway. We were at Daddy's airstrip. My tummy felt funny. Something bad was happening and she was leaving me.

She turned back to face me, a tear sliding down her cheek from under her shades.

"Mommy has to go now, alright?" she whispered, her voice shaking like she was about to cry. She reached out and touched my cheek before looping one of my wild curls around her finger. "I love you, my angel."

Everything faded away as I cried out for her.

"Harmony! Look at me! See me!"

Billie.

The darkness slipped away, and that monster released my throat with a growl. As it sunk back down into the murky depths, everything came rushing back.

The phone call with Mason.

The door.

The man.

I blinked and saw my beautiful best friend in front of me, her face crumpled with concern. "Billie?"

"Jesus, Harm," she croaked, tears filling her eyes. "Where did you go?"

I swallowed the lump in my throat and looked around frantically, looking for the man. My brows came together. "How did we get into my apartment?" I asked, my voice raspier than normal.

"I carried you," Cabe answered. I looked up to find him standing over Billie and me in front of the couch, his arms crossed over his chest. "That fucker is gone."

Nodding, I whispered, "Good."

"Honey, Mason is on the phone," Billie said, holding out my cellphone to me. It was on mute. "I can tell him—"

My heart pounded in my ears as I snatched the phone out of her hands, tapped the screen, and held it to my ear. "Mase," I pleaded, my voice thick.

"Talk to me," he demanded harshly.

"I—I don't know what happened," I admitted, tears stinging my eyes.

"Put Cabe on the phone," he ordered.

"Mase—"

"Darlin', now isn't the time to push me," he growled. "Put Cabe on the phone."

My eyes closed as I whispered, "Okay."

A moment of silence passed before he whispered, "Gonna take care of you, baby. Put him on the phone for me."

I handed the phone to Cabe, who was already waiting for it. He turned and walked away from us, his pissed off voice carrying throughout my space. "Yeah. What do you need from us?"

I went to grab my bottle, blindly reaching beside me, only to find it wasn't there. I sat up, terror prickling over my shoulder as my stomach twisted painfully. I looked around me, forgetting Billie's presence. It wasn't on the couch. It wasn't on the table in front of me.

I lost it.

It was gone.

My throat was dry, burning and pleading for water.

I needed water.

"Oh, no...no, no, no, no..." I cried, standing up, my hands flying to my hair. "God! No! Where is it?" Everything was closing in, and for the second time that day, the monster swam up to the surface.

Soft hands cupped my face, and a sweet scent surrounded me. "Hey, calm down. Breathe. It's right here," she said, taking a hand away. A second later, I felt the familiar shape of the bottle press into me. My hands wrapped around it, the cool metal comforting me in a way no one else could, not even Mason. I stepped away from her, giving my best friend my back as I scrambled to take a drink—as if I hadn't been drinking all day. The cool, refreshing water hit my throat, and the horrors of the past were washed away, shame and embarrassment taking its place.

Pulling the straw from my lips, my face crumbled and my shoulders sagged, the unbearable weight of remorse settling upon them. I looked to my feet, tears filling my eyes as I struggled to inhale a simple breath.

Such a waste.

A nuisance.

Nothing but baggage.

No one wants to deal with your messes.

"Harmony?" my sweet friend called out from behind me.

I waved her off, not wanting her to see this. She'd seen enough six years ago when she'd found me. She didn't need to see this.

My tears broke free, falling down my face and splashing on the wooden floor by my feet. Tears weren't glorious. Tears were weakness. That's all I was.

Weak.

Broken.

Undeserving.

Unable to handle the sight, I squeezed my eyes shut and twisted my head towards the window as a broke sob escaped me. This was the final swing of the hammer, and my foundation cracked, sending me and everything I'd built myself up to be crashing down. I was *nothing*.

What in the hell was I thinking? Starting a new life, pretending every-thing would be okay, escaping to music, dating a handsome bull rider who made me feel alive...

It was laughable—truly.

For the last two weeks, ever since coming home from Nashville, I'd felt it—lingering in the shadows, coiled up and ready to strike. I'd felt a heavy, dark presence. There was no other way to describe it.

The man who approached me just confirmed my biggest fear.

I tried to ignore it when the police officer came in for an appointment at the clinic, requesting me to do his preliminary testing. He claimed he was there just for his annual physical, but I'd felt his eyes on me when I turned around—I felt the chill.

I tried to ignore it when I saw a squad car parked outside my building, in a direct line of sight with my apartment. It had been there every single day for the last week.

I tried to ignore it when I was at the Farmer's Market with Cabe and Billie last Saturday, and I felt like I was being watched—not by my dark cowboy. When I scanned the area around me, no one stood out until I made eye contact with two officers casually leaning against their vehicles, drinking coffee, both sets of eyes on me.

I tried to ignore all of this—desperately wanting to be normal. Just a normal woman, with a normal job, falling hopelessly in love with a rowdy bull rider. Just a normal woman in her apartment, who had fresh tulips delivered to her door every three days sent by said bull rider. Just a normal woman who listened to her man groan her name as he fisted his cock for her in the dark hours of the night on the phone.

Two weeks of pretending to be normal, ignoring the inevitable truth. He'd found me.

As that truth slammed into me, another truth followed.

I never escaped.

"Honey, you need to eat something. Please," Billie begged.

I didn't bother moving as I whispered, "Not hungry."

"Don't make me call Dr. G," she warned.

My eyes stung from the countless silent tears I'd cried over the last few hours. My body ached—ghost pains. My heart felt the bruises coming back, the scars being ripped back open. My soul—my soul was fucking terrified.

"I knew him, B," I whispered again.

I felt her tense beside me in the bed. We'd been curled up together, and she held me as I lay in silence, trying to stop the tears. After Cabe finished his phone call with Mason, he said that he had an errand to run and that he would be back. Mason tried to talk to me, but I didn't have the energy to listen. I didn't have the energy to do anything. I'd travelled back in time to when I was holed up in that shitty motel in Michigan for weeks, spending my days staring at the walls and sipping water.

Only water.

I couldn't stomach food yet.

Not until I was forced to when I was in the hospital where Dr. G was assigned to me.

"Gonna need you to talk to me, Harmony," Billie begged softly, her arms tightening around my mid-section, pressing in closer to my back.

My throat dried at the thought of speaking about it—about that man. Clearing it, I rasped, "He's one of *his* men, Billie. I never saw the man, but I recognized his voice."

Billie shifted, crawling over me and plopping down, my face inches from hers. Her hands went into my hair, holding me in place as my bottom lip trembled. "I never really escaped him, did I?" My voice cracked.

"Don't," she warned, her voice shaking. "Don't you go there. You stay with me. You went there today, didn't you?"

I nodded.

"I'm calling her, Harm. Right now."

I dropped my gaze to the blanket between us. "I'm such a fucking burden. Everyone is always cleaning up my messes, waiting around with a mop and bucket."

Billie tugged on my hair gently, causing me to look at her. Her face was soft, masked with sadness, but her eyes held heated hatred and anger. Not for me. For *him.*

"You listen to me, and you listen good, Harmony Green. You will never be a burden to me. You get me? Not to me, not to Cabe, not to—"

"—Mason?" I finished for her. "Fuck, I don't know how he can be so patient with me. Do you know that when he is around me, I can't seem to keep my emotions in check? Nashville was supposed to be a fun trip, and I ruined it."

She raised a brow. "Why? Because you two were adults and had an actual conversation after he fucked you dizzy on the tailgate of his truck?"

My cheeks heated, but I remained silent.

"Do you honestly think he would be stupid enough to do that?"

"Do what?"

"Discover the goodness and beauty that *is* Harmony and leave her."

"I—"

"That man is deep in this with you—you aren't the only one with feelings. Part of being in a healthy relationship is navigating those feelings. You've never been in a healthy relationship, so you don't know what to expect," she explained.

"Billie—"

"Tell me you aren't a burden."

I stared at her.

She put her forehead against mine. "Say it for me, Harm."

Nothing. I couldn't give her anything.

"I'm not leaving until you do. I'll handcuff myself to you," she threatened.

"You don't have handcuffs."

She smiled. "You have no idea what Cabe likes in the bedroom."

"That's too much information for me," I winced.

"Stop changing the subject and say it," she ordered.

Seconds passed and I knew she wasn't going to let up. So, I gave her what she wanted, even though I didn't believe it. "I'm not a burden."

The front door opened, and Cabe called out for us.

"In the bedroom!" Billie called back, her eyes never leaving mine. Neither of us moved until Cabe appeared in the doorway.

He looked at me, his jaw tight, his eyes alert. "Pack a bag, sweetheart."

"Why?" I croaked, sitting up and reaching for my bottle.

"Your bull rider's orders. Grab your guitar, too."

Chapter Twenty-One

Mason

Spain

"Mason! Mason! Mason!" the arena chanted, the sound echoing throughout Barcelona.

I took off my hat, giving the crowd a smile and a wave as the bull was ushered back into the pen. *Nine seconds.* I'd held on to the bull for nine seconds, my body thrashed around like a rag doll as my mind filled with my little song's voice, her smile appearing before my eyes with each buck of the bull.

My peace was gone, my anger brewing like a thunderstorm.

I turned away, putting my hat back on, my eyes on Eddie. He met me halfway. "She's okay, Mason," he assured me, falling into step beside me.

"I need to get out of here."

The announcer praised me in Spanish while the next rider mounted his bull. It was the kid. Without a second thought, I tipped my hat to him, ignoring the glares of the other cowboys.

Once we were away from the crowd, Eddie handed me my phone. We made our way to what was supposed to be the locker room, my nerves shot, the knot in my stomach twisting tighter with each passing second.

I pushed the door open and immediately began taking off my gear. "Should've never left," I grumbled to myself.

Last night, Harmony was approached by a man. He cornered her in front of her apartment building and put his hands on her.

A man put his hand on my woman, and I was a world away, unable to protect her.

Cabe had broken down the situation for me, but when I asked for a little bit of insight on Harm's past, he shut me down.

"I need to know, Cabe. I need to know how to handle this," I growled through the phone, pacing back and forth in front of my bed.

"I can't tell you that, Mason. That's not my story to tell. B and I made a promise to Harmony years ago," he stated. Though I respected him for keeping his word, grateful she was surrounded by good friends, I wanted to break his jaw for not giving me an inch.

"Did you recognize him?" I asked. Was he the asshole who hurt my little song? Stole her voice?

"No, never seen him before. After I shoved him away and told him to fuck off, he bolted."

I pinched the bridge of my nose, trying to contain myself as the images of my baby cornered, trembling, as some fucker touched something that wasn't his washed over me.

She was mine.

She was mine, and I hadn't been there to protect her.

"Harmony can't stay there. That fucker knows she lives there," I declared, my voice dangerously low.

"I agree. She can stay with—"

"She stays under my roof. Nowhere else."

After I'd given him instructions, I tried to talk to Harmony, but she was shutting herself off from me. Earlier in the morning, at the ass crack of dawn, I called Pam into my room, demanding to go home.

Look how well that worked out.

She told me I couldn't leave until next week at the earliest, per the contract I'd signed with PBR and my sponsor.

"Mason, she's okay," Eddie said, drawing me out of my head.

I shook my head, ripping my leather vest off. "I wasn't there. She was in danger, and I wasn't there."

"Mas—"

Anger took over, rumbling like thunder as I whirled on him. "I wasn't there!" I roared. "My girl was fucking cornered—nearly *assaulted*, Ed, while I was halfway across the *fucking world!*"

Never been good enough, boy.

Weak.

Good for nothing.

"Mason," Eddie said, shaking his head. "What you're doing, what you're feeling—that's being there for Harmony. You basically moved her into your condo and hired a security detail for her. At the drop of a hat, bud. You did that."

"I need to get back to the hotel," I ground out, my jaw tight.

My friend stared at me for a moment, his head tilted slightly, his clown makeup worn. He pulled off his cowboy hat, gesturing to the door behind him. "Then go. You know I'll cover for you. Always."

I gave him a nod, my throat bobbing.

Twenty minutes later, I was back in my hotel, Facetiming Harmony.

She declined and called me instead.

"Harmony," I growled. "I'm not in the mood for this shit."

"Mase, I don't—"

"Had the longest day ever, being thousands of miles away from you when you needed me. *Let. Me. See. You.*"

Silence.

"Now," I clipped, Facetiming her again.

She answered this time, the screen filling with her beauty. She was sitting on my couch, water bottle to her chest, blanket covered, knees bent. Those wild curls were all around her, warm as the sun as her cool blue eyes stared at me. Her freckled skin was splotchy, her eyes puffy, and the rims of her eyes were an angry red.

"Baby," I murmured, my chest aching.

Her face crumbled before she dropped it into her hands. "This is why I wanted to just have a regular call, Mase."

"Look at me," I whispered, sitting on the edge of the bed.

She didn't.

"Goddammit, I want to see my favorite shade of blue, darlin'." I took off my hat, sitting it down beside me. "Let me see you. Please, Harmony. I need it." My voice was gruff; I was tired. Worry and anger had been playing tug-a-war with me all damn day.

She dropped her hands, tears falling down her face. "There's my little song."

"You didn't have to do this. I could've stayed with Billie and Cabe," she whispered.

"You mine?" I clipped, my jaw jumping.

She looked away for a moment, pulling away from me. "You deserve better."

No, I didn't. I was scum compared to her, and she deserved better, but I was too damn selfish to let her go. "I want you."

No response.

"Let me answer that question for you then, Harmony," I growled. "You're mine. You've been mine. You'll always be mine. I protect what's mine." *Which was nothing but my reputation until you, beautiful.*

Those pretty blues came back to me. "Yes," she whispered.

Thank fuck.

"That's right."

She sighed. "I'm sorry. I just..."

"I know, baby. Remember what I said in Nashville?"

"I remember everything about Nashville, sweetie," she murmured, her words piercing my chest.

Sweetie.

She'd never understand the weight that word held for me, how precious it was to me. I was at a point in my life where I hadn't thought goodness was meant for me. Then, she came along.

"Me, too." I stared at her for a moment, grateful she wasn't hurt—untouched by greedy hands. She didn't need to think about that. She didn't deserve darkness. I changed the subject. "Tell me about your day, and don't leave anything out. Was Josiah nice to you?"

Josiah was her new private bodyguard, recommended by Leon. I gave Dontell a call after hanging up with Cabe, and without hesitation, he handed the phone to his partner. Leon told me Josiah worked for a security company he used for his sister. Josiah was instructed to escort her to and from work, and then at night, he would be posted at my door. I called the building manager and informed him, along with getting Harmony set up with a key and access card to the pool and gym.

"Yes, he's nice. Doesn't talk very much, though."

Images of her trying to strike up a conversation with the big man filled my head, and I bit back a smile. "He ain't there to talk, baby," I reminded her. "How was work? Claire still being that chick flick girl?"

Harm's face split into a glorious smile as a raspy, intoxicating giggle burst from her sweet mouth. My throat thickened, my chest tightening again. Without a second thought, I took a screenshot, needing to capture this moment forever.

"Regina George?" she questioned, laughing still.

That stupid movie.

"Didn't watch the movie, Harm. Too busy kissing you to give a fuck about anything else," I said, my voice low. I watched proudly as pink colored her cheeks, her pupils dilating. I loved how easily I affected her.

My cock twitched in my jeans, but I ignored it. That wasn't important right then. "Tell me about your day, Little Song," I ordered softly.

For two hours, we talked about her day, my day, anything and everything, the miles between us be damned. The sadness in her eyes melted away as I distracted her with my stories, making her laugh. When the early morning hours came, I told her to get into bed, and I set up the phone in the bathroom while I took a quick shower, not wanting to say good-bye yet.

I hadn't intended for things to get heated, but when I pulled open the glass shower door, wrapping a towel around my waist, I saw her face, the desire in her eyes. Her blue eyes held mine for a long time, water droplets cascading down my body.

"Baby." My voice was gruff, unsure if this was appropriate right then. She'd been through so much in the last few days, and the last thing I wanted was to pressure her.

"You're beautiful, Mase," she whispered, her raspy voice thick with need.

Fuck me.

Swiping the phone off the counter, I left the bathroom. She continued to stare at me as I dried off one-handed, holding the phone in front of my face. Her blue eyes never left the screen, her pink lips parted as she watched in awe.

"Gonna kill me, Harmony," I muttered, sliding into bed. I held the phone above me, folding my opposite arm behind my head.

"I like your bed, Mase."

My dick wept at her words, and I clenched my jaw, trying to will the son of a bitch to calm down. "That's good to hear, cause it's where you belong," I noted.

She was on her side, no doubt curled into herself, her curls all over my pillow, and her blue eyes seemed brighter than before. The color in her cheeks deepened, and her pupils remained slightly dilated.

She was aroused.

At the sight of me.

"Harm—"

"Distract me. Please, Mase," she begged.

This woman had no idea the power she had over me. I'd give her anything—anything in the world. Swallowing, I asked, "What do you want, Harmony?"

"I..." She trailed off, looking down.

Frustration came over me. "Told you not to hide from me. Those blues stay on me when we're talkin'."

She looked up at me and whispered, "I want to feel good."

"Then roll on your back and let me do my job," I ordered, my voice rough with raw need, the need to pleasure her, to make her feel so good that she'd forget everything else. "Hold the phone up high." She did as I instructed and then waited for more.

"Let me see those tits, baby."

Harm whimpered as she pulled her shirt up, her amazing breasts spilling out for me, her pretty nipples hard, begging me to suck on them.

"Play with your nipples for me." I tipped my chin and dropped my eyes to her chest. Dick throbbing, I watched as she dragged her hand up, her fingers skimming over the sensitive bud. She let out a mewl, arching slightly.

My jaw ached as I bit down hard, trying to control myself, as my cock rubbed against the comforter. "That's it, darlin', that's it," I murmured, watching her alternate back and forth between each breast, squeezing, pinching, pulling.

"I know that little pussy is wet for me," I taunted.

"Yes," my little song moaned, pinching her nipple.

"You gonna be a good girl and show your bull rider his little pussy? Hm?"

Her eyes went wide, a gasp leaving her as she nodded. "I want to see you, too. Please," she breathed.

Without a word, I pulled the blanket off and angled the phone higher so she could see all of me. Those blue eyes dropped to my erection resting against my abs, another whimper escaping her.

"Show me," I demanded gently.

Her phone dropped down and I watched as she spread her legs for me, giving me a view of her pink panties, a damp spot staining the center, directly over her pussy.

A low growl rumbled from my chest as my fist dropped down to my cock, wrapping around my shaft. "*Fucking hell*, Harmony." I stroked once before squeezing, my spine tingling already. Two weeks without her had been long enough. I was ready to fly home and fuck her for a week, only stopping for food and water.

"Mase," she pleaded, "Do that again."

A low chuckle came from me. Such a dirty girl. "You like watching me fist my cock, Harm?"

Her fingers drifted over her panties, teasing me in the most delicious way. "Yeah," she mewled, her rasp making my balls throb.

"Let me see my little cunt," I growled, stroking again. My eyes never left the screen as she slowly pulled the fabric aside, exposing my favorite shade of pink.

Pure beauty.

"A fucking masterpiece, you know that, don't you?"

She angled the camera so I could see all of her as she played with her swollen clit. I was ready to bust. "You filthy girl, watching me fist my dick to you. You see what you do to me?" I growled. "You see how much *power* you have over me, baby?"

She moaned, her eyes closing. I was in awe of her. "You imagining me there with you?" I pressed, needing to hear her thoughts.

"Yes!"

"You feel my hand on your throat as I pound into you, stretching that little pussy?" My fist worked faster, precum dripping from the head of my cock. Her fingers worked faster, rubbing in quick, short circles over her clit. Neither of us were going to last long.

Fuck, but I loved it.

I loved the overwhelming desire that lingered between us.

I loved her sounds.

I loved everything about her.

I loved—

"Mase, please! Please!"

She was close, her mouth falling open, her back starting to arch as she anticipated her pleasure.

I brought the phone down to my mouth, whispering in the speaker, "Come for me like the whore you are, darlin'. Be a good girl so I can fill you up."

"Oh, God! Mason!" she cried out as her back arched, her thighs spreading even wider as she imagined me there. I felt heat gather at the base of my spine, and my hand worked faster, my jaw tight as my abs began to flex, my hips thrusting up. "Open your fucking eyes," I growled. "Give me that blue."

Her chest was red, as were her neck and face. She was drunk on pleasure, but my girl did as she was told. Her blues met mine, and slowly they descended the length of my body until they landed on my cock—*I lost it.*

"Fuck! Harmony—baby, *fuck!*" Hot ribbons of cum landed on my stomach as my body jerked, my muscles tensing. As pleasure surged through me, I kept my eyes on her, knowing that only she could do this to me. I felt like a fucking horny teenager when it came to her.

After a few moments, once we were both sated, she rolled over and curled up again. She stared at me until she couldn't any longer, her eyelids drooping as she started to fall asleep. I laid in my mess, not wanting to miss a single second of her, of her light.

Minutes passed, and words were never spoken—they weren't needed. Our bodies had done the talking tonight. She'd done it again—given me another gift.

When her eyes closed and her lips parted, I knew she was asleep. I smiled, touching my finger to the screen, right on her cheek.

"Sleep well, Little Song," I whispered, ready to hang up the phone.

That didn't happen.

Because Harmony, my obsession, whispered, "I love you, Mason."

Chapter Twenty-Two

My perfect girl, hiding in plain sight.

Right in front of my eyes.

If Moonie wasn't so angry, he would've smiled, and it would've been genuine. It'd been weeks since Hallow Ranch had burned. The dust had very much settled, half of Denver's mountain blackened.

Valerie Cross was dead.

She was pulled from the fire, and the news crews covering the story said she'd been dead when they pulled her out. There was video footage of the cowboy on his knees in his field, holding her limp body to his chest.

That was enough for Moonie.

His lawyers were drafting up something that would make him looked like a decent man, one who wouldn't want the land Langston possessed to go to waste. He was going to kill them all, but he was a man—just like Denver.

He was giving him time to mourn. It was the human thing to do.

It was fucked up, but there was something beautiful about his twisted form of mercy that he got off on. He would let the cowboy mourn for a time, and then he would claim what Ms. Cross couldn't.

Although Hallow Ranch was a valuable prize, Tim had other things to tend to: building to plan, men to hire, teams to organize. They would break ground in January.

That gave Tim Moonie plenty of time to clear that insufferable ranch and get his perfect girl back. He would have to be patient, of course, for her. She was no doubt confused and wondering where he was.

Right here, darling.

Tim sighed as his eyes scanned the length of her body. She'd put on weight, mainly in her hips. He pursed his lips, imagining how these new curves would feel in his hands. Adjusting himself, he sat back in his seat, watching as she made way over to another vender, a bright smile on her face. That was new to him. When she was his, she would've never been in a place like this.

It was beneath her.

He enjoyed her smile, missed it even. From the moment he first met her years ago, he enjoyed it. She was darling; timid, shy, and *pure*. Tim discovered, though, that he liked her tears more. Her smile made him warm, but her tears made him hard. He enjoyed her pain, and her voice had been *perfect.* Simply perfect.

The perfect cries.

The perfect screams.

She was smiling brightly up at a large black man who stood close by, in a protective away. Moonie knew he was her bodyguard—*Josiah*. The man worked for a private security company in Houston, which was interesting they weren't cheap.

His perfect girl didn't have that kind of cash.

Moonie had been back in Houston for a week, and he'd sent a man out to her. She was cornered by him in front of her apartment building—which was also beneath her. When she was his, her life had been filled with nothing but the best. Tim hated the filth that surrounded her now.

That would change soon.

She would never go back to this scum-filled life again. He'd make sure of it.

The back passenger door across from Tim opened and a man was shoved inside with a grunt. Tim ignored the man as he scrambled in the seat beside him, keeping his eyes on his perfect girl.

"Chief," Moonie drawled, "How lovely to see you. It's been a long time."

"Mr.—Mr. Moonie," the chief of police stammered, breathless.

Casting one more look at her auburn curls, disgust filling him at the sight, Tim turned his attention to his guest. His perfect girl knew her curls had to go, but there was plenty of time to discuss that later, when he had her back. He smiled at the sweaty, balding man.

"Donald, how are you?"

"Mr. Moonie—about my family—"

Tim held his hand up, his smile dropping. "I didn't ask you here for that. Please stop wasting my time. I am a very busy man, as you know," he reminded the police chief as he pulled out his cell phone. "You were instructed to bring her to me. You failed. Now, I have to make a phone call. I would very much appreciate it if you sat still and remained silent."

Donald swallowed, his throat bobbing as he nodded frantically.

Tim never understood how a such a spineless man got to be the head of the Houston police department. Then again, he didn't care.

With a sigh, he made the call.

"Green here," a man answered on the fifth ring. Moonie didn't appreciate the disrespect, so he got right to it.

"You know, Mr. Green, my father thought so highly of you. The matchmaking between your daughter and I was more than just a business transaction. It was about a mutual trust you two shared," Tim drawled, shooting a wink at Donald, who looked like he'd seen a ghost.

"Tim, I—"

"So, imagine my surprise when I discovered that Harmony is in Houston, of all places, working as a nurse in some run-down clinic," he hissed, talking over the man.

"Son, I had no idea she was back. I—listen, let me handle this," Green said.

Moonie laughed, the sound filling the cab. "No, I don't think I will. You made a deal with my father—with me. You failed to hold up your end of the bargain. Say goodbye to your stocks." He hung up, and without missing a beat, his arm shot out, fisting the chief's shirt and pulling the man across the seat. Before Donald could do anything, Tim pulled out a gun and shoved it under the man's fat throat.

"Your turn," he said with glee.

The man cried, "Anything! I'd do anything!"

Tim lowered his head to Donald's, an evil smile spreading across his face. "I've been in Colorado dealing with business, as you know. You've been here, protecting this city, isn't that right?"

The man nodded, tears running down his cheeks. Tim was disappointed; he'd expected more of a fight. He liked to fight. He liked blood.

However, his perfect girl was waiting.

"A little birdy told me someone wanted her information a few months ago," Tim stated flatly. When he'd gotten the message months ago, he was just too focused on Hallow Ranch. Now *that* problem was nearly solved, he'd focus on her, give her the attention that she deserved.

How lonely she must be without him.

"I thought your man—"

With a growl, he pushed the gun further into Donald's throat, his finger resting over the trigger. "You think your family would like to feel this? A gun in their throat? Hm?"

Donald shook his head, his body trembling with fear.

"Tell me everything. *Now*!" he barked in the man's face, losing control.

"It was months ago, Mr. Moonie," he rasped.

Tim tilted his head, the air in the SUV going cold as a shadow drifted in. "Donald, I am a patient man. I pride myself on that, but right now, you are beginning to piss me off," he sighed, looking to the ceiling. "I don't want to kill your daughter, but if I—"

"It was a bull rider! He wanted to know about her!"

Tim Moonie's spine stiffened, rage filling him.

A bull rider?

What in the ever-loving fuck did a bull rider want with his perfect girl?

She was Tim's.

A second later, he shoved Donald away. After adjusting his tie and inhaling a deep breath, he said, "Alright, Don. Tell me about this bull rider and maybe I'll forgive you for your failures."

Harmony

"Alright, you're all set! Your prescription will be sent to Walgreens, unless you have a different pharmacy," I offered, turning back to my patient.

"No, Walgreens is fine. Thank you so much for fitting me in today," he said. I smiled at the older gentleman and looked down at his wrapped hand. When he called earlier, he told me he'd stuck his hand in a bush of poison ivy by accident. He didn't want to go to the emergency department, due to his anxiety. We got him in at the end of the day, which meant I'd had to stay late.

We finished up, and I walked him up to the front desk before rushing back to mine, my nerves on edge.

Mason was coming home today—*for me*. He was leaving Spain—his dream—*for me*. After our Facetime call last week when I'd fallen asleep, he told Pam he would be leaving at the beginning of next week.

The second he told me the news, my body felt safe again after having been in a state of unease for days. Since I'd been cornered, I've been on edge, talking to Dr. G twice a day instead of a few times a week, drinking more water than I should, and carrying the bottle with me *everywhere*. Even now, it was shoved into the front pocket of my scrub tops. I had to lie to Mr. Dalys, telling him I was just dehydrated, which he believed—thank goodness. Hell, I slept with it in Mason's bed, showered with it in Mason's shower.

The monster wasn't coming up from the depths. No, it was seeping into my bones again, burying itself deep, and I didn't have the strength to dig anymore.

I was tired.

I'd failed myself—I'd failed the old Harmony, too, the girl I'd promised would never feel that way again. Yet, here I was, frightened like a stray kitten in a thunderstorm.

Only this storm wasn't Mason's.

It was *his.*

I was falling backwards into habits I'd been working so hard to break. Dr. G said this was a normal response—a way to cope with the fear that was thrusted upon me so suddenly. If that was the case, then why did I feel like such a fucking failure?

When Cabe and Billie practically moved me into Mason's condo, I'd brought my guitar along with me. It remained untouched for three days. Last night, I strummed a few chords and sang a few lyrics quietly on his bed, letting the notes fight the anxiety. It helped, but not much. Not like it used to.

Knowing Mason was coming home, relief was trying to take over the panic, but my body wouldn't allow it—the monster wouldn't allow it. I ached to see him, though. I ached to see that fake smirk turn into a real, warm, devasting smile for me and only me. I ached to see the storm in his eyes, promising me protection no one else could give.

My heart had been pounding non-stop all day, and my soul seemed to finally come out of hiding.

The man who cornered me was one of *his* men, one who used to sit in a chair across that dark room and watch me for hours on end. As I walked down the hallway, I shook my head, trying to push back the memories of those days.

The fear.

The pain.

The numbness.

Once I was back at my desk, I took my seat and pulled the bottle out, taking a generous, long, refreshing drink. It grounded me—centered me.

One, two, three.

One, two, three.

Red, blue, green.

Red, blue, green.

You're safe, Harmony.

You're here, not there.

Mason is coming home tonight.

You're safe with me.

Before his words could comfort me, my words echoed in my mind, reminding me of my stupidity.

I love you, Mason.

Those were the words I'd whispered to him right before he hung up the phone. Those words weren't meant to slip out, but when they did, I'd just pretended to stay asleep.

The worst part?

He didn't say it back, not even to my sleeping face.

"Shit," I groaned, burying my head in my hands. It was too soon for us to be saying that to each other. I knew he was in deep, like Billie said, but not *that* deep.

I was in love with Mason Langston.

I was in love even though I wasn't healed—still *damaged.*

I was in love, and I didn't deserve to feel it.

I was in love even though I wasn't worthy of it.

Do you feel worthy of love, Harmony?

Dr. G's infamous question.

"No," I whispered into my palms, the heavy truth coming out from the depths.

"No what, Ms. Green?" a deep voice asked.

I shot up from my chair with a yelp, clutching my bottle to my chest. Josiah was standing in front of the nurses' station counter, his hands raised in surrender, his brown eyes filled with a warm worry.

"Woah, cherry girl," he said gently. "It's just me."

"Oh," I breathed, shaking a bit. "H-hi, J."

His thick, dark brows came together. "I didn't mean to scare you. That last patient walked out ten minutes ago, and I—"

"Ten minutes ago?" I whispered in disbelief, my eyes widening.

"Yes, ma'am," he said softly as my eyes dropped to the little clock on my desk. When I didn't respond, the kind man asked, "Are you ready to go?"

Sobering my thoughts, I met his eyes and nodded. Quickly, I gathered my things, and as we were walking out, I apologized to him.

"I'm just glad you're alright, Ms. Green," he rumbled, holding the door open for me.

"Will you still be around when Mason gets back?" I asked, glancing up at him. He was taller than me, but a few inches shorter than Mason. Then again, my bull rider was the biggest man I'd ever seen.

Josiah unlocked the passenger door to his truck, swinging it open before looking down at me again. He stared at me for a moment, and suddenly, I felt exposed, like my pain and trauma had been splattered across the news for the world to see.

"You want me there, I'm there," he stated, an edge in his voice that told me he didn't like what he saw in my eyes.

Wordlessly, I got into the truck. Silence filled the cab until he turned into Mason's parking garage.

"A word of advice, Ms. Green," he offered, causing me to look at him.

"Yes?" I whispered.

He swung into the parking spot, switched on the truck, and twisted his upper back to face me, his forearm resting atop the steering wheel. "Men like Mason aren't stupid."

I stared. "I know that, Josiah."

He shook his head, "Nah, Cherry, you aren't hearing me. Langston and I are the same kind of a man. One look at you, and I knew."

Oh, no.

Swallowing, I rasped, "Knew what?"

He tipped his head down to my bottle in my lap. "Someone fucked you up, sweetheart," he stated, his voice still soft. "It ain't none of my business, but when Langston hired me, I needed background. I needed to know what I was dealing with, you understand?"

I nodded, dread settling on my shoulders.

Josiah leaned in. "My man didn't have anything to give me, because you haven't told him anything, just that you were healing."

There was nothing I could say, but I knew what was coming.

"My advice, Cherry, is this: tell him. Tell him everything you can. A man like that has to know his woman's pain."

"Why?" I croaked, embarrassment heating my cheeks and tears stinging my eyes.

His features softened. "He's gotta know, Cherry."

The tears began to fall, and I tore my eyes from him, my fingers squeezing my metal bottle. "If I tell him...he wouldn't look at me the same."

"That's where you're wrong. I've never met the man in person, but I could tell by his voice—*that man loves you*. Nothing will change that."

"You don't know that," I snapped, looking back at him.

He gave me a weak, half smile. "That man's a cowboy, sweetheart. Cowboys only love once, and they never stop."

As soon as the words were out of Josiah's mouth, my mind immediately went to Mason's ex-fiancé—*Cathy.*

He loved her before me.

Chapter Twenty-Three

Mason

Houston traffic was a form of torture sent directly from Lucifer himself.

"How long has it been, Mason?" Eddie asked from beside me in the back of the Uber.

I didn't say anything, flashbacks of the nightmare rushing forth and crashing into me.

"Mason, please. Fuck, you scared the shit out me," Eddie begged, exhaustion and worry coating his voice like thick molasses.

"Five years, six months, and two days," I answered, my voice monotoned.

We were halfway across the Atlantic, both of us asleep in first class, when it happened: the first nightmare I'd had about her in a long time...

"Mason! Denver! Boys! Please help me! Help me!"

The cries of our mother had Den and I sitting up straight from the swing on the porch. My brother looked at me, his gray eyes on alert as he scanned around us.

"That was Momma," I whispered to him.

He looked at me, nodding. "I know, Mase. Come on, let's go."

We were running, then, through the overgrown field.

Where was the herd? Why was the grass so tall?

"Come on, Mase! Keep up!" Denver called over his shoulder in front of me. My brother was taller than me, and I wasn't as fast as him. I watched as he disappeared into the trees, darkness swallowing him whole.

Where was Pop?

"Boys! Please! Help!" Momma's sharp, scared cry echoed from the forest. I came to a halt and watched as hundreds of black crows shot into the sky from the trees.

"Mase, where are you?" Denver roared, his young voice cracking.

I was running again, my hat flying off my head just before I entered the tree line. Denver was screaming now, and I couldn't hear Momma anymore. Heart pounding, I pushed through the branches and leaves.

The stream.

Momma would be at the stream.

In a blink, I was there, on the big rock.

Denver was on the ground, wailing in pain.

"Den!" I cried out, ready to hop down.

"Sweet boy," a voice called. Momma's voice.

I looked across the stream and there she was—flames all around her.

She smiled at me, tears in her eyes. "My sweet, kind Mason."

Before I could respond, the flames rose higher, and the sounds of her screams filled my ears, along with Denver's.

I squeezed my eyes shut, cursing under my breath. *"Fuck."*

"You need to talk to Denver, bud," Eddie's voice filled my ears. "It's time. You know that. That dream didn't just come back for shits and giggles."

I opened my eyes and dropped my head back against the head rest. "The last words I said to him were 'I hate you,' Ed. He doesn't want to talk to me."

"Maybe your next words should be 'I'm sorry,' then. Look, I know that Cathy woman came between you both, but he doesn't know the truth, does he?"

"It's not that simple," I whispered, looking out the window. Eddie didn't understand. He didn't understand that Denver had been so blinded by our father's pride, he didn't see the pain and torment I'd endured. For years, I was crying out for help, and—

"Hallow Ranch needs you, Mase," Eddie said, forcing my mind back to St. Louis and the news the bounty hunter brought me. "Moonie Pipelines isn't anything to joke around about."

That got my attention.

"You know Moonie?" I asked, snapping my head to him. My gut had been in knots since leaving Spain. I was worried about my little song, and since having that nightmare, I was worried about Hallow Ranch for the first time in over a decade.

I held Eddie's eyes as something passed through them—something haunted. My friend was in dressed in jeans and a pearl snap, his face free of any fucking clown makeup. Right now, you couldn't tell he spent his days chasing bulls and making people laugh. He looked like a regular ol' cowboy.

"Corporate blood sucker," he growled, his upper lip curling. "His father tried to come after my daddy's ranch when I was just starting out in the rodeo."

That was news to me. After years of late nights of shared stories and whiskey, I thought I knew everything about the man beside me. Granted, he didn't know everything about me...

I knew Eddie started out as a bull rider, back in the nineties. He had one full year with PBR, and his short career came to an end when he was thrown off by a monster, trampled as soon as he hit the ground. He told me that when he tried to go home, his father wouldn't let him. So, Eddie made PBR his home. Two decades later, he'd done well for himself, known around the world.

"Wait—didn't your dad eventually sell the ranch?" I asked.

Eddie nodded. "Yeah, but to another rancher."

Silence filled the cab for the next few minutes, and when the driver pulled up to my building, Eddie asked the million-dollar question.

"Do you think Denver will sell?"

Putting my cowboy hat on, I put my hand on the door and looked over my shoulder at him. "My brother would die for that ranch."

Even if he wanted to, he couldn't.

Not after the promise he made Pop.

A few minutes later, I swung open the door to my condo, the scent of Harmony filling my nose. Melons. A different kind of ache bloomed in my chest, one that I hadn't felt since I was a boy.

A throat cleared, drawing me away from my home.

I looked to Leon's man, Josiah, leaning against the wall beside me. Cutting through the shit, I got right to it. "Thank you."

He gave me a short nod as he pushed off the wall. "Everything has been quiet. Nothing out of the ordinary. Her friends have been by every day."

Damn good friends.

They were exactly what she deserved.

"Appreciate the info," I muttered, holding my hand out to him. He took it, and we shook before he looked to Eddie and nodded once in greeting.

"Before I go, you need to know that Harmony asked me to stay this afternoon," Josiah informed me, his dark eyes meeting mine.

A chill went down my spine.

My eyes shot to Eddie, a shadow of concern hovering over his features.

"Did something happen?" I asked, my voice firm.

Josiah looked into my condo, into the living room just beyond the foyer. "No, but I just know she's been through something."

"No shit? Why in the fuck do you think I hired you?" I deadpanned.

Why the hell would she ask him to stay?

Did he know something I didn't? Had Harmony confided in someone else, sharing the pain she couldn't seem to share with me?

"She asked me to stay because she's on edge," he responded, his voice calm.

Fuck, how could I argue with that?

I nodded, sighing through my nose, feeling helpless. "I know she is."

"You're here, so I'm going to go home for the night. Got a kid and a woman waiting for me. I'll be back in the AM."

After he took off, I focused on what mattered. *Her*. Not wasting another second, I adjusted my hat, charging over the threshold.

I love you, Mason.

"Baby?" I called out, stepping into the foyer, Eddie right behind me. Once in the living room, I tossed my bags on the couch, my eyes searching for my woman. Her guitar was propped up against the far end of the couch, a blanket tossed back. There was a humming sound coming from the spare bathroom. My feet moved instantly, carrying me to her sweet voice. Not wanting to frighten her, I rested my ear against the door, listening.

She was in the shower, humming a gentle tune that made my heart pound in my ears. She was safe. She was here with me. I was back.

Like hell would I ever leave her again.

Never again.

My mind drifted back to the phone call, Cabe's voice telling me that the most precious thing in my god forsaken life had been threatened, scared shitless.

I'd been helpless.

You haven't always been helpless, my sweet Mason.

Backing away from the door, I ignored the gentle voice in my head, the one that reminded me of my mother but I knew wasn't her. It was the demons in my head, plaquing me, reminding me of my failures.

The voice was right, though. There were times I could've helped. Countless times, in fact I just didn't have the strength to answer the fucking phone. Swallowing, I tried to ignore the twist in my gut, but I couldn't. Without saying anything to Eddie, I made my way to my bedroom, into the closet, straight to the safe. It was small and beat up, most likely from rolling around in the back of my truck for so long.

I'd bought it a month after I left Hallow Ranch, needing something to keep valuable things in. My intention had been to toss it over a bridge over some river, watch it sink to the bottom, and move the fuck on with my life.

When the time came, I couldn't.

The claws of Hallow Ranch were buried deep within me, its brand on my skin, leaving it scared and hideous.

My jaw tightened as I put the combination—Momma's birthday—into the lock. With a soft click, the door popped open, revealing the past I'd been desperately trying to bury. Reaching inside, my hand engulfed the small device, fury coursing through me as it did every other time I grabbed it.

This fucking phone.

"Maybe the fucker won't turn on," I mumbled to myself, flipping it open and pressing the power button.

The tiny screen brightened, showing me a logo from a different life.

Just my fucking luck.

Without thinking, I went to the call log. Two hundred and fifty missed calls, sixty voicemails.

Denver.

Denver.

Denver.

Jigs.

Denver.

Denver.

Denver.

Denver.

Jigs.

Beau.

Denver.

Denver.

Denver.

My throat thickened. It was a never-ending list of calls that spanned years. I went to the voicemails, clicking on the most recent one from a few years ago.

After the beep, my brother's deep voice filled my ear, misery shooting through my body. "Mase...fuck, man...I need you to come home. Brother, please...whatever issues you have with me, fine, but this isn't about us anymore. It's about the future of Hallow Ranch. My home, your home—our home. I need...Mase, I need you—"

I hung up, slapping the phone shut before chucking it to the floor beside me. Reaching up, I pulled my hat off and braced my hands on the wall above the shelf as my hat fell to the ground, landing next to the phone.

Denver bought me that fucking hat.

Pop never bought me a hat, but my fucking brother did.

"Come on, Mase. Every cowboy needs a good hat."

"It's too expensive, Den."

"Not for my brother, it's not."

My shoulders were shaking with an overwhelming rush of emotion when I heard boots click on the floor behind me.

"You alright?" Eddie drawling.

Eyes to the floor, I gave him the truth. "No."

"You finally getting the courage, or what?" he asked.

"The fuck?" I growled, slowly dropping my hands and turning to face him. He was leaning against the doorframe, arms crossed, hat off.

He smirked. "You heard me. I didn't stutter."

I raised my brows. "You wanna start this shit with me? You sure about that?"

I watched as one of my only friends shook his head, disappointment in his kind eyes. "He's your brother."

"You don't know shit about me or my fucking family!"

"Oh, so he's your family again?" he challenged.

"Fuck you," I spat.

Eddie huffed a harsh laugh. "Always the fighter."

"The fuck is that supposed to mean?" I clipped, taking a step towards him.

He pushed off the frame, pointing a finger at me. "It means that in all the years I've known you, all the years I've watched you soar, riding beasts that shouldn't be conquered, listening to the world chant your name, all you've done is fight! You fight yourself, you fight your managers, you fight the other riders. That's all you know how to do, Mason! When the hell are you gonna learn to stop throwing punches and actually *feel something* besides pain in your split knuckles?"

I was silent.

"You telling me you don't give a shit about Hallow Ranch?" he snapped, taking another step closer, his finger an inch from my face.

"Get your finger out of my face," I warned, my voice low and shaking.

Eddie huffed another laugh. "That's right. You can't even lie to me about that."

"You don't know shit. Now, get your fucking hand out of my face," I ordered, balling my fists at my sides.

He swung his arms out. "What? What, Mason? You gonna fight me, too?"

"You don't—"

"I know that if you didn't give a shit, you wouldn't have been carrying around that damn phone for *the last decade*! I know that if you didn't give a shit, you still wouldn't be in contact with *Jigs!*"

I shook my head, nostrils flaring. My friend's worn features softened as his brown eyes gentled. "Been watching you for ten years, boy. I know enough," he whispered.

He didn't know shit.

I pushed past him, checking him with my shoulder. That didn't stop Eddie though. He followed. Part of me knew he would—*hoped* he would—but that part was drowning in agonizing pain.

"Wanna know how I know?" he called after me. A hand landed on my shoulder and instincts kicked in. I whirled on him, grabbing his shirt and shoving him back until he slammed into the living room wall.

"I don't give a fuck, Ed," I sneered.

"You've been fighting every day because as a boy, you couldn't. If you did, he would've killed you!" he choked out.

I froze, acid in my veins like poison rushing through my body, filling my organs, rotting me from the inside out. My hands released him, and I slowly started to back away. "Don't—"

"John Langston beat you!" he boomed, pushing off the wall. My friend raised his finger again, pointing it in my face. "He beat you and you couldn't fight it. You didn't know how, but you do now. Got the scars on your knuckles to prove it, don't you?"

"Stop," I growled, my chest heaving.

"The only problem is that fucker is *gone*, and you have no one to fight! So, you chose everyone around you. I don't understand it, Mason! *He's gone*! Your father is hell where he *belongs,* and you are taking *his sins* out on *your brother—*"

"Denver didn't protect me!" I roared.

A chill settled over the room as my ears rang and time stood still.

Eddie looked wounded. "What?"

I bared my teeth, a twisted smile spreading across my face before I could stop it, the pain leaking out of me like thick tar. "*My. Brother. Didn't. Protect. Me.*"

"You mean...?"

"Denver was the golden boy. I was the burden. Put two and two together," I hissed.

"Mason—"

I threw my arms out. "He hated me with everything he had, *Pop.* God, I woke up feeling it and went to bed drowning in it, Ed. Never escaped it! He raised Denver and threw me aside. He took the pain of losing Momma out on *me,* drowning it in whiskey, pounding it out with his fists *on my body*! Denver didn't do a damn thing!"

Eddie stared. What more could he do?

There were no words in any language that could take away this pain and the nightmares that came with it.

"Denver lived the perfect childhood. He was destined for glory from the moment he took his first breath. Hallow Ranch was his. All I needed was him, nothing else," I seethed. "And what does he do? Go ahead, Eddie, since you *know* everything about me. You tell me what he did!"

Eddie's eyes looked past me for a moment, but I was too pissed to care. The dam was open—*shattered*—and the rapids were surrounding everything and everyone around me.

No one was safe.

"He left," he answered.

A manic, pained laugh ripped from me. "Ding, ding, ding! We have a fucking winner!"

"Alright, Mason," Eddie said softly. "Let's take a second. Calm down."

I was far from calm. There was a storm raging within me, ready to be unleashed. "The day my brother left to fight for our country—*to protect strangers*—Pop got drunk, went into the barn, and grabbed a brand—"

"—enough, Mason," Eddie barked, taking a step towards me, his eyes darting behind me.

My hands yanked up my shirt, pulling it over my head before I tossed it aside. The cool air of the room couldn't help soothe the burn on my skin, like hellfire being rained down upon me.

"I was asleep, Ed!" I yelled. "I was asleep, and he fucking *branded* me! Woke up in pain as he shouted 'Now you can't leave! Got the brand on you, son! You belong to Hallow Ranch.'" I twisted my torso to show him the scarred 'H' on my shoulder blade. "I begged, cried, shouted, fought...he didn't take it off me..."

"Mason," Eddie whispered, his eyes wide with disbelief.

I straightened, my jaw jumping. "Now, you tell me if I should go back to Hayden and stop Tim Moonie from claiming Hallow Ranch," I spat, venom in every word.

"M—Moonie?"

Little Song.

I turned to find her standing in the middle of the room, one of my shirts on her body, stopping at her hips. Her hair was wet, skin pale, her blue eyes wide with fear.

Pure fear.

Suddenly, nothing else mattered but her, my past be damned.

She was scared, and I needed to make sure that she wasn't scared of me.

Chapter Twenty-Four

Harmony

"Now, you tell me if I should go back to Hayden and stop Tim Moonie from claiming Hallow Ranch!" the bull rider I loved shouted at his friend.

Tim Moonie.

Moonie.

Hallow Ranch.

Hayden.

Hallow Ranch and Tim Moonie.

Mason and Tim?

Mason knew about Tim?

"M-Moonie," I stammered, my voice weak from my throat tightening as the air left my lungs.

Mason and all his raw, staggering beauty turned to me, concealing the scar he'd just exposed to Eddie. His chest heaved as his gray eyes assessed me from head to toe. When they reached my eyes again, I instantly wanted to be sucked into his storm.

Unfortunately, the monster had risen to the surface, its claws digging into my skin, ready to pull me under, chuckling in my ear.

Gotcha, darling.

"Darlin'."

Mason's deep voice tried to overpower the monster, but it wasn't enough. Despite the gentleness and warmth, it still wasn't enough. I was about to be dragged down into the pits of hell—my past—and I feared I wouldn't be able to escape it, not again.

Before I went, I had to know one thing.

"You know Moonie?" It came out as a raspy whisper. Under normal circumstances, I don't think he would've heard me, but the silence in the room was almost as deafening as my screams had been.

Mason's brows came together as his jaw tightened. He took a step towards me, and I retreated.

He froze, his eyes flashing like lightning in a dark night. "Harmony?"

"Answer me, please," I begged, my body beginning to tremble.

"Moonie Pipelines is trying to buy Hallow Ranch," he answered.

"Your home," I rasped, tears stinging my eyes as I retreated further. The monster yanked on my foot, and I was in the thick, dark water, struggling to stay on the surface.

He shook his head, his eyes softening. "Hallow Ranch ain't my home, baby."

It was too late for me to catch the meaning of his words, the sincerity behind them lost as I was engulfed in darkness...

"Darling," he scolded, his voice light.

He was such a contradictory type of man. I'd seen him threaten a man's life with a smile on his face, his eyes bright, as if he'd just won the lottery. That was the thing about my future husband: he enjoyed pain. He enjoyed inflicting it upon others.

Tim Moonie was a madman, and I was trapped.

"Please," I croaked out, my arm outstretched to the light behind him. It was first word I'd spoken since it happened. My body was spent, aching and failing, but that light gave me hope.

Freedom.

Clean air.

Food.

Water.

He scoffed, kicking my arm back. "How are you supposed to be my perfect girl when you can't even control your own body?" he taunted. "You say you want to be a nurse, but darling, if I let you chase that dream, you would fail. Do you know why?"

My throat was burning.

My eyes stung.

My tongue was dry.

My skin was brittle.

I didn't have the strength to answer.

When the door opened, I'd hoped he would bring something for me to drink and eat, like he'd done for the last two days. I'd thought he'd have mercy on me.

It wasn't my fault.

It wasn't my fault.

Thirsty.

Hungry.

My lower body throbbed, the ache starting in my abdomen, shooting down into my thighs, overwhelmed with grief. I didn't have to look at my skin to know that it was covered in black, blues, and purples. Hell, maybe even some greenish yellow by now. I don't know how long I've been down here.

I just wanted something to drink.

If he didn't give me anything to drink, I wouldn't be able to scream, and that was what he liked most.

Hearing me scream, beg, shout, and cry for mercy: it made him feel like a god.

"Are you going to answer me?" he hissed.

My head fell back against the damp, cool concrete, exhaustion and hopelessness settling over me like falling snow. I hated snow. I hated winter. That was something Tim and I had in common, our mutual hatred for the cold. Keeping my eyes on his five-hundred-dollar leather shoes, I noticed a scuff mark on the left one, right by the toe.

He was going to hate that.

His voice was closer to me, which was interesting because I didn't even notice his shoes moving closer.

All I could see was the scuff, the only thing I wanted to focus on. I knew that when he noticed it, he would throw them away without a second glance, even though they were custom made for him.

Like I had been.

Born, raised, taught, and sold off to the highest bidder.

Like cattle at a stock exchange.

Custom made for a monster.

"Harmony," he sighed, "I'm losing my patience."

I wanted to cry, but my body couldn't produce tears. I was all dried up, much like the blood between my thighs, on the walls, and in my hair.

Pain radiated through my scalp as my head was yanked off the concrete, my neck bent back so I was forced to look at the well-dressed wolf. As always, his blond hair was styled to perfection, his eyes fierce, the brightest, coldest blue I'd ever seen, his white teeth gleaming in the dark.

"You were supposed to be my perfect girl," he clicked his tongue. "My perfect little wife."

Perfect.

Perfect.

Perfect.

Always so perfect, darling.

I opened my mouth to scream as he jerked my head once more, white hot pain shooting through me, reminding my body it wasn't done, but my pretty voice didn't come out.

Instead, a raspy, choking noise.

I lost my voice.

Tim's upper lip curled in disgust.

"Fucking worthless, that's what you are," he barked, shoving to the ground, my cheek slamming into the hard surface. He was angry.

"You can't even scream for me anymore, darling."

I rolled over on my side, trying to find even a milli-second of comfort, but it was useless. He was yelling, but I didn't hear him. I didn't care anymore. He was mad, so I let him be mad. The sooner we got this over with, the sooner I could sleep.

I liked sleep.

I didn't feel pain when I was asleep.

There was a bang in the distance, once again reminding me that there was an entire world outside of this cold, dark room. A world I hadn't had the chance to explore yet, and I never would.

I wasn't leaving this place, that much I knew. I'd accepted my fate, so I just lied there, waiting for the hurt—the torture—the now-silent screams. The shoe scuff I'd been so fascinated with connected with my stomach, sending another gush of warmth out between my legs.

Maybe that was the last of it.

I squeezed my eyes shut, biting down hard as the torment began. Minutes or hours would pass; it was all the same to me.

Time didn't exist in hell.

When my eyes opened, the light was gone, and the monster had gone with it. I was numb once more, my brain trying its hardest to give me a few moments of peace.

My body was tired, but still hanging on. However, my soul was dying—and I wasn't even trying to save it. It would die along with my heart, and maybe then, my body would die too.

I didn't know why I was still alive, why my body couldn't just let go. There was nothing left for me here.

Take me, please.

Take me, like you did her.

Why did you take her and leave me behind?

Before I could muster another prayer inside my head, darkness fell over me, leaving me unconscious in a pool of my own filth and blood.

Harmony.

Harmony!

Darlin', wake up!

Darlin', not darling.

I opened my eyes again to find a shadow looming over me, a shadow with a storm in his eyes, calling out to me, promising me protection.

But it was too late.

"Little Song, baby, come on!"

I sucked in a deep breath, my eyes shooting open. Warm light flooded in, causing me to wince. My chest caved in as panic slashed across my soul like a flaming blade, digging deeper into the scar. My cheeks felt wet, my eyes stinging as they darted around, trying to make sense of it all.

With a gentle shove, I was back in reality. I felt strong arms around me, caging me once more, ready to drag me back to hell.

I began to buck, shove, and fight. "No, no, no," I whimpered, pleading with the universe to let me be free. I'd had enough torture, enough pain. "Let me go!" I shouted.

"Baby," a choked, hurt-filled murmur came from behind me. The arms fell away, and I acted, springing to my feet and whirling around to face my captor, my breaths short and ragged.

I expected to see Timothy Moonie with a snide smile on his arrogant face, but in his place, on the floor, was a shirtless man in jeans and boots.

I knew this man.

How could I have forgotten him?

A bull rider with dirty blonde hair, tanned skin, a face sculpted by the gods, a bit of scruff covering that face, and gray eyes.

My bull rider.

My Mason.

He was looking at me intently, pain flashing in those eyes I'd fallen for. His features were soft as he whispered, "You're safe with me."

"Mase," I cried, my knees buckling.

"Shit," he hissed, moving quickly. Before I hit the ground, he was there, his arms wrapping around me once more. "I've got you, Harm. I've got you," he grunted.

Those sweet words washed over me like a forgiving rain after a deathly season of drought, and I couldn't hold it in any longer.

A shrill cry of agony escaped me as I clung to his shoulders, burying my face in his strong chest, my damp curls shielding me from the outside world. His scent overcame me, reminding me of a summer day, warmth, and pure goodness. Goodness I'd never had, goodness I never wanted to let go of once I'd gotten a taste. I crawled into his lap, my arms banding around his neck, my legs wrapping around his waist.

His hand went to the back of my head, holding me steady as he began to sway. "It's alright, darlin'. I've got you now. Nothing is going to happen to you, ya hear?"

Darlin'.

My throat burned.

"Water," I rasped into his skin. "Please."

"Anything you want, baby," he said firmly. "Ed, grab her bottle for me, would ya?"

Seconds later, I felt the cool, familiar metal brush against my arm. "Drink for me, Harmony," Mason demanded softly.

I pulled away from him, allowing just enough space between us to fit my bottle. Without a word, I flipped the straw up and took a long drink, my greedy gulps filling the silent living room. The hand on the back of my head remained, and I felt his thumb sweeping back and forth, his eyes never leaving me. "That's it, take what you need," he murmured.

I closed my eyes, a single tear landing on my bare thigh. After a few moments, I pulled the bottle away and set it on the floor, needing to feel him against me again.

"Can I hold you?" I whispered, looking up at him.

A pained look crossed over his features, but he blinked it away quickly. He brought me back to his bare chest, my head on his shoulder now. As his free arm tightened around my waist, he grunted, "You never have to ask me that, Harmony."

"I'm sorry, I—"

"No," he growled. "You have nothing to apologize for. Stop that."

I fell into the silence, soaking in his warmth and safety, the feel of his skin under my hands, his steady breathing, the rhythm of his heartbeat. He continued swaying me, stroking me, holding me.

He didn't ask to get up.

He didn't ask me to move.

He didn't push me off after a short period of time.

He didn't complain.

He just held me.

"I missed you," I admitted, my breath hitting his broad, tanned, shoulder.

Mason didn't say a word; he just tightened his hold on me.

Swallowing the lump in my throat, I spoke again. "I'm sorry that I'm such a burden, that I'm so much trouble—I don't—"

"Shut. Up."

I blinked, fear gripping me by the arm. "Are you—are you mad at me?" I stammered, tears stinging my eyes again. I was tired of crying. His fingers sunk into my curls, gripping my hair gently and pulling my head back.

The second my eyes met his, I knew his patience had run out. The tension in his muscles and his jumping jaw told me he was trying very hard to keep calm—for me. My heart skipped.

Mason's gray eyes bounced back and forth between mine, studying me. My hands slid down to his chest as I began to tremble. I tried instead to focus on the steady beating of his heart beneath my palms.

You're safe with me.

"Don't say his name please," I begged. "I can't—I don't—"

"His name triggers you. Understood," he resolved. His eyes darting behind me. "Got that?"

"Sure do, bud."

"Do me a favor?" he called, his eyes still on Eddie. My cheeks heated, embarrassment washing over me along with everything else.

Overstimulated was an understatement.

"Anything, Mason." The softness in Eddie's voice caused my heart to ache.

"Get her friends here. Cabe's number is in my phone," he instructed.

There was a part of me that wanted to argue, wanted to tell him that I would be okay, to laugh this off and go back to the way things were, but nothing would ever be the same again.

He was in this darkness now, and I was too broken to turn him away. I was selfish. I needed him. Eddie's voice filled my ears, but I didn't register the words. Guilt was taking over now.

Hallow Ranch was in danger.

"Do you want to wait until they get here to tell me, or are you going to tell me now?" Mase asked.

I closed my eyes, squeezing them shut. "I had a plan, Mase. I was going to tell you about him, but I wasn't ready."

He sighed. "Seeing as how that fucker is in both of our lives, I gotta know."

My bottom lip trembled. "I just—I didn't want to be broken. For the first time in a long time, when we're together, I don't feel broken. I feel normal," I sobbed softly, my body shaking. "I just wanted to be normal."

He remained silent.

Then, he broke it. "You are anything but normal, Harmony Green," he whispered. "You are a gift to me."

I sat up, and our eyes met as he brought his hand to my face, his rough, callused thumb sweeping over my cheek. "Talk to me."

I thought of the conversation I walked in on, of the scar on his back, the terror in Eddie's eyes, the pain in Mason's voice. My cowboy read me like an open book. "Don't. Don't mix my shit with yours," he warned, his eyes flashing.

"I'm sorry," I rasped. "I'm sorry that your father—"

"Tell me about him. Please. I don't want to talk about my father. I don't want to talk about my brother and the broken, irreparable bond between us. What happened at Hallow Ranch is in the past, baby. I'm not looking there. I'm looking at you, the woman who was scared shitless by a man who cornered her. The woman who carries her water bottle everywhere like it's Baby Jesus. The woman who looks at her feet when people should be on their knees for her. The woman whose beauty knocks the breath out of me every single time I see her. The woman who sings like fucking angel. The woman who makes homemade pasta and sets tulips everywhere in her apartment. The woman who cares about the little people. The woman who dedicates her life to helping people heal while she is healing herself."

I looked away from him, tears flowing freely now.

"That's what I want to talk about. My shit doesn't matter," he finished.

"It does to me," I whispered, keeping my eyes on the lamp behind the chair.

The air around us and between us changed, the storm in his eyes picking up, the power in them ready to demolish anything in its path. His fingers gripped my chin, turning my face back to his. *"He* hurt you," he growled.

He knew this. He knew I was healing, but now that he knew the name of the man who caused me so much pain...things changed. For both of us.

"Yes," I rasped, my voice scratchy.

A venomous shadow fell over his rough features, something sent a chill down my spine.

"You will tell me every single *fucking* thing. I don't care how long it takes, how much you need to cry, scream, recover—whatever. You will remain in my arms, because, dammit, I need to touch you while you do this. Bare yourself to me, darlin'."

I needed his touch too, more than I realized.

"His 'darling' is different from yours," I confessed.

Mason went solid underneath me. "Come again?"

"You call me 'darlin', and he called me 'darling'," I explained. He stared at me, unblinking for a long stretch of time.

"You want that word out of my vocabulary?" he finally asked, his voice strained. He didn't want that, but I knew he would forget the word if I asked him to.

I shook my head, bringing my hands up to either side of his neck. "When you call me that, I feel safe."

When you call me baby, I feel desired and beautiful.

When you call me Little Song, I feel loved.

"And when he called you that?" he pressed, scooting us back until he was leaning against the side of his couch.

"Do you want to move from the floor?"

"I want you to answer my question, Harmony." His voice was stern as he leaned over to grab my bottle, bringing it to me.

I sucked in a breath, thinking back to Dr. G and her advice.

You are allowed to be loved. You are allowed to share your story. You are worthy of love.

"He only called me that to degrade me," I began, looking at Mason's chest. "When I did something wrong. When I put on the dress, wore my hair in a way he didn't like, said the wrong thing—"

"He didn't like your hair?" he clipped.

My lips tipped up slightly as a hopeless laugh left me. "He hated it. My father hated it. It was too wild for them, needed to be tamed—"

"Nothing about you needs to be tamed, Little Song," he whispered, grasping my chin and lifting my head. "Get me?"

I nodded.

"When did you meet him?"

Before I could open my mouth to answer, the door flew open, causing me to jump. Then, Billie's voice echoed throughout the room.

"Harm! Are you okay?" The panic in her voice had Mason's arms loosening and me moving to my feet. Wiping my face free of tears, my eyes met hers as I tried to give her a weak smile. She came flying towards me, her face crumpling.

Billie crashed into me, sending me back a step, but Mason was there to steady us. Her arms wrapped around my neck as her tears seeped into my shirt. Something was wrong.

Something was very wrong.

"Billie..."

"B," Cabe called softly, from behind her. My eyes lifted to him, and I sucked in a breath.

"W—why do you have a black eye?" I stammered.

My friend ignored my question, lifting his eyes to the cowboy behind me. "She tell you about him yet?"

"Just getting started before Blondie barged in," Mason drawled.

Eddie snorted from his spot in the kitchen. I'd forgotten he was here; I had been so wrapped up in everything else. His gaze collided with mine as he gave me a kind smile. In the middle of chaos, he was offering me a small ounce of kindness.

Eddie was an angel.

"We got problems," Cabe stated.

"What's going on?" I demanded, looking back at him.

"Look—"

"Don't," Billie stopped him, pulling away from me.

"Don't what?" Mason snapped.

Cabe looked at his lover, my best friend, silently communicating with her. They were hiding something from me, something important.

Because you're a burden who loses her mind at the sound of his name, goes into shock.

"Tell me," I croaked. All eyes moved to me, Mason's hand going to my waist. "If it's about him—just don't—" I sucked in a breath. "Don't say his name."

"We never do," Cabe assured me.

Billie turned back to me, her eyes darting up to Mason and then back to me. "You're in danger, Harm."

Before I could respond, Mason snapped, "Eddie, call Josiah. Get him here now." He came around me, guiding me to the couch. "Sit, please, baby," he murmured to me.

Once my butt was against the cushion, he snapped his fingers, pointing to Cabe. "Talk now," he ordered, his patience worn thin.

Billie sat at me, immediately grabbing my hands.

"He's here—in Houston," Cabe informed us.

"That doesn't make any sense," Eddie noted, pushing off the counter and coming to us. "He should be in Hayden."

"Hayden?" Billie parroted.

"Colorado," Mason muttered, his eyes to the floor, brows drawn together.

"There was something in the news the other day about Hayden. A fire," she said.

At her words, Mason's head snapped up and to us. "What?"

"Yeah, there was a wildfire," Cabe explained. "On a ranch. Hollie Ranch, I think—"

"Hallow Ranch," I breathed, looking at my bull rider.

Chapter Twenty-Five

Mason

"Hallow Ranch," Harmony corrected Cabe, looking at me.

Fuck.

Fuck.

Fuck!

"Stay here," I ordered, my feet already moving to my room and then into my closet. Harm called my name, but I couldn't—

Hallow Ranch.

A fire.

Momma.

Once in the small space, I grabbed a shirt and threw it on. Then, I grabbed both my phone and the old one. My jaw was tight, aching from the pressure as blood pounded in my ears.

Call him, my sweet Mase.

Her voice was clear as day, as if she was right beside me in this room, and I almost turned around to pull her in for a hug. I hadn't felt her touch in over twenty fucking years. Only recently had I started hearing her voice again.

I unlocked my phone, went to the contacts, and pulled up the number I only called in times of weakness.

Was Denver okay?

The herd?

The house?

The land?

Had anyone been hurt?

Why did no one call me?

Because you haven't answered in the last ten years. Why would they bother, asshole?

Without thinking, I dialed the number. As usual, I was expecting to hear the old man's voice after the third ring, but I didn't. The phone continued to ring three more times before going to voicemail. "This is Jigs. Leave a message or don't. I don't give a shit either way."

A lump formed in my throat.

Jigs always answered when I called. Why wasn't he answering now?

Maybe the flames ate him up like they did your mother.

I turned to the nearest wall, resting my forehead against it as I squeezed my eyes shut and braced myself. Great; first Momma's voice, now Pop's, like a fucking dead family reunion in my head. My eyes began to sting.

Cowboys don't cry, boy. Thought I taught you better than that.

Get the fuck out of my head!

I needed my eight seconds of peace, just eight seconds, and I'd be back to normal. I needed a fucking bull.

"Mase?"

I twisted my neck, looking over my shoulder to see the most stunning woman I'd ever seen in the doorway of the closet, her arms wrapped around herself. Her eyes were puffy and red from crying, her curls in a beautiful disarray, her pale, freckled skin flushed, and her bottom lip trembling.

She was reaching her breaking point.

The shitty thing was...so was I.

"Hallow Ranch," I growled, frustrated and scared.

"I'm so sorry," she breathed.

I pushed off the wall and turned to her. *"He* do this?" I clipped. "Did *he*—does *he* want it that bad?"

Her blue eyes dropped down to the phones in my hands and then lifted back up to me. *"He* won't stop, Mase," she rasped. The nickname was like a punch in the gut, because I knew she was telling me the truth.

"I was approached in St. Louis, baby," I confessed, my hands tightening around the devices. She opened her mouth again, but I continued, "A bounty hunter by the name of Joseph Grayson came to see me when I was visiting old friends. He'd been tracking me for a few days."

Fear sparkled in her teary eyes. *"He—"*

"Grayson was hired by my brother."

"Your brother?"

It was then I realized I hadn't told her anything about my past. "Denver is my—"

"Mason, I know who he is to you. Billie looked you up a while ago."

I ignored the chill in my spine. "And what did she find?" I asked, my voice low.

My sweet, strong little song cut through the bullshit, hitting the nail right on its flat fucking head. "Hallow Ranch, you brother, and your ex-fiancée."

Grinding my teeth, I silently cursed myself for not having Pam handle that fucking interview Cathy did.

That fucking bitch came after me a year after I caught her in my brother's bed, begging for me to take her back, but I didn't need her anymore. She was always a means to an end. Yes, I hoped that at some point we would become something more, but she wasn't the one for me.

The one for me was desperately trying to hold herself together in the middle of my closet in a condo I barely tolerated in a city I hated.

"Mason," Eddie called. I looked past Harmony to see him standing in the middle of my room, an iPad in his hands. "The fire happened a few weeks ago. No casualties."

My chest caved in as the organ in it strained.

He was safe.

Denver was safe.

I looked back to Harmony. "How far would *he* go?" I demanded.

"Don't ask me that," she whispered.

Closing the distance between us, I quipped, "I'm asking. I'm fucking begging at this point, Little Song. For months, I've known of your pain, fucking seen it with my own eyes!" I threw my arms out and brought them in against my chest. My voice was rough, filled with emotions I didn't want to face. "Kills me, baby...when I was in Spain, not here for you—" I stopped myself, taking a breath. "Been patient with you long enough, tried to be the gentleman, be good enough for you—a man who was worthy of you. Fuck that," I growled, my hands dropping.

She opened her mouth to speak, but once again, I cut her off. "You better be opening that pretty mouth to tell me what I want to hear," I warned.

"No one wants to hear this," she snapped, getting angry.

Finally, something other than sadness and worry.

"Harmony, I don't want to hear it, any of it, but I need to!" I boomed, my voice bouncing off the walls. She instinctively took a step away from me, and I couldn't blame her. Eddie took a step closer to her—I'd never liked the man more than I have in this moment.

He'd seen the anger inside me, the monster in me, passed down from my father. Eddie had his own demons to fight, yet here he was, helping me fight mine all while protecting the woman I'd become so fucking obsessed with.

"Mason, once you know—once I tell you—"

"Nothing will change!" I shouted, charging towards her. "My feelings for you will never change, Harmony! Who you are now, the amazing, strong woman I've—" I clenched my jaw, grinding my molars. Feelings were hitting me from all sides, and it was difficult to control. "I'm—*fuck!*" I threw my hands in my hair. Her eyes shined with tears, and I hated them.

"I'm damaged," she croaked out.

"Not. To. Me." My growl echoed just as loud as my shouts, and that's when Billie and Cabe appeared in the doorway.

"Mason, bud, I'm going to ask you to step back," Cabe requested.

My eyes shot to her friend, grateful once again that Harm had good fucking people in her corner. "Let me make one thing very clear to everyone in this room," I said, my voice low as I pointed to my woman. "I would put a bullet in my mouth or purposefully loosen my grip on the bull rope so that fucker could kill me before I ever laid a hand on Harmony Green with the intention of bringing her pain."

"You ever loosen your grip on a fucking rope, I'll kill you myself," Eddie barked, stepping up to me.

"He beat me, Mase."

Harmony's voice made my blood run cold, the tremble within it unlocking the cage deep within my soul, releasing something that had been hidden, buried, for years. Images of Tim fucking Moonie standing over her as she cowered on the ground, beaten, bloodied, and bruised. Suddenly, the vile man above her changed, morphed into someone I never wanted her to know about.

Pop.

No.

I was speechless, but Harmony wasn't done. Not even close. Her cage had been unlocked too, it seemed. I braced myself, my nostrils flaring.

"You don't have to do this," Billie said to her friend. "There are a lot of things hovering around us right now. Maybe—"

Harmony held her palm up to her friend, silencing Billie, keeping her blue eyes on me as my chest heaved. My fists tightened around the phones, and I heard a crack in the plastic of the older one, but it went ignored.

All I could focus on was the pain she was bringing to the surface.

"He *caged* me," she seethed, her voice rising, making the rasp I adored so much stand out even more. Billie whimpered, bringing her hand to her mouth. She looked like she was going to be sick, and her man, he looked like he wanted to kill something—or someone. Eddie was frozen, staring at the back of Harmony's head in shock, fury brewing in his eyes.

My little song was shaking, more tears running down her cheeks.

"Baby," I began, "we don't have to do this now." I pushed her too hard. She'd said enough.

Less than ten words, and I was already planning on killing the bastard.

"You don't understand! You don't see, Mason!" Harm screeched—her voice sounding forced. "*He*'s not going to stop, not until *he* gets what he wants!"

Like hell.

She took a step towards me. "If Hallow Ranch is what *he* desires, then he'll have it, no matter what it takes! He's *dirty*, Mason. His father was nothing compared to *him!* Hell, I could tolerate *his f*ather. Even after mine—" My baby cut herself off, looking away from me, bowing her head so she couldn't give me my favorite blue. She was hiding again, building walls that weren't needed.

Damaged or not, I fucking loved her.

We needed this.

No more of the back and forth.

This needed to come out, right now.

Every word from her mouth was pure music, a gift. Even if it was painful, I still wanted to hear it.

Her song.

Tim Moonie was part of her song, but he wasn't in the final chorus. No, that would be reserved for her and me, for the happiness that I would spend the rest of my days trying to give her. She could have the world if she asked, but right now, I needed her to sing for me.

"What did your father do?" I asked, my voice thick with emotion.

"He sold her," Billie spat through her tears.

"Sold her?" I quipped. When I looked back to Harmony, she was still looking at her feet.

No.

None of that.

I tossed the phones aside, erasing the distance between us, gripping her chin and forcing her to give me her blue. Holding her eyes, I ducked my head, so I was an inch away from her face. In her world, on her stage. It was just her and me.

"Bare it to me," I whispered. "Give it to me. All of it."

Her hand came up to my arm, the touch grounding me away from insanity.

"My father is a businessman; he runs multiple million-dollar companies throughout Texas. My father and *his* father ran in the same circles. I was betrothed to him before I turned sixteen," she explained.

My jaw ticked.

"I didn't meet him until after I'd graduated. I was groomed—prepped for his arrival."

What in the actual fuck?

"Why?" I pressed.

Her eyes held mine. "My father will do anything for power, including sell his own daughter. I have siblings—brothers—but I haven't seen or spoken to them in ages. Not since—"

"Harmony, please sit somewhere when you tell him this," Billie begged. I looked at them, both of her friends wearing pained expressions.

I didn't want them here, not now, but Billie knew more than me. She'd seen Harmony's episodes before. With that in mind, I walked her back to the bed, planted her ass on it, and stood up to my full height.

"I'm going to be outside," Eddie muttered. He understood.

Harm looked at me, then at her friends, then back to me. "I'm okay," she whispered.

"We'll be right outside," Cabe answered. I looked at him, giving him a nod.

Once we were alone, she didn't hesitate.

"*He* was nice at first. *He* was everything I didn't expect. Kind and gentle. *He* respected me. We officially didn't start dating until I was eighteen, and even then, *he* was...*he* checked all the boxes."

Great, she had boxes.

I folded my arms over my chest, and something flashed across her face. "Tell me what you need," I ordered.

"Please don't stand over me like this...not now."

I lowered down to my haunches, bracing my hands on either side of her hips, my thumbs rubbing against her soft skin. "This okay?"

She nodded. "A year into our relationship, something changed. *He* became distant and detached. My father was worried *he* was losing interest, and so he told me to fuck *him.*"

Yeah, I was killing her father, too. "Baby."

Bringing her hand up, she wiped her tears away. "He wasn't gentle the first time, or the second..." Harm trailed off, looking away from me.

My chest ached, and I needed her eyes on me. "Eyes, Harmony. Please."

Her eyes hit mine, and over the next few minutes—or hours, I couldn't be sure—she bared her broken soul to me, breaking mine with it. She cried, even shook, as she recalled her darkest memories —singing the saddest part of her song. She continued to shake as she told me how she got away from him and didn't stop shaking until she began talking about her therapist, Dr. Garcia.

My gut was so twisted, I didn't think I would eat for days.

When it became too much for her, she lunged at me, her arms wrapping around my neck, anchoring herself to me. Even her wanting my touch was a gift. I sat on the bed with her in my lap, rubbing her back. She soaked my T-shirt with her tears and assured me crying was healthy, telling me that when she used to talk about this with Dr. Garcia, she'd become so numb that she couldn't even express emotion.

This was just years of backlog finally catching up with her.

Holding her helped; knowing she was with me—safe—helped. What didn't help was the mind-blowing rage boiling within me, so powerful that I'd never felt anything like it before, not even the day Momma passed.

When my little song finished singing the most heartbreaking melody, she was exhausted, falling asleep in my arms. Minutes passed as I stared at her, memorizing every freckle, her smooth skin, her long, auburn lashes, her pink lips.

She was the most beautiful creature I'd ever seen, and her strength and courage shining brighter than the sun she reminded me of.

Slowly, I stood, carried her to the side of the bed, and tucked her in. As I pulled the covers over her, she whispered my name.

"Sleep, darlin'. I'll join you in just a bit."

"Alright," I sighed, moving into the living room. Billie was curled into Cabe, a mug in her hands, her eyes weary and filled with exhaustion. Cabe's eyes were alert and on me, and Eddie was staring out the window, his arms crossed over his chest.

Pointing at Cabe, I asked, "What's with the shiner?"

"She out?"

I nodded.

He sighed and looked down at his girl. "Moonie is here, in Houston."

"Yes, you told me this," I deadpanned.

Billie sat up, tucking a blonde lock behind her ear. "He knows Harmony is here. She told me the man who approached her seemed familiar to her—"

"I know. It was one of his men; she told me," I finished for her.

"She told you everything, then?" Cabe pressed, leaning forward, forearms to his knees.

"Start to finish," I clipped. Cabe opened his mouth, but I cut him off with a question that had been eating away at me for months. "Who all knows about Moonie and Harmony's...history?"

Who knew what kind of monster Tim Moonie truly was?

"Dr. Garcia, me, Cabe, and now you," Billie answered.

Good.

"She can't stay here," Billie breathed, fear in her voice. "She has to leave again."

My eyes cut to Eddie. "Pam."

He grumbled something about her yelling at him again, but he pulled out his phone.

"Moonie's guy do that to you?" I asked, gesturing to Cabe's eye.

He nodded. "Stopped by Harmony's work this afternoon, just to check."

My gut twisted even more. "Check what?"

"I've had a feeling since she was cornered, bud. I've been checking her apartment, too, looking for anything out of the ordinary."

"And?"

"There was a car parked across the street from her building today, after a week of quiet. Went to her clinic, and there was a man arguing the fucking janitor, demanding to know about the red-headed nurse."

Fuck.

"There's more," Billie whispered.

Fuck me.

My eye shot to hers, waiting.

"There's a girl Harm and I went to school with—she's dating a police officer," she explained.

Eddie looked at me, his phone to his ear. I didn't need to hear the full backstory. One was enough.

"Get to the point, blondie," I snapped through clenched teeth.

"Moonie has the cops in his pocket, and the police chief has been on edge. Apparently, the asshole stopped by for a visit, claiming the chief was an old friend. The whole bullpen was on edge."

"The night I got arrested after meeting Harmony, I didn't meet the chief, only his deputies," I muttered, trying to remember anything from the day. My mind was in a fog.

"He's applying pressure," Eddie bit off, shoving the phone back in his pocket.

Inhaling, I turned to him. "He pull this shit with your father?"

"Tried to. Tried to sway the local sheriff station with money and pussy."

My mind went to Hayden—Chase Bowen. He was the current sheriff. Chase was a good man, but any man could be swayed for the right price...

"Right," I started, "Harmony is with me. That means she's under my protection—"

"Mason, you don't understand. When it comes to a man like Moonie, you don't have protection," Billie argued. Cabe grunted in response.

I glared at her. "Sweetheart, I may be a bull riding star. My name may be plastered all over the tabloids, my bank account may be full, but make no mistake: I'm a cowboy down to my fucking soul. Cowboys don't play games when their women are involved. Not only has this asshole messed with my woman, but he's also fucking with my family's land. He will get neither," I promised, my voice dark.

She's your everything, so make it so.

"Then you take care of her," she ordered, holding my gaze. "With everything you have."

"With everything I have," I promised, "Starting with my last name."

"What?" Cabe and Billie asked, stunned.

Eddie chuckled. "Here we go..."

I looked at all three of them. "I have plan to take down this son of bitch."

Chapter Twenty-Six

Mason

August. Hallow Ranch.

My eyes were on the woman approaching the house. She was gorgeous, nothing like the sleeping woman in my truck, but still. Her beauty didn't belong here, not around cowboys. She was smiling to herself as she walked up the hill from the bunkhouse, and I could hear the laughter of the men behind her.

My gut twisted.

After weeks of trying to prepare myself for this, I knew I wasn't ready to face him, but I *could* face her.

She was a stranger, this dark-haired woman.

Once she was close, I cleared my throat. I shoved down a chuckle as she yelped and spun around to face me. I was sitting in the back of my tailgate, needing to let Harmony get some much-needed rest. The woman in front of me gave me a once over with her green eyes, and I knew she knew who I was. I bit down, my jaw tightening as the shock melted away from her features, revealing something damn near close to kindness.

"Mason," she greeted, her voice smooth and sweet as her eyes held mine. She lifted her chin higher, standing her ground. I gave her a smirk, letting her know I wasn't a threat.

"Denver around?" I asked, tension in my voice. In fact, it was in my shoulders, my back, and my gut, which hadn't stopped twisting for weeks.

The woman didn't answer; she just continued to stare.

I didn't have time for this shit, neither did Harmony or Hallow Ranch.

Sighing, I hopped off the tailgate, shut it, and made my way towards her. She held her ground, and I respected the hell out of that. "I asked you a question, darlin'," I drawled, softening my voice.

"And she won't answer it."

The sound of my brother's voice should have been a relief after all these years, but it was a punch to the fucking gut. My eyes snapped to the dark figure hovering over her. "Denver," I bit out.

"Mason."

There wasn't anger in his voice, something else lingered there. I swallowed the lump in my throat.

"Valerie, come here," my brother ordered, his eyes never leaving me, but mine dropped down to the woman who was backing up to Denver. I watched as he pulled the woman to his side, and I didn't miss the way she relaxed against his frame.

When I met my brother's eyes, he asked, "What are you—"

"You son of a bitch!"

Who in the fuck—?

Someone rushed up to my side, and before I could stop it, pain shot through my jaw. The man pulled back, ready to give a second blow, but I was ready. My eyes met his, giving him a cocky smirk. Before the fun started, as always, my big bro decided to step in, pulling the man off me. I brought my hand to my jaw, rubbing it as I glared at the young cowboy. "The fuck?" I growled.

The man was fuming, his eyes dancing with anger. What the hell was this guy's problem?

"Lance," Denver barked.

Lance shook his head, glaring at me. "No. No. Told myself if this sorry son of bitch ever stepped on this ranch again, I'd—"

Great, Denver's been sharing his feelings.

Enough of this shit.

"I'm not here to cause trouble," I deadpanned, walking to my truck and setting my hand on the door handle. "That bounty hunter you sent told me about Moonie."

"What's it to you?" a deep voice asked. I looked to the side, seeing a line of cowboys. I didn't give a fuck about anyone of them besides the older man at the end.

Jigs.

His tanned skin was worn, lines drawn into his face, and his mustache had gone from gray to white over the last ten years. My eyes went to the blue-eyed cowboy standing next to him: his son, Beau. He was a year older than me, but I barely knew the man. Jigs had kept him far from Hallow Ranch for the longest time.

When I looked back to the old man, he still wasn't looking at me, but at Denver. My eyes followed his, colliding with a pair of identical gray ones. He had a beard now, dark and short. There were crinkled lines around the corners of his eyes, showing his age, reminding me of all the years lost between us. Another punch to the gut.

"Found a way to take Moonie down," I declared, pulling the door open.

My back stiffened as multiple sets of eyes landed on my beauty.

My little song.

Valerie—my brother's woman, apparently—tilted her head slightly, her green eyes dropping to the bottle clutched to Harmony's chest. A feral, protective instinct crawled up my spine and peeked over my shoulder. Tightening my jaw, my eyes dropped to Denver's hand on Valerie's waist again, trying to comprehend what the actual hell was happening.

Where in the fuck was Cathy?

"Who the hell is that?" Denver asked.

Everything.

She's my everything.

My eyes hit Valerie for a second before going to my brother's.

"My wife," I answered, enjoying the words on my tongue, their taste.

"Mase," Jigs gaped, shocked.

"Your wife?" Denver barked.

"His wife, honey," Valerie confirmed softly, looking to Denver.

"What the fuck does *your wife* have to do with Tim Moonie?" that same deep voice asked. I looked to the cowboys in search of the owner, stopping on a dark, bearded man, around the same height and build as my brother and me. I couldn't see his eyes under the brim of his dark hat, but I could feel their anger.

No idea who the fuck this man was, nor did I care. I was here to speak with Denver, not his fucking buddies.

Biting my tongue, I ignored the man, turning to my brother.

"Got a minute?" I asked, my voice tight.

He shook his head, scoffing. "You're fucking kidding me, right?"

I just stared at him in response.

"Mason, where have you been?" Jig asked, finally looking at me.

My head snapped in his direction. "Maybe if you picked up your fucking phone, you would have known exactly where I've been."

"Picked up the phone?" Denver growled, stepping away from his green-eyed beauty. He looked at Jigs. "What the fuck is Mason talking about?"

Jigs looked pained. "Den, you must understand—"

"Understand? Understand?" my brother boomed, his deep voice echoing in the field beside us. He was getting ready to explode.

"Mase?"

My body reacted instantly to her rasp, turning to face her, my hand going to cup her face. Harmony's blue eyes were open, wide and searching.

"Hey," I cooed. "We're here."

She sat up, her hand touching my arm. "Why didn't you wake me?"

Because for the last month, we'd have been constantly moving, planning, and plotting. Because knowing you're sleeping in my truck gave me peace when I felt like I was in the middle of a war zone.

"You needed your rest," I answered, smirking at her. If she were anyone else, she would have bought it, the lie plastered on my face, the one that said, everything was okay. But she was Harmony—my wife—and she saw right through me. I was a sheet of glass, and she was the sun, her rays seeping inside, warming the cold darkness that lurked there.

"Mason," Denver snapped from behind me.

Christ, he reminded me so much of Pop. I looked over my shoulder to find him standing with his feet apart, arms folded over his chest, brows up.

"Can we talk or not?" I snapped back at him, pissed at the expectant look on his face.

"Sweetie," Harmony whispered.

I looked at her. "Remember when I told you a week ago there were things you still don't know?"

She nodded.

"A lot of it has to do with the man you're about to meet," I explained. Her eyes flashed in understanding.

"Then introduce me to my brother-in-law," she said, throwing her blanket on the center console to reveal her navy-blue romper with sunflowers on it. It was my favorite on her, one of the outfits I'd gotten for her in Spain.

I dipped my chin to her, grateful for her patience. She gave herself to me completely weeks ago, the good and the bad, and I was still struggling to give myself to her.

Because she wouldn't accept it—me—and I was entirely too selfish to let her go now.

She hopped out of the cab, landing her converse-covered feet on the dirt of Hallow Ranch for the first time. Her blue eyes scanned the group of people in front of us, her hand dropping down, seeking mine.

Our fingers laced together, my mother's ring pressed against my skin. I watched as she twisted, setting her bottle in the empty passenger seat.

Part of me wanted to ask if she was sure, but I didn't. Harmony was strong, and I supported her choices. If she needed her bottle, I would get it for her. That is, if my fucking brother ever lets us in the house.

My wife's eyes landed on Valerie, who was already staring at her, assessing, eyes guarded.

"Sorry to interrupt y'all's evening," Harmony called, her rasp like the sweetest honey.

Valerie's eyes bounced between us for half a second. Apparently, that was all she needed because she stepped forward, holding her hand out in offering, her face kind.

"Not at all. I'm Valerie Cross."

My woman—*fuck, my woman*—took Valerie's hand in her free one, shaking it gently. "I'm Harmony Langston. Nice to meet you."

Harmony Langston.

Harmony Langston.

An everlasting song filled with an everlasting beauty.

Valerie smiled, moving her hand out to me. "It's nice to finally meet you, Mason. I've heard a lot about you."

I swallowed a scoff. I bet she had. Loosening my jaw, I took her soft hand in mine, engulfing it, shaking it. "It's nice to meet you as well. Though I can say, I'm a bit confused. I was expecting someone else in your place."

I expected hate or even jealousy to emerge in her features, but she remained unfazed by my confusion.

"Yes, well, we have plenty of time to talk about that. Don't we, Smoke?" She looked over her shoulder at my brother, and I caught a look of pure love in his eyes before it vanished when he looked at me.

"Looks like it," he muttered, his throat bobbing.

Interesting.

"It's good to see you again, Mason," Jigs said, walking passed Denver, heading straight for Harm. His old face spread into a warm, welcoming smile. "Darlin', that hair is brighter than the moon tonight." He held out his hand to my wife. "I'm Jigs."

"Just Jigs?" Harm asked, smiling.

After what she'd heard that night in my condo, I told her about Jigs. She knew what he meant to me, and why I'd kept in touch with him after all these years. What she didn't know is that he, along with my father, murdered two men in front of Denver and me when we were children.

Would she still be wearing that smile for him if she knew?

Would she run away from me when she found out about the blood on my hands?

Would she still look at me with love in her deep seas of blue?

Would she still want my momma's ring on her finger?

"Just Jigs," he confirmed. Then he threw an arm out, gesturing to the line of perplexed cowboys. "My boy, Beau."

Beau stepped forward, his bright blue eyes shining as an easy grin spread across his face for my wife. The hair on the back of my neck stood up.

Something was off.

"How ya doin', sweetheart?" Beau drawled, taking her hand.

"H-hi," she stammered. Fucking Beau. Always the damn charmer.

"Nice to meet you, Harmony," he murmured, his eyes scanning the length of her. I stepped in front of her, ending their handshake.

"Long time no see, Beau," I greeted.

His eyes held mine, and for a second, I was sure he would spit in my face. Instead, he tipped his chin. "Still see you're holding on."

The bulls.

"Always," I confirmed.

"Multi-million-dollar bull rider, I hear."

I smirked. "That's right."

"Let's go inside," Denver declared. "No sense in standing out here."

Valerie smiled at him before looking at Harmony. "We have a bit of a full house tonight. My mother is here, along with her nurse, Jackie. Also, Caleb has a friend over."

"Caleb?" my wife inquired.

Denver answered, his gray eyes on Harmony. "My son."

Chapter Twenty-Seven

Harmony

Two Weeks Ago. Eddie's Ranch—West Texas.

"I've known you for over a decade, and this whole time, I didn't know you had a ranch," Mason snapped from behind me, irritated.

I giggled, shaking my head. "What he means to say is: Eddie, your home is lovely. Thank you for having us."

Eddie set his beer down on his porch railing. "Sweetheart, don't you go lying on his behalf. He's just mad because he could've been training here this whole time instead of in Tennessee," he laughed, coming down his porch steps. Without hesitation, he came to me, stopped, and asked, "You gonna be alright if I hug you? Cause this old man has missed you."

That was Eddie, a respecter of boundaries.

"Of course, you can, Ed," I allowed, throwing my arms around him.

With a grumble from Mason and a chuckle from Eddie, I was wrapped into a hug. "Glad you two are safe," the rodeo clown whispered into my curls.

"You gonna say that to me or just my wife, asshole?" Mason clipped.

Letting go of Eddie, I spun, slapping Mason's hard chest. "Be nice," I demanded, shooting him a glare.

His tall figure blocked the sunset behind him, the warm orange rays shining all around him. My eyes met his under the shadow of the brim of his cowboy hat, his storm calm for the first time in weeks. In Spain, we were looking over our shoulders.

We were safe here.

We were safe here.

You're safe with me.

"He kept this place a secret from me, baby. I have a right to be an ass."

"Your husband is a piece of work, Harm. Say the word, and I'll have the getaway car loaded and ready to go," Eddie joked from behind me.

Husband.

As of forty-eight hours ago, Mason was my husband, and I was his wife.

Harmony Green was gone, a stronger woman by the name of Harmony Langston standing in her place. Since the night he returned from Spain, the night I told him everything, I'd grown stronger and braver than ever before. Dr. G tells me that the progress I'd made was extraordinary.

"Well, let's get you inside. There's a storm brewing about sixty miles north of us, and I have a feeling it's going to hit. Soon."

There was a storm brewing here, too, inside my husband. Ever since we've been back on American soil, he's been on edge.

Something was brewing.

It was the downfall of my ex.

Once we were inside, Eddie ushered us to the breakfast table in his small kitchen and served us sweet tea and lemon cookies.

"My mother's recipe," he bragged softly, sitting back in his chair as Mason took off his hat.

I took a bite of a cookie and knew that I would have to beg Eddie for recipe...or steal it from him.

"Why didn't you tell me about this place?" Mase asked his friend, reaching across the table to grab my hand.

Eddie sighed, looking out the window. "No one knew about it, bud. It was my haven during off-season."

My eyes went to my cowboy, watching as sadness drifted over his features. Had he not had a haven to return to all these years? Where had he gone during the off-season?

"Anyhow, got an update for you on him," Ed sighed, his eyes going to me for a second, then back to Mason.

"The police chief?"

Turns out, the man who haunts my nightmares had the police in his pocket.

"Did some digging. Found out that the chief was being threatened to keep tabs on Harmony, and when you walked your happy ass up to the counter asking about her, he was instructed to report it to you know who," he explained to us.

Mason's hand squeezed mine, his rough thumb sweeping over my skin, providing instant comfort.

"How did you dig, Ed?" my husband asked, sliding his gray eyes to his friend. I watched as the men conducted a silent conversation, for which I was thankful. I didn't want to know what was being said, what their eyes were conveying to one another.

"Got friends everywhere, Mason. Not to mention, Cabe and Billie have been pulling their weight," Eddie explained.

"Is the bastard still lurking?" Mason growled, referring to the man trying to destroy our lives.

"According to Josiah and his team, no. According to Cabe and Billie, no. That doesn't mean he doesn't have eyes everywhere, though. He might be back in Colorado, bud."

Hayden.

Hallow Ranch.

That was the final part of our plan, but it was one Mase kept putting off. After hearing about his father, I understood why he didn't want to go home, but I knew there was something missing, another piece of Mason's complicated puzzle that he had yet to show me, and I was beginning to wonder if he ever would. We hadn't talked about his past, not since that night.

We needed to.

We were husband and wife now. Everything had changed.

"How was the wedding?" our friend asked, changing the subject.

It was simple and elegant, on a private beach at sunrise. I wore a white silk dress, and I'd never felt so beautiful.

My cowboy turned his head to look at me, his hard features softening. "Best day of my life," he murmured, his rough voice sending tingles throughout my body.

"Agreed," I whispered, my heart pounding. I loved him. When he asked me to marry him, offering me his mother's ring, hesitation wasn't even in the room. I'd said yes immediately, because all I could think about was my love for him.

Was it crazy? Yes.

Was I scared shitless? Yes, but not of him, never of him.

Eddie groaned from across the table. "You two make me want to barf."

"Then leave so I can stare at my wife," Mase shot back, not taking his eyes off me. My cheeks heated.

"Here's the question, love birds: are you heading to Hallow Ranch or not?"

A shadow fell over Mason, lightning flashing in his storm eyes as his jaw tightened.

It wasn't a choice.

We were bound for Hallow Ranch, whether Mase liked it or not.

"Son?"

The question came from Mason, and no one could miss the pain and confusion in his voice. *He had a nephew.* Despite the emotions in Mason's voice, I couldn't tear my eyes away from his brother.

Denver Langston.

He was taller than I'd expected—and darker. There was something about him that scared the hell out of me. One look at his painfully handsome face—features like my husband's— and I knew. I knew that there was darkness in his soul, perhaps darker than the bull rider behind me.

That wasn't the only difference between the two.

Where Denver was dark, Mason was light. Their skin was sun-kissed, a blessing from being cowboys, and they both possessed the same gray eyes. However, my husband's held a lot more anger. My husband had dirty blonde hair and scruff; his brother had dark—nearly black—hair and a full, trimmed beard.

Two brothers, opposites but similar all the same.

It was a contradiction, a puzzle that needed to be solved.

There was no mistaking the years of distance, the awkwardness, but underneath all of that, there was a need—a bond. It was clear it was broken, desperately in need of repair, and the way Valerie looked at my bull rider was confirmation.

She could see it, too.

The silence had gone on too long for my liking. "How lovely," I praised, giving Denver a small smile.

His dark, intense gaze dropped down to me, his eyes narrowing. My heart began to race, and I felt a drop of sweat from the summer night trickle down the back of my neck.

There was one more difference between the Langston brothers.

One would protect me with his life, and the other looked like he didn't give a damn. I was a threat to him, his cowboys, and Hallow Ranch.

I'd been in bed with the enemy—literally. That enemy hurt this ranch and was coming to take it. What Denver didn't know was that I would protect his brother with my life. Hallow Ranch was Mason's home, whether he wanted to admit it or not. Therefore, I would protect it with my life as well.

Whatever it took.

Hallow Ranch and my husband would be safe from the bastard who took everything from me.

"Come inside," Denver grunted, breaking his glare to look up at Mase. "We've got a decade to catch up on." He turned to his cowboys. "Dining room."

"Fucking hell," Mase muttered under his breath. We watched in silence as everyone moved towards the big, welcoming house.

I twisted my neck to look back at Mase. He was pinching the bridge of his nose.

My mouth opened to say those three little words I hadn't uttered since he was in Spain, but I stopped myself. He hadn't said it back yet, and even though the need to hear those words from his mouth grew with each passing day, he had enough on his plate. So instead, I whispered, "I'll be right beside you, sweetie."

His head snapped up, his eyes flaring. "Don't fucking deserve you. You know that?" he murmured, moving towards me.

My heart skipped a beat, and the ring on my finger felt heavier than before. I spun my body to face him fully, my brows coming together. "Mase—

His hand shot out, grabbing me by the back of the neck, his fingers sinking into my curls as he yanked me to him. Our bodies collided as I let out a gasp, but it was cut off by his lips slamming down on mine with a desperate, pleading force that made my knees buckle. I felt his free arm band around my waist tightly as his tongue slipped between my lips.

We shouldn't be kissing like this, not in front of his family, but I was helpless. Mason Langston tasted like heaven, something I was never supposed to have in my life. It'd been too long.

Even though we were married, it wasn't consummated. He hadn't touched me aside from kissing over the last few weeks. I knew why. I wasn't stupid. He was afraid to touch me. Somewhere in the back of that beautiful, stubborn brain of his, he saw me as damaged goods. Between the travelling, running, and planning, I didn't have time—that was bull-shit. The truth was, I didn't want to think about why my husband, the man I'd hopelessly fallen in love with, didn't want to make love to me.

So, when he kissed me like *this*, I held on. I was greedy. I took everything he gave and demanded more. My arms wrapped around his neck as I tilted my head to the side, giving him more access—all of me.

He had all of me, damaged or not. I was his.

A growl left him, his grip tightening in my hair as he bit down on my bottom lip. Pleasure—white, hot, scorching pleasure—shot through my body, hardening my nipples as wetness began to pool between my thighs. I whimpered when he released my lip, his tongue stroking it gently as his lips moved in time with mine.

"God dammit," he growled, pulling away from me, dropping his arms.

"I'm sorry," I rasped, my cheeks heating again.

He shook his head. "Don't you ever be sorry for kissing me like that, baby."

I was speechless and aching as he lifted his chin to the house. "Let's go. I'm sure my brother is sick of watching me make-out with my wife."

Once we were up the porch steps, I heard it: the unmistakable sound of children laughing—boys. Valerie was at the door, holding it open on the other side of the screened one. "They are playing Star Wars, I believe," she said, laughing lightly.

I was grateful for her effort, but it wasn't necessary. No matter what she did, the conversation was going to be awkward as hell. I smiled at her anyways. "I love Star Wars," I noted as Mase pulled the screen door open and settled his hand on the small of my back.

"Everyone is in the dining room. Down the hall—"

"Grew up here, sweetheart," Mase reminded her from behind me, his chest against inches from my back. "Know where it is." His voice was tight.

Valerie blinked away whatever was on her face and straightened her shoulders. "Right. I'll be in there in a moment. I must see to my mom."

Right. Her mother and nurse were here too.

A full house.

I watched as she retreated to the right, heading into a living space. I heard Valerie's smooth voice, then a hushed reply before—

"What the hell do you mean Denver's brother is here?" a woman snapped.

"Get a move on, darlin'," Mase demanded, his voice still tight. He pressed his hand into the small of my back, forcing me to move. I complied, turning to the left. We bypassed a kitchen would be envious of for the rest of my days, before entering a hallway. Two steps in, the wall opened into a formal dining room, with a long table filled with cowboys.

I expected all eyes to go to my husband, but they landed on me instead. There were clearly twins, younger and rugged, sitting side by side. Standing in the corner by the window was another dark cowboy. He scared the shit out of me. Across from the twins sat Jigs and Beau. There was a seat at the head of the table, empty, just like the one beside it. Then, at the opposite end, there was a single empty chair.

I felt Mase's lips against the shell of my ear. "Down there, gorgeous."

There was no hesitation. I moved quickly in hopes that everyone would avert their eyes, but they didn't. Mase pulled out the chair, I took my seat, and silence fell over the room. Denver was nowhere to be found, perhaps upstairs, dealing with his son.

Eyes.

So many eyes on me.

Panic began to swim up from the depths, sent up by the monster. I folded my hands in my lap, missing my bottle. I'd left it the truck as a test for myself. I didn't want to be the weird girl. I didn't want to be broken. These people didn't know me. They didn't know my story, my history, my trauma, my triggers, or my fears. To them, I was just the red-headed girl Mason married. I was a stranger.

Hallow Ranch was, in a way, a clean slate for me.

I didn't want to be broken here.

I just wanted to be Harmony Langston.

My bottle was in the car, panic was surfacing, and eyes were on me.

One, two, three.

One, two, three.

One, two, three.

Red, blue, green.

Red, blue, green.

Red, blue, green.

You're safe with me.

You're safe with me.

You're safe with—

"You boys got three seconds to peel your eyes off my wife before I rip them out with my fucking fingers and shove them down your throats," Mase threatened from above me.

The panic stopped just under the surface of his demand. I held my breath, squeezing my hands tighter, ignoring the sudden itch in my throat. I needed my bottle, but I refused.

I refused to show weakness in front of these people. They would see me as one thing and one thing only: Mason's strong, supportive wife. That's why I was here: to, support him, to protect him and his home.

The panic inside was still waiting, waiting for a moment to break free and claim me, but I kept my eyes straight ahead on Denver's empty chair as the eyes studying me peeled away. All except for the man by the window. I didn't have to look to know he was staring, analyzing me. I heard Mason shift above me.

"That goes for you too, asshole," my husband growled, his hand landing on my shoulder. His voice was hard, but his touch was gentle—comforting.

"Enough," Denver barked as he walked into the room, his cowboy hat off. He had thick, dark, unruly hair, and it made him look even more striking. His boots clicked across the wooden floors slowly as he made his way to the head of the table, his eyes on Mason and me. Once he was seated, Valerie came in, her dark hair now piled high on top of her head.

"Sorry about that," she breathed.

My eyes went to the hall and back to her. "It's no problem. Thank you for inviting us into your home. It's beautiful," I praised her.

She took a seat beside Denver—her rightful place—and shook her head. "I haven't been here that long. You should be complimenting Den."

"Re-painted the kitchen," Mase noted from above me, his fingers flexing on my shoulder.

His brother nodded once. "Needed it. Cabinets were chipped."

Silence settled over the room, the tension thick.

"Oh, for fuck's sake," one of the twins growled, throwing up his hands and slamming them down on the table. I tried to hide my flinch, but I didn't go unnoticed. Beau caught it, his jaw tight as his brows came together. The twin pointed at me, his teeth bared. "Who are you and what the fuck do you have to do with Mo—"

"Don't say his fucking name!" The roar came from my bull rider, as he moved around my chair, his hand leaving my body. He stood over the table, his face twisted in a dark fury that sent shivers through my body. "Do. Not. Say. His. Name. In. Front. Of. Harmony."

"Mase," I whispered, all eyes on me again.

"Fine, I'll ask you a different question. Why, after a fucking decade, did you decide to show your face here?" the man growled.

"Lance," Denver warned.

Lance turned to face the ranch owner. "Nah, Den. I wanna know the reason. I wanna know why this bastard deserted his home—his brother."

Mase's head snapped to his brother's. "My nephew hers?" he asked, gesturing to Valerie. "How old is he?"

Denver looked pained for a second but didn't answer. A harsh laugh erupted from my husband. "Are you fucking kidding me?"

"Mase, please," Jigs begged. "You came to us."

"Yes, he did," I snapped before I could stop myself. All eyes came to me once more, but that was fine. I was getting angry. Angry at the piss-poor welcome home he received, the judgement in the cowboys' eyes, the resentment in Denver's behavior even though his eyes told a different story, and the secret of Caleb. I was so pissed, I rose to my feet, the chair screeching against the wood. I braced my hands on the table, my curls falling around me.

"The man who is trying to obtain Hallow Ranch is not a good man, and judging by the looks on your faces, you must know that. The fire that made national headlines a few months ago? It was him. Do you want to know how I know that?"

The table was silent. Beau and Jigs had their brows up, Valerie's hand was on Denver's forearm, her nails digging into this skin, the twins looked surprised at my outburst, and that man by the window was now standing closer to the table.

Grinding my teeth, I hissed, "Because I've seen first-hand the evil that man is capable of." My eyes snapped to Denver. "Your brother is here for you and for this ranch. He didn't need to come back, nor did he want to. Yet here he is!" I threw my arm out in the direction of my husband. "He's right here, and he's discovered that you have a son, been punched in the face, and judged by strangers." It was my turn to bark out a laugh. "I've never had a home. I didn't know what home was supposed to look like, not until I met Mason. My home isn't a structure with a roof, a green kitchen, or a big porch. My home is a person," I said, my voice cracking. "How dare you treat my home this way?"

"Little Song," Mase whispered.

I wasn't done.

Keeping my gaze on Denver, I finished, "Mason doesn't need Hallow Ranch. He hasn't for ten fucking years. He is the best bull rider in the world, worth millions of dollars. He did that on his own."

"I know that, sweetheart," Denver said softly.

"Then you must know he isn't here for your help. He is here for you. He is here for your ranch—*your home*," I returned, my rasp thicker than before.

"Damn, Mason. How in the hell did you land a woman like this?" Jigs asked. It wasn't a joke. He was being completely serious.

"I try not to question God's blessings, old man." A large, warm hand landed on my lower back. "Sit, baby. Please."

With a sigh, I took my seat and Mason announced, "Now that you know our intentions, tell us about the pipeline."

Valerie and Denver looked at each other, sharing a moment. When they looked back to the room, Valerie began with, "I'm a former em-ployee of...*his* pipeline."

Chapter Twenty-Eight

Houston, TX. Police Station.

"Mr. M—Moonie," Donald, stammered as a greeting, rising from his desk chair.

Tim held up his hand, an easy smile on his face. "How are you, old friend?"

The police chief was visibly sweating as he shook his head. He knew what was coming. Tim was glad the man wasn't that dumb, because he didn't want to waste time explaining himself. With a sigh, he asked, "I would assume you are doing awful, all things considered."

Donald held up his shaking hands, ready to beg for his life. "I'm sorry—I've done everything I could. We searched her apartment—man—managed to get a warrant. Took a few weeks, but we—"

Tim Moonie waved his hand, not caring about his excuses. "If I wanted Harmony's miniscule belongings, I would have obtained them myself."

The police chief paled. Rightfully so, considering he lost Moonie's perfect girl and the insufferable bull rider she was involved with. Tim should have been worried that Mason Langston would run back to his home—Hallow Ranch, but he didn't.

Mason Langston hated that land and his brother.

Tim knew his perfect girl wasn't a brave girl; that's why he liked her so much. She was timid, shy, and complacent—everything a man like himself needed. For a time, it was bliss. She would serve him during the day and scream during the night. His cock twitched at the thought of hearing her pain once more.

Soon.

Very soon.

Unfortunately, this little cat and mouse chase he'd been on for the last two months kept him in Houston. Tim didn't need to be in Houston; no, he needed to be back in Denver. Plans were being drawn up, engineers conducting meetings he had to attend via Zoom. It was infuriating. Tim, like his father, liked to be hands on during big projects like the Colorado pipeline.

When he didn't get what he wanted, anger overcame him, seeking a sweet release. His visit to Mr. Green, Harmony's father, was less than an hour ago. It was swift, but messy. Tim liked that. He liked the feel of blood on his fingers, almost like paint, and he'd left a masterpiece at the Green Mansion for his man to clean up.

As for the police chief, there were steps to be taken before Tim could unleash his fury. So, he took a seat, ignoring the fear in Donald's eyes as he crossed his legs.

"I find it funny," Moonie began, "that you love your family so much but yet, you give them the bare minimum in regard to protecting their lives."

Donald's lip quivered, tears gleaming in his eyes. "Please, Mr. Moonie. I did everything I could."

Tim looked at the ceiling. "You gave me information on a rodeo clown, Donald. Please, be serious. Now is not the time for games."

"That man was the one who bailed Mason Langston out of here the morning after his arrest. The two were very close, and I thought—sir, I thought that Eddie character could lead you to her," he cried, coming around the desk.

Irritation prickled over Moonie's skin under his navy suit. He clicked his tongue. "You were wrong." Tim's man followed the information, and it had led him to an old, abandoned ranch in West Texas, land his father was trying to claim back in the eighties.

"I'm sorry, Mr. Moonie," the man rasped, falling to his knees before Tim, utterly broken.

Tim smiled. "You aren't. You just don't want me to kill your family."

Donald looked to his office door, and back.

Moonie was impatient. Therefore, he pulled out a folded piece of paper from his suit and set it on the desk as he rose from his seat. "Follow the instructions and your family lives." Tim's hand shot out, wrapping around the Chief's throat as he bent down close to his face. "Don't, and I get to play with your wife after I kill your daughter."

Without another word, Moonie shoved the man to the ground and left the police station, ignoring the curious eyes of the officers in the bull pen. They knew better than to insert themselves in this kind of business. Ten minutes later, he was on his way to the air strip, disappointed he wasn't going to be able to bring his perfect girl to Colorado.

Tim had no other choice.

It was time to go back to Hallow Ranch.

Two Days Later. Hayden, CO.

Harmony

"Eddie," I rasped at the sight of a familiar face.

He flashed me a handsome, quirky smile as he slammed the door of his Ram. "Hi, Harmony."

His gentle voice made my knees wobble as my lip trembled, but I sucked it between my teeth so he wouldn't see, to hide the fact that I was falling apart, crumbling from the inside out. Eddie looked up to the building behind me, the shadow of his hat covering his face now. "Place looks haunted."

A soft laugh came from me. "I haven't seen any ghosts."

He walked up to the sidewalk. "Take it the family reunion didn't go to well," he guessed.

Yeah, there was no way I was hiding my trembling lip now. "You would be correct," I whispered, my voice shaking.

"Dammit, Harm," he muttered. "Come here." His arms opened wide, and I didn't hesitate. I needed something, and my Zoom calls with Garcia weren't cutting it anymore. I crashed into his solid frame, my arms wrapping around his waist as it hit me. Before I knew it, my body was shaking, and I was soaking his pearl snap with tears.

"My boy do something stupid?" he asked, hugging me back. He sighed. "Didn't want to kill him, but I will for hurting you."

No, Mason hasn't done anything stupid.

"It's been two days," I cried, holding on tighter.

"What's been two days, sweetheart?" he asked softly, his Texas twang sounding thicker.

"Since he left me here."

Eddie's back went rigid, the hand on my back stilling. "What?"

I pulled away from him, looking up to find the goofy, easy going man's eyes filling with a dark madness, his jaw hard. "Eddie..."

"Alright, Harmony. I'm going to need you to explain to me where he is. Better yet, give me the run down on everything," he ordered stepping away from me. He turned his head, looking down the street towards the shops, restaurants, and the town bar of Hayden. Then, he looked back up to the hotel. I'd been staying here, by myself, for the last forty-eight hours. I knew coming into this town was a risk for Mason, because he'd been through something here—something dark. His father put him through years of torturous abuse, and the last thing he needed was to come back here, the memories etched into his brain. I knew he was having a hard time; it was plain as day.

However, I didn't think that he would abandon me after the first visit to Hallow Ranch. We'd stayed up with Denver, Valerie, and the Hallow Ranch cowboys, listening to Valerie's story. Aside from her former employer trying to burn her alive, I thought the story of her and Denver was beautiful. After my outburst, Mase stayed close, keeping his hand on my shoulder as he stood above me.

All that changed when he got into his truck.

"Sweetie," I called as he pulled onto the gravel path, driving away from the beautiful home.

He plucked my water bottle off the center console and held it out to me, his other hand gripping the top of the steering wheel. "Drink, baby, please."

"But—"

His powerful gray eyes slid to me as he eased the truck to a stop. "Saw the panic in your eyes in there. Please. Drink."

Taking the bottle from him, I pulled the straw out and took a long drink. The cool water hit my throat, but it didn't provide the same relief as it once did. It wasn't what I needed right now.

Right now, I needed to know what was going on inside my bull rider's head.

"Are you okay?" I asked softly.

"Nope."

My chest ached. "Do you want to talk about it?"

"No, darlin', I don't."

I tried not to let those words get to me, but they did. I'd practically opened my chest up and let him see my bruised, healing heart, then offered it to him on a cracked platter, and he was shutting me out.

Knowing only part of what he'd been through, I couldn't be mad. My trauma was my own, and his was his, plain and simple. He came back after a decade; he came back to his childhood home to help save it. I felt it in my soul that even if I wasn't in the picture, he would've come. He would've seen the news coverage about the fire and booked the first flight.

My eyes went back to him. His jaw was tight, the gold band on his finger shining from the lights on the dash, his eyes on the road leading back into the little town. He needed comfort, and for the second time tonight, I wanted to say those three little words.

But I couldn't.

He had too much on his plate and I was just being sensitive. Tomorrow, I would call Dr. G.

Ten minutes later, we pulled into the small town, passing a diner, an Asian restaurant, a post office, small clothing boutiques, and a bar before pulling up to the hotel. We'd been driving all day, heading straight for the ranch. I called ahead of time and booked a room for a week. I didn't know how long we'd be here, and the man that I could extend my stay if needed.

Mason swung his truck into a parking spot in front of the old brick building. Wordlessly, he got out and rounded the hood. He pulled open my door and said, "Come on, Harm. I know you're tired."

Yes, I was tired, but I was more concerned about him. "I know you are, too," I noted softly, hopping down.

He lifted his chin to the door. "Go on and check in. I'll get the bags," he ordered, turning away from me. I swallowed the lump forming in my throat, clutching my bottle tighter as I headed for the front door.

After opening the wooden double doors, I was greeted with warm light and the smell of cinnamon. The faint sound of snoring came from behind the check in desk. I crossed the old, cream, tiled floors to discover an older gentleman asleep in a chair. The overalls-clad man had his arms crossed over his chest, head back, mouth open.

I didn't want to startle him, so I cleared my throat.

Nothing. Just a snore.

My eyes found the bell to the left of me, and I reached out and tapped it. The man snored again, his white whiskers moving with his nose.

"Sir?" I called.

"Bart, get your old ass up. We're fucking tired," Mason barked from behind me. I jumped, letting out a yelp. The old man shot up from his position, his head jerking from left to right. "Who? What? Officer, it wasn't me!" he shouted.

"Old fucking geezer," my husband grumbled as he came to stand beside me. "Bart!"

Bart blinked and looked up at us. His eyes widened at the sight of me, but I thought they were about to come out of his skull when they landed on Mase.

"The legend returns," he boasted, standing up as a weary smile spread across his face. He held out his hand over the counter. "Welcome home, Mason."

Mase visibly stiffened, his jaw jumping out of the corner of my eye. My hand slid down and grabbed his. His fingers instantly folded with mine, making my heart skip a beat.

"Bart," he greeted. "My wife called earlier and booked a room."

The old man looked at my husband for a moment, trying to see if he could get past those walls.

Trust me, Bart. You can't. I've tried.

"Right. Well then, let's get you folks fixed up!"

Ten minutes later, Mason opened the room door and guided me inside. It was small but cozy, with a large bed and a little desk. I stood off to the side as he carried in the bags, set them on the desk, and checked the bathroom. When he was done with that, he turned to me, his eyes flashing. He stalked towards me, and I retreated, my back hitting the wall.

Immediately, he braced his hands on either side of my head, bending down so he was in my space. "You were amazing tonight," he stated, his voice gruff.

"It wasn't a performance," I reminded him. I meant every single word. Mason was my home.

His throat bobbed as his eyes dropped to my lips. I wanted him to kiss me again, like he did earlier. I wanted his lips on mine, his tongue demanding attention as his arms closed around me. I wanted his body against me. I wanted him inside me.

I wanted us to be the way it was before I told him about my abuse.

I wanted him to treat me like a human being instead of a glass doll.

I wanted to be normal.

I wanted my husband to fuck me.

"Mase," I pleaded, cupping his face.

His eyes closed as his nostrils flared. "Harmony."

My heart felt heavy. "Please, don't shut me out. I know this is hard for you and—"

"Little Song, stop."

I pulled my hand from him immediately. His eyes opened, and I saw regret. Before I could speak, he whispered, "Need you to rest. I have to go."

A chill skated across my skin. "Go?" I parroted.

He pushed off the wall, adjusted his cowboy hat, and headed for the door. "I'll be back, darlin'. Just gotta clear my head for a bit." The door opened and closed before I could utter a single syllable.

Eddie stared at me, pity in his eyes. "Harmony, you have to understand—"

"I heard him, Eddie," I interrupted. "I heard the pain in his voice and saw that fucking scar on his back." Every time I thought about it, I wanted to bring John Langston back from the dead and kill him myself.

It wasn't like me to have such thoughts. I wasn't a violent person, but I would be anything that Mason needed me to be, and right now, he needed me to be a good wife. That's why I called Eddie, and, lucky for me, he was on standby in Denver.

"Know that, sweetheart, but you haven't known him long," he started, lifting his bag up. "Been watching that man since he was just a young buck, when he was pissed at the world. Hated everything in it, Harmony. Saw it in his eyes."

I looked down to my Docs, tears stinging my eyes. I was so tired of crying, but at least now, I wasn't crying over my pain. I was crying over Mason's.

Which was worse.

Eddie muttered a curse before calling my name. When I looked up at him again, he was standing closer, in my space once more. His eyes held mine as he told me something that rocked me to my core.

"The first time Mason got bucked off...it was bad. Luckily, we weren't at a huge location, and it wasn't broadcast on TV. This rodeo was for charity or some shit like that. I can't remember. It was about nine years ago," he explained, his voice serious. "That monster threw him off, and he landed on his back."

I waited, picturing the man I loved on his back in the dirt.

Eddie sighed. "Harmony, he was awake. Saw it plain as day. He was breathing, but he didn't move. The bull turned around, ready to charge, and Mason didn't move."

My throat began to burn.

"We were trying to get the bull into the pit, but it was too late. He'd already taken off. I was too far away, running for Mason's life, but he didn't move. He was staring up at the blue sky, and I could've sworn I saw that crazy man smile."

"No," I croaked, shaking my head. "Don't say it."

"At the last second, he jumped to his feet and ran for the fence. The bull missed him by the skin of his teeth. After that, something changed in him. He became even more addicted to riding. During the off-season, he was practicing with the local bulls in Tennessee. He never stopped."

"I think coming here was a mistake," I confessed.

Eddie looked down the street again. "Coming home is never a mistake, not for a cowboy. Trust me on that." With that, he turned on his heels, walked to his truck, and tossed his bag in the back. Then, he looked at me, jerking his head to the passenger door. "Get in."

"Where are we going?"

The rodeo clown gave me a handsome smile. "I've always wanted to see Hallow Ranch."

I didn't have my bottle; it was up in the room. This was it, the test to see if I was strong enough.

I looked to the sky and whispered, "You aren't alone in this, Mason."

Then, I got in the truck, my water bottle sitting on the desk in our hotel room.

I didn't need it anymore.

Chapter Twenty-Nine

Harmony

"God dammit," Eddie muttered as we came to a stop. My head snapped up.

"What?" I asked, eyes going wide as I stared at him.

He was looking straight ahead. "This ranch looks a hundred times better than mine, and it pisses me off," he grumbled, shutting off the vehicle.

My eyes followed his, and sure enough, he was right. Hallow Ranch was a slice of heaven. When I was here the other night, I couldn't take in its beauty. There was a large red barn with a black metal roof down the hill adjacent to the house. Next to the barn was a smaller building, matching in color. My head turned and I looked past the buildings to the lush, green pasture, then to the mountain beyond it. My heart ached at the sight. Half of it was scorched from the fire *he* caused.

I hated *him*.

Oh, how I fucking hated that *man*.

Eddie whistled low. "Damn shame."

"Agreed," I bit out.

He looked at me. "Mother nature knows how to heal herself; don't worry about it too much." He looked towards the house. "Now, let's go find your husband."

"I don't think he's here, Ed."

He opened his door and shot me a look. "He's here, Harmony. Not at the house, not in the barn, not with the cowboys, but he's on this land. Trust me."

I really had no other choice in the matter.

We were almost to the steps of the house when I heard her.

"You must be what all the fuss is about," a rich voice called.

My head snapped up to find a beautiful African American woman in deep green scrubs staring at us. She rose from the swing and gave us her back. She spoke lowly for a moment before turning back to us and walking to the top of the steps.

This must be Valerie's mother's nurse.

"Hi, I'm Harmony—"

The woman laughed. "Oh, I know. Trust me, sugar." She looked at Eddie, her brown eyes scanning him from cowboy hat to toe. "Nancy, I've made my decision. I'm moving to Colorado."

I looked at Eddie, my brows coming together. He wasn't looking at me. No, he was looking at the nurse, awe-struck.

"You got a name, handsome?" the woman called.

Ed shook his head. "Perfectly fine with you calling me that for the rest of your life, ma'am."

The woman blinked. "Val! Get out here before I do something reckless and marry a cowboy!

"Ew! Are you going to marry Beau?" a young voice shouted from inside the house. A second later, a little boy the spitting image of Denver Langston emerged, a Harry Potter book tucked under his arm and a glass of red liquid in his hands. He sat the book and his juice on the railing. "I mean, that's fine, but I don't want to see you and him kissing all the time like Dad and Val do."

This was Caleb—Mason's nephew.

The woman looked down at boy, smiling. "Beau is already spoken for, kid."

"Lucky me," Eddie muttered.

I didn't have time for this. "I'm looking for Mason," I declared.

Valerie stepped out of the house wearing a lilac dress, drying her hands with a dish towel. Caleb looked at me as he jumped down the steps.

"Uncle Mason?"

Had they met already?

Did Mason come back to meet him?

"He's not here," Valerie informed us, stepping down and putting her hand on Caleb's shoulder.

The little boy looked confused, tilting his head to the side. "Do you know Uncle Mason?"

"Yes," I rasped, nodding.

His little gray eyes dropped down to the ring on my finger. "You my aunt?" he called out, shrugging Valerie's hand off his shoulder and stepping forward.

For a moment, I thought he was mad at me—at us.

Then, he broke into a run and collided with me seconds later, his small arms wrapping around my waist, knocking the wind out of me. "Oh," I gasped, raising my arms.

Caleb's face was pressed into my stomach, his apology muffed. "It's so nice to meet you. Welcome to the ranch!" he shouted with glee as he pulled away from me, offering me a child-like smile that felt like a knife in my gut.

Blinking away the potential tears, I smiled at him. "I'm Harmony."

"Dang, you have a pretty name, too. Just like Val," he said looking back to see Valerie and the nurse approaching. "And pretty hair."

"You know Denver's brother?" the nurse asked me, her brown eyes guarded.

"She married the son of a bitch, gorgeous, so yeah, she knows him," Eddie answered for me, his eyes on her.

She turned to him, crossing her arms and raising a brow. "Don't cuss around me, handsome," she ordered.

Eddie smirked and took off his hat. "A bad habit I intend to break for you."

"Jackie, you cuss all the time," Caleb noted. "You cuss more than Mags and the twins."

"Don't matter one lick to me," Eddie murmured. "You don't want me cussing, then I won't...Jackie."

Here we were, trying to find Mase, and Eddie was chasing some tail. I refrained from rolling my eyes and looked at Valerie.

"Is Denver around, Valerie? Maybe I can talk to him?" I asked, my eyes drifting down toward the barn.

"He's out in pasture four with the boys today," she answered. "And call me Val, Harmony."

I didn't give a response, because I wasn't sure if I would ever get to know her well enough to call her by a nickname.

"We figured you two left town."

My head snapped back towards her. "Why would you think that?" I asked.

Valerie looked confused. "Harmony, we haven't seen or spoken to Mason since you two left the other night."

Eddie and I exchanged a look.

"Is Uncle Mason in trouble?" Caleb asked, worry in his voice.

My stomach sank.

Where the hell was he?

Eddie shifted closer to me, throwing his arm around my shoulders. "Well, since we're family now, how about a tour?" he asked, working his charm by adding a handsome grin.

"And you remember Jigs," Valerie said, as we approached the intimidating red barn at the same time Jigs emerged. He was dressed in faded wranglers, boots, a cream hat, and a blue flannel.

Shock was evident on his face. "Harmony. It's good to see you again," he greeted kindly. Almost too kind. Something was off. I could feel it in my bones.

An awkward silence settled between us as a hawk flew over, its cry carrying through the summer heat. The chill that settled over me was a stark contrast to the sun above us. A breeze flew around us, rustling the tops of the trees behind the barn and at the end of the pasture. I put my hand to my forehead, covering my eyes from the sun. Before I opened my mouth to speak, Eddie cut me off once again.

"Valerie, is that the bunk house?" he asked, pointing to the small red building.

Her green eyes met mine for half a second before nodding. "Yes, that's where the boys stay. Caleb likes to stay there sometimes as well," she explained.

Eddie whistled again. "That sure is a big one. Mind if I have a look? I'm a rancher, just bought some land, and I'm looking to build," the rodeo clown lied through his teeth. He already had a bunk house, and two ranch hands who kept things in order when he was travelling with PBR.

God, Eddie was the best kind of friend to have. He reminded me so much of Billie in that way.

"Of—of course. That alright with you, Jigs?" Valerie looked at him, but he was still looking at me, his brows knitting together slowly. He nodded once, and when they were out of ear shot, I went straight for it.

"Have you heard from Mason by chance?" I asked, my voice thick.

The old man's throat bobbed. "Nope."

I saw right through him. "You're lying, Jigs," I stated, frustration building inside my chest.

He took off his hat and ran his hand over his balding head, mumbling something I couldn't hear. I took a step closer. Jigs was hiding something, and that pissed me off. Mason needed me.

"Jigs. Where is my husband?" I demanded. His blue eyes met mine, and I gritted my teeth. "He left me at the hotel two days ago, Jigs. Now, I don't know what in the fuck is going on at this Hell Ranch. I don't know about all the darkness from Mase's childhood, but I do know his father beat him—"

Jigs' eyes widened. "Harmony—"

He wasn't expecting that, and frankly, neither was I. Still, I pressed on, advancing towards him, my Docs crunching the gravel underneath me as he backed into the barn. His eyes avoided mine, looking behind me. That was fine. His ear couldn't avoid me. "I know that evil, vile man *beat* the man *I love* for years—tortured him for years, and his brother stood by and *did nothing*!"

Jigs winced, holding out his hand to me. "Sweetheart—"

I shook my head, pointing at him. "Do not call me that! Do not attempt to use your cowboy sweet talk on me! I'm not some fucking weak, insignificant woman. You know nothing of the hell I've been through, but I know you're lying! You kept in contact with him for the last decade, Jigs! He's close to you!" My raspy voice echoed throughout the empty barn, cracking at the end. I hadn't been this loud in years. Then again, I didn't have a reason to scream until now.

"Where is my husband?" I shouted.

"Fighting his demons the only way he knows how," he answered softly.

Mase didn't need to fight them alone anymore. He helped me fight mine, and I was damn sure going to help him fight his.

"Where?" I hissed.

He put his hat against his chest. "In the second barn, sweetheart."

I didn't have time for questions. "Take me to him."

"Harmony, he—"

"Jigs, he is my husband. I am his wife. Let me do what I need to do!" I ordered.

"Before you go," a deep voice rumbled from behind me, "tell me again how my brother was abused by our father as I stood by and did *nothing.*"

Everyone seemed to be here except for the one person I wanted. Spinning on my heel, I turned around and was greeted by Denver, standing by a beautiful brown steed. He was dressed in dark wranglers, a dirty, white T-shirt, and his black cowboy hat. His grey eyes lifted from my face to Jigs. "You and I need to have a conversation."

"Denver..."

"Take Ranger," Denver barked, handing the reigns to him. Then he looked down at me. "Talk. Now."

God, this man was an asshole. "That doesn't work on me, Mr. Langston," I snapped.

He bit off a curse and looked to the bunk house, his eyes narrowing on Eddie. "That man with you, or do I get to shoot him?"

"You shoot Eddie, I shoot you," I warned, standing up on my toes, getting in his face.

After a moment, a ghost of a smirk appeared on Denver's face. "Alright, sis. Stand down."

Sis.

"Take me to the second barn," I ordered, ignoring the warmth in that word.

"You ride?"

"No."

"Okay, then I'll take you on the four-wheeler. Ranger's had a long day, and he needs his rest," he explained. Great, he was an asshole who cared about his horse.

"Rather have Jigs take me," I said.

"Considering you just ripped that man a new asshole, I'll be the one to take you to your husband." He dipped his head, his eyes bright under the shadow of his hat. "That alright with you? Or would you like to rip me a new asshole for something I just learned?"

The breath from my lungs escaped me, and I staggered back a step. "What?"

Denver didn't give me a second to process. " I didn't stutter."

"You didn't know?" I whispered. How could someone not know what went down in their own house?

The cowboy's bearded jaw tightened, making him look more dangerous than before. He reached out, his rough hand landing on my bare shoulder. "Pop would have been dead if I knew."

"He *is* dead," I quipped. Rotting in hell, too, probably.

"Of old age, Harmony. If I'd known about Mase..." He trailed off, dipping his voice low. "Pop's ashes would have been spread on my mountain." He raised a tanned arm, pointing at the charred piece of nature in the distance. I don't know what that meant, but I knew it wasn't good. "I'm going to take you to Mason. You do what you need to, and then once you're both ready, I want you both back at the house."

"Did you know he was here?"

He shook his head, dropping his hand. Sighing he answered, "No, Harmony, I didn't. Thought you both left town after hearing Val's story."

I looked at the mountain, the lush pasture, and the herd that wasn't there a few minutes ago. When I looked back to Denver, he was holding out his hand for me to take. "You can trust me," he said softly.

I eyed his hand. "How can I?"

In an instant, he took my hand, holding my eyes with his. "Evergreen is Mason's biggest sponsor, correct?"

It was. "Yes," I confirmed slowly.

"Hallow Ranch is the owner of Evergreen. Mason's biggest sponsor is me."

Chapter Thirty

Mason

"Come on, you bastard!" I screamed down at the bull. "That all you got?"

The beast huffed, bucking again. It wasn't enough, though, as I held, steadfast and ready. The scenery around me was a blur as he kicked, thrashed, and spun me around. My hand tightened on my bull rope, my other hand in the air as the sky above began to darken.

There was a storm coming and I was in the center of it, riding a beast, in desperate search of peace.

Just eight seconds.

That's all I fucking needed.

I'd been here for two fucking days, riding this pissed off bull. No matter how many times I mounted him, my peace never came. He bucked again, sending me forward, but my thighs tightened at his sides. With a growl, I rose back up, my body aching from the stress. I closed my eyes, but all I saw was Denver, the cowboys, Moonie, Momma, Harmony.

My sweet, sweet little song.

I just wanted peace, for fuck's sake.

"Dammit!" I roared, letting go of the rope as the bull bucked again. Hitting the ground, I rolled onto my back and jumped to my feet. The monster charged after me, and I ran to the other end of the pen, hopping over the metal fence just in time for his head to collide with the bars.

As my chest heaved, I turned to face him, his black eyes filled with rage, nostrils flared out as he rammed again. I looked from him to the empty pasture behind me. Hallow Ranch didn't own this bull—I did. Bulls like this were specifically trained to throw sons of bitches like me off, and they normally didn't have these conditions.

He was calmer now, pacing the pen. I pulled off my hat and pointed at him with it. "You stay away from the heifers, ya hear? No hanky panky on Hallow Ranch." The animal huffed, preparing to charge at me again.

I cursed under my breath, knowing this was a stupid idea, but right now, I didn't care. Unlatching the lock, I threw the gate open and hopped on the fence. The bull charged for his afternoon of freedom, leaving me alone.

I pulled my legs up, rested my boots on the second railing, and leaned forward on my knees. For two days, I'd been acting like a madman, searching for something I'd clearly lost. I didn't know why. My mind drifted to Harmony.

A wife I didn't deserve.

A woman I'd left in a fucking hotel room for two fucking days.

I bent my head, squeezing my eyes shut. "What the fuck is wrong with me?"

Nothing, sweet Mase.

Great, Momma's voice was back in my head.

I was losing my mind and I didn't know how to stop it. From the moment I stepped foot on this ranch, I'd been having flashbacks of Pop, hearing his voice, seeing his face. I didn't want that evil touching Harmony.

She was too good to be touched by his darkness.

The low hum of an engine had my head snapping up. In the distance, I saw my brother on a four-wheeler, heading straight for me. The organ in my chest skipped a beat when I saw bright auburn curls flying over his shoulder. I bit down, grinding my teeth hard.

What the fuck?

Denver came to a stop about twenty feet away before he helped Harm down, his hand in hers. The sight of her made me feel like more of an ass. She was dressed in a white tank top, and a long black skirt that had little white polka dots on it. My baby was also wearing her Docs, because she didn't go anywhere without them.

There was something missing.

Her bottle.

Fuck me, where was her bottle?

"Mason," Denver greeted.

Harmony ignored him and came straight for me, running as fast as she could, tears in those precious blues. I hopped down from the fence, panic crawling over my skin.

"Baby, what—"

She slammed into me, and her arms wrapped around my neck. "Mase," she croaked into my shoulder as I banded my arms around her.

"What's wrong?" I demanded. My eyes sliced to Denver's. "What did you do?" I growled.

He looked pained. "Apparently, not enough," he murmured, his voice thick.

I flinched, my spine stiffening.

Harm lifted her head and looked behind her. "Go, Denver. Please," she begged.

He took a step forward, wanting to say more, but she cut him off. "I need to do what I need to do."

My brother nodded, looking toward the barn, a new addition to Hallow Ranch. I'd listened to his voicemail about that bad winter. I'd heard the pain in his voice and the desperation.

It went ignored for years.

"This is your home, Mase," he said, his voice carrying across the distance. "Always was and always will be."

My grip tightened on Harmony's waist.

"I'll see you back at the house. Be careful; storm's coming."

I remained still, my wife clinging to me as I watched him and the four-wheeler disappear into the distance.

"You wanna explain what the hell is going on?" I asked her, my voice low.

She pulled back from me and I set her back on her feet. "You left me," she whispered softly.

I expected anger, but I was getting something entirely different.

Her hands slid from the back of my neck to my face, cupping my jaw, her thumbs stroking my scruff. "Mase."

It was a whisper.

A plea, for something that I didn't know how to give.

My hands gripped her wrists, and I gently pulled her away from me. I couldn't handle her touch right now, not when I was so fucking deprived of it. "I'm sorry, darlin'," I muttered. She had no idea how sorry I was, how much I wanted to kiss her pink lips and show her how much I cared for her. How much I fucking loved—

"I bared my soul to you," she said, shaking her head. She brushed past me and went into the bull pen. I followed.

I would follow her anywhere, even when I shouldn't.

The ring on her finger was like a beckon as she held out her arms, doing a slow spin. "This is where you run to. You have for years, Mase. I understand that. Trust me, I know safe spaces better than anyone, but you must know that you don't have to run here anymore."

"This isn't your music room, Harm," I scoffed.

Her music and my riding were two very different things.

My wife's eyes flared as she brought her hands down. "If you think that room is my only safe space, then you haven't been paying attention."

I swallowed down the lump in my throat, fisting my hands at my sides.

"Why did you leave me at the hotel?" she demanded.

Shaking my head, I denied her. "Not doing this here, Harmony."

The sky above us darkened, the random storm looming over us now. "If not here, then when and where, Mason?" she snapped. "Stop shutting me out!"

"Darlin', don't piss me off," I warned, stepping closer to her.

"Be pissed off, Mase! Be angry! Be sad! Be something! You have a right to feel! You have a right to—"

Thunder clapped in the distance. "You think I don't feel shit?" I barked.

She shook her head. "Not around me you don't."

I scoffed again, a harsh laugh coming from somewhere deep in my chest. "Baby, you have no idea what I feel around you. You have no idea the restraint I've had to exhibit around you!"

My woman raised her chin. "You haven't fucked me in weeks."

At her words, my blood ran ice cold. At the sight of her bottom lip trembling, I felt a knife in my gut, twisting in an unforgivable way. She didn't stop there.

"You put your momma's ring on my finger, but you haven't made love to me. You rarely kiss me. Some days, I think you can't stand the sight of me, because when I look your way, you look elsewhere!"

"Baby..."

Harmony shook her beautiful head once more as a tear trailed down her freckled cheek. I watched, uncertain of which hit her tank top first: her tear or the raindrop. The storm had arrived, ready to unravel and cleanse this land. "Do you even want this?"

"What?" I breathed, my brows lifting.

What the fuck was she talking about?

She was all I wanted; from the moment I saw her in that hallway, she consumed me. The breath in my lungs was for her. The beating of my heart was for her. Everything I'd done since then had been for her. How could she not see that?

Let them go, Mase. Let your demons out.

"After you and your brother take care of Tim fucking Moonie, do you still want this—*us—me?*"

She said his name.

"Don't you speak his name," I growled, closing in on her. We stood in the middle of the pen now, thunder clapping again—this time near us. My hands grabbed either side of her head and I bent down to get to her level. "His name doesn't deserve to be on your lips. His name doesn't deserve to be heard from your angelic voice. You don't speak that name, you understand me? I don't care what you've overcome, darlin'. He doesn't get a single part of you, got me?"

"Mase," she whimpered.

"Yeah, you say my name, all day long, all night long. You hear me?" I clipped.

Raindrops were falling around us now, hitting like ice against my skin, the day's heat slipping away.

"He's the reason my voice is this way."

Didn't give a fuck how we found him—when we did, I knew I was going to be the one to kill him. I would be the one to make him scream.

"You shut me out, Mase. When I bared everything to you...you shut me out and treated me like the one thing I don't want to be," my wife croaked, the pain in her voice heavy.

"What's that?" I whispered, hating myself.

"Damaged."

I let go of her then, backing away. "You aren't damaged, Harmony Langston."

"Don't use that last name if you have no intention of letting me keep it!" she cried.

In a flash, just as quick as the lightning above us, I was on her, backing her up until she was against the metal bars of the pen. My hand shot out before I could stop it, gripping her throat but not squeezing. "Oh, I have every intention of letting you keep my last name, Mrs. Langston," I hissed darkly. "Just like I had every intention of fucking you in the hallway of your apartment the first time I kissed you. Wanted to tear off your clothes and sink my cock into what's mine, but I couldn't. Do you know why?"

Desire flared in her eyes, and she whimpered my name.

"Because you were healing—still are," I growled.

She had nothing to say, nothing to give—she'd given herself to me completely already. It was time I gave her a piece of me.

"I've been out here for the last two days, riding a fucking bull, trying to chase after my eight seconds."

"Eight seconds?" she parroted, her hands coming to my sides, clinging to my damp T-shirt.

"My eight seconds of fucking peace," I answered, my voice hard.

Understanding washed over her features, followed by pity. "Sweetie—"

My upper lip curled. "Don't need or want your pity, Harm. Never have."

She shut her mouth. I didn't.

"Been chasing after my eight seconds for ten fucking years. It's like a drug. When I'm on the back of a bull, my head is silent. I don't hear Pop. I don't hear Denver. Nothing. I'm just a man on a bull. I'm not some piece of shit brother who deserted his home. I'm not the rebel rider of the PBR. I'm not a playboy. I'm just a cowboy. I just needed my eight seconds, and then I would have been good."

"And for the last two days? What have you been?" Her raspy voice was gentle now, her lips an inch from mine.

"A piece of shit husband."

Harm shook her head, her hands climbing the length of my torso. "No—"

"The only other time I've found peace is with you—being inside you," I informed her. "Been trying so fucking hard to be the gentleman you deserve, the kind of man you want."

"Don't. Don't try to..."

Another flash of lightning came, followed by a clap of thunder. Then, the sky opened, letting down a maelstrom of raindrops, coming faster and harder than before, roaring around us. My jaw tightened, my hand flexing on her throat. "Don't."

"Find your peace with me," she begged, her blue eyes bright in the gray that surrounded us. "You're my peace, Mase." Her hands moved to my forearm, gripping it, and pulling it towards her so my hand put more pressure on her throat. "You don't need to restrain yourself around me anymore."

"Don't—"

"I trust you," she whispered, her nails digging into my arm. I didn't feel the rain hitting my skin, the sound of it pelting down around us, the earth beneath us shaking as lightning struck the ground, the wind whistling, thunder cracking the sky. All I could hear, see, and feel was my little song.

The darkness inside of me smiled.

"You want me to unleash on you, huh?" I growled, pressing my body against hers. She nodded, and my control *snapped.*

Chapter Thirty-One

Harmony

The storm around us didn't compare to the one brewing in my husband's eyes. His was darker, stronger, and far more dangerous.

I trusted him completely. I belonged in his storm, where I felt the safest.

After years of misery, of dragging around the ghost of the chains that once bounded me, I felt free. "I trust you," I whispered as I pressed his hand harder against my throat.

Mason's dark cowboy hat loomed over his face, shielding his beauty from the rain, making him look more beautiful than words could describe. I knew what those three little words meant to him, to us. They were just as important, just as heavy as the other three words. His soaked shirt clung to his muscles, outlining every dip and curve of his abdomen and chest, making him appear god-like. He bared his teeth, closing the distance between our bodies, the contact making me feel alive.

"You want me to unleash on you, huh?" he growled, his fingers pressing into my flesh. My body hummed with excitement, a basic, raw need shooting through me, heading straight to my core.

"I'm yours," I rasped.

That's when he did to me.

He brought me back to life after weeks of doubt.

White light flashed before my eyes, thunder boomed, and Mase's lips crashed down onto mine with a force stronger than anything I'd ever known. He held me in place as his lips ravaged mine, his tongue dominant and demanding as he pushed in. My tongue touched his, and we both moaned, desire coursing through our veins. His teeth nipped and pulled, sending zaps of pleasure straight to my clit. My nipples were hard from the chill of the rain, aching for his heated touch and his overwhelming mouth. My knees buckled as his other hand came around to my ass, palming a cheek roughly.

My head was yanked back by his fistful of my hair, exposing my neck to him. He dove in, his scruff rubbing and burning against my wet skin as he sunk his teeth in, a delicious pain pulsing through me. I cried out, and he pressed himself further into me, his hard cock against my belly. "This is what you do to me, Harmony," he taunted darkly, his lips hovering above my neck.

"Alive," I rasped, gripping his biceps, arching into him.

He knew me. He knew what I meant. "Yeah, I know, baby. You make me feel alive. Been dead for ten fucking years," he clipped. Immediately, he shoved his thick, jean-clad thigh between my legs, causing my skirt to ride up. I was famished for release, for his touch, for his power to obliterate me wholeheartedly, for his *love*.

"Drove me mad not knowing your name. Drove me mad watching you in your window, night after night, teasing me with those cute little pajamas. Wanted to kick your door in and fuck you on the floor like the little whore you are. Mark you, claim you, fill you over and over, again and again until your legs gave out," he grunted, kissing my skin, his lips trailing up my neck. His hand on my ass dragged up to my hip, his fingers digging in. My husband pulled me up and down against his thigh shamelessly, building an addicting friction against my throbbing clit. I whimpered, clinging to him and moving my hips faster.

"Fucking my leg in the rain," he murmured. "Needy little *wife.*"

I gasped, shoving my hands under his hat, pushing it backwards. My fingers snaked into his hair and pulled his face up to meet mine. We collided again, the walls we'd built to protect ourselves from the world crumbling, the dust around us settling as we devoured each other.

Our pain didn't matter when we were together like this.

His hat fell back, but he caught it and settled it on my head before gripping my throat again. "Gonna fuck you every day for here on out; morning, afternoon, nighttime, whatever. Don't care, darlin'. I'm going to fill my wife up every single fucking day," he promised, his voice rough. "You good with that?"

"Yes, yes!" I cried, moving my hips faster. There was too much fabric between us. "Mase, please," I rasped, kissing him again as thunder rumbled around us.

Releasing me, he spun me around to face the fence, bending me at the waist, and placing my hands on the top metal bar, which was eye level with me now. His lips found my ear. "I'm done holding back with you, Little Song," he clipped. "You want all of me? Here I fucking am."

"Yes, sweetie," I breathed, arching back so my ass could grind against his hard, bulging crotch. "All of you."

"Keep your hands right there," he ordered, releasing me. I did as I was told, gripping the railing tightly. I heard him move behind me, and then, he was gone.

I trust him.

I trust him.

My hands were on a metal bar in the middle of a thunderstorm, and I trusted him.

You're safe with me.

A second later, he was back, his hand gripping my left wrist. Something rough brushed against my skin, and then he moved to do the same to my other hand.

He was tying me to the bull pen...in the middle of a storm.

His arm wrapped around my mid-section, his hand splaying over my stomach.

"Still trust me, baby?"

Chest heaving, heart pounding, I twisted my neck to find him staring at me, his eyes dark and wild. *Untamed.* This was the man who was trying water himself down for me.

I didn't want the watered-down version of Mason Langston.

I wanted the good, the bad, and the ugly, every single day for the rest of my life.

"From the moment I saw you," I whispered, my eyes stinging. My husband kissed me hard then, showing me without words how grateful he was.

His hands were at my thighs a second later, pulling up the slick fabric of my wet skirt, bunching it at my waist, exposing me. With a rough tug, my panties were pulled free from my body, only making me more impatient. I was dripping for him, ready to be claimed, ready to be his peace. His eyes held mine as he worked his belt, the rain continuing to pour down on us.

We didn't give a shit.

This was us.

Broken but complete. Together.

Without warning, I felt the head of his thick cock against my entrance, his rough hands on my hips. This would be the moment where he would tell me that if it got to be too much, I would just have to tell him to stop, and he would. He didn't do that. He didn't say anything to me. He just waited.

"Take me," I begged, straining against the knots at my wrists.

With a growl, he thrusted into me, filling me in the most blissful, stunning, and glorious way. I tossed my head back as a guttural cry left me, my pussy quivering around his length.

"Fuck, yes," he groaned, pulling out and snapping his hips, filling me again, over and over. The sound of our skin slapping was louder than the thunder. I wanted more—needed more.

Moving my hips back to meet each of his thrusts, I moaned his name. His cock hit that beautiful spot inside me each time, bringing me closer and closer to my peak. "Yes! Mason, yes!"

I felt his body heat on my back, his hand wrapping around my throat as I felt his scuff against my ear. "Look at you, Harmony," he groaned. "I wish you could see what I see, my good little wife taking my cock anywhere she can get it." His pace was unrelenting, his breath harsh in my ear, his cock stretching me in the most delicious way.

My eyes rolled back in my head as the pleasure overwhelmed me. "I'm—Mase!"

With another growl, his hand left my throat and went to my tank, yanking the front of it down roughly so my breasts were free, bouncing with each powerful thrust. His rough hand engulfed one, squeezing hard. "You my wife?" he clipped.

"Yes!"

"Is this my cunt?"

"Yes!"

"You gonna let me fuck her any way I want? Hm?" he taunted.

I gasped, pleasure rippling through me. I was close, so wonderfully close. His hand snapped back to my throat, his thrusts halted. I whined. "No, no, no! Please, please!"

Thunder clapped again.

"I asked you if you were going to let me fuck my little, sweet, beautiful cunt any way I want. Answer me," he barked, turning my face towards his, our lips inches apart.

I nodded. "Any way you want," I confirmed, breathless.

He pulled out and slowly eased his way back in. "Such a good little whore for me," he whispered. A moan left me, and he groaned deeply in approval. "You missed your cowboy's dick, darlin'?"

"So much," I rasped. I missed him. I missed all of him.

"You gonna milk it for me, gorgeous?"

"Yes! Please, please, please," I sobbed, my body trembling with anticipation.

He picked up his pace, the hand at my hip snaking around to my front, his fingers finding my sensitive, throbbing clit. My knees buckled, but he held the lower half of my body up, still fucking me, relentless and animalistic.

His eyes met mine. "That's it. Such a good little wife, taking her husband's cock so well."

Oh, goodness.

"I'm going to—Mase—" I moaned louder than I ever had before, the sound clashing against the storm that surrounded us.

"Fuck yeah," he hissed, standing back up and gripping a fistful of my wet hair, yanking my head back as my pussy tightened around his rigid length, my body overcome with a white-hot bliss. His hips slammed against my ass, my body moving with him, my tits bouncing. I gripped the railing, holding on for dear life as he fucked me into oblivion.

"I love you!" I cried out.

My declaration sent him over the edge. "Oh, fuck, baby. *Harmony!*" he roared, releasing my hair. His hands covered mine as he swelled inside me, filling me. His lips were against the back of my head as he whispered, "Loved you the second I saw you and every second after that, Little Song."

Tears filled my eyes, the bruises on my heart finally healed.

"Are you cold?" he whispered, his breathe skating over my forehead.

I shook my head, snuggling closer to him. My hand was directly over his heart, savoring the steady, strong beat of it, his skin warm under my palm. He shifted his hips and started stroking my back again. We lay in the backseat of his truck, parked on the other side of the second barn. After he told me he loved me, he picked me up, carried me through the barn and hauled me into the vehicle, where he cranked the heat and pulled me into his arms.

For the last thirty minutes or so, we had just held each other, listening to the storm die down outside.

"Thank you," he said softly, his voice thick—vulnerable.

I looked up to find his eyes on me, scanning my face with a rare gentleness I never thought I'd see from a man like him.

"For what?" I croaked.

"For being my peace."

His heartbeat sped up, getting faster by the second. "I love you," I promised.

"Shit's about to hit the fan, Harm. When we go back to that house, it's all going to come out, and I don't want you to be blindsided," he began. Pressing my lips together, I nodded, and he kissed my forehead. "Lie back down and let me tell you why I left Hallow Ranch."

My stomach dropped. "Okay."

Once my head was back on his shoulder, he laid it all out for me. "Before I get into this, I need you to know that you are the only woman I've ever loved." I closed my eyes, trusting him. "The night I left—that was the last straw. I've lived in my brother's shadow all my life. It's common for most siblings across the world, I guess. Parents aren't supposed to have a favorite child, but Pop did—Denver. My parents struggled to conceive for years, and when they got pregnant with Den, and Momma gave Pop his boy, that was all he needed. Denver was intentional. I was a happy accident."

My heart rate was faster than his now, but the monster in the depths didn't move. It stayed down deep, feeding off the pain that would come with the memories.

"Denver is the spitting image of Pop, and if I had to guess, my nephew is too," he sighed. "I look like Momma. Got her hair, her cheekbones—that's what Jigs used to tell me all the time. Before she died, Harmony, we were the perfect family. I don't remember anything bad happening before that."

I braced myself, holding my breath.

"Momma was murdered," he whispered, like it was dirty secret. "There were bison hunters on the ranch, and Momma—she had a special spot up on the mountain. She was a photographer, and she liked to go up there in the mornings to take pictures of wildlife. She'd done it for years; Pop even marked the trail for her. Denver and I helped. When I was younger, she would take me with her, but as I got older, I wanted to be down in the barn with Pop and Denver. I wanted to learn how to take care of the ranch. At the time, I didn't know Pop had no intention of giving me Hallow Ranch. I was too young to understand."

"Did you want it?" I asked.

He sighed. "Before she died, yes. After, Hallow Ranch became a hellhole I wanted to crawl out of."

I raised my head. "You did," I rasped, tears stinging my eyes. "You got out."

"Little Song, I'm about to tell you something that might trigger you," he warned, his voice gentle and cautious. "If I say something that does, you say 'pasta,' okay?"

My lips tugged up slightly at his safe word. "Okay."

"Do you want to look at me when I say this?" I was surprised at his question, at the thoughtfulness behind it.

"Your eyes never left mine when I told you about him, Mase. Yes, I would like to look at you."

He nodded, and his throat bobbed. "Harmony, three days after my mother was murdered by those hunters, Jigs and Pop took us into the woods to track them down. We found them. Pop made Denver and me sit on a rock. He made Denver cover my ears and told us to close our eyes."

Oh, no. Please, God, no. "Sweetie," I breathed.

His jaw tightened. "I didn't close my eyes, but I knew my brother did—he always did as he was told. Denver heard their screams, and I watched my father get justice for my mother the only way a cowboy knows how—with blood. He slaughtered them and had Jigs burn their bodies."

My hand cupped his face. I didn't want to hear anymore. All I could see was my bull rider as a child, watching something he shouldn't have. He must've been so scared and... "Mason, your father was wrong for doing that."

He nodded. "I know, but that was the night the monster was born. When the men were dead, his anger didn't die. It only grew and festered, morphing him into an angry, hateful, cruel son of a bitch. He needed something to take his anger out on. He needed to forget his wife. How the hell could he do that when his son looked just like her?" There was anger in his voice, but also hurt.

"I'm so sorry. I'm sorry you went through that." There weren't enough apologies in the world. Nothing could change the past, but he got out. He took control of his fate and found bull riding.

"Don't apologize for John Langston, baby. He isn't worth a single ounce of your goodness."

My thumb stroked his cheek. "Bull riding was an escape for you," I stated.

"Figured if a bull couldn't kill me, then he sure as shit couldn't," he deadpanned, his eyes flaring.

My mind went back to Denver's words. "I need to tell you something, Mase," I confessed.

His brows came together. "What is it?"

"Your brother may have heard something I said earlier...when I was yelling at Jigs."

Another sigh came from him, and then he told me something that made my world tilt on its axis. "Denver fucked Cathy."

My eyes went wide. "What?"

"Denver enlisted in the Marines the day he turned eighteen, went away for five years. I was so pissed at him for leaving me with Pop, who was mad Denver left and that's how I got—"

"Pasta," I blurted, looking down. I couldn't hear that part again. I didn't want to hear how my husband was branded by his father. "I know what your father did, so you don't have to repeat it."

Fingers gripped my chin and pulled my face back up. "Do you want me to continue?"

I nodded. "I just—I don't like hearing about your pain." My voice was shaking.

His features softened as he murmured, "Ditto, darlin'."

"What happened when Denver came back?"

"The five years he was gone were hell. I couldn't leave the fucking ranch, not when the old bastard was losing his sanity. If I did, the herd would've been lost. The ranch wouldn't have made any profit, and the cowboys would've lost their home. So, I stayed. When I was trying to run the ranch with Jigs, I was riding bulls. That started before Den enlisted. He told me I was crazy, and he didn't know the half of it," he said, shaking his head. "I didn't speak to him for five fucking years, Harmony. He didn't know about my life, and I didn't know about his."

He stopped and looked out the window, at the clouds parting above us.

"I met Cathy at a local rodeo. From the moment I saw her, I knew what she was, and she knew what I was. We were two kids, trying to make it out of a shitty little town. Her father was a drunk, beating her any chance he got. She had no money, but I did. When she cleaned up, she looked like the type of girl who would impress Pop. For some fucked up reason, even back then, there was a small part of me that wanted to please him."

When Mase looked back at me, my gut knew what he was about to say. So, I said it for him. "You used her."

"And she used me. I proposed to her and promised her a good life. Never loved her, but I thought maybe someday, I would. Our engage-ment was a deal, nothing more. Her dad was old-fashioned. He told her the only way she would get out of his house is if she married. She couldn't run. She was piss poor broke, Harmony. No one took pity on her because of his reputation. No one cared about her. I was her ticket to freedom."

God, this man. "If that was the case, then why the fuck did she sleep with Denver?" I asked, getting angry at her betrayal.

"The last six months of our arrangement, she took a turn. The demons in her family claimed her, and she started drinking every single day. When I was working on the ranch or at a rodeo, she was at the bar, wearing my ring and getting plastered."

I stared.

"Got a call after a ride one night. I was in the neighboring county, and the bartender called, telling me Cathy was trashed, that she'd been cut off for the night. I rushed back into Hayden, pissed off. When I got to the bar, a man outside told me it was great that Denver was back in town. Didn't know he was, and in that moment, Harmony, I forgot all about her. Something in me wanted to see my brother so badly, I headed back home. Never expected to find Cathy in his bed when I got there."

"Mase," I choked out. He sat up, taking me with him.

"That was the final straw. I can't explain it. Denver had come home a decorated war hero, ready to take over the ranch I'd been taking care of, and he took the last chance I had to earn Pop's approval."

My hand slid into his hair, and I kissed him. Hard. When I pulled away, tears streamed down my cheeks, and his throat bobbed. "In that moment, bull riding was all I had...until I met you." He put his forehead against mine. "Cathy didn't get Momma's ring. I didn't want her to have it."

The band on my finger felt heavier than before. "Sweetie, I need to tell you something about Denver, okay?" I whispered, my fingers running through his hair. I didn't give him a chance to respond before I told him the truth, just like he didn't give me a chance to get into the front seat before his truck was flying out of the pasture and onto the gravel road.

Shit had hit the fan.

Chapter Thirty-Two

Denver

"Denver, are you alright?"

My hands tightened, gripping the edge of the kitchen counter harder, at Nancy's question. No, I wasn't alright. That morning I'd woken up wondering if Mason's arrival had been a dream, wondering if I would ever be forgiven for my sins. An hour ago, I discovered my sins weren't the only reason my brother didn't want to come home.

Because my home wasn't his home.

I bowed my head, my shoulders tense, jaw tight, trying to process how the hell I could have missed it. His pain. His fear. I had been so wrapped up in my own life, my own dreams, my own responsibilities, that I'd completely missed what was right in front of me.

After I dropped Harmony off with Mason, I came straight to the house in search of Valerie. She had been on the couch with her mother, relishing what little time they had left together. Nancy stopped her chemo treatments. It was her choice, and though it was hard on Val, she was supportive of her mom's choices. My woman had spent her entire life fighting for her mother, and she was about to lose her. We didn't know how long it would be, but Nancy was staying with us until the end. Valerie was working on putting Nancy's house in Texas up for sale, and we planned on taking a trip down.

Then, Mason showed up at my doorstep.

"Denver?" Nancy called, her soft voice weak.

Inhaling through my nose, I raised my head and looked over my shoulder. She was sitting at Caleb's favorite stool, holding a cup of tea in her hands. Her baby blue silk wrap matched the blue roses on her shirt today.

"I apologize, Nance," I grumbled, turning to face her. "What did you ask?"

She tilted her head, sympathy painting her frail face. "I asked if you were alright."

I wanted to laugh. "No."

She took a sip of her tea, looking out the window. "Valerie is an only child. You know this," she began, setting her cup back on the island. "When I found out I was pregnant, I knew one wasn't going to be enough." She smiled to herself. "I wanted a house full of babies and happiness. I wanted my kids to grow up loving, fighting, and making up with each other. No family is perfect, and siblings fight. I was prepared for that."

I leaned my ass against the counter, gripping the surface again. "What's your point, Nance?" I asked softly, swallowing the lump forming in my throat.

"I didn't have that. Your momma did, and I can tell you right now, she is looking down on you and Mason, hoping you two will fix it."

I clenched my jaw. "Things just a got a little bit more complicated for us."

"Life's too short for complicated. Simplify it and live."

She was right, of course. All I could do was nod. My enchantress walked in then, her green eyes meeting mine and reading me instantly. "Are you okay?" she asked, stepping up to her mom's side.

"Your mom is helping me work through it," I said honestly.

Nancy made a show of batting her lashes and whipping the ends of her head wrap. "I'm just full of wisdom."

"You are," I confirmed. "Thank you."

"Alright, I think I'm in love!" Jackie yelled as she came back into the house.

Val looked to the ceiling, Nancy laughed, and I scowled at the nurse as she came into the kitchen, dancing. "You talking about the rodeo clown?" I clipped.

I didn't know who that man was, but when Mason's red head stood up for him, I knew I couldn't shoot the fucker. Not yet, anyways. For now, he was a stranger snooping around my ranch.

"His name is Edward," Jackie shot back. Then, she looked to the women opposite of me. "I'm not kidding this time, girls. The second I saw him, I felt it. Do you know what I'm talking about?"

My gaze collided with my woman's as she agreed. "I know what you're talking about."

Fuck, I wanted to kiss her. Scratch that, I wanted to carry her upstairs, sink my cock inside her and get lost in everything that is...her. Unfortunately, I couldn't do that, so instead I turned back to Jackie. "Where is he?"

"He got a phone call from Mason."

My spine stiffened. Then, I was moving, leaving the women in the kitchen and heading straight for the front door. As soon as my boots hit the porch, I clocked him. He was standing down by his truck, pacing back and forth, still on the phone. As I got closer, I caught the end of his conversation.

"Mase, I swear to you on my life, I didn't know."

Silence.

"What do you mean Pam knew?" the cowboy barked. "The whole time?"

"The fuck are you talking about?" I growled. The man's back straightened before he slowly turned to face me. His once-kind eyes were cold but alert.

"Mase, bud, just get back to the house. It's time," he said, hanging up the phone. His eyes studied me for a half a second before he lifted his chin. "I'm Eddie. You're Denver. We both care about Mason. I've always looked out for him and will continue to do so, unless you plan on shooting me."

Harmony had a big mouth. "Not going to shoot you," I snapped.

Eddie offered a wide, offset smile. "It's nice to finally meet the CEO of Evergreen Feed."

I didn't have time for this. I needed to talk to my brother. "Is he coming back?"

"Should be."

"Him and Harmony alright? That storm got a little crazy for a few moments," I noted, pissed I couldn't check on them. I couldn't pick up the phone and call him. Hopefully, that would change by the end of the day.

I prayed to the good Lord above that it would. I'd been selfish and greedy with my prayers the last few months, but I just wanted my family back.

Eddie nodded, looking down at the barn. "Your boys don't trust them or me. Hope you know that."

They didn't trust Val, either. "They'll come around. What do you know about Harmony and Moonie?" I asked.

His eyes met mine, and I knew that look, seen it a thousand times before. "Moonie's getting one of my bullets for what he did to her."

Before I could respond, a brand-new Chevy pulled down the gravel drive. It came to stop two feet from me, and in a flash, my brother was out and charging towards me. His hat was off, and he had on a different shirt than when I last saw him. His gray eyes were filled with rage, pinned on me, holding me in place.

Just take it, Denver.

Take your punishment.

Mason

"Mase, please. Listen to me," Harmony pleaded as I turned onto the gravel drive up to the house, my foot heavy on the gas petal.

"Baby," I quipped, my voice shaking with anger.

"Just—"

"Harmony, dammit, I love you. You are my wife. I intend on spending the rest of my days with you and the children we create, but right now, I need to punch my brother," I explained through clenched my teeth. My eyes looked ahead again, seeing the son of a bitch standing out front with Eddie.

"Look at me," my wife begged. I hit the brakes, put the truck in park, and gave her a look. Her blue eyes were calm and void of judgement.

"Just one punch. Then you talk to him, you hear me?" she ordered.

I chuckled darkly. "I get two, darlin'. Stay in the truck." I was out before she could say another word and slammed the door.

My brother was staring at me, his jaw set, shoulders squared—waiting for me. I formed a fist at my side, ready to lift and pull back. "Gonna get two, Den," I called out, readying myself.

He nodded once. "Make them count."

In the next second, the years of pent-up anger, resentment, frustration connected with my brother's jaw, sending him flying back. My fist throbbed, pain radiated up my arm, but for the first time in what felt like an eternity, I felt the tug at the bond between us. He gained his footing, inhaled deeply through flared nostrils, and rose to his full height, meeting my eyes. "Got one more, Mase. Don't hold back," he ordered, hatred in his eyes, but it wasn't directed at me.

My chest heaved, and I heard the screen door open.

Great, an audience.

Where was the fucking popcorn for the Langston Family Drama Special?

I couldn't take my eyes off Denver. He was angry, but not at me.

"Come on, Mase. Hit me," he barked, fuming.

He wanted this.

It was punishment for him.

I found myself lowering my fist, a sharp pain slicing through my chest. "Harmony told me," I stated, the air thick and tense around us.

Denver didn't move, aside from his eyes going to the truck. "Hit me again, Mase."

"Did you know?"

"You said you were going to give me two. Still owe me one more. Do it," he demanded, looking back at me.

"Did you know?" I yelled, my body shaking.

"Hit me, god-dammit!" he roared, taking a step closer.

I closed the distance between us until, we were toe to toe, nose to nose. "Did you know?" I shouted in his face, my voice cracking at the end. He put his hands on my chest and shoved me away from him.

"I'm gonna make you hit me," he growled.

He was punishing himself.

"He used to do it when you were out in the fields or off with your friends," I told him, memories crawling out of their graves, their claws sinking into my skin, right over my brand. Pain flared over the skin there like wildfire, spreading down my back. "Started with a hit here and there, when he looked at me for too long. I look just like her, you know?"

"Stop it," he hissed.

I wasn't even close to stopping. The words hung in the air, being sucked up by the greedy monster of toxicity that lingered in our bond, and it wanted more. "Fuck, he hated seeing me cry, Den. He couldn't stand the sight of my tears. Used to sneak into Momma's dark room when everyone was sleepin' so I could cry and mourn her in peace. I missed her so fucking much, and I wasn't allowed to! Fucker told me cowboys don't cry," I spat, fuming as Pop's words rang in my ear.

Cowboys don't cry, you stupid boy.

No one cares about your tears.

Denver looked broken, utterly defeated, his entire body stilling. "Please, Mase. We don't—"

Oh, but we did.

The wound was open now, years of hurt flowing down its river of blood, a fucking massacre. "Denver Langston, the golden boy! Captain of the football team, next in line for the great Hallow Ranch. You had it all. You had everything in the palm of your fucking hand, and you still couldn't see how much I needed you. Why the fuck do you think I started riding bulls? Everyone called me crazy!"

My brother was silent, his throat bobbing.

I looked out to the pasture, my jaw tight. "Figured if a bull couldn't kill me, then Pop sure as fuck couldn't, right? If I could conquer a beast, then I could handle that bastard. I was so fucking pissed at you for leaving me," I spat, looking back at him. I bared my teeth, leaning towards him. "You fucking left to defend our country, while I was here—"

My brother charged towards me then, shoving his hands up in his hair, knocking his cowboy hat off. It landed on the damp dirt, upside down.

"Mason, I didn't know!" he roared, throwing his arms out.

I was too far gone to turn back—it was time. It was long overdue. "He was mad, too, ya know? Never seen him so mad, not since the day Momma died—"

Denver's shoulders were shaking, his gray eyes filled with rage and hatred, and yet his voice was soft as he begged, "Mason. Please. Stop."

"Drank a fifth of Jack that afternoon," I continued as I grabbed the bottom of my shirt. His eyes dropped to my hands, his chest heaving, matching mine.

"Mase," a raspy, sweet voice called from behind me. I looked over my shoulder to see Harmony at the front of the truck, tears in her blues.

"Turn away for a second, Little Song," I ordered, pulling the shirt up. Throwing the fabric over my shoulder, I looked back at my brother. His cowboys were standing behind him now, concern masking their faces. Beau's eyes dropped down to Denver's hat on the ground, then lifted back to us. His father looked as if he'd seen a ghost.

"When the bastard got done drinking, he came up to my room when I was sleeping," I began, my voice filled with venom and pain. "I don't sleep on my stomach anymore, because the last time I did," I gave Denver my back, my scar on full display, "I was *branded by a monster.* He held me down while he did it, told me he already lost one son, and he was going to make sure the other stayed." I turned back to Denver just in time to see him fall to his knees, tears in the grown man's eyes. He bent his head as his entire body started shaking.

"Denver," Val rasped, running down from the porch and dropping down to her knees behind him.

A soft hand touched my back. My obsession, my safe space, my sweet Harmony, the blessing who brought me home.

"Mason," Jigs croaked, stepping up to us. "My strong boy, why didn't you tell me?"

My strong boy.

Jigs was more of a father figure to me than Pop ever was. My eyes stung, but I blinked the tears away. *Cowboys don't cry.* "How could I? He was your best friend," I countered, pulling my wife to my side. Immediately, she anchored herself to me.

"No, why didn't you tell me?" Denver growled, looking up at me. "I'm your fucking brother!"

"And his fucking favorite!" I snapped back. "Pop was a *god* to you, Den! You fucking worshipped him."

He was on his feet then, pulling his woman up as well. His finger pointed to his chest as he vowed darkly, "I would've put his ashes on the mountain, Mase! The second you told me, I would have!"

I was silent, my hand tightening on Harm's hip, trying to register his words.

Denver killing Pop—for me?

I started to shake my head, but he spoke again. "Momma told me to protect you, Mase. Why the fuck do you think I wouldn't have protected you from Pop?"

Listen to him, my sweet Mase.

Silence fell between us.

"There wasn't a day that went by I didn't worry about you," Den vowed. "I watched every single ride. Every single time, for eight seconds, I was scared shitless. When you got thrown off that first time, I bought a plane ticket. I was going to come to you—but when I got to the airport, I couldn't get on the plane. I didn't think—I knew you hated me. I was a coward, Mase."

"Why Evergreen?" I asked.

He looked toward the house for a moment. "Hallow Ranch was my dream, PBR yours. Wanted to make sure you had it," he answered, looking back at me.

My chest constricted.

A cell phone ringing interrupted the conversation and Momma's voice. It was Eddie's. I swung my gaze at him just as he answered. "You got Eddie." He looked at Harmony. "Yeah, she's here—Harmony," he called, "It's Billie."

I felt her nod against me before I saw her eyes. When my eyes landed on her blues, she whispered, "I can have her call back later, if you want me here."

I looked at the people around me. This visit wasn't about me or healing old wounds. It was about saving this fucking hell hole. The Langston Family Shit Show was over. Billie calling was a saving grace. She and Cabe probably had an update.

My eyes landed on Denver. The secret was out. He knew the truth and there was nothing more to say.

So, I shook my head. "Go, then report back, yeah?"

My strong woman looked to the Hallow Ranch crew and back to me. "I love you," she said, her raspy voice carrying so everyone could hear. She let everyone know how she felt about me, where I stood in her life, and in that moment, I lost it.

Turning her to face me completely, I grabbed her face, and pressed my lips against hers. I didn't give a fuck about anyone or anything around us in that moment. My wife just told me she loved me in front of the people who thought I was a piece of shit.

So yeah, I was going to kiss her. Hard. Until she was breathless and clinging to me.

When I pulled away, resting my forehead against hers, I whispered, "Only you, my little song."

Chapter Thirty-Three

Mason

I watched Eddie and Harmony walk to the back of my truck. Denver called my name, but I was done with the conversation. He knew the truth, I knew his, and that was that. We didn't have time for emotions, plain and simple. Before going for my shirt, I went for Denver's hat, picking it up, dusting it off.

"Here," I said, holding it out to him. "Glad to see you still have it."

I'd gotten this for him for his eighteenth birthday, before I knew he enlisted. His hand reached out, taking it from me gently. I didn't give him a chance to say anything else.

Once my shirt was back on, I faced the cowboys. "We need to have a discussion in the barn about fuck face," I declared, referring to Moonie. Harmony was still in earshot, and even though she had said his name earlier, I meant what I said and then some.

Tim Moonie doesn't get to be anywhere near her, and that included his fucking name.

Without waiting for them, I headed for the barn, ready to get this shit over with. Two minutes later, I entered the building where I spent most of my childhood. My eyes lifted to the loft, wondering if Denver was making use of it—then, a thought occurred to me.

"Mase, we have to talk about this," my brother said from behind me.

"Where is Caleb?" I asked, worry coating my voice.

Jesus, I haven't even met the kid yet. He probably didn't even know about my existence.

"He's at friend's house down the road," he answered. "Why?"

"Just making sure he didn't see any of that," I muttered.

"Mase—"

"Our past doesn't touch him," I growled. "That clear?"

He didn't say a damn thing, just stared.

The cowboys came up behind him, Beau leaning against the barndoor on one side, Mags on the other. The twins flanked Denver as Jigs lingered behind, unsure of what to do.

"Why did you keep in touch with Jigs all these years?" Denver asked.

Beau's brows knitted together, his blue eyes studying me. I looked at his father. "You tell him?" I asked.

"We had a conversation," Denver answered for the old man.

My eyes met my brother's. "Some things are harder to let go of."

Pain flashed across his features. "You didn't have to let go, Mase."

Continuing to cut through the bullshit, I said, "Cathy was the last straw for me, Denver, but you have to know that I never loved her."

The men exchanged looks. "You asked her to marry you," Beau deadpanned.

"She was a means to an end," I explained.

"To what end, Mase?" Denver asked, his brows drawn together.

"Pop's approval. She was in a bad spot with her father, needed to escape him and the abusive household she grew up in. Being young and naïve as I was, there was a huge part of me that wanted to please Pop. I wanted his approval, and I thought by marrying a sweet girl like Cathy, I would get it."

"That woman ain't sweet," one of the twins snapped. He was the one who punched me—Lawson? Lance? Who the fuck knows.

"So that night..." Denver trailed off and looked away from me. He blew out his breath. "Look, you and I have a lot to talk about, but here's the fucking truth. I don't regret that night. I regret the pain I caused you, but I can't regret that night—because of Caleb."

A chill ran down my spine. "What?"

"Caleb is Cathy's son," he confirmed. "After you stormed off, I sent her away. She came back a few weeks later with a pregnancy test, told me we could get married. That was the last thing I fucking wanted, but I tried to do right by her—and Caleb. After he was born, Cathy disappeared and went—"

"—after me," I muttered, pinching the bridge of my nose. What a shitshow.

"She told me you two were in love."

Dropping my hand, I sighed. "If she'd stayed away from the booze and broke her generational curses, then in time, we might have been. I never loved her. The only woman I've ever loved is sitting on the back of my truck, trying to save this fucking ranch."

Mags scoffed. "Right, and we should trust her because...why?"

My head snapped to him. Tilting it, I argued, "I'm sorry, but didn't Valerie work for Moonie?"

"We knew that from the beginning. We have no idea what your little red-headed—"

"Mind your tongue, or I'll rip it out, cowboy," I seethed.

The man's dark eyes flashed, and slowly, he dropped his arms. Before he could say anything, Denver asked, "How is my sister-in-law involved with Moonie?"

"She isn't."

"Mason, you have to tell us," Jigs said, coming from behind Denver and standing in front of his son.

"Harmony's story is her story," I clipped.

"And we need to know it," Denver said softly, requesting more.

Harmony bared herself to me, sharing something so precious with me, leaving a permanent mark on my soul. If someone wanted to get that information out of me, they would have to hog tie me and do something worse than a brand, because my wife's story is safe with me. Forever.

Therefore, I denied my brother once more. "You won't be getting that information from me."

"Then why the fuck should we trust you?" Mags growled, pushing off the wall. "How do we know you're here for the good, for the future of this ranch? How do we know your surprise appearance with a wife who claims she has a way to take this fucker down isn't just a ploy?" All the men in the barn stilled, bracing for his final blow. "How do we know she isn't in on it, working with him behind the scenes, ready to reap the reward—and share it with the brother who hates this place?"

One of the twins stepped forward, nodding. "She's a pretty girl with a sob story. How life-changing. Do you think we're supposed to believe her—"

"Lawson," Denver warned.

"—and when you've ignored Denver's calls for years? Didn't even come to your Pop's funeral. You left Hallow Ranch in the dust while you built your bull riding empire—"

The other twin stepped up. "—while your brother was sponsoring it the whole time. You spat on the Langston name and the legacy of this ranch. Now, you show up here ten years later with a woman just months after that Moonie had Val kidnapped and intended to burn her alive? And you just expect us to trust you—after you punched Denver?"

I raised my brows, crossing my arms over my chest. "You wanna talk about punching people? That's rich coming from the fucking stranger who took a cheap shot at me."

The cowboy smiled. "I'm sorry, did you need a warning? I'll remember that next time—"

"You touch me again, you'll be in the fucking hospital sucking apple-sauce through a straw," I threatened darkly. My eyes snapped to Denver. "My wife is the one who convinced me to come here—this was her idea. She didn't want me to lose this place."

"You? Lose this place?" Beau scoffed. "You haven't cared about this—"

"Son, that's enough," Jigs said, trying to be the peacekeeper.

"Yes, before I lost this place, Beau. Despite what everyone here thinks, I worried about it. Hallow Ranch might have been my hellhole, but it was your sanctuary, Denver," I said, my voice firm as I looked at my brother. "I'm here to make sure you never lose it."

"False words from the show boy," Mags growled. "This isn't just Denver's home. Its mine, Jig's, Beau's, and the twins' too. Your little wife—"

"—was sold to the devil by her father."

The men turned to find a woman standing in the entrance of the barn, wearing a deep green sundress, her red curls piled high on top of her head. We'd gone to the hotel to change before coming here—I didn't want her to get sick. She was holding Eddie's cell phone to her middle, her hands curved around it—

She heard us talking about him.

Fuck, she needed her bottle.

I rushed to her, checking Mags' shoulder in the process. My hands cupped her face, my fingers stretching into her hair, my eyes searching hers for signs of panic. "You don't owe them anything," I assured her.

"If we're going to do this, then they have to know," she croaked.

My jaw ticked as I shook my head. She'd made a lot of progress over the last several weeks, and we haven't had another episode. After that night, she talked to Dr. Garcia about our plan, and the woman approved. Of course, we just told her about us getting married. What we didn't tell her was that I was going to put one of the wealthiest men in the country six feet under with my bare fucking hands.

Harmony brought her hands to my wrists, gently easing them off her. She gave me a small smile, and whispered, "Stay close to me?"

"Always."

She turned to face the men, who were all stone faced aside from Denver, who was showing concern. My wife dove right in, not missing a single beat. "My father is a wealthy businessman in Houston. He and—" She cut herself off, taking a breath. "I have trouble hearing his name.

So, for now, I'm going to refer to you know who as Navy Blue—that's his signature color. Is that alright?"

None of the men moved or said a word. Finally, Jigs spoke up. "That'll be fine, sweetheart."

She nodded and reached back to grab my hand. I took it instantly, giving it a squeeze as she began. "My father was in business with Navy Blue's father. When I was child, they made an agreement. When I was of age, I would be handed off to Navy Blue for a price. Navy Blue's pipeline invested a lot of money into my father's company over ten years in exchange for me. I was trained for him. I was taught to act a certain way and expected to do anything Navy Blue required of me.

"When I met him, he wasn't anything like I'd pictured. I'd pictured a monster. Navy Blue was handsome and even kind. He was gentle and attentive. When I told him I wanted to go to school to be a nurse, he seemed alright with it." My wife let out a shaky breath before continuing. "After about a year of knowing him, he wanted to be intimate with me."

My entire body went solid, my hand tightening around hers. This marked the second time I'd heard this, and I felt myself getting angry all over again. The thought of any man touching her set me on edge—but him? I was on fire.

"He wasn't gentle," she said softly.

Denver bit off a curse, looking murderous.

Beau stared at his boots, shaking his head. The twins just looked pissed. Mags—Mags just stared at her, a shadow forming over his features.

"At the time, I didn't know any better. I thought that was just how it was, something I had to deal with. My mom—I-I don't remember her well. She left when I was very young, so there really wasn't anyone that I could talk to, aside from Billie, she's my best friend. She told me that the first time always hurts."

I wouldn't have made it hurt, Little Song. I would've taken care of you. Fuck me, baby, I would have treasured you.

"As time went on, he moved me into his house, saying that when he was settled within the company, we would get married. He promised me the world. During the day, he was gentle and kind. At night, he was completely different man." She ducked her head. "My therapist says people who endure domestic violence often give up and just deal with it instead of fighting it. That's what I did. I gave up. I smiled for him when I needed to smile. I cooked for him when he was hungry. I opened my legs for him so he wouldn't hit me too hard."

At this point, the air in the barn was thick. Rage lingered in the air, the promise of revenge spinning in our heads. Differences aside, I knew by the look in these cowboys' eyes that we agreed on one thing: you don't touch women. That was good, considering the next part of the story. I took a slow breath in through my nose, trying to make sure I stayed present for her.

"One day, he came home and found me in the bathroom. He didn't like what he saw. He—" She cut herself off again, her voice shaking. It was too much—for both of us. She didn't owe these men anything. Her story was her story, and the world didn't need to know it.

I spun her to me, my arms wrapping around her. "We're done. That's enough."

Her face was in my chest as she cried, "No! I have to tell them. They need to believe me. They need to know—"

My eyes shot to the men. "Do you need more, or is that enough?" I growled. "Does that check all your fucking boxes? Does she pass the Hallow Ranch acceptance test? You don't want to hear the next part—trust me. That man hurt my wife. This isn't an act. There is no prize other than her safety and the security of this ranch."

Denver nodded, and the rest of the boys followed suit.

"She's protected," my brother vowed, his eyes snapping from her to me. "You have my word."

My throat was tight, my chest was aching. All I could do was nod.

Harmony turned her head to face them. "That monster took everything from me," she rasped.

Mags stepped forward, not stopping until he was in front of her. "What did he take?" he asked, his voice soft for the first time since I'd met him.

"Back off," I barked, tightening my arms around her. Mags' eyes snapped up to mine, and all I saw was pain.

What the hell?

"Sweetie, it's okay," she said, lifting her head. My hand eased her back onto my chest without looking at her. I didn't need to look to know her beautiful, freckled face was red and blotchy, eyes swollen. I hated it.

"You stay right here when you re-open this wound," I clipped. "Got me?"

She nodded and circled her arms around my waist.

"What's your name again?" she asked the man softly.

"Mags."

"Just Mags?" she whispered.

He nodded. "That not enough for you? Cause' it's all I got." Behind him, I saw Denver's eyes darken.

My little song decided to accept his name. "I'm Harmony."

His lips twitched. "I know that."

God, I wanted to punch him, too.

I felt her body expand as she inhaled a deep breath, steadying herself for the incoming pain. "Mags, Navy Blue found out I was pregnant. He didn't want me to be..." The air in the barn got colder, and the eyes of every cowboy flared. I braced as she delivered the final blow, tightening my hold on her, my fingers weaving into her curls, her heart beating against me. She took another unsteady breath. "He—he took care of it himself," she whispered, broken and weak. I felt her body shaking, and a second later, I felt wetness on my shirt.

A sharp, burning pain struck me in the chest as I clenched my jaw hard, hoping the pain would take away from the agony in my chest. My fists ached to hit something, and the darkness inside me craved blood.

Tim Moonie's soul was mine to reap.

Chapter Thirty-Four

Harmony

Six years ago. Michigan. Dr. Garcia's office.

"Harmony, do you remember me?"

The owner of the pretty voice was looking at me, and just like her voice, she was pretty.

She was put together.

This was her job.

She was normal.

I watched as she carefully set her tablet down on the small table beside her. My body went on alert when she leaned forward slightly. What was she doing? Why did she want to get close to me? I didn't want to be touched. I wanted to be alone. Even though it still hurt to speak, I cleared my throat, ignoring the burn.

"I'd like to go back to my room, please."

Tears stung my eyes, and I couldn't believe it. My voice.

It wasn't my voice anymore.

It was rough—ugly.

How was I going to sing?

I loved to sing.

"I just wanted to get to know you a bit before you had supper. Is that alright?" the woman asked, her voice smooth and beautiful. Rich. Worthy.

I shifted in my seat, my fingers flexing against the cool metal bottle in my lap. It was teal blue and bright. I liked bright colors. They made me feel happy. It had been so long since I'd seen anything pretty. Now, I had pretty—right in my hands. I also had water to drink whenever I wanted.

Mine.

Only mine.

No one could take it from me.

"I'm Dr. Garcia."

I nodded. "I know."

"So, you remember me?" she pressed, her voice gentle.

"You were at the hospital," I whispered, wincing at the sound of my voice. Was it going to be like this forever?

How was I going to sing?

"That's right. Do you know where you are?"

Panic wound through me like a shot of morphine. She was going to tell him how to find me. "Please! Please don't tell him where I am. I-I-I—he can't know! Please! Oh god, please!"

He can't find me here.

He can't find me here.

He would lock me up again if he did. I would never see the sun again if he did. He would take my voice from me if he did. He would kill Billie if he did.

He would take another one from me...

"I don't want to be his perfect girl anymore," I cried, standing up.

Dr. Garcia followed suit, raising her hands. She nodded. "You're safe, Harmony. He isn't going to hurt you again," she assured me, giving me a false promise.

He was here—I could feel him. He was watching me! My ankles ached, feeling the weight of those dirty chains as he laughed in my ear.

"No!" I screamed. "No! No! No!" I closed my eyes and brought my hands to my hair. "No! No! Please! He took her! He took her! No!"

"I need some help in my office," Dr. Garcia said in the background.

I fell to my knees, yanking on my hair. "He hates my hair," I sobbed. "She would've had my hair!"

"Alright, Harmony. We'll try again tomorrow."

I felt a prick in my neck, and then I was sucked down to the depths by the monster.

Mason

Mags' eyes found mine. He gave me a single nod and that was that. When he looked back down to Harmony, he whispered, "Forgive me."

She sniffled. "Already forgotten, Mags. I understand why you had doubts. I have trouble trusting people, too."

"Alright, bud, Billie's father got a lock on—"

I spun us to see Eddie standing just outside the barn, the nurse beside him. Her brown eyes darted to my wife as she read the scene and instantly jumped into action.

"Baby doll, you look like you could use a cup of tea."

Harmony dropped her arms and lifted her head. "That actually sounds really lovely, Jackie. Thank you."

Jackie looked at Eddie, shot him a smile, and came to us, offering her arm. "Edward tells me you're a nurse."

Edward?

Harmony stepped away from me. "I'm an RN at a clinic in Houston. Mason graciously donated to our new building, which is going to be on the opposite side of the city."

"Did he now?" she mused, raising a perfect brow. "Bet he did that to get your attention."

My wife looked back at me, her eyes red and puffy still. "He had my attention long before that."

From the moment I saw you.

"Ditto, baby," I murmured. I lifted my chin. "You good?"

She nodded. "I'm going to get some tea."

My strong woman. God, I loved her.

As Jackie led my wife up to my childhood home, I turned to the men. "Harmony's friends, Cabe and Billie, are in Denver. They've have been doing some digging."

"Let's hear it, brother," Denver said.

Brother.

We held our gazes for a long time. There were things that still needed to be discussed, but we didn't need to hash anything out. The past is the past, and that's where it needed to stay. Right now, Moonie was the primary focus.

"You still in touch with Chase?" I asked.

Denver lifted his chin to Beau. "Call Chase and get him out here."

Harmony

"Jackie tells me you're what all the fuss is about this week."

My eyes met a pair of jade ones, and in that second, I knew they belonged to a kind soul. I'd seen enough bad ones during my time to know the difference. Jackie brought me up to the house for tea. Upon arrival, she burst through the front door, yelling to Valerie that I was here and that we would be in the living room, where her mother currently sat. She set her E-reader down and gestured to the empty spot on the couch beside her.

"Come, come, take a seat. I want to hear all about you," she invited, a weak smile on her face.

No, she didn't.

Valerie came rushing downstairs, a stack of folded blankets in her hands. "Hey, Harm—is it alright if I call you that? I don't want to make you uncomfortable. I was going to get these linens in the wash real quick. The office bed will be ready in just a bit for you and Mason."

Uh, what?

"Excuse me?" I breathed.

Valerie waved her hand, like what she said was nothing. "Den bought the bed for Jackie, but she's leaving tomorrow."

"Yeah, I have to get to my sister's wedding," Jackie explained, rolling her eyes. I looked back at her as she continued. "It's her fifth damn wedding and frankly, I don't have the time for it...but family is family, you know?"

No, I didn't.

Shaking my head slightly, I looked back at Valerie. "I'm sorry, I'm confused. Mason and I are staying at the hotel in town."

She immediately pressed her lips together. "Yeah, about that...Denver called Bart this morning after you went to look for Mason and canceled the rest of y'all's stay. Lawson is going to pick up your things after dinner."

I blinked. After what went down in the barn, I didn't believe her. Those men trusted me about as far as they could throw me. Aside from Mags...I felt like I'd made a step in the right direction with him, even if it was bonding over pain.

Today had been a whirlwind of emotions, and I was looking forward to a quiet night with Mason. After everything that'd gone on these last two days, we needed seclusion. I wanted to go back to Spain, to our little apartment by the sea, far away from all of this.

Since I was speechless, Valerie turned and disappeared down the hallway.

"Drama, drama, drama," Jackie clicked her tongue. She looked at Valerie's mother. "And you thought I was a handful."

"Jackie, you're more than a handful," she laughed.

"Listen here, Nancy..."

I tuned the women out when my eyes landed on an antique rocking chair in the corner by the window. It was beautiful, clearly hand-made. There wasn't a blanket or pillow on it, making it inviting for anyone. I knew in my gut that no one was allowed to sit there. That chair belonged to someone special.

My mind immediately went to Mason and Denver's mother.

"Harmony, is it?"

Valerie's mother's sweet, smooth voice, much like her daughter's, brought me back to reality. I looked down at the stunning woman, giving her a small smile. "Yes, sorry." I held out my hand to her, and she took the opportunity to pull me down onto the couch with a grunt. I twisted, righting myself as I gaped at her. She shot me a smirk. "I'm Nancy. It's a pleasure to meet you. Valerie tells me you're Mason's wife. I've had yet to meet him, but I've heard wonderful things from Caleb."

What the actual heck was going on?

"Caleb knows about Mason?" I blurted.

"I'm going to make the tea," Jackie muttered before leaving the room.

Nancy tilted her head. "That boy is Mason's biggest fan. Talks about him all the time. Though recently, he and Denver have been watching a lot of baseball. He's been going on and on about a player named Dean Connors..."

Once again, I was speechless. Denver didn't hide Mason from Caleb, and I guess that makes sense, because of Evergreen and all. "Mason can't wait to meet him," I rasped. As for me, I could use another one of the boy's hugs. It felt nice—welcoming. She hummed in agreement.

"How long have you and Mason been married?" she asked.

"Oh, not long. Just a couple of months." The best months of my life.

"How did you meet him?"

He pulled a man away from me, called me baby, beat that man up, and got arrested. "At a PBR event. By chance." Not the whole truth, but still the truth, nonetheless.

"Jackie told me you're a nurse at a clinic, yes?"

I nodded. "Yes, ma'am."

"Have you always wanted to be a nurse?" she asked.

It was an innocent question, and normally, I would be able to smile and nod.

After today, it was much harder.

My eyes stung with tears before I could stop them, and I bowed my head, inhaling a greedy gulp of air.

When we arrived at Hallow Ranch days ago, I didn't want anyone to know my story. I didn't want anyone to see me as weak and pathetic. Now, the cowboys knew the harsh, ugly, disturbing truth about me, but it would save this ranch. Dr. G's voice popped into my head at just the right time.

Chin up, Harmony. Accept the past for what it is, but remember that it doesn't define you.

"I apologize, Nancy. It's been a very emotional day," I said softly, lifting my chin. Nancy was smart woman, that much was clear. So, when she decided to change the subject, I was relieved.

"Enough about work. What do you like to do when you're off?" she asked.

"I like to go to the Farmer's Market on the weekends, where I buy my tulips."

Her pale face lit up. "Tulips? What a wonderful flower. They're my favorite. I used to put them into all my arrangements." She paused for a moment. "I used to own a flower shop outside of Dallas."

Suddenly, I found myself in a deep, rich conversation about flowers and life, distracting me from the darkness that lingered over the day. Minutes passed, Jackie came and went, and Valerie eventually sat on the floor beside her mom and joined the conversation. I found myself feeling safe in a house where Mason didn't as a child.

However, the presence of John Langston wasn't here. There was a different kind of presence, welcoming and warm.

When the front door flew open, all of us looked to the foyer as two, tall cowboys stepped through, both sporting looks of surprise as their eyes landed on us. Mason didn't linger. He came directly to me, ignoring Nancy and Valerie. "You alright, darlin'?" he asked, his gaze intense.

I nodded. "I was just talking about flowers with Valerie. This is her mother, Nancy."

My Mase lifted his head just a fraction to look at Nancy. "Pleasure to meet you, ma'am. Mason Langston."

The woman looked stunned, to say the least. I didn't know what she was expecting, perhaps for him to look like Denver, but either way, her eyes widened at his introduction. He didn't wait for her to respond; instead he looked to Valerie. "Val," he greeted.

My heart skipped a hopeful beat at the use of her nickname.

"Mason."

Denver came into the living room, sans the cowboy hat, carrying two beers. He handed one to his brother and as if they'd been doing it their whole lives, they clanked the tops together and took a healthy swig. Val looked like she was about to cry, Nancy looked satisfied, and my jaw was on the ground.

Mason just punched Denver an hour ago.

Was this how cowboys made amends?

"Val, is the office ready, or did you need my help?" Denver asked, bending down to give her a quick kiss.

"The sheets are in the washer. Should be done after dinner," she breathed, looking up at him. I'd never seen such powerful love, not even between Cabe and Billie.

"Den, we won't be staying for dinner. Harm and I have got to head out shortly," he informed the room.

Val's eyes shot to me before she sighed. "Well, I'm going to pick up Caleb. Mom, would you like to sit out on the swing for a bit?"

Nancy looked at me, then to the men, and then back to me. "That sounds lovely, Vallie." Then, she winked at me.

Denver helped Nancy up, and once they were out of the room, Denver took a seat on the couch next to me. "Actually, you two are," he said causally.

Seriously, what the hell was happening?

My husband shook his head. "Harmony needs to rest, and I need to call Pam."

"She can rest upstairs, and you can call Pamela from anywhere," Denver countered, reaching for the TV remote. He looked at me. "You like baseball, sis?"

"Uh—"

"Denver," Mase growled.

Denver didn't take his eyes off me. His handsome, bearded face split into a grin nearly as beautiful as Mase's. "It's alright if you don't. We can watch something else. I'm just following this ball player named Dean Connors. Five years ago, he was announced dead in his apartment when he played for the Cubs, and a few months back, he started for the Yankees."

"What in the hell is happening?" I whispered, breathless. My eyes bounced back and forth between the brothers.

Denver took a long swig of his beer before sitting it on the coffee table and angling his body to face me. He threw his massive arm over the back of the couch. "You're Mason's wife," he stated.

"Yes...?" Was this cowboy crazy?

His eyes fell to the ring on my hand. "That's our momma's ring on your finger."

"Not taking it, Den," Mase warned, coming closer to me.

"Wouldn't dream of it, brother," Denver said, his voice earnest, keeping his eyes on me. "Harmony, you are family now. You probably didn't expect or ask for it, but you got it. I protect my family, I stand by my family, and I love my family. Do you understand what I'm saying to you?"

That sounded lovely, truly, but I knew my Mase. I knew the pain he'd been through in this house. Now, his brother was looking at me like he was thinking of asking me to make desserts for Thanksgiving dinner. "My husband just punched you an hour ago."

The rancher nodded, rubbing his bearded jaw. "Yeah, and he punched me again a few minutes ago—"

"Mason," I scolded, glaring at my bull rider.

He took a pull of his beer and shrugged. "Told him I wanted two, baby. He let me have two."

Just two punches, and they were going to forget a decade of pain?

"So what?" I started, "You two are better now? Two peas in a pod again?"

Mason cleared his throat. "Not yet."

"But we'll get there," Denver finished for him. My brother-in-law's eyes swung back to me. "My family has been broken for ten years..." He trailed off, regret clouding his features. "Until Valerie stepped foot on the ranch a few months ago, I was only living for my son."

Mason stiffened beside me.

"I have a lot to make up for, Harmony. I'm a desperate man. When a cowboy is desperate, nothing will stop him. Your things at the hotel will be picked up and brought here." Denver looked at Mason. "We fight this fight under one roof, understand?"

The two cowboys were in a stare down. "I've never had a family," I blurted, desperate to relieve of the growing tension. "Aside from Cabe and Billie, of course."

Denver blinked and looked at me. His features softened. "You got one now, sweetheart."

"Honey, the sheriff is here," Valerie called from the foyer, opening the door.

"Valerie," a deep voice greeted. "Den, sorry man. I got here as soon as I could. We need to talk about Cathy—" The sheriff cut his words off at the sight of my husband, his eyes going wide.

Mase nodded to the man. "Sheriff."

"Mason. Hey bud, it's good to see you," he said, still stunned.

"We just going to pretend that the last time I saw you, you weren't trying to arrest me?" Mason asked.

Oh, good Lord.

"Do you get arrested often? Because you said what happened in Spain was a fluke," I noted.

"Spain?"

"Darlin'—"

"What the fuck happened in Spain?" Denver clipped.

"Let's go back to Cathy," Mason suggested. "She in my nephew's life?"

"Not anymore." This declaration came from Valerie. She held Denver's eyes for a moment before looking out the window, chewing on the inside of her cheek. The truck keys were in her hand as she crossed her arms over her chest.

"What happened to her?" my husband pressed, looking back to the sheriff.

The man was good looking, young but seasoned. Clearly, he knew Mason's ex...apparently, everyone in this town did, because even Bart mentioned something about her on my way out this morning. With a sigh, the sheriff put his hands on his hips, resting them above his badge and gun clipped to his jeans. "What have you told him, Den?"

Denver stood. "It's been a hell of an afternoon. What's one more trauma dump?" he muttered. He looked down at me and said, "Has Mase told you about Cathy?"

I nodded.

"Cathy is Caleb's mother."

A lump formed in my throat, and I looked at Mase. He wasn't looking at Denver or me; instead, his eyes were on the rocking chair in the corner. We'd only talked about children a few times, but given my history, if we do decide to pursue that, we would need to be mindful about the possible outcomes. Good or bad. I knew in my soul that Mase's feelings towards fatherhood were complicated, but I also knew that if God gave him a child, he would love him or her with everything he had.

Without a doubt, my bull rider would make his entire universe that baby.

And you would be at the center of it, Harm.

"She's working with Navy Blue," Denver finished, bringing me back to the present. Had he been talking this whole time? Navy Blue got to Cathy?

Mase crossed the living room, muttering a string of curses that would make a nun blush. "Greedy woman."

"She tried to take Caleb away from Hallow Ranch," Valerie explained, coming into the room, her eyes lingering on Mason. "I punched her. Sorry."

"Why are you apologizing to me for protecting my nephew?"

She looked perplexed. "I—I don't know. Just felt like I should say it."

My cowboy's lips twitched, and when he looked back to the sheriff, he demanded, "Tell us everything. Don't say his name; refer to him as Navy Blue

The sheriff, Chase, not questioning the need for a code name, proceeded to tell us everything about Cathy, her working with Navy Blue, and her skipping town. When he was done, I was gripping the edge of the cushion, trying desperately not to slip under the surface where the monster lay waiting.

The evil man had beaten her—like he did to me. She worked at the strip club on the outskirts of Hayden, and upon investigation, the office was trashed, blood stains on the carpet, furniture in disarray. There was a man sleeping in her apartment when Denver searched it a week before her disappearance. They told us about the contract, Valerie went into further detail about her time working at the pipeline company. Like that first night, she stressed that she'd never met the man in person until he flew her out to Denver for lunch.

"We found her car on the state line, broken down and emptied. We talked to Bart, and he said that Cathy would stay with Navy Blue most nights when he was at the hotel—"

"He was here?" I stammered. "At—at the hotel? He didn't stay in Denver?"

Chase nodded. I looked down to my lap, my mind running in overdrive. "I need to call Billie."

"You sure?" I pressed.

"Harmony—"

"Billie, please. I need to know that this is going to end," I begged.

I heard typing on the other end of the line as she sighed. "Yes. I have tons of maps and documentation, Harm. Dad said that only desperate men act this way, that the bastard must have a lot of friends on Wall

Street. If you look at the numbers closely, you can find the trends, but it would take a professional," my best friend explained.

"Like you," I surmised, biting my thumbnail. My throat was burned, but I pushed the hurt away. I wasn't thirsty. I wasn't thirsty. I was here with Mase. I was safe.

"We need to change the plan," I decided, ready to go back inside.

"About that...I was trying to tell you when you called...Harmony, he's in Denver," Billie whispered.

My feet stopped moving, my blood going cold, freezing me in the middle of the porch, phone to my ear. "How do you know?"

"Grayson is tracking him."

After Mase and I were declared husband and wife, we spent two glorious days together before he made a call to the bounty hunter Denver hired. We had another job for him: keep tabs on the bastard trying to ruin our lives. Mason and Eddie had been handling the updates, keeping me away from it. Before coming to Colorado, I'd focused on healing, getting stronger mentally and emotionally. Like every journey, there were ups and downs.

Since we'd been in Hayden, I pushed Mason's pain to the forefront. We were here to save his home, Billie and Cabe helping from the sidelines, Eddie being there for us as well. In my head, I believed we could save Hallow Ranch while the asshole was still in Houston looking for me.

"How long?" I breathed, my voice scratchy.

"He landed twnety minutes ago."

He was desperate. His need to own Hallow Ranch wasn't about the pipeline. It was something bigger, considering he was willing to put his search for me on hold—

The temperature around me dropped, the wind picking up, promising another round of storms, a shadow looming over me as the monster chuckled.

I'm coming for you, darling.

He knew about Mason.

Marrying my bull rider was to divert him. Taking the Langston name was supposed to be the element of surprise...

He knew about my love.

He was coming for my sweet Mase.

He was going to take everything from me again.

Fear struck me like a venomous snake, its fangs sinking into my blood steam, flooding it with illogical thoughts. My mind drifted back to the basement, the darkness, the cold dampness, the filth, the blood....

"Billie—I—" I choked on nothing, my body ready to go back into survival mood. The phone slipped from my hands, colliding with the wood of the porch, and suddenly I felt dizzy. My body swayed, ready to collapse. Blackness seeped through my vision, clouding my reality as my heart pounded in my ears.

"Harmony?"

My knees buckled.

"Shit—" Strong arms wrapped around me and when my vision started to come back, I expected to see gray.

I saw blue.

"He's coming," I rasped.

"Mason!" a man shouted, lowering me to the ground. My chest was hurting. My head was pounding. It was happening again. I was losing my grip, the rope slipping through my fingers. I was going to go away again. The last time this happened years ago, I lost an entire week.

Time was precious. I had to fight it.

"What the—Little Song?"

I needed to fight the panic. I needed to be strong. I reached up, searching for my bull rider, my wild cowboy. "Mase..."

I felt like I was being shifted, and then I felt something huge and warm all around me.

"Right here, beautiful. I'm right here." There was fear in my love's voice.

He didn't know about the lost time. I didn't tell him.

"Dr. Garcia, Mase. I need her."

The monster's claws were wrapped around my ankles, and I heard the chains. He was shackling me.

Not yet.

I had to tell my love.

He needed to know about—about—

"He doesn't want the pipeline," I rasped, my vision blurry.

"Harmony? Harmony! Baby, what's happening? Talk to me, please," he begged. I shifted again. "Billie! I don't—she's—no, she is—I don't!"

All I could make out was my husband's outline, and with a shaking hand, I tried to reach up so I could touch his cheek. "He wants the *gold.*"

Everything went black.

The monster pulled me under, my lungs filling with tar, causing my throat to burn.

Water.

I needed water.

Chapter Thirty-Five

Harmony

"Hold me, I'm on the edge.
And I'm scared of falling, I'm scared to fall.
I'm scared to fall for you,
I wish I wasn't afraid.
I'm prone to making mistakes.
I'm tired of grinding my teeth, thinking that maybe you'll leave."

I brought my brows together, strumming the guitar strings once more. I was tired of singing my favorite song, thinking it would sound pretty coming from my lips.

"It's not pretty enough," I whispered, shaking my head at the guitar.

"I thought it was rather beautiful."

I yelped at the new voice, my head snapping up, searching around me. Someone was in my music room with me. I looked towards the doorway, only to find it empty. How weird. Billie and Cabe weren't coming over today; they were the only ones who had a key.

My eyes scanned over space, noting how everything was in its place.

"Hello?" I called. I was sitting in my green chair, by the window. It was after a long day of work, and instead of making dinner, I felt drawn to come in here.

Playing music washes away my days sometimes.

"Did you write that?"

Suddenly, before me stood a blonde woman.

I let out a small cry and leaned further back in the chair.

She was beautiful—striking almost. Her blue eyes were soft as she gazed down upon me. Her thick hair was swooped back into a low ponytail, and she was wearing light blue jeans and a navy shirt with an "H" on the front, right over the heart. She had a warm smile on her face, her blue eyes scanning over me.

There was an intruder in my apartment, and I was staring at her like an idiot. This only proved Cabe's theory, of course. If I was in a scary movie, I would be the first one to die.

"Why are you in my music room?" I rasped, eyes wide. Yes, because the stranger could be in my apartment if she wanted to, just not in my music room. Geez, Harmony.

She giggled. "If you would prefer a different place, we can go there," she said casually, turning away to inspect my bookshelf. I blinked.

"I would prefer it if you left my apartment before I call the cops," I deadpanned, leaning over to set the guitar on the stand.

The woman hummed, turning back to me. "Oh, take that with you. I want you to sing me a song."

My head snapped up to hers. "Take what—"

I watched as my music room, my place of peace and safety, transformed, morphing into a completely different space. Suddenly, I wasn't in my favorite chair, I was sitting on a metal stool. The bright colors of my space faded away and my vision filled with a red light. White sheets of paper hung down around me, and a counter popped up beside me, running the length of the walls, square bins sitting on top of it, each filled with liquid.

My hand tightened around my guitar, and my breath came faster, my chest heaving.

"Oh, sorry. It's a force of habit to leave the light off in this room," she laughed lightly. She flipped the switch on the wall beside me, and a warm light filled my vision. I scanned the area quickly.

"Why are we in a dark room? Who are you?" I asked, trying to get a grip on reality.

She looked up to the ceiling, as if she was listening to something. After a second, she looked at me. "You've been through so much, Harmony. You didn't deserve to get lost in the darkness again."

I blinked. "No offense, lady, but that didn't clear anything up, and—"

She knew my name.

"How do you know my name?" I demanded, standing from the stool.

She ignored my question, walking over to the curtains and pulling them open. With a quick flick of the latch, she opened the window. Sunlight warmed the room even more, and though I had no idea what was going on, my intuition was telling me I was safe. Peeling my eyes from her, I looked around the room, a sense of familiarity washing over me, settling on my shoulders.

As she walked back across the room, the floorboards creaked underneath her. Then, I realized I'd been here before.

"Are you a friend of Cabe's?" I asked, remembering Cabe had a friend who was into photography.

"No."

Well, that was helpful.

"Did you write that song?" she asked.

"No, but it's my favorite," I told her truthfully.

She hummed. "Why?"

I shrugged my shoulders. "I just...I can relate to it, I guess."

"Your voice is beautiful," she replied, coming closer to me. "My boy loves it when you sing."

I cleared my throat and ignored that comment. "Can you tell me why I'm here?" Panic was beginning to crawl up my spine. I wanted to go back home. I had to get to work tomorrow, and—

"You were about to be lost again, Harmony. You two can't lose each other in a sea of pain, not after you've found each other in the storm."

Lose who? What storm? "I don't know what you're—"

The woman took another step closer, her face full of grace and patience. "My boy loves you, you know?"

Something in my chest fluttered. Her boy? Love? Loves me?

"I'm sorry?"

"He's stubborn, actually. Both of them are," she muttered, looking out the window. Outside a gentle breeze blew, causing the curtains to flutter. "You saved him, Harmony. I was worried he couldn't be saved, not after everything...not after the pain."

Was he a patient?

I set my guitar down, leaning it against the counter. "Ma'am, I have no idea what you're talking about."

She came to me then, and I froze. Her soft hands cupped my face, her fingers brushing back some of the curls. She was taller than me by a few inches, and she smelled of vanilla. Her blue eyes bounced back and forth as she studied me.

"You are beauty, inside and out. I was scared he wouldn't find such beauty, that my boy would live in anger forever," she whispered.

Tears stung my eyes at the compliment. Beauty. For so long, I'd hated my body. My ex made me hate my body, telling me all the time how I was nearly ready.

Ready to be his perfect girl.

"That vile man isn't welcome here," she warned. "Push him from your thoughts."

"I—I—how did you—"

A clock chimed from somewhere outside, and the woman sighed. "Sweet girl, we don't have much time."

"Time for what?"

Suddenly, the room and everything around us faded away into a bright, white light. The woman's touch disappeared from my face. The light was too bright for me, and I squeezed my eyes shut, holding my hand in front of my face. I heard a splash of water beside me, and a cool, thick liquid landed on my leg.

"Oh, that's done. You can open your eyes again. Sorry, it's bright here. Takes some getting used to," the woman said.

I opened my eyes and gasped at the sight before me. We were in a small wooden boat, the woman sitting across from me. Her clothes had changed. She was in a cream dress now, looking over the edge, down into the dark, murky lake that surrounded us. She clicked her tongue. "That's quite the monster you've been fighting."

My eyes followed hers.

A dark, scaled claw with black talons covered in tar shot out of the water, coming for my throat. The instant it made contact, it squeezed hard, choking me and cutting off my air. My hands went to its slimy arm, trying to fight it and yank it away. I noticed the woman wasn't doing anything. Her head was tilted slightly, her brows furrowed.

"He doesn't control you, Harmony," she said, her voice loud but still soft. Pretty.

"Please," I wheezed, trying to gasp for air.

"He hurt you, sweet girl, but he didn't break you."

"Harmony, baby please. Come back to me," a deep male voice echoed over the water, causing the monster to growl. It yanked me forward, my upper body leaning over the water, my face an inch away.

I was fighting, kicking and clawing. I tried to scream, but I couldn't.

He was going to take my voice away.

"Tell the monster to go away," she ordered. "You have the power here!"

I didn't. I'd never had any power, not when it came to this.

"Little Song, please."

That voice. That nickname.

"My boy is calling for you, Harmony. He needs you, more than you'll ever know. I'm sorry I won't be there to see it. I've never got to see him ride, but you have."

Flashes of a bull rider filled my vision, his body moving with each buck of the beast. A black cowboy hat. The sound of a buzzer going off rang in my ears. A handsome smirk. Gray eyes.

Gray.

A storm.

A raging, everlasting storm.

"He loves your voice, Harmony. He loves it when you sing."

Images of my apartment came then, a man standing outside of it, watching me—protecting me. A cowboy kissed me against the wall, promising me he'll be back. Nashville. Tulips. Phone calls. A confession. A brand.

A wedding ring.

A voice from a memory, the same deep voice I just heard, echoed in my mind. "This was Momma's. Before I left Hallow Ranch, I snuck into Pop's room and stole it from the safe. I needed to have a piece of her when I left. Now, I need to have it on you, every single day. I need to look at the most treasured thing in my life and see that ring on her finger."

The claw around my throat loosened and I raised my left hand to find a ring on my finger. A simple gold band, with a tear-drop diamond.

"Loved you the second I saw you."

Mason.

The woman's boy was Mason.

Her boy was my bull rider.

"Mason," I cried, pushing the monster's arm away from me and falling back into the boat.

"Atta girl," the woman praised.

Everything shifted again, and then, I was on the ground. I looked around. I was in a field. The sun was high and the sky was blue, fluffy, glorious clouds scattered across it. The grass beneath me was soft and lush. I shifted, my body aching from the struggle, and I felt a warm liquid ooze between my legs. I sat up, my eyes going directly there. It was blood.

"Mommy?"

My head whipped to the right to find a little girl with auburn curls. She was in blue jean overalls with a sage green shirt. She had blue around her lips, as if she had been eating berries. My heart convulsed, pain shooting through my chest.

He told me that couldn't have her, and that I couldn't be a mother. Pain formed in my stomach, and I lifted my hand to it, pressing in.

I was empty.

I lost her.

Now, she was standing before me.

"Sammy?" I croaked, tears flowing down my cheeks. The blood. She couldn't see the blood. I looked down. The blood was gone, and my clothes were clean.

I looked back to her, fearing she might be gone, but she wasn't. My daughter smiled at me. "Hi, Mommy!" she yelled, breaking into a run, her curls flowing behind her, the sun guiding her to me. A second later, she collided against me, her little arms wrapping around my neck.

I held on.

Oh, how I held on.

Her little body was warm against mine, and I could feel her breath against my neck. She was healthy—whole. My face crumbled as a grateful sob left me, and my hand went to the back of her head, cradling it. My sweet girl. He didn't take her. He didn't take her. She was right here. In my arms. Alive and happy.

"Why are you crying?" Sammy asked, her sweet, smooth voice music to my ears.

Sucking in a shaky breath, I whispered, "I missed you, my flower."

She giggled and pulled herself away from me. "Mommy, I see you every day."

I brought my hand to her face, tilting my head. "What do you mean?"

Sammy pointed, and my eyes followed her finger. The woman who brought me here, Mason's mother, was standing a few feet from us. "Grandma lets me see you every day. She said you are make her son happy. She said that you're love."

I looked back and forth between them. "What does she mean?"

"I've got her for now, Harmony," the woman promised.

My daughter kissed me on the cheek before she made her way to the blonde. I scrambled to my feet, reaching for Sammy. My precious girl. "No, wait—"

"As much as you want to let go, you can't, sweet girl," Mason's mother said, taking my daughter's hand. "My boy needs you."

"What do you mean?" I cried. "I want to be here!"

She shook her head as she began to fade away. "The monster is gone. He won't ever try to drag you under again, but you need to live. You overcame the pain. You're strong. It's time to go back."

"I can't leave Sammy!" I tried to get closer, but I was frozen, unable to move. I felt a tug in my chest.

Little Song.

My daughter smiled at me. "Grandma Jane takes care of me, Mommy! She keeps me safe."

I was supposed to keep her safe.

I was her mother.

That was my job, and I failed.

I couldn't leave her now.

"Little flower, I can't leave—" I choked back a sob.

"You have to go back, Mommy. Don't worry, Grandma and I will be waiting!"

The bright light returned, and something started pulling me away.

"Darlin', please. Please, baby! Every day, remember? You and me?" Mason whispered, his voice filled with agony.

I looked over my shoulder to see a storm coming for me, lightning striking in the distance over the mountains. It called to me, needing me.

"Do me a favor, Harmony?" Jane called.

I looked back at the woman and my child. They were holding hands. She was going to keep my baby safe, and for that, I owed her everything.

"Anything," I rasped.

"When my wild boy asks you to sing for him, remember we can hear your songs. There's power in your voice, daughter, use it."

"Bye, Mommy!"

"Harmony!"

He needs me.

She's safe.

I took one more look at her, memorizing her beauty, and not seeing a trace of Tim Moonie.

"You've defeated him, sweet girl," Jane declared. "Go live."

"Harmony, please!"

"Baby?"

My eyes opened to find Mason hovering above me, his features filled with devastation and anguish. His eyes met mine and I felt his rough hand against my cheek. Something wet hit my other cheek.

It was a tear—a tear that came from *my husband.*

"Mase," I rasped.

"Shh, don't. Let me look at your pretty eyes," he ordered softly, rocking me back and forth. "I gotta see my favorite blue."

"Every day," I croaked.

"I said hush," he growled, his fingers pressing into my head slightly. He was angry, but he was also scared. He didn't know how to cope with this fear. "You went away, Harm. You took two steps from me and—you went away. No one could wake you up. It was like you were in a coma..." His voice cracked as his upper lip curled into a snarl. "Don't you ever do that again, you hear me?"

My throat tightened. I nodded.

"Know this, my beautiful, precious little song; I'm going to kill him. Sooner rather than later."

"Mase, he wants the gold," I breathed, panic rising again.

He didn't blink once as he said, "Harmony, whatever gold was on this land was found by my ancestor, and he used a chunk of it to build his legacy, gave some to the town, to the tribes surrounding us, and that's it. We haven't found any in over eighty years. That bastard thinks we have some still." He dipped his chin, his lips hovering over mine. "The last of it is currently on your finger, and that's where it will stay. If you want to pass it down to our kids, fine. You wanna wear it when you're buried next to me, fine. It doesn't leave your finger until you make that decision."

Whatever air I had in my lungs was gone, and I was overwhelmed with a heavy, intoxicating love for this wild man, this loving son, broken brother, fighter, bull riding cowboy.

"He was going to drag me under again," I whispered.

Lightning flashed in my Mase's gray eyes. He knew what I was talking about; I told him about the monster when I bared myself to him. "Did he? Did he try to drown my wife?"

Tears stung my eyes. "No," I sobbed, shaking my head. "I beat him, Mase. I finally beat him."

I was lifted up in his arms, pressed against his chest. He twisted, and then I was over him, sitting on his lap. Wait—where were we?

I pulled back from him and looked around. We were on a bed, white linen below us, the smell of lemon in the air. My eyes went to the window, taking in in the night sky. I knew this room. I'd been here before.

"Where are we?" I asked, looking down at him. His back was against the metal headboard, his hand at my waist, and he was looking at me like he'd just seen me for the first time.

His grip on my dress tightened. "The spare-spare bedroom. Before that, it was my brother's office, and before that...before that, it was my mother's dark room."

I closed my eyes, my hands drifting up to his chest as a single tear fell down my cheek. Mase's steady heartbeat was unwavering and grounding beneath my palm. Visions of my dream...message...whatever came back. I squeezed my eyes shut, trying to remember the details. There was a photo hanging above the counter, a photo of two little boys in a pasture, the mountain behind them.

"Baby?"

"She loved you so much," I whispered, my voice raspy and broken. My eyes opened when his chest heaved. "Jane loved her boys so much, Mason. Oh, how she loved you and Denver."

Mase's eyes were red again, tears forming. His scruffy jaw tightened. "I never told you her name."

My bottom lip trembled. I cupped his face with one hand. "I know, sweetie."

How do you explain that you had a visit from an angel? That she graced you with just a moment with the child you lost? How do you tell your husband that without sounding utterly insane?

"It's going to sound crazy," I murmured, my gaze unwavering. I was done being scared.

"I want to hear every single second," he choked out.

Unable to take it anymore, I crashed my lips down to his. He sat up, his hands tangling in my hair. Our lips moved together in an aching, pleading kiss. Our breaths collided with unrelenting, powerful need. Our hands clung to one another, afraid of getting lost. Our bodies pressed against each other, completing one another like a puzzle. Some of our pieces were damaged, scared, bent, but that didn't stop us.

He was made for me, and I, him.

When I broke away, leaning my forehead against his, I told him about her.

About how she looked.

How sweet she sounded.

Then, when our cheeks were covered in tears, I told him about Sammy.

My precious little wildflower.

When I was done, he told me something, too, healing my soul completely, making me whole again.

"Sammy is mine, you hear me? He doesn't get her. That's my daughter. If somehow, a cowboy like me gets into heaven, that little girl is mine. Fuck, I love her so much."

"Mason..." I buried my face in his neck, crying.

"I love her mommy, too. Fuck, baby, I love you both so much," he cried, his arms tightening around me.

We laid there, holding on, and crying—mourning.

Hours or minutes later, whenever sleep came to bless me, I heard my husband whisper to the ceiling. "I forgive him, Momma. I forgive Denver for the sins he didn't commit. Take care of our wildflower for us, yeah?"

Chapter Thirty-Six

Mason

Two Days Later

"Where are her photos?" I asked, trying to sound calm as I through the room that used to be Momma's dark room. Harmony had made the bed and was downstairs talking to Nancy and Valerie. This was the first moment my brother and I had alone in forty-eight hours. The last time we were alone, I punched the fucker in the jaw, taking my final swing.

It was done.

I thought I'd channeled all my anger into those two punches, and I was prepared to struggle. I was prepared to fight the anger and resentment. All that changed when Harmony told me about her angel visit.

"In the attic, preserved properly," Denver answered from behind me.

"Before you had this bed put in here, it was your office?" What the fuck was I doing? I knew the answer to that.

He sighed. "Yeah, needed a place to keep everything organized, but when we moved Nancy in, Jackie needed a place to stay," he explained. "Had the boys move everything up to the loft in the barn for now."

It made sense. It made perfect fucking sense. To move Momma's photographs, to make it a functional room for his growing family...

He'd admitted his mistakes, was working hard to make up for them.

Tell him, sweet Mase.

Momma's voice called to me again, calming the anger that didn't want to forgive. I knew that was Pop inside me, the monster he'd passed down to his sons. I wasn't the only living Langston with demons.

"Do you ever hear her?" I blurted, turning to face him. I leaned against the door frame and folded my arms over my chest.

Denver knew exactly who I was referring to. Taking a sip of his coffee, he nodded. "A lot more since Valerie came into my life. You?"

"I have for years," I muttered, looking down at my boots. "Mostly after I get my eight seconds, but lately, I've been hearing her more because—"

"Of Harmony," he finished. When I looked up at him, I found him staring. "The day of the fire, I saw Pop."

A chill went down my spine, and I smelled burning flesh—my flesh. The brand.

"No shit?" I pressed, raising my brows.

"It wasn't anything worth repeating, trust me," he promised.

Silence fell between us.

Tell him, tell him.

Fuck, you idiot, just tell him.

"When Harm passed out," I began. My brother's eyes darkened. That day, he had been just as scared as me. We'd tried everything, but she didn't want to wake up. I'd called Dr. Garcia, and because the situation was so dire, she'd broken the law. She told me about Harmony's extreme episodes during her early days of treatment. She told me that my wife's PTSD became too much for her, that her mind would become overthrown with memories. She told me that the longest episode lasted a week. They hooked her up to monitors, gave her an IV, and watched her. Her body would shut down, putting her in REM sleep, as an act of self-defense. Thankfully, Harmony's most recent episode had only lasted three hours.

Longest three hours of my life.

"Mase?" Denver prompted, raising his brows.

"She had a monster that manifested from her trauma in her brain. She told me that whenever things got bad, if she felt like she was in danger, if she was anxious, the monster would come up from 'the depths' and try to drag her down. When the bastard succeeded, she would black out."

He made a low noise in the back of his throat. "How long has she been in therapy?"

"Six years."

He nodded. "I just started."

My chest ached. I knew he was in pain; I saw it the first night, the second his eyes landed on mine. He was deep and twisted, like me. However, I had PTSD from my childhood, and he had it from his time in the marines.

Two different types of beasts to conquer.

Tell him, Mase.

Tell him now.

I blew out my breath. "Denver, Harm saw Momma."

He didn't move an inch, didn't blink. He was still as stone. "Come again?"

"When she blacked out, she told me she was being dragged down and then she was in her apartment. That's when Momma showed."

"How do you know?" he questioned.

"Because Harmony said her name, Den."

He flinched.

"I never told her Momma's name."

My brother cleared his throat. "When I pulled Val from the fire, and they were trying to bring her back..."

I tightened my jaw.

Denver looked out and down the stairs. "She told me Momma came to her. Told her that she needed to breathe. Breathe for me."

A gust of wind hit the house, and inside the spare bedroom, the curtains lifted as the summer air blew through the open window. Keeping my eyes on the window, Denver came up beside me. We stood together in silence, watching the curtains move in the gentle breeze, sunlight pouring in the from the heavens above. The chatter downstairs carried up, followed by the beautiful melody of laughter.

Denver grunted, shaking his head, looking down to his boots. "Thank you for coming home."

I looked to the ceiling, my heart aching. My eyes closed as a sense of peace rained down on me. "Thank you for keeping the door open."

"I'm sorry," he exhaled.

"Me too, brother."

"Look at me, Mase."

I took a deep breath and held it in as I looked at my brother. His eyes were glossy, his jaw tight. He put his hand on my shoulder, turning me to face him. "Nothing I say is going to change the past, but hear me when I say this: you have nothing to apologize for—"

"—bullshit," I argued. "I ignored your calls. I put this ranch behind me. I—"

"And I left my little brother alone with the devil," he shot back. His grip on me tightened, and he lifted a finger to my face. "You make me work for it."

Forgiveness.

"Too late, Den. I forgive you."

His shoulders fell slowly, and he dropped his hand as his head started shaking. "You—I don't deserve your forgiveness."

"I don't deserve to be sleeping under your roof, but here I am."

"Mason."

"Denver," I stated, looking back into the room. "It's time to be a family again."

"Caleb is dying to meet you."

I still hadn't met the little cowboy. Denver had been keeping him at his friend's house, his father standing on guard until we took care of Moonie.

"Den!" Val called from the bottom of the stairs.

"Marrying her in the fall," he murmured, looking at me. I nodded. Good. Valerie was good woman, and my brother deserved some good in his life.

"Want you standing beside me, Mase."

My throat felt thick. I swallowed. "Wouldn't miss it," I promised.

"Den, Lance is here!"

The air shifted.

Lance was here, which meant the boys were back from the errand we sent them on this morning. Two days ago, Moonie touched down in Denver, with a bounty hunter on his tail, changing the plan. Two days ago, my wife overcame the pain he'd caused. Two days ago, after we'd gotten Harmony settled upstairs, Denver told Chase to look the other way. He agreed.

Now, it was time to end this.

"You ready?" my brother asked, adjusting his hat.

"Always."

He nodded. "I'll be downstairs."

As his boots thundered down the wooden stairs, I twisted my neck to look back into the room, memories coming back. Momma and me dancing in the middle of the floor, her laugh filling the entire house as we spun around. Denver sitting on the stool, reading a book, smiling. Momma showing us her pictures, proud of them. Denver and me playing hide and seek. Momma jumping out from behind the door in an effort to spook us. All three of us sharing a hug as she watched the storm outside, her hands stroking our hair.

I tipped my hat to the empty room. "Thanks, Momma."

"No," I said firmly, shaking my head.

"Mase."

"Little Song, I said no," I warned, getting more and more pissed.

My wife hugged herself, looking out to the herd, her red, wild curls shifting in the breeze. "I don't want him hurting you."

I wanted to laugh. There wasn't a chance in hell Tim Moonie would hurt me, but I had to respect her fear. She was afraid of losing me, and that made me love her more. "Darlin', you ain't getting rid of me," I said, closing the space between us, pulling her arms apart. "You're stuck with me for life, Harmony Langston," I whispered, wrapping my hand around the back of her neck, the other holding her at the waist. I bent my neck, getting into her space, my eyes holding hers. "It's done, Little Song. You can rest now."

"Promise me you'll come back," she croaked.

"Haven't you been listening?"

"Mase, please."

I turned us, walking her back until she was pressed against the side of the main barn. My body was against hers, and her breath hitched. "Every single night, you'll been in my arms. Every single morning, I'll kiss you silly. I'll make love to you every single day. Every single day, I'll come home to you. You hear me, wife?"

"Yes," she rasped.

"I want you to go with Val and Nancy to get Caleb. She's taking you three to lunch. If you go to the diner, get the Rueben and onion rings. If you go to Ching's, get fried rice. Stop by the Farmer's Market and get some of Mrs. Patt's blueberry pie, if she still has it. When you get back to Hallow Ranch, I'll be waiting."

"Mase," Denver called. I looked to the right to see him on his horse, another one beside him, saddled and waiting.

"I love you," my wife whispered.

"From the second I saw you, baby." Not giving a shit whether Denver was watching, I kissed her. Hard. When I was done, she was breathless. I adjusted my hat and shot her a wink. "Gotta go do cowboy shit, darlin'."

I felt her eyes on me as I made my way to Denver. He handed me the reins. "Been a while," he noted. "You sure you can keep up?"

Once I was on the horse, I looked back at him. "Keep saying shit like that, and I won't help you catch the bull roaming around here somewhere."

Den's eyes flashed with anger. "The fuck did you just say?" he growled.

I shot him a smirk and snapped the reins. In seconds, I passed the pens, then flew out to the pasture. The horse's hooves pounded the earth, flying through the land, the scene around me a blur. The sun was high, the sky blue, the grass green, and the scent of revenge in the air.

It was a damn good day to be a cowboy.

Chapter Thirty-Seven

Mason

"Grayson," I greeted him.

The bounty hunter was leaning up against the second barn, dressed in black cargo pants, black combat boots, and a black long, sleeved thermal. His dark eyes were alert as Denver and I left our tied-off horses and came to him.

"Glad to see the Brady Bunch back together," he noted, his voice rough and low.

"You don't have to be here," Denver said. "You've done your job."

"Actually, he does," I countered.

My brother raised a brow. "Why is that?"

"Because it's part of his payment." Eddie. My lips twitched as I watched my friend as he emerged from the barn, wiping dirt and blood from his hands with a black bandana.

Denver looked at Grayson, narrowing his eyes. "Why?"

"Made a mistake with Valerie. This is me fixing it."

"Look, that wasn't your—"

"Your woman was kidnapped and nearly burned alive because of me," the bounty hunter growled, pushing off the wall. He jerked his head to the dark barn. "I get to be the one who tells him his empire has fallen."

"Then let's get it done," I said, meeting their eyes.

As the four of us headed back into the barn, the smell of fear and blood filled my nostrils. The deeper we got, the more my eyes adjusted to the light, and I was pleased to see the pipeline prince hanging from the deer hook, the tips of his dress shoes scraping against the dirt below him. His navy-blue suit was saggy and torn in various places, his face was beaten and bloodied, his hair was dirty with a red tint to it.

A wicked smile spread across my face.

"Well, it's about time I meet the great Timothy Moonie," I drawled.

The other cowboys leaned against the walls, clearly amused. Mags chuckled darkly, the twin shared a fist bump, and Beau was sharpening a large hunting knife, his father beside him, watching.

Moonie lifted his head, and the second he registered who I was, an unhinged growl left him. "Where is she?" he shouted.

"Are you referring to my wife?" I asked casually, walking to the table of blades, clamps, and pilers.

"She's *mine!*" he roared.

I lifted a pair of pilers, inspecting them. "Timothy, we don't have the time for games."

"We have other business to discuss," Denver informed him.

"Fuck you," the fuck face spat.

"Mind your tone, Moonie," Mags warned. "Wouldn't want this to end before we've had our fun."

"Funny thing, actually" Eddie began. "I was looking to invest in some stocks the other day and I came across yours."

Moonie's eyes shot to my friend's.

"Your stock is doing fairly well for a man whose company is about to go under," the rodeo clown mused. "It's a good thing I have friends in high places."

Joseph Grayson stepped up, coming into Tim's line of sight. Everyone in the room saw it when it happened.

The fear took over.

"You," he gasped, straining against the ropes, his body wiggling.

I watched as an evil, satisfied smile spread across Grayson's face. "Me."

"You drained my accounts!"

"Oh, I didn't do that. The IRS did—well, technically, Agent Casey Gomez with the Federal Bureau of Investigations did on behalf of the IRS. You see, when you tricked me, thought you had an innocent woman burned alive, thought you won Hallow Ranch, I decided to do a deep dive. Imagine my surprise when a few weeks later, the bull rider I was hired to find calls me."

Moonie's eyes shifted to mine.

"He tells me he met a woman whom you've had relations with. Apparently, she was sold to you in a deal struck by her father and yours. I did some digging on Mr. Green," Grayson shrugged. "Have to be honest with you, Tim, killing him in his house with cameras I hacked into wasn't the best idea."

The boys chuckled, and I smirked.

"I like to think of myself as a decent citizen, Tim," Grayson said. "Of course, I had to report it to the lovely men and women in blue in Houston. Then, I came across something else: your strange friendship with the chief of police out there. He, being the desperate man he is, and only wanting to save his family, tells me everything."

"No!"

"Yes," Beau taunted with a sickeningly sweet smile.

"Oh, and your friend? You know the one who kidnapped my woman?" Denver chimed in. Moonie was seething now, glaring at my brother. I watched as Denver moved to him, his hand shooting out, wrapping around Moonie's throat. "His ashes are on my mountain now, but don't worry—you'll be joining him soon."

"Moonie Pipelines Inc. was declared bankrupt this afternoon. The company is being broken down and sold," Lance said.

"Your stocks are gone. Your accounts are emptied, and your contracts with the last five ranches you bought are null and void. The ranchers will be keeping the money and getting their land back, if they want it," Lawson explained.

In a last-ditch effort, Moonie turned to me. "You know, she used to have the most beautiful voice," he sneered, smiling at me. My spine went straight. "Smooth and rich. God, it was pure music."

The temperature in the barn dropped as darkness drifted between us.

"But I'll tell you the best part, Mason: hearing her scream."

My feet were moving, slowly and calculated, towards my brother. My eyes didn't leave the madman who'd made my love suffer, who'd taken away Sammy, who'd starved her.

"The best part was when she miscarried."

Mags pushed off the wall, but I held up hand, stopping him.

"That's when I got to lock her up," Moonie explained, chuckling. "She had to learn her lesson. She had to learn that I was the only one she could love. If her attention was on a baby, how could she serve me? How could she worship me?"

The pilers fell from my hand, hitting the dirt with a soft thud.

"The chains looked so beautiful on her," he sighed. "I liked it when she was weak, when I could hold her down, but she could still scream for me. I didn't give her any water, and it only made it better!" The bastard laughed. "For days, she would scream and scream, and her voice changed."

I held out my hand to Denver, and he twisted, grabbing something out of one of the bags on the ledge. Moonie was still laughing like a fucking lunatic when Denver handed me what I wanted, the metal warm from sitting in my truck for the last two days. I made my way to the hanging man, my breathing ragged as I took off my hat and held it out to Mags. "Hold this for me, would ya?"

He took it, staying silent.

Tim looked at the bottle in my hand and back up to my face. "Are you going to give me a drink?" he laughed again. "That's what she *begged* for, even as I beat her and ra—"

With a growl, I fisted the bottle and swung. The metal connected with his face, and I relished the sound of something breaking.

"I took her voice," he screamed.

I shook my head. "No, Moonie, you didn't," I said, pulling my fist back. "You gave her one."

The bottle slammed into his head over and over as Mags took hold of the rope, lowering the man so I could beat him harder. The space around me faded away. Bones cracked, blood spewed everywhere—my wife's teal bottle was covered in it, concealing the dents his face was making in the cool metal. I didn't stop—I couldn't stop.

Eventually, Tim Moonie was under me as I beat him into the dirt. My body ached, but still, I couldn't stop. As I beat the man who haunted my woman's dreams to death with the bottle she had to cling to for years, he morphed into the man who haunted mine.

On that bright summer day, in the middle of Hallow Ranch, I killed two men with my bare hands.

Tim Moonie and John Langston.

When it was done, I fell back, ready to hit the dirt, but Denver was there, waiting and ready to support me. I leaned against him as we all sat in silence, our eyes on an unrecognizable lump of flesh.

We left our sins in that barn, and later, when we spread the ashes of a monster on our mountain, we let go of our anger. My brother and I rode back to the house on horseback, the wind whipping around us, our home in the distance.

We finally had it.

Peace.

Epilogue

Harmony

One year later. St. Louis.

"Mase," I breathed, my fingers yanking on his hair. Too much. It was too much.

My husband's hands tightened on my thighs, holding them wide as he flicked his tongue against my over-sensitive clit. I'd just come down from my second climax, and he was going to make me come again.

"You my good little whore?" he taunted, his deep voice vibrating against my pussy.

"Mase, I can't—"

"You can and you will," he growled.

I didn't want to come on his tongue again. I wanted to be filled with him. I wanted him to stretch me. "Fuck me, cowboy," I begged.

"I'll fuck you; I'll fill your fertile little cunt up with my seed. You hear me?" he smirked.

I nodded, watching him rise to his full height. He was in his riding gear; he was supposed to be on a bull in half an hour. He was due for a press conference in ten minutes. We were in our RV, and I was lying naked on the dining table. My husband reached up to take his hat off.

"Leave it on," I whispered.

He ducked his chin, and all I could see was his smirk as he pulled out his thick, hard cock from his jeans. "You want to be fucked by your husband, or the bull rider?"

"Both." My fingers pulled and pinched my nipples, my body reacting instantly, my back arching for him. I was giving him a show, and I dropped my eyes to his cock, whimpering at the sight of pre-cum leaking from its head.

"Please," I rasped.

"You gonna sing for me, Little Song?" he asked, lining himself up. He didn't give me a chance to answer as he slammed his hips forward, ramming his cock inside me. My pussy fluttered around his length, stretching and soaking him. His grey eyes rolled back as a groan rumbled in his throat. "Fuck, yeah."

I moaned, wrapping my legs around his waist, as his hand went to my throat, squeezing gently. My clit throbbed, begging to touched. As I dropped my hand, my fingers rubbing my bundle of nerves in quick circles, he growled. "Dirty little wife. My cock not enough for you?"

I whimpered. "Fuck me, Mase."

He snapped his hips, setting a quick, harsh pace, the table beneath us rocking. "Supposed to be out there, telling the sports stations I've turned over a new leaf," he taunted. "That I'm a good boy now. Yet, here I am, balls deep in my needy whore."

"Oh, god!"

"Gonna fill you up so when I ride that bull, I know you'll be watching with my cum leaking down your thighs." He lowered himself over me, his hand flexing on my throat. The leather of his vest scrapped against my nipples in the most incredible way. He pulled out and slammed back in, holding himself deep.

My husband dipped his head and put his tongue against my ear. "You mine?"

"Yes!"

"This my cunt?"

"Yes," I whimpered.

"Say it," he growled, *finally* snapping his hips.

"I love you!" My legs started to shake.

He hummed in approval. "I love you, Harmony."

He fucked me harder then, his harsh breaths against my ear. "Take your fingers off your whore pussy."

I clenched around him. I was close. "Please, please!" I didn't move my fingers; I kept rubbing.

His hand went to my jaw, and he forced me to look at him. "Stop playing with my pussy, or I'll leave you empty and aching."

Snaking his free hand between us, he yanked my hand away. "Gonna fucking breed you, wife. You want that? You want my cum filling you up and your belly swollen with my child? Hm?" he huffed, moving faster. He was unhinged, and someone was banging on the door.

Oh, god.

"Yes!" I cried.

There was another knock on the door and his hand covered my mouth, but he didn't let up.

"Mason! Open up!"

My husband chuckled. "Should I open the door, baby? Let them see what a good girl you are for me, spread on this table like a feast, and taking this dick like the whore you are?"

I moaned against his palm, my eyes rolling back. My peak was there; one more word and he would send me over the edge.

"My beautiful wife," he whispered. I met his eyes. "Milk your bull rider's dick for me."

I was *gone.*

I screamed into his hand, pleasure warping my body as my back arched. My pussy tightened around him, wanting him to stay inside me forever. He groaned my name loudly, and the knocking stopped.

Minutes later, Mason kissed me goodbye, leaving me sated on the table.

"Eight seconds, and Mason Langston is still going!" the announcer roared through the speaker system.

"Uncle Mason is badass," Caleb whispered in awe from beside me.

"Caleb," Val scolded on the other side of him, her hand on her swollen belly. "No cussing."

"Dad cusses, so why can't I?"

"Boy," my brother-in-law warned from behind me. I twisted to see him glaring down at his son.

"You told me cowboys cuss, and last week you told me that I was cowboy," Caleb told his father.

Val and I shared a look.

Denver mumbled something under his breath before taking a pull of his beer. Last fall, Valerie married Denver, and three months later, she adopted Caleb. Caleb's mom, Cathy, was found working at a casino in Las Vegas. She was handed court papers personally by Denver's lawyer, but she never showed up. Cathy lost all parental rights to her son, and if she ever stepped foot in Colorado again, she would be arrested. Caleb tried to brush it off and act tough, but not being wanted by a parent was difficult for a child.

Mason and Caleb's weekly rides seemed to help though. Those two are inseparable.

Valerie found out she was pregnant, and a month later, Nancy passed away, the cancer having finally run its course. It wasn't a shock; we knew it was coming. In her final days, no one worked on the ranch, Jackie and Eddie came from Texas, and even Cabe and Billie joined us. All of us sat with her in the house, and after a night of weak smiles and cowboy stories, she passed in her sleep. Valerie didn't leave the bed for two weeks. Denver didn't leave the house. Caleb sat outside the bedroom door and read *Harry Potter* out loud.

When they found out the sex of the baby, Valerie told me the name she'd picked out. Denver didn't know that his daughter would be Nancy Jane Langston yet, and I couldn't wait to see his face when he found out.

As for Mason and me, we were officially trying to have a baby...while building our house on the other side of Hallow Ranch. Once the dust had settled, after you know who's "disappearance," Denver gave Mason half the ranch. After giving it some thought, we'd decided to settle there. It was Mason's home, and the place I found my family. There was too much pain in Houston.

The clinic I used to work for ended up naming their second building after Mason, and every quarter, he made a special visit. According to Pam, he had to. Speaking of Pam, she was now Mase's official manager. Denver's company, Evergreen Feed, was a major sponsor for multiple young bull riders, offering lessons to those interested. Jigs was one of the mentors.

Cabe and Billie are expecting their first child in about a month. They'd usually visit Hayden for Thanksgiving, and I missed them dearly, but Billie and I spoke every single day.

I still had Dr. Garcia as my therapist, though we only have bi-weekly meetings. I'd made a lot of progress, and even though the journey to healing hadn't been an easy one. I was still focused on music and song writing. I didn't have any desire to become famous or perform, but I didn't mind singing to the cowboys in the bunk house on Friday nights, or to my husband when we were on the road.

"Twelve seconds once again! Folks, Mason is wild tonight!"

I snapped back into reality just as my bull rider hopped off the bull and ran. Eddie and the other wranglers jumped in, steering the bull back into the pens.

"Mason Langston, everyone!"

The crowd roared, and Caleb shot up from his seat, clapping.

"My crazy ass brother," Denver called.

Mason took off his hat and gave the crowd his signature smirk. When he finally found us in the crowd, that smirk morphed into a genuine smile. Then he jogged to us. He climbed up the rail to us and held out his hat for Caleb.

Their normal routine.

"Hold on to that for me, bud," my cowboy said.

Caleb immediately set it on his head. "I'll keep it safe for ya, Uncle Mase."

"Atta boy," he replied, smiling at his nephew. Then, he turned to me. "You enjoy the show, Mrs. Langston?"

"You're my favorite bull rider," I breathed, gripping his vest and pulling him to me. Our lips collided and, as always, my wild cowboy kissed me breathless.

When he pulled away, the cheers around us were deafening, but I didn't miss it when he murmured, "You're my favorite song."

My wife curled against me, clinging to my warmth as I stretched to get my ringing cell phone. For fuck's sake, it was three am.

"Sweetie?"

"Shh, darlin' go back to sleep," I soothed, lifting the phone up.

Jeremy Jones.

"Shit," I muttered. Quickly, I eased Harmony off me and exited the bed. I walked to the front of our RV and looked out the window, my eyes going to the Arch standing tall about a mile away.

"Jer?" I answered.

"What's up, cowboy?" My friend's voice was good to hear, but not at 3 AM. Something was wrong.

"You alright?" I asked, cutting through the bullshit.

I listened as the leader of Oasis, the prince of St. Louis, sighed, "Told you about that Mafia shit, right?"

"A bit," I replied, leaning around the counter. "You got trouble?"

"Mason—fuck—I hate to ask this but—"

"Ask it, Jer. Anything you need."

"Heard you made up with your brother..."

I nodded to myself. "Yeah, man. Thankful as hell for it, too. We had some trouble along the way, but we took care of it. You need my brother in on this?"

He was silent for a moment. "Mason, I need to use Hallow Ranch."

A chill went down my spine. "For what, Jer?"

"I think it's best if I tell you in person. You still in town?"

"Leaving tomorrow," I answered, looking back to where Harmony was slept.

"Feel like pushing that back and coming to Oasis?"

My jaw jumped. "You gonna tell me everything?"

"Everything he'll allow me to tell you, yes."

I pushed off the counter, not believing what I was hearing. "Someone controlling you, Jer? Are you in a bind?"

He scoffed. "No, it's just that the new leader of the Italian Mafia has stuff he wants to keep under the table for now. If you agree to this, I'll tell you everything I can. Normally, I would say fuck it, but he's family."

My brows wrinkled in question. "Whoa, whoa. There's a new leader? Who the hell is he?"

"My brother-in-law."

Son of a bitch.

"I'm bringing Denver. He owns half the ranch. If he says no, then I say no. That clear?"

What the fuck was I doing?

"Be at Oasis tomorrow at noon."

He hung up, and I pulled the phone away, staring at it in my hands.

Cowboys, street racers, and the Mafia.

What could go wrong?

Author's note

Babes,

I told you it was going to hurt. There aren't enough words to describe the pain that I felt when Harmony told me her story. I'd had been in the living room, playing with my daughter when she came to me. I cried for two hours and tried to convince myself to not write this story. It needed to be written. Harmony's past is dark, but her strength? Glorious. Her journey is awe-inspiring. I hope that you loved her just as much as I do. I hoped that you accepted my wild bull rider in the end.

I want to thank you, new and returning readers, for taking a chance on my dark cowboys. This was the most painful story I've ever written, and I am so grateful for each and every single one of you.

When the Langston brothers first came to me, I was in the middle of writing **Grand Slam**, the fourth book of the **Batter Up Series**, and they took me by surprise. I knew I had to write their stories—*soon*. The duet that I'd planned on creating was intended to be short, hot, and extra spicy. Instead, it transformed into these two beautiful, dark, gut-wrenching romances about love, lost, and healing. Of course, we couldn't forget the spice. ;)

Returning readers, welcome back! I'm sure that you noticed some little easter eggs that I hid in this book...hinting at what is to come.

It's time to go back to St. Louis. Buckle up, babes. My **Burn Out** men are going to give you whiplash.

I've gotten a lot of questions in regard to the rest of the Hallow Ranch cowboys. The answer is yes, they will be getting their own stories. However, I have a certain bounty hunter who is patiently waiting for his story to be told...

A note to my new readers: Hi, I am so happy you are here. FYI, all of my books take place in the same universe. There were characters mentioned in reference to the ***Batter Up Series*** and the upcoming ***Burn Out Trilogy***, a dark street racing romance series. If you're in the mood for a dark baseball romance that involves that mafia and the FBI—check it out! Start with Dean and Gwen's story, ***Batter Up***!

Acknowledgements: To Alexa *(The Fiction Fix)*, thank you for everything. You are amazing and so special to me. I love you. To Sam, thanks for listening to all my voice messages without complaint. I love you so much. To my team, you already know I love you to the moon and back. Thank you for supporting me, making me laugh, cry, and being the *best* team a little author like me could have. To my family, thank you for supporting my dreams. To Dean Connors, none of this would be possible without you popping into my head seven years ago, thank you.

Don't forget to leave your review for **Sing for Me**! Reviews help authors out so much!

Leave your review here: https://a.co/d/56Cha8s

For more updates check out:

Home | Brittany Ann (brittanywitte1495.wixsite.com)

Follow Brittany Ann on Instagram!

@authorbrittanyann_

Follow Brittany Ann on TikTok!

@authorbrittanyann

About the Author

Brittany Ann is an indie author.
Batter Up *was her debut novel, published 09/2021.*
Brittany's dream has come true, and she has her readers to thank for that.
She has been writing since she was eight years old, creating worlds in composition notebooks underneath her math homework.
The story of BU came to her years ago in a dream and it changed her life.
Writing romance makes her soul feel whole.
Her favorite meal is mac n' cheese and her first crush was Batman.
Brittany Ann is working on multiple projects, and she cannot wait to share them with you!

Titles

The Batter Up Series
Batter Up
Swing Batter, Swing
Strike Zone
Grand Slam
Slugger (a Batter Up Novella)

The Langston Brothers duet
Breathe for Me (Denver and Valerie)
Sing for Me (Mason and Harmony)

The Burnout Series
St. Louis isn't done with you yet, babes. Buckle up.
Breakneck (Dontell and Mina) – 09/01/2023
Clutch and Shift (Leon and Amara) – Early 2024
Full Throttle (Cain and Dominque) – Spring 2024